IT THAT PLEASES THEM

Also by G. A. Brandt

As Beautiful As This: A novel of the reconciliation of war and peace within an American family

IT THAT PLEASES THEM

The Awakening and Redemption of Chaucer Giroux

G.A. BRANDT

Wild About Words Publishing
Rochester, N.Y. | 2022

It That Pleases Them
The Awakening and Redemption of Chaucer Giroux

By G.A. Brandt

©2022 G.A. Brandt

All rights reserved. No part of this publication may be reproduced, redistributed, or transmitted in any form by any means without the prior written permission of the author, except in the case of brief quotations embodied in critical reviews and certain other noncommercial uses permitted by copyright law.
For permission request, email the author at gab10@cornell.edu.

To purchase additional copies, contact the author or write to
27 Landsdowne Lane, Rochester, NY 14618-3847.

Library of Congress Control Number: 2022920751

ISBN: 978-1-7329881-7-0

Cover and book design by Susan Welt
Cover photo by G.A. Brandt and used with permission.

Manufactured in the United States

Please note that throughout the book are links to songs to which the reader is encouraged to listen at that point in reading the novel.

To the memory of Joe Brandt and Lorraine Kieffer Brandt of
Rochester, New York, and Joe Sutter and Barbara Louden Sutter
of Burlington, Iowa. They set the rules to guide us long ago,
and we still follow them;
To Rhett K. Brandt and Rhianna M. Brandt Bangs.
They have given me purpose and clarity since the day
they were born, and nothing has changed in that purpose
and clarity over the years;
and to
W.P. Kinsella, author of Shoeless Joe, and Phil Alden Robinson,
writer and director of the movie Field of Dreams (1989),
for giving us Ray Kinsella, who made a pilgrimage,
heard a calling, and lived it.

Jane Sutter Brandt with Phil Alden Robinson
at the George Eastman Museum.

Contents

Preface *8*
Prologue: From Chaucer's Journal, 2004 (age 57) *11*

BOOK ONE: POWER

1. The Giroux and Wellesley Families: The Early Days *17*
2. Ottawa *21*
3. Remy and Olivia Pas de Deux *25*
4. Western Canada *28*
5. Strong Winds Make Bold Trees…Sometimes *32*
6. Spinning the Wheel *34*
7. The Sun Also Rises, Said Hem *39*
8. Time Moves, Life Moves *47*
9. Return to Vancouver *59*
10. Do Not Go Gentle into That Good Night *64*
11. It's Summertime and the Livin' Ain't Easy *71*
12. Running Far *75*
13. Thank you, Kathleen *83*
14. Naples *88*
15. Little Switzerland *96*
16. Joanie and Whaleback *102*
17. Cheshire Dump Sunday *109*
18. Confessions *115*
19. The Western Light *120*

BOOK TWO: WANDERJAHR

20. You'll Never Believe This, But Try *127*
21. Moon over Mexico *136*
22. Away on a Broken Wing *147*
23. West Coast Terminal *153*
24. Lighten the Load, Brother *163*
25. Michael, Row the Boat Ashore *168*
26. Wandering Days of Wonder *176*
27. The Wisdom of Solomon *187*
28. Rode Hard and Hung Up Wet *191*
29. To Leo the Lion Again *199*
30. The Pillars of Hercules *202*
31. Angels Fly On *214*

BOOK THREE: CONVICTION

32	St. Émilion	217
33	To Normandy	222
34	The Bear	227
35	London	231
36	And Mother Dear	239
37	To Pamplona	249
38	There was a Gentle Whisper	259
39	The Mystical Days of the Camino	269

BOOK FOUR: APPLICATIONS

40	Suzette	277
41	Running on Empty	282
42	The Stephanie and Tessa Book of Children	288
43	Six Weeks Later – Early September	297
44	More Questions	303
45	Glasgow	307
46	Naked on the Naked Earth: St. Francis of Assisi	314
47	Spring Comes to Despair	319
48	Family Matters	321
49	To the Drawing Board	334
50	The Beginning	339
51	Ottawa Jumps	343
52	St. Jerome's Shadow	346
53	The Final Phase for St. Jerome's	349
54	Melba Jacobs	352
55	Ottawa Redux	357
56	For Love	360
57	A Secret Hidden in Victoria	368
58	Mobile Bay	377
59	Life Happens	380
	Epilogue	
	Chaucer's Journal Entry 1: July 14, 1995	388
	Journal Entry 2: Remy's letter to the family on Canadian Thanksgiving Day, Monday, October 9, 2000	390
	Journal Entry 3: Chaucer's letter from Christmas 2018 to his children	393
	Acknowledgments	396

Preface

Canterbury Tales II

Now pray I to them all that listen to this little treatise or read it, that if there be any thing in it that please them, that thereof they thank our Lord Jesus Christ, from whom proceeds all wit and all goodness.

— Geoffrey Chaucer, Canterbury Tales, written from 1387–1400

Anyway, I keep picturing all these little kids playing some game in this big field of rye and all. Thousands of little kids, and nobody's around-nobody big, except me. And I am standing on the edge of some crazy cliff. What I have to do, I have to catch everybody if they start to go over the cliff-I mean if they're running and don't look where they are going I have to come out from somewhere and catch them. That's all I'd do all day. I'd just be the catcher in the rye and all. I know it's crazy, but that's the only thing I'd really like to be. I know it's crazy.

— Holden Caulfield, in Catcher in the Rye , by J.D. Salinger, 1951

Well I went to rearrange a little pile'a change
That was accumulatin' on the bar
I set my mind on home, but never got that far

Ordered one for the road, and whaddya know
I end up cryin' on the back room phone
And I'll understand if you want to go-home
Then I got to wond'rin' how ya are

— From the song "Blue Eagle" by Bat McGrath, 1976

If you look for me, Maria, you will find me in the shade;
Wide awake or in a dream it's hard to tell
If you come to me, Maria, I will show what I have made;
It's a picture of our lady of the well
  —From the song "Our Lady of the Well" by Jackson Browne, 1971

…but to all who received him, who believed in his name, he gave power to become children of God; who were born, not of blood nor of the will of the flesh nor of the will of man, but of God…

—John 1:12

Prologue

From Chaucer's Journal, 2004 (age 57)

IT IS A QUIET, CALM, AND SUNNY AUTUMN late afternoon in Ottawa. Some maple trees in the yard are beginning to show the first signs of color. I miss Maggie this day more than most days when we are separated by our work. I can smell and feel New Orleans as I sit on our porch overlooking the Ottawa River. Father is napping as most people do at age 82 in the afternoon. My son McCarthy is off on a hunting trip to Newfoundland with his own son this week, so it is just Father and I at the family home for a few days.

These soft days often send me into my den where I will put pen to paper with the plan of recording thoughts that I may lose. Today I have written about my history, in an honest way, which is not always how it is done I am told. But I will let you, the reader, judge things for yourself. Here is where I start for you, with this entry:

I did not know of all our strange and odd family history as a young boy 50 years ago, and perhaps it was better that way. I think that had I learned that true family story early in my life that I likely would not have learned it as I did, by living it first. I had to find my own light, rather than have Mother or Father shine it in my face and blind me more.

If I were to describe myself based on my early life, how I was raised and my own self-indulgences years ago, I would see myself as a young, peace-seeking, hedonist Christian. My nature was to have fun, avoid confrontation and arguments, and portray kindness. But then the events of the next two decades forced me to relearn my earlier predisposition to universal kindness and love. I learned that falling hard teaches you much. Fall hard I did, and the lessons and bruises were many.

My sister, JOA, and my cousins were there to aid and comfort me in my greatest times of confusion, self-doubt, and self-loathing, and I am thankful for their love and kindness. I learned from JOA and cousins Jean Marc, Ollie, and Kathleen how precious each life is. I learned from Cousin Logan and Maggie how to listen to the spirit to show me the way, to re-shape my way in life. And I learned from many important women in my life how and why we must guard, protect, foster, and advocate for each life. I came to understand to not try to play God, and to not even think I could. You have seen those who have tried. That has always been a fool's game. I have learned many rules of life by living them. For that I am grateful as it was the best teacher for me.

* * *

My mother, Olivia Juliette Wellesley Giroux, was an eccentric, even for an artist. Her mother, my grandmother Photina and my grandfather Plantagenet Sebastian Wellesley, were from England. I believe Photina and my grandfather raised my mother to be agnostic and a rebel on purpose, not by chance. My English relatives were not normal or common, and never pedestrian in anything they did. In England, they had their own family parade each year to protest the Queen's birthday and to celebrate pagan holidays, some of their own creation. And thus my mother's approach to raising JOA and me was to let us be free to fall, and fall we did. JOA's undisciplined early life almost set her on a destructive path; however, my father did as all good lifeguarding parents do; he rescued her before she went under.

My failure as a young man to understand the word "responsibility," resulted in my poor treatment of women and makes me ashamed to write about it now. But through the grace of the heavenly spirit, I learned to fix my broken parts, and then to help rescue others who were also so corrupted, and who had no one to speak for them or to help them.

These days I give thanks every day that our heavenly spirit did not give up on me, as I gave up on my own mother years ago. As for my father, Remy Giroux, what can I say? If all men had just a small part of his love and kindness and responsibility, then our world might have the light that our God wished for, as it is written in the book of Genesis:

When God began to create the heavens and wind...and he

said 'let there be light' and there was light, and God saw that light was good, and God separated the light from the darkness...

For me, that light was my father. His life made sense to me — for he helped, he built, he showed charity, and he didn't complain despite having plenty to be angry about. Is he a saint? Perhaps. I have come to understand that nearly all saints in our Christian faith were not fully understood and recognized during their lifetimes. Regardless of what the future church leaders may or may not say about my father, he was a saint to me and many others. His memory will live on in his work and deeds and perhaps in the work and deeds of me and JOA.

The prayers and counsel from my sister and cousins and Pastors Louden and Wagner were the force that brought true love and understanding into my life when my father was absent, which he often was because of his many travels for his shipping business. I came to understand that without my father, my family, and these clergymen to guide me, how could my transformation have happened? I was told that the spirit works in mysterious ways, and I have come to accept that as an *a posteriori* existential truth in my life.

* * *

My father served in World War II and when the war ended, he entered the business world in which he was very happy and successful. He met my mother in Ottawa when he was first home from the war. He was infatuated by her beauty, as most men were, for her beauty was in her face and in her smile and in her captivating manner of speaking. When she spoke, those around her stopped what they were doing to listen to her voice and examine her gestures, for her body language would display an elegance like no other. She could captivate any man in a matter of minutes, even those who believed that they were immune. They were not.

Initially, I loved that the temperament of my parents was very different and became more so after JOA and I were born. Mother, being who she was, named my baby sister Joan of Arc, but soon we just called her JOA, not Joan or Joanie, which my mother prohibited us from ever using as her name. Within a decade or so after their marriage, the ties that had bound my parents together loosed, then fell off and finally they parted. I was thirteen and JOA was eleven.

Perhaps I grew to be too much like my mother in the years after the divorce. Perhaps I could have been more like my father or like JOA. But I was not. To this day, I have left that matter for God to sort out. I love my sister very much, as she is much like our compassionate father, and I am so very grateful for that.

In 1961 Mother left our home in Ottawa and took us away from our father, first to far-flung Vancouver, then to the city of Victoria on Vancouver Island. Father was devastated, I later learned, but he held it back from my sister and me, often saying it was the best for all of us and that he would provide for us and he would come to visit us often. And he did. Our father never, ever was absent from our lives as we grew up. I did not fully understand how Father could be so calm, so brave to see Mother when he visited us. For I knew how much he still loved Mother, and how much he loved JOA and me. It was not until I was older and had made my own mistakes with women and my children, that the enormous love and moral rectitude that my father had lived during those post-divorce years was fully understood and felt by me. I believe it is called the acquisition of "life's wisdom," which we gain over time.

In the early post-divorce days, Mother tolerated his visits, probably because it kept his checks coming to support her and us. In those days after we moved to Victoria, she mostly sequestered herself in her writing studio in the barn behind our house overlooking the Haro Straight, where she wrote novels and poetry. She had some men call on her, though she did not seem to fancy any of them in particular, perhaps because she had already fallen in love with her solitary writing life. Maybe because she knew that at any time, when she was ready, she could have almost any man that she would want. Perhaps she was conceited or maybe she was wrapped up in her own fiction. She never said much, and JOA and I didn't ask much since we had enormous freedom and did not want to jeopardize it by getting Mother distracted from her writing life.

Soon Mother had produced a novel about a woman who left her family to experience life alone in the Canadian West, (*Enfin Seul – Alone At Last*, 1963). The novel quickly gained the favor of a large Canadian and American reading public who then wanted more, and she gave it to them. It seemed she was just our mother one week, and then she was a celebrity on CBC radio and TV. She had asked for my father's help in negotiating a contract with a publishing house in

Toronto, and he did help via his company lawyer, thus guaranteeing her a good annual income from her books. That accomplished, she became even more distant from Father, JOA, and me.

Whatever the reason, Mother never did marry again. She became exceedingly eccentric as the years passed and much more absent from the lives of JOA and me. Being older, I was able to leave for university, with Father paying my tuition for my study at the University of Toronto. I mostly stayed with Father in Ottawa during summer breaks, only visiting Mother at home on Vancouver Island for a week or two and for the Christmas holiday even though Mother did not celebrate it with any special joy.

By then Mother had alienated JOA by being so disengaged that JOA would take the ferry to Vancouver and stay away for a week at a time. Mother never questioned her absence. It did not work for JOA as by the end of her freshman year at the University of British Columbia in Vancouver, her use of drugs and alcohol had rendered her helpless to control her own life. Fortunately, Father intervened and took her to Ottawa to live with him for four months. He stopped any non-essential business travel to stay with JOA while she worked with a therapist and Pastor Louden to get herself well again. Father's love and attention helped, and JOA returned to Vancouver and transferred to Simon Fraser University in September. Once a month, Father flew to visit her during her first semester there, taking me with him on two occasions.

Together we were able to help JOA back to being the best version of herself, but it was a struggle for Father. She did not disappoint Father (or me), making the Dean's List in the spring semester. Mother seemed to just ignore JOA's struggles, continuing to write and cultivate her network of liberated women friends in Victoria and western Canada. I believed that Mother staying away from JOA at that time was the best for both of them. In the years ahead this was how it was; Mother continued to withdraw from us, her children.

I recite this history because it explains the basis of who I was as a young man. My early family life wreaked havoc on my calmness, and how I saw relationships and marriage. I know now that neither of my parents wished this upheaval on me or JOA, especially not Father who had become my mentor and adult friend. I wished that I had had him all the years when we were separated by nearly 3,000 miles across Canada.

Father had enormous patience with me. His ability to see my mistakes and help me correct them with firm but loving advice is what drives me today in my beliefs and actions. Perhaps without my mother and her many extravagancies and indulgences, I would not have rebelled. I will never know. But without her heritage, her family, and their history of being descendants of Geoffrey Chaucer, my namesake, she may never have emerged into a successful author. God works in strange ways, I know. If you watch and listen, are silent, observe, and learn, then you will love and understand this about God. Some of us call it just life or coincidence. I call it God's teardrop because God is so sad to witness the cruelty of humans to one another.

BOOK ONE: POWER

Chapter I

The Giroux and Wellesley Families: The Early Days

CHAUCER GIROUX WAS BORN IN SEPTEMBER 1947 in Ottawa, the national capital of Canada. His father, Remy Giroux, was the son of a Canadian military officer, who himself was the son of a Canadian military officer. Remy, like his brothers, was expected to distinguish himself and his family name by serving in the Canadian military, which he did in World War II. But after the war, he decided to leave the Navy and go into business with two military men that he had met in the war, a fellow Canadian and an American. They decided to start a shipping business using the ports of eastern Canada and the northeastern United States as their places to build warehouses to store products to export and receive products imported for distribution via rail or truck. Soon they expanded to container shipping, at first leasing freighters, then buying their own.

Thanks to the American Marshall Plan to revive Europe, the need for more freighters was immense, and Remy and his partners took advantage of personal contacts made during the war and found banks friendly to loaning them the capital needed. Another American they had met in the war was an attorney who specialized in maritime law, so the company made him its legal counsel and off they started, with big ideas, some money, and the energy of young veterans. They had little idea how successful that they would become in the years ahead.

Remy's mother, Gillian, had been in a literary group in Ottawa that had started as a women's book club of old friends long before WWII. It evolved into a bigger social and political group that often would meet for dinner parties prior to symphony, ballet or theater performances in town, and on occasion, the group would host gala political fundraisers for a particular candidate that they could mostly agree on. One of the women that Mrs. Gillian Giroux gravitated to was Photina Wellesley, a woman with allegedly historical English roots. Her mother's family were descendants of Geoffrey Chaucer and her husband's family were descendants of the Duke of Wellington.

Yet Photina with all the regalia of her historical British links at her beck and call, was without presumption or falsehoods in her personality and social graces. She dismissed it all as so much depleted and pompous status with little dividend of true success if one was to be honest with herself. Photina was quite happy being a nouveau painter and a minor essayist, sometimes having her new work in art showings at local galleries and occasionally having an arts essay printed in the *Ottawa Citizen*.

Photina and Gillian Giroux spent some time together over the years and had introduced their spouses to one another, although the families (one being military, the other patron of the arts) did not usually socialize but for a special occasion. Their children were often away, and all had not been introduced. And then near the end of the war years, Photina's husband Plantagenet, (he preferred his middle name Sebastian), suddenly died during a trip to England. His career had been as a liaison between the Canadian and British governments in matters related to communications technology. He and his fellow Canadians were in the Golden Fleece Pub in London after a meeting in Westminster when he had a heart attack and died in a booth while dining on his favorite Shepard's Pie and consuming his regular numerous pints of Samuel Smith. For Photina, it was not unexpected, for Sebastian was a smoker, heavy drinker, overweight, and considered exercise a poor man's endeavor. Nevertheless, her daughter Olivia Juliette was deeply sadden in losing her father as he had read to her nightly as a child and helped instill in her the appreciation of the beauty of words, verse, and literature.

In July 1945 after the end of the war in Europe, Remy and his two brothers reunited for the first time in many years at the family home in Ottawa. To celebrate, Remy's father and mother hosted a grand party for extended family and friends. At that party Gillian and Photina introduced some of their children to each other for the first time. Remy was overtaken by Olivia Juliette Wellesley's beauty, and soon after, by her intellect and creative nature. She was two years younger than Remy and as beautiful a woman that he could remember seeing. Remy himself was slender (as were most men just home from years of war), and his black hair and brilliant blue eyes set him apart from most other men to whom Olivia Juliette had recently met.

At the introduction, Remy politely bowed when his mother introduced Photina's daughter. "Olivia Juliette, such a lovely name," Remy said.

Olivia Juliette smiled, happy with Remy's admiring look. "Mother insisted I be Olivia Juliette, as she named me for her favorite Shakespeare play, and Father acquiesced."

She then gave Remy her best seductive Scarlett O'Hara smile with slightly averted eyes. "I simply wished to be called Olivia as a young girl, but mother never called me that at all, and required anyone in her presence call me Olivia Juliette. That was embarrassing when I was a young child but I learned to accept it for the beautiful name it is."

"Yes, count me in as one of the admirers too. Your mother seems wonderful, very delightful, and quite beautiful. I can easily see where you acquired your beauty and charm," Remy replied with a polite smile.

"Thank you, Remy, you are so kind." Oliva looked straight into his eyes knowing the time was right. "And can I assume you are a virtuous man?" a question she inserted into nearly every conversation when she met an attractive young man.

"Well, thank you, and yes, if you mean virtuous in the sense that one puts country before self," Remy replied with a soft nod.

She seemed puzzled at first, hearing a response unlike most men to whom she had posed that question. "Please elaborate for me, Remy."

"You see, the Giroux family is a military family, and we see a man's virtue as the depth of his love of country above all else." Olivia Juliette, her eyes wide, simply stared at Remy as she pondered this surprising response. "It emanates from our understanding of Cato and the creation of honesty and ethics in government." Remy knew he had her full attention now. "And it also follows our French brother Montesquieu, who 200 years ago spoke to the need for virtue to keep and preserve the government and thus the nation state before all else. I know that others likely answer your question in a different manner." He smiled broadly at Olivia Juliette, who was left without a retort. She mildly blushed, having never heard a man be so honest with her. She found it wildly attractive to be spoken to in such a way.

For years later, Olivia Juliette often said that while Remy smiled at their first meeting, he did not come on forceful at all, as had so many other men that she had met. Remy quietly asked her about her work, which she explained was writing stories and biographies for a company in Montreal. When she inquired about his time in the war, Remy, unlike other men, gave her no braggadocio bluster about his service time. He simply said that he had served in Canadian Naval Intelligence, mostly as a liaison with the U.S. Navy. This greatly pleased Olivia Juliette, for it was rare to meet a man who was actually interested in her work and not bragging about his own merit.

And so it went, from a cordial beginning to a romantic love affair to a marriage all within a year. They were married in June 1946. Remy's older brother Jean Luc, who was referred to in the family as Le Guerrier (the warrior) and who was a colonel in the U.S. Army, was the best man. Jean Luc had arrived from Boston with his American wife, Elizabeth, and they both were taken aback by the grace, intellect, and beauty of Olivia Juliette. It seemed to be a fine union, and Le Guerrier made a grand toast to his brother at the wedding dinner. The families had not heard such a grand recitation of the Giroux family legacy as was given that day. General Giroux and Gillian Giroux was so very proud of their sons on that auspicious day. Olivia's beauty and charm on her wedding day became legend in Ottawa.

Chapter 2

Ottawa

As Remy's shipping business, known as Canadian American Transport Inc. (CAT), grew rapidly, Remy and Olivia Juliette bought a large traditional home in what was called the Diplomatic Section of Ottawa, a neighborhood of homes used by foreign government ambassadors. Remy traveled to Toronto, Montreal, Boston, and New York City frequently to meet with his partners and to manage the new contracts and locations of CAT. Occasionally he would fly to London and Paris to negotiate an agreement with a new client. His regular travels were fine with Olivia Juliette as she was well occupied with her job and her writing, plus her female friends were always meeting to discuss new books, visit an art gallery opening, or see the latest American film in town. She was happy to join her friends in Remy's absence. She did travel occasionally with her husband but almost never after the children came.

In late 1946, Olivia Juliette found that she was with child, much to the delight of Remy. This did not slow her literary pace at all as she was young and strong and engaged in researching and developing her own poetry and short stories. The next year she gave birth to a baby boy and insisted to Remy that he be called Chaucer in honor of her mother's heritage as well as to let the family and the world know that she was serious about her future in writing. Remy reluctantly agreed but not before he insisted that his middle name be

French, so they settled on Thierry. Since they were on the discussion of names, Remy announced that he would heretofore call his wife Olivia, not Olivia Juliette, except of course in the presence of his mother-in-law. Olivia Juliette reluctantly agreed.

In September 1947, a healthy, dark-haired boy was born. His parents and grandparents adored him. Olivia decided that she would not be held down by childcare or breast feeding. Within six weeks after Chaucer was born, she insisted on hiring a nanny five days a week when the child was not at either the Giroux or Wellesley grandparents' home, which was frequent. The nanny was a wonderful older woman named Helen Cabot, who had been the nanny for the Giroux family when Helen was a young woman. She had helped Gillian Giroux manage her hostess duties over the years, so she was a logical choice for Remy when he learned that Olivia had no intention of cutting back on her writing career and her work for her employer in Montreal.

When Chaucer was two, Olivia learned she was pregnant again, much to the surprise of Remy as he had been traveling extensively in recent months. She was not overjoyed. In February 1950, Oliva gave birth to a beautiful, healthy, light brown-haired baby daughter with the most joyful smile. Again, Olivia insisted on choosing the name for the baby. Remy just nodded, expecting another creative surprise. A week after Olivia was home from the hospital and she had not yet volunteered a name for the baby, Remy asked one afternoon, "What do you wish to call this beautiful baby of ours?" he asked with a wry look.

Olivia stared out the window for a moment or two and then spoke: "We shall call her JOA," she said with a serious look of superb dignity.

"Joe-uh?" asked Remy. "Where is that name from? How do you spell it?" he asked in a tone of mild exasperation.

With a smug look, Olivia replied, "JOA is Joan of Arc. J-O-A. The bravest of women, who was condemned and killed by weak men for showing her intelligence and courage in the face of danger. Plus, she was French; you should like that," Olivia smiled slyly, awaiting Remy's reaction.

"Oh, I see," Remy said, unsure whether he loved or hated the name. He kissed his wife on the forehead, then walked to the table and poured himself a glass of whiskey before walking out on the porch. There he lit a cigar, a rare occurrence, and stood in the winter chill staring at the snow-covered English garden and frozen river. Now Remy knew for sure that Olivia was an untethered iconoclast with zero inhibitions for convention. Nevertheless, Remy loved her and had learned long ago to expect the unexpected from Olivia.

* * *

As JOA grew from infant to child, she manifested little of the independence for which her mother was noted. JOA was a child who liked to be held and read to. Remy did this with love and consistency whenever he was in Ottawa. JOA also loved to watch and copy her big brother, Chaucer. By the time JOA was age three or so, Chaucer read children's books to her. Over these early years, JOA and Chaucer became very close, and Chaucer grew to feel that he was her protector. Remy noticed this and it made him very happy. Olivia, engrossed in her writing career, barely saw it, or if she did, failed to acknowledge it. Nevertheless others in the family had already taken notice of the love and kindness that Chaucer bestowed on JOA.

When Chaucer was ten, Olivia enrolled him in a children's ballet class at the National Arts Center downtown. A new dance group called the Ottawa National Ballet Troupe had formed when some displaced members of the Canadian National Ballet Theatre departed Toronto and moved to Ottawa. Through connections, their director, Elizabeth Browne, was able to obtain a funding commitment from the federal Arts Office in Ottawa. Part of the grant was to provide for a new youth and children's ballet school. Olivia learned of this from her mother and promptly enrolled Chaucer and JOA.

When Remy returned home from a two-week trip to Portugal, Olivia couldn't wait to tell him of the new ballet class for Chaucer. Remy said nothing, but again poured a glass of whiskey and lit a cigar on the porch, steam practically rising from his forehead. After making a phone call in the privacy of his home office, Remy announced to Olivia over dinner that a local business friend had accepted Chaucer as a player on the Pee Wee hockey team he coached. Practice would begin in two weeks.

Olivia sipped her drink and eyed Remy. "As long as you understand that hockey shall not be allowed to conflict with his ballet classes after school," she stated.

"It should not be a problem. Buddy (what Remy sometimes called Chaucer around the home) misses playing hockey. Last season was cut short by his broken arm remember? Buddy, are you ready for more hockey with your friends now?" asked Remy as he looked at Chaucer.

Chaucer looked at his parents and smiled, knowing that an argument was about to happen. "Yes, Dad, I want to play this year. But I need new skates as my feet are bigger now."

Olivia pursed her lips but said nothing more, unhappy to have her prerogative undermined by the often-absent Remy. The dinner conversation was stilted that night, unusual for a dinner hour when both parents were home. JOA just smiled through it all, as did Chaucer, both rather enjoying seeing their father getting his way for a change.

Chapter 3

Remy and Olivia Pas de Deux

BY HIS TWELFTH YEAR, Chaucer had grown tall and looked so much like his parents. His hair was deep black and wavy like Remy's and his smile was like Olivia's when she seemed truly happy. Although somewhat thin, Chaucer had a lean toughness to him, much like an adult runner. Olivia wanted her children to be appreciative of the arts, which was why she had enrolled both Chaucer and JOA in ballet classes two years earlier. Chaucer remained in the classes to please his mother, but by age 12, his tolerance for leotards and practicing was over as puberty was fast upon him. He often found it difficult to concentrate on his dance movements as he preferred stealing glances at the older girls whose breasts were developing.

Twice in the final weeks of his classes that year, he grabbed his stomach and bent over pretending to gag and cough, abruptly leaving class to hide a protruding erection in his leotard. He told his class instructor that he felt sick and had to hurry to the lavatory. He was embarrassed and when he later told his best friend, Bobby Chandler, at hockey practice the next night, Bobby, who was a year older, explained the connection between his eyes, his brain, and his penis.

Two days later in ballet class, the middle-aged female instructor noticed Chaucer's predicament before Chaucer even did. "Chaucer, you may excuse yourself if you wish," she said softly, at which point Chaucer's face turned red and he bent over grabbing his stomach and grimacing in fake pain. He ran out the studio door without any of the other students catching on. He never returned to class. His days as a young male dancer were over. He explained to his mother that he was no longer interested in dance. She had a brief discussion with him about how quitting one thing could become a habit in life, but he promised that would not be a problem for him. Of course he never did he tell his mother the real reason.

Remy was happy that Chaucer had now moved on to play more hockey. He and Chaucer did not have a specific discussion about his reasons for quitting ballet class although Remy soon learned of it through Bobby Chandler's father whose son hadn't kept his conversation with Chaucer a secret. Remy's reaction was just to smile broadly, knowing that his son was developing into a man.

*   *   *

In the months just before Chaucer turned fourteen, he realized that his parents were often having heated discussions. Olivia's raised voice could be heard through the closed door of Remy's study. He wasn't sure what it was all about but he felt a gnawing ache in his stomach as these discussions seemed to be happening with growing frequency and weren't going away. Remy had a steady personality, rarely raising his voice, while Oliva could, and did, get animated about many things. Olivia's way of managing life was often thinking out loud, while his father was far more circumspect and measured, perhaps from his upbringing but likely more as a deliberate counterbalance to his wife. This worked for years and seemed normal to Chaucer and JOA. Often their mother would be upset, raising her voice and arguing her point passionately. Their father's response usually was to listen, say little, then retire to his office with a drink and a cigar, emerging an hour later, which as the children learned, was the approximate time it took for their mother to move on to another matter of less controversy.

However, this time was different. A few days after the latest heated discussion, Remy packed his suitcase for another business trip to Europe. Before leaving, he gathered both children in his office. His face was long, and he looked sad. He hugged both Chaucer and JOA and asked them to sit down on the old leather sofa next to his desk. Finally, speaking softly and deliberately, he said:

"I am going to be gone with my partner Bradley Ekstrom for about two weeks. We have a new operation beginning in Spain, and we both need to be there to get it set up properly. I want you both to take care of your mother for me. I will write to you, and I will bring you each back a special gift from Spain. Remember, I love both of you very much." He then gave them each $50 for spending money. He forced himself to smile and hugged them both for a long time. Chaucer noticed with alarm that his father's eyes looked watery, but Chaucer did not say anything. Chaucer carried his father's suitcase to his car in the garage, while JOA carried his hat and coat. Remy hugged them both a third time, said he loved them, then he was gone.

The next day, Olivia announced that their Grandmother Photina would be staying with them in the house for a week or so.

"I have a work assignment in Vancouver, and I am flying out tomorrow. I will be gone for seven days. Please listen to your grandmother and help her with the chores. Make sure you do your homework," she told them with little emotion. Her detachment was noticeable to both children. While JOA did not seem bothered by this sudden news, Chaucer felt a sense of foreboding; it was an uncomfortable feeling that he disliked.

Chapter 4

Western Canada

OLIVIA GIROUX DID IN FACT HAVE AN ASSIGNMENT that took her to British Columbia, researching the status of the performing arts in the emerging city of Vancouver. The population was growing rapidly with many Asians getting permission to move to Canada, and most of these new immigrants were settling in the rainy but temperate Vancouver area. As they came, they brought their religion, their cuisine, their art, and their literature. Olivia's publisher wanted to know exactly what was developing there, as he contemplated opening a Vancouver office soon.

Olivia had set up meetings with some of her art and literature friends in Vancouver to gain the information she needed. To her surprise, Olivia found herself falling further in love with the city of Vancouver, the people, and the climate. She had been to Vancouver twice before but only for a couple of days each time. She had been much younger and Vancouver had been a smaller city. In the fifteen years since the end of World War II, much had happened in Vancouver, and she wanted and needed to learn about it and experience it.

Olivia scheduled her business meetings in the mornings, leaving her free in the afternoons to wander around the town lost in thought, ever dreaming. Within three days she decided to leave Remy and move the children to Vancouver and start a new life there. Remy had been a good father but his business and his constant travel had essentially taken him out of her life as both a lover and a confidant. For much of the time she felt that they were married in name only. He had paid less and less attention to her as the years went by, and while she needed him in her life at one time, now her thoughts and emotions were guiding her in a different direction. She had wanted to share her creative life with him, her poetry, her stories.

Remy was always so busy that he seemed to have forgotten to love her like he had in their early years. She felt that her needs were not unreasonable: just a long kiss each morning and night, making love a few times a week when he was at home, a special dinner a few times a month, and perhaps a separate vacation once a year without the children, even if only for three or four days. This was not her life now, and it had not been for a few years. Her only indiscretion in all their years of marriage had been long ago while Remy was in France on a business trip. She had been at a gallery opening in Ottawa the previous year when she had too many glasses of champagne, and she allowed a visiting Englishman to take her to dinner that night. Her resulting guilt was abundant the next day in a conversation with her mother at lunch.

"How was your dinner last night with that fellow you met?" asked her mother, who had also been at the gallery opening.

"He was boring after the appetizer; it seemed he was mostly interested in getting me to go to his hotel room for a glass of port," Olivia replied.

"You didn't, did you?" Her mother asked, sounding overly concerned.

Olivia grabbed her forehead and rolled her eyes at her mother. "Of course, I did! I wanted that glass of port, but then I left him wondering." She laughed out loud.

Her mother smiled, clearly relieved. "Wise move, and I hope no one saw you at dinner with him."

Olivia had only wanted the Englishman's attention for an hour or two, and it felt good that night.

The Englishman returned to his home country after a couple of days. Before leaving he tried to convince Olivia to meet him again but she refused. In the following months he mailed her three letters, sent to her publisher's office, but she never responded and he never contacted her again, which is how she wanted it. She had an experience that she would later use in one of her novels, so it was of benefit to her, beside the glass of port that night.

※　　　※　　　※

Soon Olivia's life returned to what it had been, before the dinner with the Englishman. She believed that she was in love with Remy, she just needed more from him. Olivia was confused, knowing though, after many years, what Remy would always be: an excellent provider, a loving father, a calm and thoughtful man, but not the man she had hoped he would evolve and grow to be. They had grown in different ways, at a different pace, and her hopes that he would change were fading. She did not feel like a failure but only that she knew this: Who they were at their best, in their early days of their love, would likely never return. And so she decided it was time to end her days of aching loneliness and constant hoping. She would make her own life and have her own happiness. Applying lessons she had learned from her parents, she decided she would not be bitter; she just needed to move on.

Olivia also understood that Remy was a realist; he had proven that in his business life. She knew he would be hurt by losing her and the children, yet she also knew he had, could, and would continue to get lost in his work, to mitigate any hurt. That was her reason for moving to the Pacific coast, across the continent. She wanted to be away, for her peace and his sense of finality...and it had to be final.

Staying in close proximity to Remy, even in Montreal or Toronto, would not create the separation she needed to advance her own career and not be distracted by having him making too frequent visits to see the children. Remy had an office in Montreal, so she did not want to live there even if her employer requested it. And she detested the size and business environment in Toronto, "a large city with a small imagination," she had always thought. She was finished with Ottawa too. It was a cold, boring town of small visions and occupied by an army of dull government bureaucrats and clerks. Eastern Canada had served her well for her early life. The West and Vancouver would be her opportunity, the salvation for her writing life. She wanted and needed to have the complete break from the past fifteen years. She believed that Chaucer and JOA would adapt to Vancouver, and she knew that Remy would support them financially and visit them. Olivia had been casually contemplating a breakaway. These past days in Vancouver had allowed her time and freedom to make the final decision: She would announce it to Remy when he returned to Ottawa from his business trip in two weeks.

*   *   *

Having made her decision, Olivia spent her free time in Vancouver finding suitable living quarters for her and the children. She planned to return to Ottawa in a few days, so her need was immediate. She remained confident that her employer would transfer her to Vancouver to start and manage the new office that she would convince him to open. Regardless, her mind was made up: She was coming west with Chaucer and JOA. Remy had plenty of money to support her if she lost her job or the books she planned to write didn't sell. Olivia was excited to get started.

Three days later, she rented a four-bedroom house on York Avenue near Kitsilano Park. A professor from the University of British Columbia was taking a year-long research and teaching sabbatical to Manilla in the Philippines. Olivia had met his wife at a business meeting a few days before, and Olivia had casually mentioned her search for a rental house. Her timing was just right. The professor and his family were leaving the following month. Olivia decided that she would offer her mother, Photina, the fourth bedroom if she wanted to join her. She wasn't worried about paying the rent. She knew that Remy would send money for the children. Her own employment might be in doubt for now, but she was confident that she could always find work, even if not as a writer or editor. This was her decision, and she would find a way to make it successful. Remy was a good husband, but she was not in love with him anymore, not in the same way as before. She wanted more, and she was going to take this chance since she knew Remy would never leave Ottawa. Plus, she didn't want him to follow her. She would take the risk.

Chapter 5

Strong Winds Make Bold Trees... Sometimes

A BREAKUP IS RARELY EASY. Whenever a family is broken apart by its own volition, not by death or war or natural disaster or crime, the family members all suffer different levels of hurtful emotions and pain knowing that the cause of the separation was internal.

In Olivia's case, her suffering was minimal. She was moving to Vancouver, even if she had to go alone. For Remy, his commitment to his business partners, employees, and clients was so great that he would not leave them. As always is the case, it is the little ones, the ones with no part in the final decision that get hurt and suffer the most. And so it was and would be with Chaucer and JOA.

JOA was almost 12 years old, with plenty of young female anxiety already, and now she would be extracted from her father, her friends, her grandparents, her school, and her future in Ottawa.

For Chaucer, he was leaving his hockey team and friends, his school, a girl he had just started to take an interest in, and most of all, worst of all, he was leaving his father behind, the one person whom he felt was consistently in his corner, willing to stand up to Olivia's whims. Chaucer held his emotions in check at first but they soon morphed into his nighttime dreams once Olivia announced her decision to him, JOA, and Remy.

Olivia was back in Ottawa for a week before Remy returned. She wrote up her findings about Vancouver and sent them to her boss, Randall, in Montreal. Three days later, he called her to say that he was almost certain that the president of the company would agree to expand to Vancouver, and because Olivia had been a fine employee and knew the company well, it was likely that she would be offered the position to manage the new office. "Thank you, Randall, that is great news. But regardless of whether I'm offered the job, I plan to move to Vancouver in two weeks, so I'm giving you my notice right now."

"Are you sure that you want to do this, Olivia?" he asked, surprised at this news.

"Yes, Randall, I am moving to Vancouver in two weeks. I'll give you my address. I know it's the right thing for me. I'm tired of Ottawa. I'll be happy to work for you out there if you need me, but I am leaving Ottawa with my children. Once I get a phone installed, I will call you with the number."

"Well then, Olivia, I hope that my boss will open that office, and also have the wisdom to keep you on our team. I will recommend that we keep you in the organization, but I can't guarantee anything just now. I'm sorry, but is that clear?"

"Oh, Randall, how does your beautiful wife put up with you and your cautious behavior! You know damn well that our company will be opening an office in Vancouver, and that you will be calling me in a few weeks to hire me back. Shame on you for your silliness. Now you have my address out there, and I will call you and give you my phone number. In the meantime who in the company will manage you while I am moving?" Olivia said, chuckling. "Bye now, Randall. I will call you soon."

Olivia hung up, smiling smugly. She would prove to Randall and everyone else that she could manage quite nicely on her own. In fact, she couldn't wait to get started.

Chapter 6

Spinning the Wheel

WHEN REMY RETURNED FROM SPAIn the following week, he had barely walked in the door before Olivia met him in the front hallway. She asked to speak to him in his study. Chaucer and JOA were still at school. Remy looked tired as he sat down in a wing-back chair, but Olivia was oblivious. She sat down in the chair opposite him and perched on the edge. Olivia could barely contain herself. "Remy, I'm leaving Ottawa, and I'm taking Chaucer and JOA with me. We're moving to Vancouver. I rented a house when I was out there while you were away," she blurted out.

Remy sat there, stunned but only for a moment. He'd had a premonition that Olivia was secretively making some plans. His head was spinning as he absorbed the news. Olivia waited, watching him, wondering if her revelation would finally ignite some passion in him, the passion she remembered from years ago. Finally, Remy just sighed. He seemed just to accept her decision, much as a bull in a Spanish Corrida de Toros knows that he is not walking out of the bullring.

"You are doing what?" he asked calmly.

"I've decided we are not the same people that we were fifteen years ago," she said.

Remy's face showed little emotion. "Perhaps you are right; perhaps we have grown apart but we can surely fix it if we try." He paused then nodded to her. "I love you, Olivia, and I love our children. Let us talk this through and see what we can do to make you feel better about us."

Olivia stood up and put her hands on the back of the chair where she had been sitting. "That is exactly what I expected you to say, Remy. 'Let's just fix this' and carry on...Remy, I have changed too much now to stay in Ottawa. I don't like it here. It constricts my creative nature, and I have all these stories to write now. I tried telling you this for the past year or more but you either don't listen to me or you are not here to talk with me. Frankly, I don't see you changing now, but I have, and I need to go far away to satisfy my need to write. Vancouver will do that for me."

Remy looked defeated. He knew that his company had taken a big measure of him the past years but he loved the business, and he and his partners had been a very successful team. His world seemed to flash before him in a panic of thoughts. He knew Olivia well, knew that she rarely changed her mind. He closed his eyes, took several deep breaths, then looked at her determined face.

"OK, I think I understand. But let the children stay with me in Ottawa. They have their friends, their relatives, and their schools here. Give yourself a year and if you are not doing what you want to, you can move back. And if you are doing what you want to, then I will move to Vancouver and open an office there." He looked at her with the face of a negotiator.

"Remy, if the children and I do not make a clean break from Ottawa, then I will never truly know if I am able to be the creative writer that I think I am, that I can be. I would always have that Ottawa decision hanging over me, and I have decided that if I want to be honest, then I need to go without a safety plan, and the children need the same opportunity to break from the East, to get out of Ottawa, see the West, become the people that a new place will allow. No, I am not planning to come back, whether I am successful in Vancouver or not. I need to have in my mind that the children and I will not be coming back east." Olivia, her arms folded on her chest, looked Remy in the eyes.

Remy wondered whether she was testing his resolve about losing her or that she might be using the discussion as a test for a scene in one of her stories. He didn't say anything for a few minutes, just looked at Olivia, looked around the room, trying to figure out his next words. Then he sighed. "Ok then, if your mind is made up, go. But I want us to keep it civil for the children, and I want your promise that when I come to visit them that you will support my visits and allow me to see them, and you'll let me bring them back to Ottawa in the summers. They will want to see their grandparents, cousins, and friends. Will you agree to that then?"

Olivia said nothing. She just nodded and left the room.

* * *

Later that afternoon, Remy walked into the living room where Olivia was sitting in her favorite chair, feet up, and reading an arts magazine. "Let me help with the arrangements to move," he proposed. "I want the children to be happy and not be burdened with any more issues than that we are separating. Will you allow me to do that?" he said.

She glanced up from the magazine and calmly replied, "My rental house is furnished. It is the house of a faculty member at the university who will be away for a year, so our move will be relatively simple, Remy."

"OK, then leave as much as you want here, and at some time later, I will ship it to you, when you are ready."

"Yes, that will be fine. What we will take is our clothes and our books and papers. The children will want their things too."

"Yes, I will have a mover come here, and you can tell them what to take, and I will have it sent to Vancouver for you, so please do not worry, we will make it easy for Chaucer and JOA."

"Thank you, Remy, I expected you to behave exactly like this," she said with a firm look at him.

They both were quiet for a few moments. Remy was refilling his glass of sherry when she got up and began pacing the floor.

"I am sorry that I have hurt you, Remy. You knew that perhaps this time would come, didn't you, with all your travel, being away so much, year after year?"

He thought for a while, looking out the big window at the river.

"Yes, I am not surprised, Olivia," he sighed. "We have had a good life together, and I know that you have a different calling than do I. So I understand, and in time my disappointment and pain will go away, I suppose. I will miss Chaucer and JOA every day, as you know, and I will visit them as often as I can. You approve of that, don't you?"

"Of course, Remy, they love you very much, so please come any time. We will work it out, and we will do it for them."

They did not have much to say after that.

*   *   *

The next day, Remy told Olivia that he would be staying in Montreal until she and the children were gone. He gave her the name and number of the moving company that would come to pack their things.

That night, Remy took Chaucer and JOA to his golf club for dinner. They talked well into the evening about the changes that were coming for all of them. Remy made sure not to blame Olivia in front of the children, although it was a difficult task for him. He was angry at losing his children, yet he knew that he could not show that to them. They would have it difficult enough without feeling that perhaps that they had caused the breakup, and Remy would not do that to them. They were still too young to really understand what had happened, so he spent the time at dinner talking about the move and their educational goals. He mentioned that perhaps he would be able to convince their mother that they could spend the summer back in Ottawa with him.

Both Chaucer and JOA were quiet during the dinner discussion. Remy wondered if perhaps they thought that this was just a temporary thing for the family. Neither child had guessed that such a radical change was coming, so neither could really frame questions about their feelings now, especially since Remy had said the decision had been made, and that he would be visiting them every few weeks until they got settled in Vancouver.

Chaucer seemed angry but did not say so. He more or less just listened and stared at his father. JOA seemed to think the entire matter was just a story and that moving to Vancouver might just be a long vacation. The enormity of the forthcoming changes simply did not compute with them, being so radical from their current, stable life. Since Remy had been such a good provider, which gave them that stability, he was not surprised at their quietness.

By the end of the dinner, Remy was spent emotionally. They drove home, and that night he tucked each child into bed as he had when they were younger. He told them that he would always love them, no matter what happened in the future. He said that he was leaving in the morning after they went to school, and he would be in Montreal until they were gone. Both children hugged him as tightly as they had ever done. He told each child that he wanted them to watch over their mother and care for her the best that they could, and that he would come to Vancouver in a few weeks to see them during a coming school break.

Remy turned the light out in each of their rooms after kissing them. He went to his office then and locked the door. He poured himself a big glass of scotch, sat in his favorite chair, and proceeded to weep for a long time, eventually falling asleep on the old leather sofa with a pillow and a throw to warm him. It was one of the longest nights of his life.

Chapter 7

The Sun Also Rises, Said Hem

ONE MORNING A COUPLE OF DAYS LATER, Chaucer awoke feeling at peace. He was so happy. He had had a dream during the night that he and his father were sailing. They had left his mother and JOA standing on the long pier, and the wind had taken the two of them in their boat out to sea. They sailed in the sunshine, with a perfect tailwind, eating sandwiches in the aft deck, feeling the wind on their backs with the mainsail and the jib in a tight haul, carrying them further and further from land. They spoke of many joys and future days together. Then, suddenly in a surprise, JOA emerged from the cabin below and came up the steps into the cockpit. She took the wheel. She turned around to Chaucer and her father and smiled. Chaucer said, "You were on the pier with Mother; how did you get here?"

"No, that was not me. That was someone else. I have been hiding in the cabin all morning waiting for you two to take me away from her. I want to be with you, the both of you, I do not want to stay with her anymore," she declared, still smiling as she held the wheel. She had the same mischievous smile that Olivia had when she had one of her big ideas.

Remy smiled too, then Chaucer laughed out loud, very loud, very, very loud, and then he woke up. In his dream, he had a dream within a dream, thinking that when he awoke that he was awake, only to realize that it all was a lengthy dream. This confused Chaucer for most of that morning, seemingly unable to tell reality from fantasy.

* * *

In the last days before Olivia and the children left for Vancouver in January 1961, Chaucer, who was not yet 14, took a train to Montreal for the day, and he and his father had a serious conversation about Chaucer coming back east in four years to attend either the University of Toronto, McGill University in Montreal, or Carleton University in Ottawa. Remy promised Chaucer he would pay the tuition, and he said that by then Chaucer would be 18 and old enough to make that decision and convince his mother that it would be best for him. Chaucer liked that promise from his father, and he held it close for the next few years.

* * *

In the days ahead, Remy paid to have both his children attend private schools in Vancouver: JOA was sent to the Crofton House School for girls, and Chaucer was enrolled in St. Patrick's Secondary. He also would join a youth hockey team in the local league.

In the first weeks, the children were not happy. Their father had been their loving and trusted parent and friend, and now he was gone from their daily lives. Neither child had ever had to respond to a parental subtraction like this before. It became their time of great sadness. The perpetual gray skies of Vancouver perfectly portrayed the emotions of both Chaucer and JOA as the weeks turned to months.

* * *

There is little need to detail much more, for any readetr who was separated from a loving parent as a child knows the anguish it creates. Olivia did not seem to notice her children's unhappiness, or perhaps she thought it would organically work its way out of them, or worse, she did not seem to care all that much. She quickly got into her daily routine of work and writing. The cooking was usually left to either Chaucer or JOA, and many meals were just frozen dinners from the oven, or simple pasta and rice with some meat and vegetables tossed in for color. Many nights Olivia would have dinner with her new friends in Vancouver who came to visit her. They would sit in the living room, build a fire, and eat small plates of food while drinking wine. She would leave dinner instructions for the children on the kitchen counter and ask them to clean the kitchen before doing their school work. Olivia was happy in her new city, with her new life, and she seemed to believe that her children were old enough to care for themselves now.

In March 1961, Olivia's company in Montreal did open a new office in Vancouver, and they made Olivia the deputy publisher, a position that Randall had created just to keep Olivia with the organization. Her move and the transition plan had worked well for her. She truly believed that the children were feeling fine with their new schools, the good schools that Remy had paid for. She met some of the new friends that both Chaucer and JOA brought home. Olivia, like her own mother before her, had assumed that children were resilient and all matters would be resolved. Chaucer and JOA, if asked, would not have agreed.

A month after the move, Remy came for a week to visit, staying in the guest room. Olivia was away on a work assignment to Calgary for six of the seven days that Remy was in Vancouver so she decided that he should stay in the house with the children. Olivia's mother, Photina, had decided to remain in Ottawa where she had her loyal circle of literary old friends and not relocate with her daughter. She wrote to Olivia that she thought it was a task for a younger grandmother, so she politely declined.

On the day before Remy was to return to Ottawa, the day that Olivia returned from Calgary, all four of them went to a fine restaurant for Remy's farewell dinner. Olivia was proud to announce that her first novel, the book that she had spent the previous three years working on, had been purchased by a Toronto publishing house, and that they had made her an offer to produce another book within twelve months. She asked Remy to please review her contract, which he passed to his company attorney. The attorney deemed it a good contract. Both Remy and Olivia were pleased with her new success.

Privately, Remy knew that this would be the end of any hope that Olivia would ever move back to Ottawa. She had achieved success in her writing life. He knew what that meant for him and the children: permanent separation. Remy was big enough to accept it, and he would display grace in his days going forward. But in truth, Remy was aching inside. He missed his children so much that at times, his entire body was in pain. He had started to drink more as well. His life without Olivia's companionship could be survived. He was a handsome man with a good business, and he could surely find other female companions if he wanted, but that was not on his mind.

He was learning that he could not live without his children, and soon his periodic gloom was morphing into a daily state of depression. He had thought that he could manage his emotions, with the hope that Olivia would change her mind and move back east. Then with Olivia's book contract, he realized that a return to the former life in Ottawa with an intact family was gone. He felt a knife to the heart and a cloak on his soul. Neither the war nor any other matter heretofore in his life had ever possessed and distressed him like this. Remy was lost at sea with only a small lighthouse — his successful business — shining any light to save him.

*   *   *

Within a month after Remy returned to Ottawa in May 1961, he received a call from Olivia informing him that once the school year ended in June, she would be moving with the children to Victoria on the big island across the Strait from Vancouver. She told him that using her advance from the Toronto publisher for her next book, she was buying an old farmhouse. She was quitting her job as deputy publisher with the Montreal company and would spend all her time now writing. She had never sounded happier.

She told Remy that her literary friend Francine, who worked at the Vancouver bookstore MacLeod's on West Pender Street in Gas Town, was selling her mother's old farmhouse outside of Victoria. Olivia had gone with Francine a few weeks before to get the house ready for sale, and she herself had fallen quickly in love with the property because it had a small two-story barn behind the house. From the hay-loading door on the second floor of the old barn, one could look down a grand hill and see the Haro Strait and the islands to the east. She liked the house, which had three bedrooms and a large stone fireplace in the living room.

Yet it was not the house that she fell romantically in love with, rather it was the upstairs room in the barn. Standing in the wide door on the second floor of the barn, next to a hoist that had been used to haul bales of hay up for storage, she could see far. She could see water. The land had some large old trees in the meadow where the cattle used to graze, and a dirt road cut through the apple and pear orchard into the nearby forest. It also had the most important quality that a writer needed; it had an abundance of quiet for it lay on a farm of twenty acres. She knew that this place, at this time, did not come to her by chance, rather by the spirit that had given her the gift to write. She knew right then that this would be her chosen place, and she had been guided there for the purpose of writing. Her joy was palpable. Remy was happy for her, but now he knew that any chance of Olivia ever returning to Ottawa was gone.

Francine had told her of the price put on the property by the appraiser, who had been hired by the attorney that was the executor of her mother and father's small estate. Francine's only sibling, her younger brother Carl, had moved to Los Angeles long ago and had not been to see his mother in four or five years, so she was allowed to guide the settlement of the estate. She told Olivia that the price would be below market value because so much work needed to be done to make repairs prior to placing it on the market, and that if Olivia would buy the property as it was, that they would be able to set a good price for her.

So with this unexpected opportunity, Olivia quickly checked her finances, and with the recent advance she had received and a small contribution from Remy, she could buy the property. Remy made a quick trip west to see the house and barn with Olivia and the children. He could see the merit and potential that Olivia had described to him over the phone. He liked the proximity to both the city of Victoria, which would be good for him to make travel connections and secure lodging when he visited Chaucer and JOA. Plus, while he still loved Olivia and had hoped that somehow one day that they might even reconcile, he also felt pleasure in seeing her happy. He hoped that if Olivia were happy, she'd be more relaxed and loving to the children. And so Remy constructed a purchase contract that placed the property in the names of Olivia, Chaucer, and JOA, and Remy would have the power of attorney for the children until they each reached the age of 21.

Olivia agreed, and with that Remy made a fifty percent investment into the property, leaving Olivia with a small mortgage and no need to use her book advance, which Remy wanted her to use to renovate the property. He also said that he would continue to deposit $1000 per month into Olivia's bank account for the care of the children, and he would continue to pay for their schooling. Olivia could not have been happier.

The property would close with the local bank in thirty days, so in agreement with Francine, Olivia hired a local contractor to begin immediate work on the renovation of the barn. She had the contractor winterize the second floor of the barn, cut two large windows into the east side of the second floor so she could put her desk in front of one of the new windows allowing her to look out to see the Haro Strait and San Juan Islands in the distance. She upgraded the electrical service in both the house and the barn. She had new cabinets, a new oven, a large sink, and a dishwasher put in the kitchen, and had a washer and dryer installed in the mud room between the house and the garage.

Over time, she would create an English garden between the house and the barn, paint the barn a deep red and the house a federal blue, her favorite house color. Olivia had made her break and in the course of just a year, had completely rebuilt her life. In doing so, she had also substantially crippled her children emotionally and left Remy with an empty house and broken heart in Ottawa.

* * *

The next two years moved quickly and relatively quietly for the family. Remy's company continued to expand, gaining access to more ports and cities, and Olivia continued to write, although her personal life and living habits were becoming more and more eccentric as she sequestered herself in her writing barn in Victoria. Her second novel achieved greater critical acclaim than did her first breakthrough book. Sales were very good, and her financial status was thus settled with this success.

Olivia had so loved her writing room in the barn that soon she added a powder room, and she moved a loveseat with a pull-out bed to the room. When it was late at night, as her writing was finished, and perhaps it was raining or cold, she could sleep on her thoughts next to her desk and typewriter, ready to continue at 4 a.m. or 6 a.m. or whatever time she rose. She had taken to smoking a pipe, her father's old meerschaum pipe, the tobacco bowl of which was carved into the shape of a whale, and it had turned a complex brown-and-orange color from the years of him smoking it.

Olivia remembered the whiskey smell of his tobacco but could not find any of his former tobacco brand in Victoria, so she simply bought an expensive tobacco brand in a two-pound metal container from the Cicero's Smoke Shoppe in town, then sprinkled a few drops of Kentucky bourbon into her leather tobacco pouch, which when absorbed into the tobacco would recreate the smells of her father's pipe smoke from her youth. This pleased her very much, and her habit of smoking the pipe with the whiskey-flavored tobacco lasted the remainder of her life.

Her other habit that evolved as her writing life matured was her love for champagne. Her routine was to buy two cases from her local provincial wine outlet each month, almost always a French non-vintage Blanc de Blanc brut, and open a bottle to have a glass or two with her dinner. She would recork the bottle, and then when writing in her loft the next day, she would sip the remainder of the bottle from the night before, which by this time due to the lack of bubbles, tasted more like a glass of chardonnay. This suited her needs for a creative stimulant just fine. The love of her writing life knew no bounds, and since Remy had helped with her income until her book royalties were sufficient, she was able to afford the indulgence.

Olivia rarely spent time in the main house anymore, usually going only to gather food to take back to the loft, use the shower, or occasionally sleep in her large bed rather than in the loft. Every other week, she would host her group of three or four other women friends in her living room, or she would drive to one of their homes nearby as they rotated the hosting of the group. Once a month the group would have a farm supper event. The supper event was where all the others, with or without husbands, lovers and kids, would show up at the designated host house. The host that night had the responsibility of preparing all the food, ensuring that enough whiskey and wine were available, then cleaning up once the guests left. The ending time was always 9 p.m., and they all enforced that rule. Other than for these supper events, Olivia seldom left the property except for groceries or an occasional trip to the local Canada Post Office, when the employees were not on strike, and the Post Office was open. She always called ahead.

* * *

The move to Victoria Island meant that Chaucer and JOA boarded at their respective schools. Olivia's only mandate was that they take the ferry every Saturday and spend the night, so Olivia could have Sunday dinner with them. The rest of her days, she was alone with her typewriter, and that was how she liked her life. Sometimes she and one or two of her Victoria friends would take the ferry to Vancouver to see a play or a dance company, always stopping at MacLeod's Books to see Francine and others. At first Chaucer and JOA missed being with their mother. Yet as time moved on, each made friends at their schools, and the desire to take a bus to the ferry, then the ferry to Victoria, then back again the next day held little joy. For when they were home, Olivia rarely seemed interested in their lives, their classes or their friends, instead taking her refuge in the satiety of her new circle of women companions, all of whom were also engaged in some artistic pursuit, be it painting, photography, sculpture, or writing.

When the children were home, she surveyed Chaucer and JOA on a particular plot line or character development in the novel that she was writing at the moment. Neither child enjoyed this, inducing a state of acedia in each. At times, one or the other or sometimes both (when they conspired) would call Olivia and offer an excuse for avoiding the solemnity of the Sunday dinner that week. Olivia was rarely troubled by this since it gave her more time to write and take long walks in the woods on her land.

For Olivia, writing didn't feel like work; it was therapy from the life that she had felt trapped in, first by her parents, then to a lesser degree by her earlier career and her marriage to Remy. Some days she did miss Remy, his handsome smile, his touch, his voice. Yet as the months, then years past, the solitude of her writing life and the freedom and income it offered her built up a soft curtain to her old life, and the memories perhaps were most vivid in her dreams rather than in her conscience thoughts and mind. The family that once was now had become four separate lives only connected by past common history and bloodline.

Chapter 8

Time Moves, Life Moves

CHAUCER GRADUATED FROM ST. PATRICK'S a year late, having added on an extra year due to poor grades his first year when he was still reeling from the divorce, and then adding classes to ensure his admission to university. He applied to the University of Toronto (UT), McGill University in Montreal, and Carleton University in Ottawa, and all three accepted him for the fall 1967. He chose UT because three of his friends from Ottawa were enrolled there; UT had some academic options that he liked, and one of his Ottawa friends played on the university club hockey team and assured Chaucer that he would make the team if he wanted to play, which he did. UT also was just a four-hour drive from Ottawa in good weather, and he could visit his father on any given weekend when needed. Choosing a university more than 2,000 miles from his mother felt liberating to Chaucer, an end to the unhappy life his mother handed him when she yanked him away from the home and friends he had been so happy with nearly five years before.

In 1966, Remy had been dating a local Ottawa woman, Monica Perkins, for about a year. Once Chaucer spent time with both of them, he totally approved of the relationship because Remy seemed happy. Monica paid great attention to his father and had a sense of kindness that Chaucer liked and made him feel comfortable around her. Monica had a career and her own home and money. She now controlled the multi-office travel agency in Ottawa that her father had created after World War II. Remy had known her father, and he had met her some years before, as the Perkins Travel Agency always made the flight and hotel arrangements for Remy and his partners for their trips abroad.

The summer after his graduation from secondary school, Chaucer got a job with a landscaping company in Victoria that was owned by the husband of one of his mother's writing group friends. Remy insisted that Chaucer stay with his mother for the summer before coming east. Chaucer knew it would be his last time of any length spent with Olivia, so he agreed. Being outside appealed to Chaucer, and he could work late and make plenty of money that summer before going east to college in Toronto. His mother was as reclusive as ever, and many days he would not see her, given her late night writing or writing group meetings and her propensity for sleeping late each morning if she had been up late writing or drinking too much champagne. They communicated, when they did, by notes on the kitchen table. This was fine for Chaucer. His mother remained in her own cosmic universe, and it seemed that neither he nor JOA rarely fit into it anymore. The mother who had held him, stroked his hair, taught him to read, and taken him to plays and music recitals now hardly even touched him anymore. Chaucer wondered about her emotional stability, her happiness, her health, but he remained silent. He felt ignored, lonely, and at times resentful. He missed his father, and he missed Ottawa. At first, he had been loath to understand why they had separated and divorced, but now his observations of her behavior made it all the more clear to him.

Regardless of how she had evolved since the divorce, Chaucer missed the times when his mother had made him the center of her attention, read to him, helped him with his homework, kissed him goodnight as a boy. He was conflicted about this denial of his mother's love for him. He wanted his mother back in this life, to talk with him, approve and validate his feelings, share her life with him. But because of the divorce and the relocation to Vancouver, he was resentful and the growing pain in him had developed into a salty dislike for his mother over the past few years. He did not like what she had done to his father; he did not like her social circle; he felt no love or enduring attachment to Victoria Island or British Columbia.

* * *

In the middle of his fourth week on the landscaping job, he came home after dark to find a note on the table:

"When you get home, come into my office. I will be with my writing friends but knock. Important," and so Chaucer did just that.

Knock, knock. "Chaucer, I will be right out." He could hear Olivia telling the other women that she would be back shortly. Her office door opened, and she walked out, shutting it behind her.

"Good, I am glad you are home. I received a call a few hours ago. It's about your father."

"Why, did something happen?" asked Chaucer, feeling a small tightening in his chest.

"Well, yes. Your father is in the hospital in London. They think that he will be fine."

"Why, what happened, Mother, tell me," he said firmly, almost rudely.

"It appears that your father was in a business meeting with some people at the Royal Admiralty offices, and something exploded near the building. Your father was injured and is being treated. I do not know anything else at this point."

She handed him a piece of paper with the phone number of the hospital on it.

"Call this number and see if you can find out his condition. It will be about 5 a.m. in London now and let me know what you learn. I must get back to my group," she said with little emotion.

"Wait, what exploded, what is going on?" Chaucer asked in a desperate voice.

Olivia looked at him impatiently. "Just call, maybe they can tell you more," and she turned, opened her office door and disappeared behind it.

Chaucer couldn't believe how dispassionate his mother was in sharing this news. No concern at all about Remy or how upsetting this was to Chaucer. His father, the man he looked up to before all others, was lying in a hospital bed in London, and Chaucer knew nothing else. His mind started to whirl. He ran down the stairs of the barn and back into the house. He called the number in London via a local operator, but the line was busy. "Call back again," she told him.

He walked to the small TV set that his mother had and turned it on to a local British Columbia/Vancouver news and weather station. A few minutes later, at 9:30 p.m., a reporter at the news desk came on:

> We have an update on the IRA bombing yesterday of the Royal Admiralty Office in London. It appears now that three are confirmed dead, and many more are in local hospitals. We will bring you more information as we receive it from London.

Chaucer dropped to a chair. "What the hell?" he said aloud in a state of growing confusion. He folded his hands, closed his eyes and bowed his head and became very quiet. He took a few deep breaths to calm himself, and thought of his father, the man he loved more than anyone in the world. "Dear God, please protect my father, heal him, and bring him peace and comfort." This soothed Chaucer somewhat, and his mind stopped racing. He breathed deeply, and thought of his father's broad smile, his laughter, how he always held JOA in his arms when she was a child. He thought of himself and his dad skating on the Rideout Canal when he was a boy. He whispered to himself, "I love you, Dad, I don't want you to die, please don't die on us, Dad," and soon the tears of fear and uncertainty wet his cheeks. He cried loudly for several minutes, his face in his hands. He didn't care if anyone heard him. He just wanted to be with his father now.

Chaucer found a half full bottle of red wine in the refrigerator and poured some into a glass. He decided to call Monica in Ottawa. It was nearly 1 a.m. back east, and his call awakened her. "Hello," she answered groggily.

"Have you heard from my father? How is he?"

Monica could hear the urgency in Chaucer's voice. "No, I haven't. I know he's in London. What's wrong?"

Chaucer told her that his mother had received a call that Remy had been hurt in the bombing and was in the hospital, and he hadn't been able to get through to find out more.

Monica said she had heard about the bombing on the radio earlier that day but it never occurred to her that Remy might have been hurt. The call from Chaucer frightened her.

"Monica, please book me on a flight from Vancouver to London tomorrow. I am going to see my father. Bring me through Ottawa with a layover as I need to stop home for my passport and some clothes. Please use the business account." Monica got out of bed and quickly made the arrangements, then called Chaucer to fill him in

He left early the next morning to catch the first leg of the flight from Vancouver. There was no sign of Olivia, so he assumed she was sleeping in her studio. He scribbled a note that said simply, "Flying to London to see Father. Will be in touch when I get there."

With the flight times, time zone differences and a stopover in Ottawa, Chaucer was able to arrive at the hospital in less than 36 hours from when his mother had given him the information. He had also learned during the Ottawa layover that his father was in stable condition with a broken leg and arm and many cuts from glass. Once he had this news, he called JOA to tell her what had happened. She had opted to stay at her boarding school for the summer and was working part time in a boutique in Vancouver. Chaucer reassured the tearful JOA that Remy's life was not in danger. Knowing this comforted Chaucer enough so he was able to sleep on the flight from Montreal to London. He took a cab from Gatwick Airport to the hospital and soon found his father resting in his room. It was 11:15 a.m. Greenwich Mean Time (GMT).

Walking into his father's hospital room, he rushed to Remy's bedside. "What happened, Dad?" he asked, his voice trembling from both anxiety and love.

Some white bandages covered part of his father's face, and there was a plaster cast on his left forearm and a boot cast on his right lower leg. Chaucer was relieved to see Remy sitting up in bed. He beckoned Chaucer to come closer as Remy's hearing had not yet recovered from the concussion caused by the bomb blast. Although Remy was already in good spirits, he felt even better when he saw Chaucer. Remy explained that he was in London to negotiate new provisions to his company's contract for allowing his bigger ships to dock in Liverpool, Belfast, and Glasgow. They had just sat down in the commander's office when a bomb went off in the lobby area. It blew the office's door off and pieces of it hit him and the commander, who was also suffering a broken leg and a more serious concussion. Two Admiralty staff in the very next room were killed as was a member of Her Majesty's Naval Service Security Marine Guards in the lobby. Remy considered himself fortunate. He actually laughed a bit and said to Chaucer that these injuries were worse than anything that he had received in his five years in the war.

Chaucer stayed three more days until his father was discharged from the hospital, and then they flew back to Ottawa together. It served Chaucer well to know that he could look after his father at home. Being there now was generating a heightened level of resentment for his mother. He wondered what level of contempt could she have harbored for her husband, children, her mother, Photina, and for Ottawa, that would give her the will, the desire, the license to bring such conflict and emotional harm to him, JOA, and Remy. "How could she do this?" he thought, but he found no answers.

During the second week home, Chaucer took Remy (who could not drive due to his broken right tibia) to his local physician. The exam resulted in Remy learning that he did not have any permanent hearing loss. The doctor took off the bandages and pulled out all his stitches, and he told Remy that in two more weeks he should be able to drive and walk without a cane. When Chaucer, who was sitting in the waiting room first saw his father come out of the doctor's office limping with his walking cane, he looked at his face and started laughing.

"What humor am I missing, Son?" asked Remy.

"Have you looked in the mirror since the doctor removed the bandages?" Chaucer asked.

"No."

"Well, you look like Jean Beliveau might look after a fight with Gordie Howe," said Chaucer, laughing. When they got to the car, Remy pulled the rearview mirror toward him and peered at his face. Chaucer was right, he had multiple red lines on his face from where the physician had just removed the stitches. He did look like an NHL player after a fight, and he smiled broadly and they both laughed heartily, as only a father and son can in such a moment.

* * *

In the next week Chaucer called JOA every day to discuss the progress of their father. Remy himself spoke to Olivia about the explosion and his recovery. Monica came to the house every evening to prepare dinner for Remy, Chaucer, and herself. Chaucer soon learned how kind and intelligent Monica was and why his father would have developed an affection for her. Her brilliant eyes and disarming smile were wonderful for his father's recovery. Plus she was very fluent in the language of travel, just like his father. This brought contentment to Chaucer as the days went on. Seeing his father happy again was therapeutic for him.

Soon it was decided that Chaucer would return to Victoria, gather his personal things and then return to Ottawa with JOA. JOA would stay for two weeks or so to see her father and some of her old girlfriends in Ottawa, then return to Victoria to live with Olivia until school started in September.

Before dinner one evening after JOA had returned to Ottawa, she went to Remy in his study and sat down next to him calmly. "I want to stay with you until school starts. I don't want to go back to live at Mother's house anymore."

Remy put his arm around her and looked at her with reassuring comfort. "And why is that, JOA?"

"Mother hardly speaks to me or Chaucer when we are there. She just sits in her barn and writes and then goes out with her women friends. I get really lonely there, especially when Chaucer is not around. I just don't want to go back. Can't I stay with you until school starts, please, Dad?'

Remy stood up and pulled JOA beside him; he hugged his daughter, stroked her hair, and kissed her head. He felt so very sad inside, hearing this from JOA. He felt his eyes swelling but stopped before any tears could fall. How could this family have been changed so much from the one that had occupied this house just a few years before?

They both sat back down. "Yes, I would love it if you stayed the extra weeks. I will call and let your mother know, OK?"

JOA smiled broadly and grabbed her father's hand. "Oh thank you, Dad, thank you, thank you, thank you." Her smile was off the charts.

So it was set. JOA would stay in Ottawa until her classes resumed in Vancouver and her dormitory opened for the fall semester. Remy called Olivia to explain the change in plans for JOA. Olivia sounded surprised. "I didn't know that JOA would be coming back to Victoria. I thought she'd just return to school in Vancouver." Remy just shook his head at Olivia's lack of interest in spending time with JOA. He replied, "OK, thank you...goodbye," and he gently placed the phone receiver down.

Remy asked Chaucer to spend the remainder of August in the company office in Montreal so he could help out while some of the employees took their August annual holiday time. "I'd really like that,

Dad," Chaucer said, pleased that his father was entrusting him with this assignment. Chaucer could stay in the home of a senior manager in Montreal, a man he had known since childhood who also had a son the same age as Chaucer. On the weekends, Chaucer could drive back to Ottawa so he could see his father and his mates in town. He also wanted to start on the freshman reading list that the University of Toronto had sent to him. He was excited about being back in the East and he wanted to be prepared for school in September. His life with Remy was giving him meaning and order again.

JOA and Chaucer would be together in their childhood home in Ottawa for the rest of the summer. Chaucer thought that true grace had blessed him and his sister. How did he and JOA earn this luck, he wondered. It was where they both wanted to be again. They wanted those lost four years in Vancouver restored, but that was impossible; they had been lost to them forever, and they needed to move on now.

*   *   *

JOA, now 16 and physically mature, was happier than she had been in four years as she spent the time in Ottawa with her old friends. They went shopping and to movies together downtown. At a teen dance with her friends one night, JOA met a young man named Michael, whom she really liked. Michael was 18 and had just joined the Canadian maritime service and was awaiting his training orders. Remy initially was interested in Michael's career plans based on what Michael had told him the first time they met, until one evening two weeks later when Remy came home early with Monica after a dinner party.

Michael and JOA were sitting in Michael's car in the dark in Remy's driveway, listening to the radio, smoking marijuana, and drinking whiskey out of a half-liter bottle. Driving up slowly, with the car's headlamps off, Remy pulled his car quietly next to Michael's car. It was a warm summer night, and Remy's car windows were down. He smelled the pot smoke and then saw JOA drinking from the glass bottle. While Monica was aghast, Remy calmly got out of his car and walked up to the driver side of the car. Remy thanked Michael for bringing JOA home, then instructed his daughter: "JOA, please go into the house with Monica," which she did with no resistance or comment.

After Monica and JOA went inside, Remy stood at the window of Michael's car, arms folded, and gave Michael the look of an angry hockey coach.

"Michael, when are you leaving Ottawa on your training?"

"Sorry, sir, we were just having a little fun. JOA is a great girl."

"I didn't ask you about JOA. Tell me about your training schedule."

"Well, sir, I have my training to complete in Montreal and then I will be assigned to a ship."

"Michael, let me give you some important advice. First, you are not to see JOA again, here or anywhere. And second, if I find out that you have, I will call my good friends at the Merchant Hall in Montreal and make sure that you are assigned to the longest cruise, on the worst boat, and with the most hardened captain that they know. Do you understand what I am saying, young man?"

Michael's eyes almost popped out of his head. "Yes, sir, I didn't mean any harm to your daughter."

"That's not the point. The point is you were smoking an illegal drug with my daughter, and giving her whiskey and heavens knows what else tonight and before, and that is completely unacceptable to me and likely to your parents as well. She is 16 years old! You have acted in a completely irresponsible manner and now you are not to come around here or see her again, period. Do I make myself clear, sailor?"

Michael nodded his head, started the car, and drove off quickly.

Once inside, Remy said that it would be best if JOA went to her room and he would speak to her in the morning. JOA nodded and disappeared up the stairs, her guilt intact for the moment.

*   *   *

The remaining weeks that JOA, Chaucer, and Remy spent together that summer of 1966 went smoothly. They attended a gala dinner and concert by the Ottawa Symphony and even went with Photina and Gillian to a private preview of a new ballet by the National Ballet Company of Canada that they would introduce in late September. The three of them soon felt like their former lives had been restored, if only for a few weeks. Their happiness was palpable, as thick and warm as before.

Soon JOA boarded an Air Canada flight to Vancouver to return to school. Remy drove her to the airport, and they joked about old family stories and even about how Remy had handled Michael the sailor a few weeks before. JOA admitted that she had made a big mistake, and Remy held her hand in the car. She squeezed her father's hand in return, showing him her love.

At the airport, Remy parked the car and carried JOA's big duffle bag and suitcase to the Air Canada counter. When her boarding gate was called, Remy stood with her near the gate, holding both her hands and looking into her eyes as only a father can.

"JOA, I want you to remember that I love you with all my heart. If you ever need me to come to Vancouver for you, just call me and if I am in Canada then, I will be there the next day, OK?"

"Thank you, Dad. I love you too. I just don't understand why Mom did this to us, to you and me and Chaucer. I just don't understand it." Her eyes filled with tears as she looked up at her father.

Remy put his arms around JOA and hugged her tight. He stroked her hair softly. He did not want her to leave ever again. His old feelings of pain came rushing back.

"I don't understand it either JOA, but I will always be here for you, and you will always be my daughter. We all need to accept what your mother did, and we need to understand that it will never be like it was." Remy swallowed hard, trying to find the right words to comfort JOA. "You and I and Chaucer, we'll be the family we want. We'll make it work for us. Now it's important for you to finish up at school these next two years, and if you want to come back east for university like your brother, we can make that happen, OK?"

"Yes, Dad, I understand. I'll really miss you and Chaucer. I will call you when I get to Vancouver. Take care of yourself and give a big hug to Chaucer for me…I love you both very much."

With that, she kissed Remy on the cheek, turned, and walked to the gate. Turning around as she went into the tunnel, she saw Remy mouthing the words "I love you" and she gave him a big smile that belied her broken heart.

As the plane readied for takeoff, JOA sat in her seat and allowed her tears to flow freely. Seeing the distraught young woman, a flight attendant stopped next to JOA's seat and asked "Are you OK? Can I help you?" JOA sighed and said softly, "I'll be OK," and turned to the window next to her seat to hide her face. She dabbed her eyes with a tissue, blew her nose, and within in a few moments after take-off, she was asleep.

* * *

Driving home from the airport, Remy could hardly contain his anger with Olivia, and not for the first time in the last three days. Two days before, Chaucer had essentially the same talk as JOA had had with Remy. Even though the separation and divorce had happened more than four years ago, both Remy and the children were still hostage to the events and the past joys of their former life together. It was a pain that afflicted them all, and Remy continued to wonder "Will the pain never end?"

A few days later, Remy drove Chaucer to Toronto to start his life at UT. No tears were part of this trip, just father and son discussion about Remy's travel schedule, planning holiday events for the fall, and Chaucer's weekend visits to Ottawa. Remy said that he would get tickets to a Maple Leafs hockey game from a friend who lived in Toronto, and the two of them would go to a game or two. "That would be great, Dad," Chaucer said. They talked of the coming Christmas, and how JOA would be joining them in Ottawa. Father and son were joyful that Chaucer had chosen to come east for his university years.

After Remy and Chaucer unloaded his bags in his dorm room, they went to a local pub for dinner. Remy departed and was back in Ottawa just after dark. He drove directly to Monica's house where they sat on her deck, had drinks and talked, and Remy spent the night. It was a good night.

* * *

At the University of Toronto, Chaucer continued to play recreational hockey, playing for the UT club team, which had two nights of practice per week and a game or two on the weekends. Late in his teen years, Chaucer had grown to six feet tall. He was a strong skater and happy he could keep playing the game. Remy was quite proud of how Chaucer had matured both physically and in his scholastic efforts. Most important of all to Remy was his belief that Chaucer was a kind young man, a trait that he believed that Chaucer had gained from spending time with Remy's mother, Gillian, during his boyhood years in Ottawa. Grandmother Gillian had been a great listener, a kind counselor, and a teacher of good habits and polite behavior for Remy and his siblings in his childhood days. Remy had made sure that both Chaucer and JOA spent as much time with her as they could. Olivia had never objected. She was always busy reading and writing thus any quiet time at home was lauded by her. How she had defined her family life then was different than Remy. He had tried to understand it. He had failed.

Chapter 9

Return to Vancouver

WHILE CHAUCER WAS MATURING IN TORONTO, JOA was not faring so well back in school in Vancouver. She found her classes to be boring and couldn't figure out how discussing the novels of Jane Austen or learning about World War I had anything to do with real life. Her school friends were girls who had plenty of time and money to explore the things that young girls should best avoid until they are more mature and have a better understanding of male hormones and how they govern behavior in young men. She and her friends started attending University of British Columbia fraternity parties. The laissez-faire drinking and pot smoking finally caught up to one of the older girls in the group when she got pregnant, quit school, and ran away to San Francisco with the UBC student who was the father of the baby.

Once they arrived in Haight-Ashbury, the boyfriend wanted to sleep around and told her to do the same, which devastated her fantasy that he loved her. He also tried to convince her to get an abortion. She refused. Swallowing her pride, she returned to Vancouver still a pregnant 18-year-old. Her parents surprised her by welcoming her back with understanding and love rather than the severe admonishment and rejection that she had expected. Soon, she delivered the baby and decided to continue to live with her parents. They adored the little boy and cared for him while she completed high school. A serious life lesson had been learned.

* * *

Despite seeing the serious predicament of her friend, JOA failed to see a lesson in it for herself. JOA continued to misbehave by skipping classes, drinking with her girlfriends, and being essentially non-compliant in school. Her behavior reeked of her emotions and the predominant belief that her own mother didn't give a whit about her. Then in the spring of 1967, after multiple counseling meetings with JOA regarding her behavior, the dean of the school suspended her. He called Olivia and left her a message on her answering machine, asking her to come to a meeting with him and JOA at the school in two days' time. Olivia listened to the message but forgot to put it on her calendar and didn't notice that the meeting conflicted with her Women's Writing Group meeting, and thus she never showed up to meet with the dean. Frustrated, the dean called Remy who was alarmed to hear the trouble JOA was in. Remy immediately flew to Vancouver and met with the dean and convinced him to readmit JOA on probation.

That night, over dinner in the Vancouver hotel where Remy was staying, he had the necessary "father talk" with JOA. "We had a good summer back home, you and me, you and your brother, and now this, JOA. I need you to help me understand this latest episode," he began with a stern but kind look.

JOA squirmed in her chair and looked at another table of people sitting nearby. Remy patiently waited for her to talk.

"I was so happy last summer, Dad, just to be with you and Chaucer and to be back home," and she emphasized the word "home," as her tears were near falling. Remy saw this and reached over and grabbed her hand to calm her.

He let out a sigh, and said, "JOA, these last years have been very difficult for you and your brother and me, too. But we need to manage things today, where we are, where you are. You see what you do today, if you make bad decisions, those can affect you for the rest of your life, and that is why I came out here right away. I want to listen to you and see what we can build together to help you, can you see that?" he said sympathetically.

JOA felt so lost and confused. She looked at Remy, took a deep breath, and calmed herself. "Oh, Dad, I just want to leave this place and come with you back to Ottawa and have things be like they were. Mom doesn't pay any attention to me. When I am at her house,

I feel alone, like I am with someone I don't know anymore. How can she be like that to her own kids? Chaucer feels the same way I do."

Remy nodded. "Yes, he has said that to me as well." Remy sat back in his chair and sipped his coffee. He had expected her words about coming back home with him, so he was prepared. "JOA, let me propose a plan for us — a plan that I can sell to your mother and that will work for us too." He paused, looking closely at his daughter. "Here's what I think will be our best plan. I will agree to let you come to Ottawa and I believe that I can convince your mother, but here is your part. You'll need to complete this semester here, stay out of any more trouble in school, and get all passing grades. If you do that, then I will convince your mother to allow you to spend the entire summer with me. This way, I will know that you are serious about coming home with me when school is over, and it will benefit you in learning self-discipline, and also having the grades for college too. Can we agree on this?

JOA knew that her father was right. She smiled softly, then nodded yes.

Remy told her that he knew this was the most responsible path for now and her future. He promised to arrange for a summer job for her in Ottawa too.

JOA tried one more ploy with her father. "If I do all this and behave in the summer, can I attend my senior year at the school near our house in Ottawa?"

Remy smiled. "Let's get the first part accomplished, and once that is done perhaps we can discuss the second part about next school year, OK?"

JOA smiled, knowing that her father loved her, and that was the most important thing that night.

The next day when Remy went to see Olivia in Victoria to discuss the matter, Olivia did not take the matter that seriously.

"The school will keep her. They want your money," she told Remy bluntly.

"When the semester ends, let me take her back to Ottawa for this summer; she needs a new environment right now," Remy explained. Olivia acquiesced immediately, offering no resistance as her fourth book was behind schedule, and she had just been offered a deal to work on a screenplay in Hollywood. Her work was consuming her life. This idea of Remy's would help her stay on her writing schedule.

* * *

Three days after the school year ended, JOA flew to Ottawa. Remy had set up a summer job for her with the local recreation department, overseeing day-camp activities with kids in an Ottawa playground. JOA made new friends with the other counselors and reconnected with some old friends. Remy spoke with his good friend, Presbyterian Pastor Leo Louden, to ask his granddaughter Selma to spend time with JOA and plan some "girl activities." Selma and JOA were both 17 and knew each other from church events before JOA moved west. Over the summer, JOA and Selma slowly became close confidants. JOA opened up to Selma about her anger at her mother and her dislike of her boarding school. Selma, whose personality was quieter and less boisterous than JOA, proved a good listener. In those summer weeks Selma and JOA bonded in many ways, each becoming a counselor to the other about the common issues of parents, school, boys, etc. They went to hear music together whenever they learned that a folk group was playing locally. They took two canoe trips on the Ottawa River north of town, and Selma introduced her to other teens that were working on a local "Save the Wetlands" environmental project. It seemed that JOA was making good progress in getting back to her better self. Knowing that JOA would turn 18 in the winter, Remy thought it critical to watch her closely and give her all the attention and love he could. These are the things that fathers who are true fathers do for their children, and he did these things with and for JOA in those months.

A few weeks before JOA was to return to Vancouver for her final year, Remy and she reviewed her plans.

"JOA, you've had a great summer here, and I am happy to see that you are not fighting me about going back to finish school in Vancouver," Remy stated.

JOA felt happy and spoke in a positive tone to Remy. "You were right, Dad, I really needed to fix myself and rethink how I was looking at school there. I thought it was a prison, but I've realized that I could fix my attitude, and I did, because I wanted so much to be here this summer. And then I started having the best time with Selma, and I loved our canoe and camping trips. I'm definitely going to apply to schools back here for college, and I plan to really study and apply myself this last year at Crofton. Selma will come visit me, and I'll be home for Christmas and then start applying for college. The time will go fast, Dad. You were right; I did need to take school more seriously, and I did after the time you came out to Vancouver when I got kicked out." She smiled and hugged Remy. Remy's grin stretched ear to ear.

At the end of the summer, JOA returned to Vancouver for her final year at Crofton Academy. Selma was excited to visit her in the fall semester, courtesy of Remy's largesse, and JOA looked forward to returning to Ottawa for three weeks during the Christmas break. It seemed to Remy that her rebellious period was on hold, and he believed that he had Selma to thank for much of it. He spent time with Pastor Lowden explaining the bond that JOA and Selma had developed. Remy and the pastor agreed that the good Lord had extended a beautiful grace upon the two young girls. It certainly appeared that way, and who were two mortal men to argue with the work of a merciful God.

Chapter 10

Do Not Go Gentle Into That Good Night

WHEN CHAUCER ENROLLED AT UT as an English literature major, it had been against his father's advice. He remembered the conversation they had the previous summer before he was to leave Vancouver and come to Ottawa for two months to live with his father

"Do you still have your heart set on being an English major?" Remy asked him that morning.

"I'm not absolutely certain, Dad, but I need to start somewhere. You and Mother raised me to love reading and drama and theater arts, remember?" Chaucer responded with a grin.

"I also raised you to play hockey, but that doesn't mean I want you to be a professional hockey player! I know your mother put you in drama and dance classes, and perhaps we pushed you too hard, too early," he said, thinking of his wife and her eccentricities picked up from her English mother, Photina.

"Is your concern because of Mother?" Chaucer asked, knowing that his father still had both a deep love and a mild contempt for his mother.

"Well, yes, probably it is." Remy hesitated. "Son, you see I would like you to have a stable life, a predictable life, and I think a career in the sciences or engineering may be better for you, don't you?"

"I see your reasoning, Dad, but I think my choice was made long ago for me, being that my mother is who she is. I just have this feeling that if I didn't stay in the arts and literature that I would be unhappy, you know, that my fate has been stamped on me long ago. Can you understand how I feel, Dad? I don't want to change my plans now because if I get into the sciences and do not do well, then I would have to go back and start over, and I don't want to be stuck in school forever. I want to get out and do things, just like you did when you got home from the war."

His father crinkled his brow and uttered a soft laugh. "OK, I see what you mean, I can understand that argument. You know I love you, and I just want to see you be happy and be successful as well." Thus said, they worked out a compromise. Chaucer, with a first name to turn heads in the English department at the University of Toronto, would be an English literature major. He would also take a math and a business class as well each semester. The deal was set.

* * *

At the start of his second year at UT in 1968, Chaucer befriended and started dating an attractive student named Tessa Fenholt. She was an American from Buffalo, New York, and a year older, in the sophomore year in her studies in the theater department. She soon persuaded Chaucer that his real interests were in drama and performing, and because Chaucer was so charmed by her beauty, he changed majors in his second semester of his second year, abandoning his English lit program for the theater department. Tessa had been dating a couple of other guys on campus, but she created such a firm grip on Chaucer that she stopped seeing any others. She had been to Ottawa with Chaucer for a weekend when Remy was away on business. She smelled the money, loved the big house on the river, and decided that since Chaucer was willing to accommodate most of her needs and desires, he would be a good boyfriend for the time being, especially since he had joined her in the theater department where she could keep a close eye on him. Chaucer had been taken by Tessa from their early weeks of dating. She had bedded him regularly, and he had learned to follow her suggestions on most all of their social and economic decisions. She was bossy, and he let her be, as he was happy with the fringe benefits of their dating.

Eventually Chaucer hesitantly broke the news to Remy that he had switched majors from English to theater. He expected a lecture and dissenting opinion from his father. So he sweetened the explanation with the proviso that he would continue to take a business and science/math class each semester as before. Remy just chalked the change up to Chaucer being a young man and trying to find his way. Remy was happy that Chaucer had informed him at all. Nevertheless, Chaucer did not enroll for his winter semester that year, instead, taking a job in the Toronto library system, playing hockey at night, and still seeing Tessa. He seemed lost in his quest to decide on a career and the courses to take to get him there. He worked with his father at the Montreal office periodically while not in school, and he seemed to like working there, but in the end, he re-enrolled at the university and continued in the theater department, now almost an entire year behind in his studies due to switching majors and sitting out a semester. His earlier plans of finishing college in four years had vanished.

The following summer of 1970, after completing her junior year, Tessa was hired for three months as a backup singer in the Broadway production of *Jesus Christ Superstar*. Her cousin was the lead singer, and he negotiated the job for her. Chaucer followed her to New York City where they shared a small apartment off Bleecker Street in Greenwich Village with eight other members of the cast, who were backup singers or stagehands. Chaucer and Tessa had their own tiny bedroom. The idea of spending the summer in the city was exciting to Chaucer, and Remy reluctantly agreed.

It turned out that the apartment that Chaucer and Tessa moved into was a dump. The building owner only cared about the monthly rent and large security deposits, not about maintenance or the city codes for landlords. He didn't care how many people were in the small unit, another flaunt of the fire code. He knew that the location of the building was such prime space that he could rent it out in a matter of hours if tenants got pissed off and walked out. Plus, his brother was an attorney who knew his way around the Manhattan County Housing Court and was not adverse to slipping city inspectors a C-note to overlook some violations.

After a week in Manhattan of dodging speedy cabs and annoying cockroaches, Chaucer secured his own job as a stagehand with the production of *Superstar*, thanks to a complimentary word from Tessa's cousin. Chaucer replaced a stagehand, who also happened to be a tenant in their apartment and had abruptly left town late one evening. The very next morning a process server from Manhattan Court came looking for the guy. The process server left his business card and asked the roommates to have their friend contact him as soon as possible. Chaucer and the others all smiled when the server left and agreed that nobody really liked the stagehand but he had supplied them with cheap marijuana, so that was a good reason to tolerate his creepy personality and dirty habits.

One warm Manhattan evening when Tessa and Chaucer were not working at the theater, they decided to walk to the White Horse Tavern. Tessa wanted to see the place where the poet Dylan Thomas drank himself into legend that night in November 1953.

They strolled from Bleecker Street to Bedford, then up Hudson to West 11th Street until they saw the old blue neon sign of the White Horse. Tessa had read much of Thomas's poetry, and at first she was almost afraid to go inside, given that the work of Dylan Thomas was so iconic to her. She had the same anticipatory yet nervous feeling that many travelers have before entering the centuries-old churches and cathedrals in Europe on their first visit. For once Chaucer prevailed because it had been a long, hot walk, and he was thirsty for a beer. Tessa held his hand tightly, and they walked in. It was early evening and the place was crowded with locals and people dressed like tourists. Chaucer saw the picture of Dylan Thomas in the corner on the wall over the radiator, and the table below the photo was empty so he pushed Tessa into a seat to hold it while he went to the bar. He returned with four bottles of Rheingold Beer, about the cheapest drink in the place. Chaucer was essentially broke until he'd get his first paycheck from the theater company, so the Rheingold looked just fine.

They sipped their beers and sat back to absorb the atmosphere of the legendary pub. The conversational noise of the patrons was to Chaucer like the sound of the Ottawa River in full roar after a long summer rain. It relaxed him, and he sat with the grin of a wee lad who had just been handed a bowl of ice cream by his father. As he and Tessa discussed the writing of Dylan Thomas and drank their beers, an older man, poorly dressed and with unkempt long white hair, walked over to their table. He stared at them intently. Chaucer determined that the man was pretty much shit-faced, so he just smiled at him. The man then put his hand on Tessa's shoulder and said in a heavy Scottish brogue, " 'Tis mee table gurl, old Dylan gave it to me before his passing on."

Tessa smiled at Chaucer, then faced the old man with contempt and said, "Sure he did; I bet he gave you his watch and writing pen too."

Chaucer just rolled his eyes and shook his head. "Tessa, let's just ask him to sit down with us, OK?"

Tessa gave the man a repulsive look, such as you would a stray, smelly dog. She said, "You know who this man is?" pointing to Chaucer sitting across the table from her. "He is Chaucer Giroux, the 14th next cousin to Geoffrey Chaucer, the best poet ever to come from England. Dylan Thomas would certainly want us at his table if even he was a Welshman," she said smugly, her face reflecting her sense of entitlement.

Chaucer said softly, "Tessa, don't do this, the man just wants to sit down." Chaucer started to stand up to offer the man an empty chair when the old man slapped Tessa across the face, knocking her beer over.

Chaucer whispered, "Oh shit," and grabbed the man's arm and twisted it behind his back, pinning his head against the wall.

"Calm down, buddy, that's enough," said Chaucer as he held the old man steady. At that instant, one of the bartenders, who had been watching this customer earlier, walked over.

"Come on now, Charlie, don't start this again. This is just a nice couple having a drink, and they will be leaving in a few minutes and you can have your table, OK?"

Chaucer released Charlie, who rubbed his arm, the one that Chaucer had twisted behind him. Charlie turned to walk away, but then looked back at Chaucer and said, "Your lassie's an eejit, best watch out for her, laddie," and he walked away. Chaucer pulled a single dollar bill out of his jeans and softly handed it to the bartender. "Sorry for this trouble, please buy him a beer for us." The bartender smiled with relief that the situation hadn't gotten out of hand. He walked away and quickly returned with another bottle of Rheingold and placed it on the table. "He spilled one of yours, so this is on me, folks."

Chaucer looked at Tessa and saw that the left side of her face was bright red from the slap. She glared at Chaucer. "Why the hell didn't you knock him to the floor, he assaulted me! I'm going to call the police now" and she started to get up from the table to walk to the pay phone on the wall a few feet away. Chaucer grabbed hold of her forearm to stop her. "Tess, please sit down, please," he pleaded as he held her arm.

She kept standing, feeling the eyes of the patrons on her back. "Please, sit down," Chaucer whispered. After several tense seconds, she did. Her nostrils were flared, and she just stared silently at Chaucer.

"He is just the house drunk, Tess; he didn't mean any harm. You shouldn't have provoked him, you know."

"He had no right to hit me. I won't take that behavior from any man, an old drunk or not!"

"OK, look, he was wrong…but you weren't right…let's just finish our beers; it's a long walk back."

And so they finished drinking, not talking, just looking around. Then Chaucer started to grin.

"What's so funny?" Tessa said with a disgusting look.

"Well, here we are sitting under the photo of Dylan Thomas, in his pub, and the local drunk whacks you for embarrassing him. I just think that Dylan Thomas's spirit, which I can feel in here right now, is somehow laughing, too, don't you?"

Tessa grimaced. "You're such an asshole. I wanna go home now." As they got up from the table to leave, Chaucer looked at the large photo of Dylan Thomas and smiled. As he followed Tessa, who was headed to the door, Chaucer nodded a "thank you" to the bartender. The White Horse had not disappointed Chaucer.

*   *   *

On the walk back to their apartment, Chaucer asked, "So why were you so rude to that old guy? He really didn't mean any harm, did he?"

"Hey look, all I wanted was to drink my beer and meditate with the spirit of Dylan Thomas, to see where he met the end. I didn't want the local drunk to take that moment from me. He was a complete jerk, Chaucer. I should have called the cops."

"That would have just completely ruined the night. I almost had him understanding the situation, and you really should have left it alone at that point."

"That's crap, Chaucer. He was a bully, and I wish you had punched him out."

Chaucer retreated into silence for the rest of the walk home.

Chapter 11

It's Summer Time and the Livin' Ain't Easy

FOR THE NEXT WEEK, the relationship between Tessa and Chaucer suffered, as all such relationships can when one of the partners is wounded. They talked some, but not with their old commonality of lovers. Chaucer could feel the change. Conflict was not his style of life. Plus, his excitement of living in Manhattan was waning quickly and turning into a dislike, what with the noise and the traffic and the many self-absorbed and rude people he had encountered. Fortunately, given the hard rub between Chaucer and Tessa, Chaucer's work hours on the *Superstar* set at the Mark Hellinger Theatre had been changed by his boss, Galen McKinley. The show's director and producer wanted set design modifications so Chaucer and two of his housemates were requisitioned from the night shift to the day shift, meaning Chaucer got off work at 3 p.m. Tessa's job was nightly from 4 p.m. to midnight so they would not see much of each other for the next three weeks of the work shift changes.

One night during the first week when Chaucer had his evenings free, he called his father at home to see how he was. He had not spoken to his father in nearly the whole month that he had been in Manhattan.

"Hi, Dad, I wasn't sure if you'd be in Ottawa or not. How are you?"

"Hi, Buddy. I'm good. I just got back from being in Stockholm and Glasgow for ten days. We've got a new shipping partner in Sweden, and I had to meet my new resident manager over there to set him up with our systems and the customs protocols. How is New York City treating you?"

"Oh, it's OK, I guess. I'm getting some good experience in real Broadway theater now. Tessa is loving singing in the musical too."

"That's good. You have two letters here from Bee Lawrence in Toronto. Didn't I meet her once when I was in Toronto visiting you at school?"

"Yes, her parents are major players in the annual Shakespeare Festival in Stratford. I really like her. She's a great painter and getting a good reputation for her work."

"Yes, yes, now I remember her. Fine young woman as I recall."

"Dad, are you going to be home for a while now?" Chaucer asked.

"Yes, I don't have any trips planned until next month when I need to be back in Glasgow and London."

"OK, maybe I'll catch a bus home for a few days when I have time off. You can just keep those letters for now. How is JOA doing?"

"She's fine. She loves working with the kids in the recreation department in her summer job. She's out with her friends tonight. I'll tell her you called."

"Yes, please do. Love you, Dad."

"Love you too, Son, goodbye."

The whole next day Chaucer had Bee Lawrence on his mind. She was an emerging arts star and a warm woman, plus she really liked Chaucer. Maybe it was his smile, the cute dimples, or maybe it was his love of acting and quoting Shakespeare or Geoffrey Chaucer or W.B. Yeats. Whatever the reason, Bee Lawrence enjoyed her time with him, as he did with her. Their relationship had been just as friends with a lot of flirting both ways. With Chaucer getting depressed in Manhattan in early July, and his recent emotional distance from Tessa, he found his thoughts often gravitating to Bee.

* * *

On Friday, when Chaucer showed up at the Mark Hellinger stage door for work, a posted sign said, "Daytime Stagehands Off Today,

Report Back on Monday" and it was signed by Tom O'Horgan, or somebody that used his authority to sign it. With time on his hands, Chaucer decided to walk up to Columbus Circle, then through Central Park to the Metropolitan Museum of Art. He showed his student ID so he could get in on the cheap. He walked around thinking that he'd have to stay all weekend to see everything, so he decided to ask at the Information Desk if they had any Canadian art or exhibits. He was directed to that floor where he saw the works of Jack Bush, Emily Carr, Norval Morrisseau, and others. All talented Canadians, and this made Chaucer both proud but homesick too. He wandered around about another hour, then looked at the wall clock and saw it was noon. He was hungry as he had skipped breakfast that morning. He decided that he would come back another time, and he left, walking out to Fifth Avenue, filled with Canadian pride and wanting to know even more about these great Canadian artists. He wondered if Bee Lawrence would one day have her work at the Met.

Chaucer caught a bus downtown, stopped to buy a burger from a street vendor, and at 1 p.m. he climbed up the steps to the apartment. He walked in the door and saw that no one else was in the kitchen, but a half empty bottle of wine was on the table. He heard music, voices, and laughter coming from his bedroom. Chaucer wasn't sure what was going on; perhaps one of the other guys in their group had his girlfriend in Chaucer and Tessa's room. He did not want to embarrass them. He saw that the door was slightly ajar, and he peeked in to see who it was. His eyes popped open and he felt faint. Tessa and some guy were lying naked on the bed, laughing and touching each other, seemingly oblivious to anything else as the radio was loudly playing some Joni Mitchell song.

Chaucer quietly walked back to the kitchen to think. He heard the guy with Tessa say, "When is your boyfriend coming home?"

"He works 'til 3. We have plenty of time. He's getting to be a pain anyway. Shut up and kiss me." She made no attempt to conceal her voice.

Chaucer looked at the small key rack next to the refrigerator and took the keys to Tessa's old Renault sedan that was parked on the street below. She and Chaucer never used the car because they did not want to give up the one parking spot that they were fortunate to have found weeks before when they had moved into the apartment.

With the car key in his hand, Chaucer left quietly, not saying a word. He just wanted to disappear.

*   *   *

Chaucer walked the neighborhood for a while then stopped to have a coffee at the 7-11 store about a mile from his apartment. His thoughts were off the charts. He had known Tessa for almost two years, and they had only dated each other, or so he was led to believe. He thought back to the event at the White Horse Tavern two weeks before and how Tessa had reacted, a manner that was new to him. In the days since, she had been very quiet and distant from him, and then he realized that what he just witnessed in the apartment likely had been going on for weeks. He had not seen it coming. She was closing him out of her life but not telling him.

He then remembered another male cast member who had been showing up at the apartment the past few weeks and seemed to be looking at Tessa in a way that was now making more sense to Chaucer. Was he being duped and used? Surely he had been naïve, he thought. He was getting angry. He sat for a moment on a bench. He realized that he didn't want to carry those ideas too deep that afternoon. He would make some other important decisions instead.

Chapter 12

Running Far

ABOUT FIVE O'CLOCK that Friday afternoon, Chaucer went back to the apartment, knowing that Tessa had likely gone to the theater an hour before. Three other roommates were home so they talked about work and the hot weather. Chaucer found some bread and cheese, an apple, and a couple of empty bottles. He filled the bottles with water and tossed them and the food into his backpack. He gathered up the few clothes he had and stuffed them into his small suitcase. He crammed his books, toothbrush and comb into his backpack and fastened it.

"Hey, Chaucer, where you going, man?" asked Marty, the nice kid from Syracuse.

"I'm going out to Montauk for the weekend. Need to visit some friends out there. Can you tell Tessa that I'll be back on Monday?"

"Sure, I'll tell her in the morning," Marty replied.

Chaucer bounced down the stairs, no longer sad but now feeling liberated. He had made his decision. He was going back to Ottawa and borrowing the old Renault to take him there. He would settle up with Tessa some other time. She would be working in Manhattan until at least early September, almost two months from now. Two months can be a long time when you are 21 years old. Chaucer would not look back now.

* * *

Before Chaucer crossed the George Washington Bridge and headed north up the Palisades Parkway to the NYS Thruway, he drove the Renault to the Mark Hellinger Theatre. He had written a one-page note for his boss, Galen, the good man who had hired him in late May. It read:

Dear Galen,

Thank you for the opportunity to work on this great production. You have been good to me. Unfortunately, things have happened, and I must now return immediately to Canada. If possible, would you be so kind as to send my last paycheck to me at:
2110 Sixth Line Road, Ottawa, Ontario, Canada
Very sorry to have to leave on this short notice.

Sincerely, Chaucer Giroux

He had put the note in an envelope addressed to Galen. He went in the backstage door and saw a couple of his co-workers. He handed the envelope to a guy named Mitchell that he had come to like.

"Mitch, please give this to Galen after the show tonight. See you around. Thanks." He shook Mitch's hand and winked. Mitch understood.

Once Chaucer crossed the George Washington bridge, and he could look across the Hudson River and see the skyline of Manhattan, he started to relax. He pulled into a filling station not far up the Palisades to fill up on cheap gas in New Jersey. There were a couple of picnic tables next to the building, and they looked down the cliff to the Hudson and east across to Yonkers. He could still see the towers of the GW Bridge to the south. He bought a map of the metro area and sat at the table just looking at it, knowing he would not be back to New York City for a long time. It was now about 7 p.m., and he still had two hours of daylight for the drive, which he calculated to be about six hours to get home to Ottawa.

While looking at the map, he remembered that his cousin Jean Marc Giroux had transferred from Ithaca College to SUNY Purchase. The map indicated that the college was only about twenty miles from where he was. Maybe Jean Marc is there, and Chaucer surely could use some good advice from him. He pondered the thought and decided he would call his Aunt Elizabeth in Geneva, New York, and ask about Jean Marc. He had her phone number in his wallet so he got some change in the gas station store and used the pay phone to call.

"Hello," a woman answered.

"Hello, Aunt Elizabeth?"

"No, this is Kathleen. Who is this?"

"Hi, Kathleen, it's me, Chaucer!"

"Oh, Chaucer, hello! Are you in town?"

"No, I'm down near New York City. I wanted to give Jean Marc a call and maybe stop in to see him. How are you and everyone?"

Kathleen smiled. She always had loved her cousin Chaucer. He had been a happy boy and would talk with her at length at family gatherings. "Well, all the boys are in the Army now. Logan is in Vietnam, Clint is in Vietnam, and Ollie is at basic training. Mother and Father are fine, especially Father with three of his four sons in the military now. I'm going to be a senior at Keuka College this year, and I hope to have a teaching position by this time next year."

"That's great for you, Kathleen. I'm sure your father is proud of the boys all serving now. I'm driving to Ottawa now, and I thought I might stop to see Jean Marc if he is at school."

Kathleen replied, "Actually, he's in New Paltz right now at a summer theater camp. He called me last week and gave me his phone number at a dorm where he is staying. Do you want it?"

"Sure, New Paltz is not far from where I am right now." Chaucer wrote the number on his hand.

"Are you OK, Chaucer? You sound like something is wrong."

"No, I'm OK. I'd just like to talk to Jean Marc if I can. Thanks for his phone number, Kathleen. I hope you graduate next year and get that job you want; you'll be a great teacher. Please say hi to your parents for me. Bye for now."

Chaucer found more quarters and dimes in his pockets and immediately called the number Kathleen had given him.

The phone rang a while and just before he was going to hang up, a male voice answered.

"Hello."

"Is Jean Marc Giroux there, please?"

"Aaaah, yeah, I think so. Hang on a minute." Chaucer heard footsteps walking away. Then he heard a shout, "Hey, anybody seen Jean Marc?" then silence. About two minutes later, Chaucer heard footsteps coming toward the phone.

"Hello, this is Jean Marc."

"It's Chaucer, your cousin. I need to talk. Can I come see you now?"

"Chaucer! Chaucer! No lie, where are you?"

"I'm not far from you right now. I really need to talk, can I come see you?"

"Sure, you know where the campus is? The dorm where I'm staying is called Peabody Hall."

"Don't worry, I'll find it. I'll be there soon."

Feeling mildly relieved, Chaucer drove north past West Point and into New Paltz.

*   *   *

Within an hour Chaucer was sitting on a sofa in a SUNY New Paltz dormitory commons room. The long summer sun was still warming the campus, and Chaucer was tired from the emotions of the day. So much had changed in just a few hours. He only wanted to talk softly to someone he could trust, and his cousin Jean Marc was just that person. They were both the same age, cousins, and had built a trust in each other over the years. About the only thing that they differed in was women. Jean Marc was, in his self-description, "focusing all my energy and time on my studies to building the foundation to have a good career in the theater and dramatic arts." He was postponing any serious interest in women to focus on getting good experiences and making connections in the theater and film industry in New York City. Jean Marc was fond of saying, "Women are all over in the performing arts. I'm more interested in establishing myself as a young artist or producer now. I can always find the right partner when I am ready."

Jean Marc, while not conceited, was confident. He knew his looks were more than adequate to shop around when the time came. He was slightly above average height and size and in good shape, having played high school and college baseball until an injury ended his pitching career two years before. He also had the Giroux classic French Canadian wavy black hair and a charming smile of warmth and confidence that came from his beautiful Boston mother. Jean Marc had his house in order, with clear goals and ambitions. He just needed the training and experience to get him into a career in the arts scene in New York City. Chaucer knew this about Jean Marc, and that is why he had sought him out this day.

"So, what is going on, Cuz?" asked Jean Marc as they both sat on the sofa and drank cups of bad coffee from a vending machine.

"Everything in the last ten hours has gotten really messed up. All since I woke up this morning."

Chaucer proceeded to tell Jean Marc about his job as a stagehand on *Superstar* for the past five weeks and how he and his girlfriend Tessa had been living in a cramped apartment in Greenwich Village. He explained the incident from earlier at the White Horse Tavern with Tessa and the old drunk, and the incident just six hours ago of finding her making love to a strange guy in their own bed.

"Sounds to me like a messed-up woman, not the kind of girl you can put faith or trust into, heh?" said Jean Marc, just shaking his head in amazement, confirming his credo of avoiding female entanglement at this point in his life.

"Well, I really liked her, Jean Marc, and she was different at school in Toronto, not acting like this."

"Ha ha ha, that's as far as you know," said Jean Marc with a broad smile. "Remember cousin, past performance is prelude to present and future performance, as we say in the theater. Lucky for you that you found out now before you got serious with her."

Chaucer, grinned and then broke out laughing. "This is why I came to see my Yankee cousin. I needed some perspective. Today has been a whole month of emotions," he said, stifling a yawn.

"Where are you staying tonight? You're not going to try to drive to Ottawa tonight, are you?" asked Jean Marc. "You'll fall asleep at the wheel."

"Well, I was going to drive for a couple of hours and then pull over and sleep in the car."

"No, no, no, here's my plan, dear cousin. We have an extra sofa in our dorm room upstairs, you sleep there tonight. You and I are going into town right now for some food and beer, and we'll talk until we fall asleep at the bar; plus, I'm buying the first two rounds. How does that sound?"

Chaucer let out a deep breath and smiled. He suddenly felt

hungry and thirsty. Yeah, a beer would taste good. He stood up, and he hugged his cousin robustly, and they both started laughing, then laughed harder and louder until some guy stuck his head out of a door and shouted, "Quiet down out there, we're studying."

This was what the boys needed. Off they went to where Chaucer had parked the Renault, then into town they sojourned, not to return to the dorm for four hours, with full bellies and the problems of the day resolved sufficiently for a good night of sleep.

* * *

The sun rises early in July in New York State, and Chaucer had slept soundly through the night on the old sofa. At 6 a.m., he got up and went to the bathroom. As no one was in the shower, he stripped quickly and took a hot shower to awaken and soothe him. Jean Marc came in to pee while Chaucer was in the shower.

"Cuz, I have a workshop starting at 8, so let's grab some breakfast in the cafeteria, and you can get on your way, OK?"

"Yes, that works for me, Jean Marc. I'll be right out," Chaucer replied as he grabbed a towel.

After breakfast, Jean Marc went to his workshop, and Chaucer went back to the room, grabbed his backpack, and left Jean Marc a note on his bed, which read:

> Thanks for everything, Jean Marc. It was good to see you again. Thanks for the advice and counsel. I'll stay in better touch. I have your new address at school. Let's try to visit at Christmas.

On the way out of the dorm, Chaucer stopped and grabbed another coffee to go. He hopped in his car, drove back to the NYS Thruway and was driving north within fifteen minutes. He would cross the border and be home in Ottawa in less than six hours.

* * *

The monotony of driving on a boring, speedy highway is the perfect catalyst for dreaming and creative thinking. The sound of the tires on the highway, and the wind blowing in the windows were birdsongs to Chaucer. He was relieved to know the revealed Tessa.

He had been growing attached to her for reasons that he now knew were wrong for him. Perhaps he thought that sex was love, a fault of most all men. Surely his forebearer, Geoffrey Chaucer, also knew this 500 years prior, as he told it in the *Wife of Bath* and other tales.

His relationship with Tessa was over. She had screwed another guy in his presence; he had seen it himself. He no longer had to worry about his feelings for her. He would move on...but then the words of the New Riders of the Purple Sage song came into his head...highway driving does these strange things to you...

You keep laying names on me
And you keep playing games on me
And you keep playing all your tricks on me
And all I ever wanted, all I ever wanted
All I ever wanted was your loving
Is that too much to ask
You keep bringing your friends to me
And you keep bringing your men to me
And you keep bringing all your world to me
And all I ever wanted, all I ever wanted
All I ever wanted was your loving
Is that too much to ask

https://www.youtube.com/watch?v=tJuKC8X92aQ

*   *   *

With half the summer still to be lived before the fall semester at UT, Chaucer needed to find more work. He would discuss his options with his father when he got home that night.

Then the thought of the "borrowed" Renault jumped at him. What to do about it? He was tired now, having been on the road for three hours. He pulled into a rest stop, used the men's room, and took a nap in the car. An hour later back on the road and daydreaming, he decided that he would buy the car from Tessa. He would send her some money for now, and when he went back to school in September, he would negotiate a final price with her. Good, he thought, his conscience was as clear as it needed to be for a former girlfriend who had ended their relationship with such contemptable behavior. Fair enough, good enough.

He then drifted into thinking about his history with Tess. She was an underachieving academic student and a girl that liked to go to parties. Chaucer could see this more clearly now that his hormones had been radically detached from her. "I should have seen that coming," he thought ruefully. "Now I see the connections; I thought I had done this or done that and misbehaved." But he hadn't; he had been blinded by his longing for her pheromones, which he had allowed to dominate his emotions and intellect, or better stated, to disrupt his intellect. No longer would he have to endure her crazy behavior. How wrong he had been to be with her for this long. A valuable thing for him to have learned. He was just a twenty-one-year-old guy getting an early education in love too.

Chapter 13

Thank you, Kathleen

IT WAS A BEAUTIFUL LATE SATURDAY afternoon when Chaucer pulled into the driveway at his father's house. Remy had kept the house where he, Olivia, and the children had lived as a family. Chaucer and JOA were glad he had done this. They both had so many good memories of the house, the neighborhood, their schools, and of Ottawa. Chaucer did not want his father to do what many other men in divorce do: sell everything and start all over. Remy had deliberately decided against that tactic, primarily because he knew that the children would always want to have a home in Ottawa, no matter where Olivia would take them, or if Olivia remarried and the children did not like the new husband, then they could come back to Ottawa to live with their father. Remy wanted specifically to preserve that possibility for Chaucer and JOA. Olivia's dagger in his heart had bled him near empty of emotions, but it did not kill him.

Chaucer used his key to enter the house and immediately went to the refrigerator to survey the culinary options. To his disappointment, he found few. His father usually ate at work, or after work at his golf club. Chaucer was sure that was where his father was on this sunny Saturday.

Chaucer found some mail. He looked at the envelopes and saw that two had a return address of Stratford, Ontario with the sender name of Bee Lawrence. He recognized Bee's handwriting on the letter. He had met Bee at the Shakespeare Festival two years ago, and he had seen Bee a couple of times at a Toronto music club and at a party at the University. He thought that she was beautiful and so very artistic in her manners, and then he learned that her parents had been part of the group of local benefactors who had started the Festival in Stratford in the 1950s. He and Bee had flirted during that time but that was all, although Chaucer did see her as a possible girl to pursue under the right circumstances. Maybe he wanted to consider that now.

He opened the letter, and it was a brochure about this year's Shakespeare Festival with a hand-written note from Bee.

Hi, Chaucer,

I hope this finds you well. The festival team is putting together an experienced group of actors to play various back-up roles during the festival this season. I thought you might be interested. Plus, I'd like to see you again.
Please call me when you get this so we can discuss.

Fondly, Bee

It was dated May 25. Chaucer had left with Tessa for New York City two days before. His father had been in France and Sweden on business for many weeks and never forwarded the mail to Chaucer.

As his mind was seeing Bee Lawrence in his vision, the phone rang.

"Hello," he answered.

"Chaucer, it's me, Kathleen."

"Hi, Kathleen, it's great to hear your voice again. Thanks for helping me find Jean Marc yesterday. We had a good time last night; he's such a great guy. What's up?"

"I spoke with Jean Marc during his lunchtime today, and he told me that you were going to be looking for a job for the rest of the summer, until you go back to school."

"Yup, I need to earn some money until school starts. My father will not want me sitting around here not working."

"Chaucer, you just might be in luck. A good friend of mine from Keuka College and I were talking last night. Her mother is the manager of the Bristol Valley Playhouse near Naples, New York, and they just found out that their stage manager got drafted and has to report for Army duty in a week. His lottery number came up, and they revoked his temporary deferment. They could really use someone like you right now. Interested?"

"Holy cow...Kathleen, are you serious? Really? Where is Naples?"

"It's about thirty miles from our house, about forty-five minutes driving the back roads. I just talked to Mother, and she said that if you get the job, you can stay with us. We have plenty of rooms with all the boys away now."

"Well, this sounds very interesting. What do you think?"

"Jean Marc told me that you had been working on the set of *Jesus Christ Superstar* in the city, so I doubt that there is anything about this job that you would not be able to handle. They are just halfway through their summer season. They have two more productions of four weeks each, and then they'll close down. This could be perfect for you. You have a car, don't you?"

Chaucer grinned. "I do now."

※　　　※　　　※

Within the next twenty-four hours, Mrs. Thorsen, the manager at the Bristol Valley Playhouse, spoke with both Kathleen and Chaucer on the phone and hired him. She needed him at a meeting in three days to review their next production of *South Pacific*, which would begin in three weeks. They needed to finalize the plan on the sets required to put on a production from a big Broadway set to a smaller set at the playhouse. They had musicians and actors ready, and the ticket sales had been excellent. Their season sponsors from Rochester were Xerox and Eastman Kodak, so money was not an issue, but building the sets was.

Chaucer would be the assistant to Jack Montgomery, who Mrs. Thorsen had promoted immediately after she knew that her senior stage manager would be leaving in a matter of days. Jack was an older man, and he needed the energy that a young Chaucer Giroux could bring, having just been working on a big production in the city. Mrs. Thorsen knew Kathleen Giroux through her friendship with her daughter, and she considered Kathleen a responsible young woman, so she trusted Kathleen's recommendation of Chaucer.

* * *

Back in Ottawa, JOA was on a camping trip with her friends, so Chaucer had dinner that night at the golf club with his father. It was a sweet reunion. Remy had still not healed fully from the breakup of his family six years before. Whenever he was with his children, his thoughts would automatically kick back to being with them and Olivia, as they had been for 15 years.

Remy's parents had taught him the lessons of the Book of Proverbs. He was especially enamored with Chapter Eight, where King Solomon wrote about creation and wisdom, and how God loves being with his daughters and sons. Remy had experienced a good childhood, and he wanted to give his children the same gifts that he had received. His reluctant divorce with Olivia had taken it all from him, and the hole in his heart remained unhealed. Losing a wife is not the same as losing your children, especially if you loved them as much as Remy loved JOA and Chaucer.

Any occasion that Remy spent time with either Chaucer or JOA he savored, for these were his best moments. It was not his shipping business, not his male friends or the few women that he had dated, but the best time for Remy was being with his kids. And that night, he had Chaucer all to himself. Life was good, if only for a few hours.

That evening Chaucer explained to his father about his breakup with Tessa (sparing Remy some of the explicit details). They spoke about the different kinds of relationships that men can have with a woman. This was father and son talk at its best. Remy wished to give Chaucer some thoughts about showing love, accepting love, the kind of talks that most boys do not get from their fathers. They had a good talk. Truths were spoken.

"Yes, you learned some important things in your time with Tessa. I am happy to hear your words, and it is important to remember them so you don't repeat these mistakes, right?" he said to Chaucer as they were sitting in the wood-paneled dining room at the golf club with paintings of horses and hunting dogs on the walls.

"How did you get your education about women, Dad?"

"Well, some of it was with women I met during the war, but the war really prevented any decent opportunity as we were moved so frequently as intelligence officers," he said.

"So are you telling me that in five years you didn't have any relationships?" Chaucer said with a questioning look.

"No, I didn't say that; what I didn't have was any stability to develop one until I returned to Canada and met your mother."

"Mom swept you away when you met her, Grandmother told me."

"Well, yes, she and I thought we had found the right partner, and we were right, at least initially," Remy said, slowly and thoughtfully. "I believe that I took too much for granted after the war, that a woman and a man once married could fix anything that went wrong between them if they were truly in love. I messed it up by putting my business first, and that is an important lesson that I hope you understand. A woman who loves you wants you with her for many good reasons, and I wrongly assumed that an independent woman like your mother was fine with my travels for work, and before I learned differently, it was too late, hence the vast importance of good communications and honest talk. Don't assume too much; you always need to talk to your wife or serious girlfriend and make sure it is a meaningful, thoughtful discussion. And learn her needs and weaknesses so you are there for her," Remy said, sounding like both a father and a good friend.

Chaucer smiled, nodded, and filed the conversation away for his future reference, then told him about the job in New York.

Remy liked the idea of Chaucer accepting the temporary position at the Bristol Valley Playhouse for the rest of the summer. Even better, Remy was happy that Chaucer would be living with Remy's brother Jean Luc and his wife, Elizabeth, in Geneva. That made great sense to him. This was a happy and emotionally rich night for Remy. His son seemed content with his choices, and that gave Remy great joy.

Chapter 14

Naples

THE NEXT MORNING AFTER COFFEE and breakfast with his father, Chaucer packed a big, old suitcase borrowed from his father and loaded it into the Renault. The suitcase originally belonged to Chaucer's Grandfather Giroux, and it had been used by his Giroux grandparents when they had taken an ocean trip to France before World War I. It had large travel stickers from Paris, Marseille, Lyon, Geneva, and Zurich affixed to the outside. Chaucer loved the old suitcase for it gave him a great sense of his larger family and a sense of adventure. Remy gave him a check drawn on his American bank account and handed him some Canadian loonies for gas and food before he left town. Then Remy picked up Chaucer's suitcase and walked with him to the Renault.

"So, I will see you in early September then. Please come back home for a few days before you return to Toronto for school. I will be traveling to Sweden and Italy, but I will be home by mid-August. JOA will be staying with your grandparents while I'm away. If you need anything, your uncle and aunt in Geneva will help you, and I can always repay them if needed. Perhaps when I get home JOA and I might even drive down to see you and the others. What do you think?"

"Sure, Dad, I'd love to see you both, you know that. JOA hasn't seen the Geneva clan in a while. I know that she thinks the world of

Cousin Kathleen, almost like an older sister."

"Yes, I got that idea too. Kathleen is so much like her mother, your Aunt Elizabeth. Yes, I think I will bring her down for a few days, and I hope that this job will be a good learning experience for you, Chaucer. I am happy that you are finding an interest in the theater. I can see that being a good career if that is what you decide for yourself. I can always use you in our shipping business, but you need to follow you heart, Son. I'd like you to find a passion for something, and then turn it into your life's work. You will be much happier that way."

"Thank you, Dad. I love you...I know I don't tell you that as much as I should, but JOA and I both know how you always came to see us in Vancouver, how you always would write to us and call us. We really needed that when Mother first took us away." Chaucer's face was stoic but his voice weak.

He continued, "I guess we, especially JOA, thought that it might just be temporary, that we'd always move back here, or maybe you'd move to Vancouver with us, but after a while, listening to Mother, I knew it was not going to happen. JOA and I made new friends, had new schools but we missed it here, and more than that, we missed you and our grandparents."

Remy took a deep breath and fought back his emotions. Chaucer had touched the deepest part of his father, a depth of emotion that only men with beloved children can understand. Remy put down Chaucer's suitcase, and he turned the moment of great regret into a fine moment of joy by hugging Chaucer tightly, and then laughing. "This reminds me of when you were a boy, and I said goodbye to you when I left on a business trip. I would say to you 'Chaucer, you are the man of the house now, and I am counting on you to take care of your mother and JOA. Will you do that for me?' And you would say 'Yes, Father' and then salute me like your grandfather taught you. Do you remember those days?"

"Yes. I remember them well. I was always so happy that you would say that to me. It made me feel so very needed and loved. Those are good memories for us."

Chaucer had been looking at the ground while talking, but now he looked directly at his father and smiled. Remy's eyes were moist, and he took a handkerchief from his pocket to wipe them. He was silent, just looking at Chaucer, his twenty-one-year-old son, who looked so much like him, but still had the cheeks and lips of Olivia. At this moment, Remy did see Olivia in Chaucer, and that vision of her plus Chaucer's words had been too much this morning. Saying goodbye to Chaucer or JOA was never easy, and today was just terrible for Remy.

Remy hugged Chaucer again and stroked his hair. Then he put his hands on Chaucer's shoulders and extended his arms and looked his son in the eyes.

"You are a smart and talented young man, Chaucer. You use it in a good way. We'll have a good life; you and I and JOA still have so much to share. We are still a family, the three of us, please don't ever forget or doubt that. OK?...All right, your old man has made a fool of himself this morning. Now you go down to Geneva and have a good rest of the summer with your cousins and Uncle Jean Luc and Aunt Elizabeth. I'll likely see you the end of next month with JOA when we come to Geneva. Try to call me or JOA once in a while. I'll tell her all about your work in the city and this new job."

"Thanks, Dad. I'm so glad you're my father. I'll call soon. Love you."

"Love you, too, Son. Stay safe." Remy's emotions were all over the place now. He loved his children so much and missed them dearly. Even though he had been through years of counselling and had many talks with Pastor Leo, it did not protect him this day. The years without his children had seemed like decades, the weight of them being so far away had buckled his legs, bowed his back, and given him dreams reliving the separation. He had been broken, and the hurt was like having a third arm that you can hide only for so long but hide it you must, lest people see it and shower you with sorrow, or contempt, or both. Remy knew the truth of this as well as anyone.

With the goodbyes said, Chaucer started the old Renault and headed down the driveway for the border crossing on Wellesley Island and the Thousand Islands Bridge to the United States. He would be in Geneva in about four hours and then at the Bristol Valley Playhouse soon and ready to work. He was happy.

As he drove, his thoughts turned to Tessa. He remembered that he had dreamed about her the previous night, that their intimacies over the past months had resulted in her being with child, and he didn't know how to tell his father or what to do about it. In the dream, Tessa said she wanted to have an abortion, and she wanted Chaucer to give her the money for it. He was confused. He loved children, and he did not want her to take the baby away from him, from them. She laughed at him and said, "You're only a boy yourself, what do you know? I should never have gotten involved with you in the first place. Give me the money I need and then go away." Thinking about his dream, Chaucer swallowed hard. How could Tessa say those things to him after the year and a half of their dating and sleeping together? The hum of the tires had lulled him into this daydream about the previous night's sleep dream. Then he saw a road sign on I-81: "Syracuse 45 miles" and he snapped out of his thoughts. He turned on the car radio to ironically hear Simon and Garfunkel singing "The Sound of Silence."

https://www.youtube.com/watch?v=NAEppFUWLfc

The song brought a soft smile to Chaucer. It was just what he needed to hear at that moment. As the song ended, he laughed, and his smiled turned into a smirk. Tessa could now be some other guy's problem. He was done with her.

*   *   *

Chaucer arrived at the Giroux house in Geneva early that afternoon. He spent time catching up with Kathleen and Aunt Elizabeth. They wanted to hear all the latest news of Olivia and JOA, which he dutifully provided. His Uncle Jean Luc (nicknamed Le Guerrier) was away for a couple of days on business for his employer, Cornell University. Chaucer got settled into Logan's old room and spent the night and the next day on the farm, helping Kathleen with some work projects.

On the third day, on schedule, Chaucer arrived early for his meeting with Mrs. Thorsen and Jack Montgomery. He was quite impressed with the organization of the playhouse and the professionalism and experience exhibited by Mrs. Thorsen, given what he had just experienced in New York City. He liked Jack, who was fifteen years his senior. Jack was a thoughtful and generally quiet man who had earned his degree in theater at Ithaca College after he served two years in the Army, working in the Personnel Office at

Fort Dix for his entire service time. Jack was no fan of the Vietnam engagement but rarely spoke about it. He was very happy to have his military duty in the past.

During the first week of work at the playhouse, Chaucer established his bona fides with Mrs. Thorsen, Jack, and the others on staff. One day during his lunch hour, Chaucer was sitting alone on a picnic table outside of the theater when a young woman approached him and introduced herself.

"You must be the new guy that Mrs. Thorsen just hired," she said with an adorable smile as she extended her hand. "My name is Melissa, and I am the ticket manager here."

Chaucer had a mouthful of sandwich and tried to smile. Melissa laughed. He swallowed his food then shook her hand.

"Hi, I'm Chaucer, sorry to not smile but I had a mouthful of a cheese sandwich." Melissa just kept smiling; she was smitten with Chaucer already.

"I'm here until the end of the season I guess. The other guy got drafted, I was told. Did you know him?"

Melissa just kept smiling, staring at Chaucer. Then "Oh, yes, his name was Liam O'Toole. I thought he was a little strange myself."

"In what way?" asked Chaucer.

"Well, he really didn't socialize with the rest of us. He lived in Joe Henderson's barn up on the hill near the winery. He kept to himself, and," she paused, as if thinking of what to say.

"And then?" asked Chaucer, thinking she was being a wee bit weird.

"And then early last week, a state trooper showed up here. They were looking for Liam but that day he had taken our truck and gone to the lumber yard in Rochester, and so they didn't hang around. Jack told me that the trooper gave Mrs. Thorsen his card and asked her to call him when he showed up. When Liam came back late in the afternoon with the lumber and other supplies, Mrs. Thorsen asked him if he could explain why the State Police were looking for him. He told her it was about a traffic accident from a couple of weeks ago in Rochester, and then he said that he had just gotten notice from his draft board that his lottery number was selected, and he had to report in a few days for his Army physical in Buffalo so he would be leaving the job ASAP."

Chaucer watched her intently, admiring her cute face and tight figure in her short skirt. Melissa had grown up in Naples; she was a local. She had an innocence about her that Chaucer liked.

"Liam said he thought it was about a traffic accident or ticket or something," and she hesitated.

"This sounds like a movie," Chaucer said with a grin. "You're joking with me, aren't you?"

Melissa already was in love with Chaucer's dimples and demeanor. And Chaucer could sense it, so he just kept his cool, knowing that he would be seeing her every day now. No need to rush anything.

Melissa continued. "Well, the next day, Liam didn't show up here for work, and we had this new production deadline, so Mrs. Thorsen sent Jack up to the barn where Liam was living." Melissa looked serious, as if for effect. "Jack came back and said that Liam had packed and left first thing that morning, not even telling Mr. Henderson that he was leaving or coming here for his pay. We all figured he had done something and decided to take off before the police came back."

"Rather strange, don't you think Melissa? He must have been dealing," Chaucer laughed.

"Dealing? Dealing what?"

Chaucer shook his head and smiled. "He probably was selling dope around here, and the police got a tip, so they came here to see him."

"Really? You think so?"

Chaucer just smiled, knowing that Melissa was naïve and being from this small town, had perhaps not been exposed to the pot crowd yet.

"Where do you go to college?" he asked

"I'm at the University of Buffalo; I'll be a junior this fall."

"Don't people smoke pot in Buffalo?" Chaucer asked, it being a rhetorical statement, for he knew from his dating Tessa and visiting Buffalo with her a few times for party weekends that Buffalo was a heavy weed-smoking town, especially around the university.

"Well, not me...my sorority sisters...no, I can't say that they do either," said Melissa, hesitantly.

Chaucer changed the subject as he concluded that Melissa was either a serious student, or just not very hip, or likely both. Instead he asked her a few questions about Naples. As he watched her speak, he smiled, thinking that her innocence was probably a good thing for her. Her youthful figure and her cuteness would make her a magnet for college boys in Buffalo. Chaucer liked her and thought that she was a nice girl. He would leave it at that.

To change the subject, he asked Melissa to tell him about Naples as he hadn't visited the village yet; the playhouse was a few miles north. She described her hometown as being in a big, beautiful verdant valley at the south end of Canandaigua Lake, just a mile from Woodville where the marina, Pep's Tavern, and the county boat launch sites were. Large old maple, oak, and willow trees lined the roads. On the east end of the lake stood the 1500-foot peak called Whaleback, which sat ensconced in the state's High Tor Wildlife Management Preserve. She told him about how the south end of the lake bled into a huge wetlands area, not deep enough for much navigation but fine for birds, other wildlife, and a small stream, sort of like the swampy jungle in which Humphrey Bogart and Katharine Hepburn were lost in their boat during the movie *African Queen*.

Melissa then told Chaucer the story that her grandfather had told her about Humphrey Bogart. "Grandpa Schenck said that the Bogart family lived in Manhattan in the years before World War I, but during the summers they would come to their house on Seneca Point, a few miles up the west shore of Canandaigua Lake from Woodville. One summer when Humphrey, who Grandpa said was known locally as 'Hump,' was about 14 or 15, he and some of the summer boys from the city started to come into Naples on weekends to see what was going on. They made friends with a local boy, Tommy Wayne, who was a wiseguy and a hustler. Tommy was older, about 18, and he and some of his friends would play cards, gamble, drink, and smoke on Friday and Saturday nights behind the Naples Hotel on Main Street. They would get some beer from the hotel bartender and have a good time being where the sheriff could not find them. Grandpa said that he was one of Tommy's friends, so he knows this story."

Chaucer was loving watching Melissa talk. Her face was so radiant and expressive that he was watching her more than he was paying attention to the Bogart story.

"Well, Tommy invited the rich Seneca Point boys to play cards with them one night, and Tommy, Grandpa, and the other local boys won all the money from Bogart and his rich friends. He said that

Bogart got really mad, saying that Tommy had cheated them, and he kicked over a pitcher of beer. So Tommy stood up and punched Humphrey Bogart in the nose, and blood spurted out everywhere." Melissa made a disgusted face. "Then Tommy told the rest of the rich kids to get the little jerk home, and if they ever said anything about it to their parents that Tommy and the rest of his boys would come looking for them on Seneca Point. I guess that Grandpa loves that story because Humphrey Bogart always played a tough guy in his movies, but Grandpa knew that he was just a wimp."

Chaucer laughed out loud. "Seriously, this is all true?"

"Yup, my grandpa later became the sheriff in town, so I guess he wouldn't fib to me."

Chaucer grinned, thinking of the movies that he had seen with Humphrey Bogart as a gangster or a tough guy. And then he wondered, if only for a minute, what kind of parents that Bogart had, certainly not a father like Remy or his uncle Le Guerrier.

Chapter 15

Little Switzerland

MELISSA CONTINUED TELLING CHAUCER more about Naples. "It's a beautiful village. If you drive into Naples from the road coming from the east, from Italy Valley or from the south Cohocton Road, you feel as if you've been transported to Switzerland. The hills and lake will remind you of the mountains there. I lived there for a year when my father was assigned by his company. I was never homesick because it was so much like Naples and Canandaigua Lake. Naples is abundantly green and shady, it's almost a paradise in the spring, summer, and autumn. Winter is another story," she paused and smiled, "unless you are a skier, because then you are only fifteen minutes from Bristol Mountain if you drive north on Route 64. Bristol Mountain has the longest downhill ski trail between the Adirondacks and the Rockies. It makes the winters in Naples so much better, if you can afford the lift tickets, that is!"

Melissa explained to Chaucer that Naples had just one prominent throughfare, appropriately called Main Street, along which sat all the businesses and churches. The large Widmer winery was located off Main Street to the west, and you could see the offices, storage buildings, and shipping docks where the trucks loaded the pallets of wine. Between the buildings and Main Street were acres of vines that produced some of the annual harvest. The elementary and high school sat on the west side of Main Street, as did the Naples Art

Center, housed in a converted railroad building. The rail service to Naples and the winery had been long gone as the trucking industry had made it obsolete decades ago.

Melissa finished giving Chaucer her virtual tour of Naples. As she started to get up from the picnic table to return to her office, Chaucer asked, "Any local music going on around here?"

Melissa grinned. "Funny you should ask. There is a guy playing at the Naples Hotel tonight. I heard him two weeks ago, and he's really good. He plays in some clubs in Rochester, but he lives over in Italy Valley. Want to go with me? I can introduce you to some other people in town."

Chaucer smiled. It was Friday, and he had had a full week since leaving New York City, what with spending time at home in Ottawa, and now three days of work and commuting from Aunt Elizabeth's house in Geneva each day. "Yup, I'm ready for some fun. How do I get there from here?" he asked.

"Where are you going for dinner?" Melissa asked.

"Well, I don't have any plans. I'll buy something around here. I won't go back to Geneva until after the music tonight."

"OK, then when you are finished here with Jack, come to the ticket office, and I will take you into town. We'll get some dinner and then go to the Naples Hotel together."

"Soooo…is this a date then?" he asked, smiling like a fox.

"It's the start of a beautiful friendship as Bogart would say," Melissa quipped, and she smiled a naughty girl smile, then turned to walk back to her office. Of course, Chaucer watched her walk away as her derriere bounced in her skirt as she walked. He smiled. Then he thought of Tessa and laughed and shook his head, comparing her bossy personality to this sweet girl Melissa.

Chaucer got up from the picnic bench and walked back inside to work on the new stage set. As he did, the Byrds' song "You Ain't Going Nowhere" came into his head, and he starting humming it, and his smile just got bigger and bigger.

https://www.youtube.com/watch?v=s2JnDKvuNzw

* * *

Later that afternoon, Chaucer called Kathleen in Geneva to explain that he would be getting back home late, perhaps midnight. "I met a nice girl at work, and we're going to hear some music at the Naples Hotel."

"That's great!" she replied, and Chaucer could tell she was smiling. "I'll leave the back porch light on. Have fun!"

As the workday at the playhouse came to a close, Chaucer stopped to give an update to Jack about the construction of the *South Pacific* set that he'd been working on with the rest of the crew.

"Chaucer, we've been making good progress," Jack said. "Your experience working on the *Superstar* set has been really helpful. I want to remind you in two weeks, when the production opens, your work hours change to 2 p.m. until closing, which is around 11 p.m."

"That's fine, Jack. I'm thankful to have the job," Chaucer replied, then decided to ask Jack about something he was wondering. "So what is the social life like in Naples?"

"There's not much, you just need to make it up as you go," Jack replied with a grin. Jack and his girlfriend, Sandy, had moved to Naples in late spring from Key West. They both had worked on Cape Cod the previous three summers at the Wellfleet Harbors Actors Theater and the Provincetown Players Theater the summer before. Then they decided to winter in Key West where they got jobs at the Key West Arts Studio. Key West was beginning to gain favor with the snowbirds from the north, and together with the local avant-garde, they were able to get sponsors from the Tennessee Williams Foundation and start to produce a regular winter season of stage drama.

Jack and Sandy had been lucky to make connections in Provincetown with Key West people, and thus they were able to get jobs there during the past winter season. There they met a man from Rochester, an old blue blood Eastman Kodak man, who took a liking to them one afternoon at Sloppy Joe's bar on Duval Street. The conversation led the man to suggesting that if they did not have plans for the following summer, that he was sure that his friend Sorenne Thorsen, the director at the BVP, could use the two of them. He wrote her name and contact information on a napkin, finished his third martini, and left with a handsome young man who came in a taxi to pick him up. He shook hands with Jack and kissed Sandy on the cheek saying, "Perhaps I'll see you here again" and disappeared out the side door onto Front Street and into the cab.

Little Switzerland

That is how Jack came to work at the BVP. As things came to be, Jack met his benefactor again at the season opening cocktail party at Bob & Ruth's Vineyard Restaurant that May. His name was Seyven Thomplinsonn; his father had been a close associate of George Eastman, the founder of Eastman Kodak Co. in Rochester. Thomplinsonn was very passionate about the theater and loved to help endow some of the various small regional theater groups in the Finger Lakes area of New York. He would also soon become a substantial donor to the Glimmerglass Opera near Cooperstown, New York, and the annual Skaneateles Classical Music Summer Program. His former wife retained her position on the board of the Rochester Philharmonic Orchestra, especially since her new husband was the famous oboe player Chad Greenstreet with whom she had run off when she discovered that Seyven had been found frequenting the house of a young man in Key West during his many "business trips" to Miami over the past decade.

Jack's chance encounter with Seyven Thomplinsonn had turned out to be just the lucky break Jack needed. It lead to advancing his career into major set construction and subsequently set design. Sandy, who had been trained in textiles and design at Bowdoin College, quickly realized that she and Jack had been given the opportunity of a lifetime, and they decided to pursue it. Thanks to contacts that both Thomplinsonn and Thorsen had set up for them, both would be moving on after the coming winter season in Key West to head to New York City to work on the set design and construction of a new play called *The Sunshine Boys* scheduled to open in late fall of 1972. Chaucer would learn much from Jack over the coming weeks.

* * *

After Chaucer and Melissa finished work at the playhouse that afternoon, they stopped at the local sandwich shop in Naples. They ate outside on a bench, washing down their dinner with a couple of beers and watching the local traffic going up and down Main Street. At 9 p.m. as the summer sun was setting beyond the high hills to the west, they walked to the Naples Hotel. Bat McGrath was setting up to perform. McGrath and his small band of fellow musicians had gained a loyal following in Rochester. They now lived on a farm in Italy Valley, about ten minutes out of Naples. The boys in the band were young and played their own creative music just right for the times. Many of the local girls were hoping to meet McGrath and his band and get invited to a party on the farm, but most never did get the coveted invitation. McGrath and his band were protective of their farm, their privacy, and their need to avoid any conflict with the locals. Their equipment set-up man, Greg, did, however, manage to get beat up by the father of a local gal one night after the father found Greg smoking a joint with her in the parking lot of the IGA on Main Street.

McGrath even wrote about it in a song:

https://www.youtube.com/watch?v=ptTlBWvx6B0

*   *   *

On summer nights in Naples, the twilight lingers until past 9:30 p.m., and darkness comes slowly. Chaucer and Melissa approached the porch of the Naples Hotel, waiting for the blackness to come and the stars and moon to shine bright. Young locals were drinking beer and laughing. One girl called it "God's Twilight," and it was to be savored each summer night. Only then would they pay the $5 cover charge and go inside. The town filled up with a lot of young people during the summers — students home from college and students who attended classes at the Naples Craft and Arts Academy. These students, few of whom were from Naples, boarded with or rented from locals. The Arts Academy had a fine reputation, and it attracted faculty, artists, and students from all over the eastern United States, people who would come to Naples for either one or both of the six-week sessions on pottery, textiles, painting or metalwork.

Instructors from the Rochester Institute of Technology and other schools as far away as North Carolina and Maine arrived in Naples to teach in the summers. The Arts Academy was held in a converted railroad-siding warehouse building. While not all the locals liked the Arts Academy, they certainly appreciated the business it brought, for Naples was a small town in a beautiful valley, but far from the commerce and industry that could bring prosperity to a town that was increasingly being divorced from its earlier agricultural roots and history.

After darkness fell and the students and locals were properly lubricated by laughter and alcohol, they went inside to hear McGrath. Most of his songs were love songs; songs of failed relationships and tender reunions, traveling far away then coming home; real life moments that cut to the heart and drew up raw emotions. Occasionally he'd lighten it up with a joyful song, but that was the exception. One wondered about his childhood and his loneliness, as artists reveal their souls when they sing or paint or write.

While Melissa and Chaucer were sitting on the porch earlier, Jack and Sandy walked up to join them. They chatted about the playhouse and the beautiful summer night. After a few minutes, Sandy recognized two younger women that she had met in her class at the Arts Academy earlier in the week. She called to them, and they came over and sat down. Sandy introduced Joanie Hargrave and Karen Perillo. The eye contact between Chaucer and Joanie was telling. Fortunately, only Jack had noticed, for if Melissa had seen it she may have walked off the porch. Jack said nothing then.

Chapter 16

Joanie and Whaleback

JOANIE WAS FROM THE NORTH SHORE of Long Island and a fulltime student at the Arts Academy that summer. She was a textile major at Rochester Institute of Technology and about to enter her senior year. Like beautiful, rich fabric, she had a natural beauty to her, with her blue eyes, full cheeks, and a high forehead framed by her sandy blond hair. She was neither tall nor short and her small shoulders and somewhat round rump made her plenty attractive enough for any man to look at and want to be close to. But Joanie, with all these assets, was not a young woman who sought attention for her physical beauty. Rather, her mother had bestowed upon Joanie a kindness of spirit that was best given by her grace and joy in living. This is not to say that Joanie would never employ her smile or her soft voice if she felt it would advance her needs, but she did not see herself as a manipulator of men, or anyone for that matter. Her mother was a parent who was honest and kind, and such kindness and honest behavior had been a good role model for Joanie. A new acquaintance of Joanie, if paying attention, would see it first thing.

Sadly, back home her parents were in the middle of divorcing. Her father was a successful attorney, and her mother was an English teacher in the local high school, the school Joanie and her brother had attended. Her father was a bon vivant, a trencherman, and a legendary debauchee whom her mother had tolerated for the last decade of their "marriage." Finally her mother hired a private investigator to uncover the extent of his disloyalty to her and the children. Joanie's mother had the goods on her father, but for the sake of the children, she never shared the obscene and perverted details.

These events were all playing out for Joanie, her brother, and her mother now in their home in Port Jefferson. Joanie had asked her father to pay the tuition money so she could spend the entire summer at the Arts Academy and avoid the emotional family divorce drama. Joanie's younger brother had come to live with her for a few weeks earlier in the summer but found Naples far too remote and rural for his tastes, so he opted to enroll in summer school at the State University at Albany, where he was to begin his freshman year in September.

Joanie was enjoying the classes at the Arts Academy, where she had met some wonderful faculty and promising young artists. She was living in a small two-room loft apartment in the converted barn of a home just blocks from the Arts Academy. Her landlord was Mrs. Emily Schoenfeld, a widow who had retired from Kodak in Rochester and moved to Naples for the slow pace of life and the absolute beauty of the Naples valley. She lived in the main house — a century-old, eight-room stately Georgian house that she shared with her older sister — about 100 feet from the barn. The barn and the house had separate driveways, and the old beech and cottonwood trees that grew along the small stream that separated the two buildings gave any tenant in the barn some privacy. Mrs. Schoenfeld was kind and quiet and liked having Joanie as her summer tenant.

She and Joanie had become friends despite the forty-year age difference. Their favorite thing to do together that summer was to hike the local trails on the weekends. Their absolute favorite hike, which they had done three times already that summer, was to hike up to Whaleback farm. Whaleback is the high peak, some 1500 feet, above the eastern end of Canandaigua Lake. It was undeveloped, as it was located on the High Tor Preserve, and the only inhabitants at the top of High Tor was the flock of sheep that lived and grazed there. It was owned by the family of one of the original investors in Kodak, a personal friend of the founder, George Eastman. Emily Schoenfeld knew the family from her years at Kodak, so when she told the family that she was moving to Naples, they gave her a copy of their family map and survey of Whaleback and invited her to go visit, using the hiking trails at any time.

The family, the Javets of Rochester, sixty years before had bought 2000 acres of the entire top of the peak and staked it as "Private Property" but over the years, they never enforced it. The locals in Naples and Vine Valley below Whaleback loved knowing that they could go to Whaleback and hike all day as long as they were orderly, left no mess or caused any trouble. The Javet family knew from their friends in Naples that the locals did enjoy their visits and hikes on the land. The only thing that the Javet family opposed was hunting on the property. They felt that the local deer, turkey, and black bear population that still survived needed a secure refuge from the local hunters, so each year they had their land manager re-post brand new signs designating the land as private and no hunting permitted under New York State law. This designation of their massive property as a wildlife preserve, as they wisely knew, also afforded them significant state tax breaks as well.

When viewed from the southwest side of Canandaigua Lake, the High Tor appears as if God had placed a large whale lying on a high hill on the east end of the lake, hence the name Whaleback. Below the property is South Lake Road, with many old waterfront homes. Three streams carry the water off the top of Whaleback into Canandaigua Lake. One stream feeds into the lake directly, and the other streams flow down the south side into the marshlands that feed into the lake. These streams, over the millennia, have forged deep gorges through the shale rock. In the summers, the mists from the waterfalls in each stream cools hikers that use the trails, the trails that the Iroquois carved through the woods next to the gorges. Often a hiker would find an arrowhead or two from the Iroquois that used to live near High Tor. To think of Iroquois people sitting next to the deep pools of water at the bottom of the falls as recently as just 200 years ago was satisfying to a hiker with a knowledge of local history.

Such an educated hiker knew that the Iroquois would have been just as happy to be sitting in the very same spot now, right where you might be sitting at that very moment, and if the understanding of time was different than that of Einstein, if it were like Chief Red Jacket believed in the multi-dimensions of the spirits and the ancestors from long ago, then you could close your eyes, and if the magic was just right, then you could open your eyes and see the original human inhabitants of the Canandaigua area with you, and you could sit with them, looking at the beauty of the falls and the deep fresh clean water, and if you were kind to one another, and trusted one another, then you could be silent and just listen to the water splashing down into the pool below you, and that time and that day would be a magical time for all those there, Iroquois and hikers, and if you were really fortunate and very quiet that day, then some deer would very slowly emerge from the trees and bushes around the water pool, and they would stop and listen, and look carefully, then, and only then, they would walk up to the edge of the pool and drink...but then someone would cough, or snap a twig, and the deer would scamper away into the trees and your chance to live just for a few minutes with the deer and these special Iroquois people would be gone; both would disappear and you would breathe deeply and smile softly for you knew, you really knew, that the time had been real and you were there, part of it, to remember for all your time on this earth...

*   *   *

That night at the Naples Hotel, when Joanie had seen Chaucer, she immediately wanted him for herself. She loved his eyes and believed a man with kind eyes also had a kind heart. Her guess about Chaucer was right.

So that night, it was not but another ten minutes before Chaucer and Joanie moved away from the others to go to the bar for another drink, and rather than go back to their friends, they just stood talking at the bar, mesmerized with each other. They had not wanted to be rude to their friends, but some special aura of initial infatuation had supplanted their social etiquette. In the meantime, other locals who knew Karen, Melissa, Jack, and Sandy filled in the space that Chaucer and Joanie had vacated, so the changed social situation of the group, while not as it was, had been repaired. But Melissa kept glancing at Chaucer, hoping he would return to sit with her.

It is not easy to describe how intense the relationship between Joanie and Chaucer became, because it happened so quickly, almost as when a lightning strike hits a dry forest and soon it is ablaze. It was also the timing for the both of them. Chaucer had been collateral damage for Tessa in her NYC unraveling and liaisons. Joanie had been numbed by the recent family divorce scenario. They both were in the right place at the right time that summer night in Naples to find a new friend who could understand the hurt of the other. And they did.

That first night together, Chaucer and Joanie talked for hours. They sipped their drinks slowly because the night was best spent talking and listening to the other rather than losing thought through booze. They opened their life books for each other, leaving the bar eventually and then sitting on the porch as the hours went by. When the others walked inside to hear the music, Joanie and Chaucer sat and talked and talked and looked deep into each other's eyes, seeking comfort and understanding.

Around midnight, when the bartender shouted, "Last call!" the two broke from their reverie. "I didn't realize how late it is," Joanie, almost embarrassed, said to Chaucer.

"Me neither. It is late, but I wanted to listen to you and learn about you. You have such a beautiful voice. Perhaps it was me who talked too much. The thing with Tessa is very difficult, but I think that by actually witnessing it instead of just hearing about it made it more understandable to me right away, kind of a gut punch."

"I understand, Chaucer. My mother is the one who is carrying the bigger burden than me or my brother. I love my mother so much, and her sorrow and pain are also my pain too."

Joanie, now holding Chaucer's hands in both of hers, whispered, "I just don't know how some people who you thought were so special, loving, and caring can turn the opposite on you." Her beautiful eyes grew sad as she spoke.

Chaucer looked at her with a closed mouth and a half grin. "Perhaps they really don't even know themselves, and care about others even less. You just wonder what was the event that started their selfishness and the contempt for the others who love them. It's just so strange that when you think you know someone and then they do these things that hurt you and others so much."

Joanie replied, "Point to where it hurts the most." Chaucer pointed to his heart. Joanie grinned. "Me too."

And so they shared each other's sadness that night, and for a few more nights after that. Soon, their time was spent learning more about each other and talking less about Tessa and Joanie's father. They were content in each other's company, safe from their pains and sadness. They had created their own happiness together, and it was good for them; they wanted it to be that way.

By the second week, Chaucer was spending nights with Joanie in her barn apartment; they were not lovers but deep friends who talked about books and the places that they had traveled to, places they loved. She always said "good night" to him with a kiss and a long hug, and then even at that late hour, Chaucer drove back to the Geneva farm. He told Kathleen that he had found a new friend, and she was so special that he had fallen over a cliff for her. Chaucer talked about her smile, her love of her craft, how they talked late into the night while sitting under the summer stars in Naples. Kathleen was happy for him and told her mother all the details too.

"Well, we'll have to keep our eye on that boy; we don't want him to do anything that his father would object to," Elizabeth said to her daughter. "We certainly can't ask him to be here with us every night; he's almost 22 years old now."

Kathleen agreed and smiled at her mother. "But that doesn't mean he can't get himself in trouble does it, Mother?" and they both laughed.

*   *   *

But Chaucer did get himself in trouble that summer in Naples. It started soon. Two weeks after he first met Joanie, he finished his workday at the playhouse and then met Joanie at the hotel again to hear the music of Bat McGrath. Like that first night, they sipped glasses of wine on the front porch and talked late into the night in the quiet of the small village. And then the spark came.

"Have you heard about the big event on Sunday?" Joanie asked Chaucer.

"No, what event?"

"I found out at the school today that there is this annual local music event called the 'Cheshire Dump Party' and local musicians get up on a hay wagon and play music all day. People by the hundreds come and dance in the field until the music stops."

"Really? Sounds like a local Woodstock! Where is this going to be?" he asked.

Joanie explained that the event was at the local Fur, Fin, and Feather Club adjacent to the High Tor property just north of Whaleback. Some of the local groups that had played in the past month at the Naples Hotel would be playing, and some from Rochester and Ithaca, too. "Are you inviting me as your guest?" asked Chaucer with the grin of a bear who just saw a big salmon jumping out of the stream right in front of him.

"Well, a lady always wants to be accompanied by a gentleman to such an event," replied Joanie with her seductive smile that could floor any guy.

* * *

When Sunday arrived, Joanie pulled open the curtains of her bedroom window and saw a beautiful sunny day, a day perfect for music and a party. She always believed that God wanted people to be joyful, and this was the day that God was giving for that purpose. In the Naples valley that morning, the air was cool as usual, but by noon, the temperature would reach the 80s as it had all week. It surely would be a good day.

Chaucer awoke in Geneva that morning and had breakfast with Kathleen and her parents. "It's so nice to be here," he thought. His four male cousins, Kathleen's brothers Logan, Clint, Oliver, and Jean Marc were fortunate to have these good parents. His uncle looked so much like his own father that Chaucer felt secure and happy being able to live with them for the rest of the summer. He told them about the Cheshire Dump Party, how the event started at a small-town dump in the Village of Cheshire up the west side of Canandaigua Lake from Naples on a summer day a decade before when some local guys took their guitars and fiddles and some beer and drove to the town dump to be away from neighbors and townspeople so they could play music and not bother anyone.

From that first event, it grew and grew by reputation, and this year it was being held in a more appropriate location — a new venue that could accommodate the now hundreds of locals and others who would show up.

After breakfast Chaucer went to church with his aunt, uncle, Kathleen, and Oliver, who had just completed Army basic training and was home. A family friend and trusted Presbyterian theologian, Pastor Wagner, gave the sermon. His ties to the family were long and special and his religious calling had been a dedicated one of service and shepherding his parishioners in the ways of the Lord. Pastor Wagner had met Chaucer a few times over the years at Giroux family events, but he did not know him well.

Chapter 17

Cheshire Dump Sunday

CHAUCER ARRIVED AT JOANIE'S PLACE in Naples about 1 p.m. He was happy. He wanted to see her and have the experience of being with her at the party on such an absolutely perfect summer day. In the summertime in the Finger Lakes of New York, God makes up for the frigid winter days of snow and the early sunsets at 5 p.m. The reward given is a multitude of gorgeous warm, dry days like this one. A few fluffy high white clouds, plenty of sun, a gentle breeze and temps in the low 80s are what God delivers for these perfect summer days, like this one in the Naples Valley. It makes one want to just stop time, freeze the day to keep it forever.

Chaucer knocked on the door and Joanie was quick to answer. She was more than beautiful this day. Her long hair was pulled back so her broad cheeks looked brilliant. In her white shorts and tank top, her slightly tanned fair skin was shining, and her frangipani fragrance ringed her smile.

"Right on time, not bad for a Canadian," she said with an even bigger smile.

Chaucer just laughed. "Can you believe this weather, not bad for New York," and Joanie laughed too.

"I heard last night from some of my friends that there will be some great bands showing up today. Are you ready for some fun? Did you bring your dancing shoes?" she asked.

"Girl, you are looking at a classically trained ballet student!"

"Really, you never mentioned this to me," she replied, clearly surprised.

"Yup, mother had me in classes in Ottawa for a couple of years. I played hockey two nights a week in our league and took ballet two classes a week. Fortunately, my father helped me get out of ballet before my friends thought I was really weird," he said, shaking his head and laughing.

"Why, I think it is great that you were able to explore ballet at a young age. Your mother was smart. I'd like to meet her sometime. She sounds like a fine woman."

Chaucer hesitated. "Let's discuss your definition of a 'fine woman' first."

He smiled and changed the subject. "How far is this party from here? Will they have food and drinks there?"

"No, my dear, it's BYO everything. This event is in the middle of a hay field, near a pond. It's about fifteen minutes from here. Let's stop at the IGA on Main Street and get some beer and food to bring. I have a bottle of wine in my bag, and a thermos of water too. OK?"

Chaucer winked at her, and they set off in the Renault, down to the IGA store, getting gas, beer, chips, and sandwiches and then off to the Village of Middlesex and up the road to the Fur, Fin, and Feather Club. There were no signs announcing the "Dump" party. That was the rule. "If you couldn't find it, you shouldn't be there" was the motto and history of the party.

They pulled off the paved road, turning on the gravel road that had a tiny sign that read "Fur, Fin, and Feather Club" so Joanie knew they had found it. Chaucer drove about a half mile through the woods and "voila," there it was — a big hay field with about 100 cars and trucks parked haphazardly. Joanie and Chaucer spotted the hay wagon and the small generator next to it. Two guys were setting up the two speakers and mikes on the wagon. A few guys with guitars and fiddles were tuning up in a circle next to the wagon. Adults and kids were spread all over the field, some with lawn chairs set up near the wagon, others on blankets, and a few even had small charcoal hibachi grills smoking. The pond had already been invaded by some kids, and they were jumping and screaming as the boys splashed water at the girls, who reciprocated. There was a sense of relaxed excitement in the air, and whiffs of marijuana smoke as well, for this was the essence of unscripted, unsupervised joy and play on a beautiful afternoon in the New York Finger Lakes.

Joanie and Chaucer looked at each other and smiled. They were content to be there together. Soon Joanie found a few of her Arts Academy colleagues sitting on a blanket, drinking cans of beer, so she and Chaucer joined them, laying out their blanket next to them.

The music and sun and joy continued. Groups on stage played bluegrass, folk, and dance tunes so catchy that it was nearly impossible to not want to get up and dance. Girls with long pigtails in homemade dresses flowed around the men in their cut-off jeans and t-shirts, mesmerized by the music and other stimulants. It was like a Grateful Dead concert, except without Jerry Garcia and his long guitar riffs, but more like David Grisman and Jerry playing "Shady Grove."

Shady Grove - YouTube

This day, the repertoire was more Irish fiddle, mandolin, traditional non-electric music. The local Swamp Root String Band was on stage, and this was their music. Everyone eventually was dancing, the children most of all. It was a day of total peace, surely a small Woodstock in the Finger Lakes. As the hours advanced, more and more people waded into the pond a capella, without clothes. No one said a word or complained. It was as peaceful and as beautiful a day as perhaps God had ever made. It is believed that the first man and woman were created naked, so perhaps this was an imitation of that day.

*   *   *

Joanie and Chaucer were having a wonderful, uninhibited day together. They both ran into people they knew, and they talked about the playhouse stage schedule and the new classes that had just started at the Arts Academy. No one talked of Vietnam or Nixon or politics. The news of the world was just forgotten and ignored, and Chaucer loved that.

It was a day without a clock, only the sun moving to the west gave any indication of the expiration of hours. Sometime later, as the sun dipped a little lower in the sky and after Joanie and Chaucer had a slow dance near the stage wagon, she grabbed his hand and led him to their blanket. She picked up her bag, water, and wine, and said, "Come on, Mr. Ottawa, I want to show you something that is very special." Taking Chaucer's hand, Joanie led him out of the field to a path that perhaps had once been an Iroquois trail, and then into the nearby woods. They walked far, until you could not hear the music and the voices and the screams of the people in the pond. They kept walking, staying on the path. They could only hear the birds and the ruffle of the leaves on the trees when a breeze blew them to sway together. It was nature's quiet. Finally, Chaucer said, "I hear water," and Joanie smiled. "Yes, we are almost there now."

Joanie knew this place. Her landlord, Mrs. Schoenfelt, had earlier in the summer taken Joanie on long, nearly all-day hikes around High Tor and Whaleback. She had shown Joanie various trails and gorges on the property, but she saved the best for last, this place, this gorge, this waterfall, this pool of water. Mrs. Schoenfelt called it "DEKANAWIDA" meaning Peace Maker Pool, because she said that it was the "Canandaigua of Canandaigua," or "the chosen spot of the chosen spot," and that if man and God, or the white man and the red man ever wanted to find a place to reconcile, to talk out things, to make peace and smoke the peace pipe, then this was surely the spot, for no other place offered such magnificent peace and quiet, buried as it was deep in the woods, high above the lake on Whaleback.

Joanie took Chaucer's hand, and they came out of the woods at the end of the trail. In front of them was a near 100-foot waterfall, which ended at the bottom into a broad deep pool of sparkling clean water. The shale rock around the spot was covered in moss. They stood at the edge and watched the water collapse over the edge and descend into the pool below, the mist visible and cooling them as they both stood quiet and in amazement.

"I was here about a month ago. Is this not a chosen spot of God's natural beauty?" Joanie said quietly. Chaucer was speechless, just gazing in awe.

"Come on, let's go down to the pool. Follow me, and be careful of the moss, it's very slippery," she said.

So Chaucer followed her down the steep path next to the gorge, and in a few minutes they reached the pool below the falls. She held his hand now. Both of them were sweating from the walk, as the afternoon heat had penetrated the shade of the forest.

Chaucer stood quiet and looked around, seeing more small

gorges and large boulders nearby. He turned to Joanie and there she was, without her clothes, as in the brief moment he had turned to look around, she had pulled off her top and dropped her shorts to the ground. "I'm going in, come on with me!" she said as she finished removing her tennis shoes and panties.

Chaucer did a quick blink at this unexpected scene. He looked at her small firm breasts and the tan line on her broad hips. His nostrils flared and his eyes were bulging. "Holy crap!" he thought. He had drunk three or four beers during the afternoon and had just a quick toke of pot, so he was far from wasted. For a brief second he thought of Tessa, and the last time that they had made love in the city. But that thought evaporated as Joanie dove headfirst into the water, a deep pool with no logs or obstructions for swimmers.

Chaucer laid his clothes in a pile and looked around. He saw no one and heard no sounds except Joanie quietly treading water and watching him. He jumped in. It was not as cold as he had anticipated. They splashed each other and laughed, swam from one side to the other side of the pool two or three times and then eventually she pulled herself out, as did Chaucer.

"Well, that was fun," he said, not knowing what else to say. She put her finger up to his lips and whispered, "shhhh" very softly. She grabbed his hand, and they walked over to her bag where she took out a towel and wiped his face dry, then her own. She put the towel around his lower back and pulled him to her, then kissed him. She kissed him again, longer than before. Then she said softly, "I want you to make love to me now," and she took the towel and laid it down on some leaves near the edge of the water. Chaucer started to say something, and again she put her finger up to his lips. And so it was to be for them, an afternoon in the "Garden," Adam and Eve at the Canandaigua Dekanawida Peace Maker Pool, learning about God's pleasures and wishes for the happiness of people on earth.

Time passed slowly for them, and soft kisses and gentle words passed between them. They decided it was time to go and just as they had finished dressing, a group of people started talking high above them near the top of the falls. They could hear their voices even over the plunging water in the pool beside them.

As they walked up the side trail to leave, they passed this group. It was two couples, and one was a girl that Joanie recognized from the Naples Hotel music nights. "The water is beautiful, you will love it," she said as they passed them.

"We will," the girl said with a broad smile. "What's this place called?"

Joanie looked at Chaucer and said, "heaven," and he smiled softly too.

What a Wonderful World - Iz KamakawiwoĐole - YouTube

Chapter 18

Confessions

A FEW HOURS LATER, sunburned and tired but full of joy, Joanie and Chaucer sat on a bench, sipping tea, in front of her barn in Naples. The summer sky glowed the deep orange of twilight at 9 p.m.; darkness would soon be upon them.

"So where do we go from here?" Chaucer asked with a sheepish half grin.

"What are you thinking?" she replied, a bit cautiously.

Chaucer didn't say anything for a few moments. "I need to tell you more about me than what I have so far."

"Probably a good idea," Joanie replied, feeling more confident. "Then I want to tell you some things that I haven't said yet either, but you go first."

"Well, like I told you that first week we met, I had been going with Tessa for a year and a half at school." His throat became tight, and he swallowed nervously.

"We were working in Manhattan, living in a group apartment, and after a month, something happened to us, and she basically dumped me for another guy. It happened so fast; it was confusing. It blew up my emotions like nothing before. I felt like I just needed to get away, so I quit my job and went back to Ottawa. Then as you know, was I lucky to land this job here, and lucky enough to meet you at the hotel that night."

"You've already told me about her, Chaucer. Is there something else you haven't told me that I should know?"

He hesitated again, thinking. "I thought I loved her. I thought we were so good together. Then this summer I guess I found out more things, and then it was over. And now you have come into my life. I guess I am a little confused." He chuckled and shook his head.

Joanie smiled softly and squeezed Chaucer's hand. "I think I understand...relationships can be beautiful and terrible all at once...I think the important thing is to stay honest and be kind...don't throw hurt around because if you throw it, it will come back like a boomerang and hit you right back, usually pretty hard too."

He looked into her deep blue eyes. "Yeah, you're right."

"So let me be honest with you now," she paused and smiled, then slowly continued. "I wanted you to make love to me today, you didn't have to say or do anything, but I am probably not ready for any relationship now." She glanced down, then looked at Chaucer again. "You already know that my parents are messed up, and school is very important to me. So for now, I need to stay, well, unattached...Can you understand?"

Chaucer smiled. "Yup, as long as we can visit the Peace Maker Pool once a week, I'll be fine with that."

Joanie laughed. "You're such a jerk, you know! Well, I'll keep that request under advisement, OK?"

And with that, he stood up, pulled Joanie up, and wrapped his arms around her. They kissed for a long time, then made love again in her bed in the barn. He slipped out about 11 p.m. and was back in Geneva by midnight.

Kathleen was sitting in the living room reading a novel when he walked in.

"Hi, Kathleen. You can't sleep?"

"Hi, Chaucer. I'm just wanting to finish this book tonight. How was the infamous 'Dump' party?"

"It was spectacular. I need to take you down to High Tor and Whaleback sometime, the place is so beautiful. My friend Joanie took me to this most beautiful waterfall. It was like the best mental therapy; you would love it."

"OK, I'm in. Promise me that you'll take me before you go back to school next month."

"I promise. Love you, good night." Chaucer walked up the

stairs, tired but with the most happiness he'd felt in a very long time.

※　　※　　※

During the next month as the calendar days slid away, Chaucer remained unsettled, not certain if he wanted to return to school. He and Joanie spent most evenings having dinner together. On Wednesday nights when there was live music at the Naples Hotel, and then usually on Fridays and/or Saturdays, Chaucer would stay the night with Joanie. While it wasn't love, it was pretty close, but they both knew in another month that they would be in different places physically and maybe emotionally as well. When you are young, your patience is never what it will grow to become later, when you learn that the real world pushes you so hard, and patience becomes essential. Being young in summer is the time to run in the fields, make love in the warm afternoon grass, sleep late, not think about a promotion at work, just think about today and maybe tomorrow. But Chaucer did think about his big question: "What to do about Joanie?" He needed to have that conversation with Joanie soon.

In the third week of August, with a week to go until the Arts Academy closed for the summer and Joanie would leave, and a month before Chaucer was to return to the University of Toronto, he decided to speak with Joanie about what was to happen to them. Their summer weeks had been dreamlike. She was smart, funny, and beautiful. When he held her in his arms, her smell was an erotic drug to him, and he had become addicted to her soft voice, her ready smile, and her deep passion for life and her art.

On that Wednesday night, after Bat McGrath finished his second set of songs at the Naples Hotel, Chaucer and Joanie sat down on the front porch drinking beer. It was around 11 p.m. and Chaucer planned, as usual, to spend the night with Joanie at her room at the barn.

"I love his music so much, he just sets me at ease," Joanie remarked, one hand on Chaucer's leg and the other around her beer. "He tells me truths of himself and of people. How does he write such beautiful songs?"

Chaucer did not say anything, he just smiled and nodded, as he wondered how this guy, maybe seven, eight, nine years older than he was, could be so brilliant and talented. His voice had a pathos of love, longing, hurt, and hope all in one voice. His words were the words of all men who have ever loved, ever waited for, found and then lost that special woman. Women also found his words revealing, helping them to understand their lovers better. No one can write and also sing such songs, unless they have lived them, and for him to have lived his songs was then to admire him for writing them, and to sing them to his friends and his audience, as he did this night, as a romantic troubadour. Was he perhaps the patron saint of love, Chaucer thought?

"I guess Bat has just lived longer than you and me, Joanie. I think if we are true to ourselves, that eventually we all fall, get hurt, get up, and have the scars to remember and learn from," Chaucer said.

"Will we have scars, Chaucer?" she said, looking at him with her most beautiful gaze, even in the weak light on the hotel porch that night.

"My father told me after my mother left him and went to Vancouver, that those that love the most have the biggest scars to live with. My father was so very hurt when she left. He was not mad, he showed no anger, which I guess means that he still loves her very much."

Joanie smiled, lips pressed together tightly, and nodded her head. "Yes, I think that he does still love her. He must be a fine father to you and your sister if that is true. Not many men can be so honest and unselfish. I wish my father was half the man yours is," she said as her eyes showed the wistfulness she felt.

Chaucer unknowingly let a single tear drop onto his cheek, and wiped it away quickly, but Joanie saw it, even in the dark. "Let's go home now, Chaucer, we have a lot to talk about."

And so they walked back to the barn that night. They drank tea, made love with the windows open and moonlight shining in. They could hear the church bell on Main Street strike 1 a.m. as the valley was very quiet, except for a motorcycle leaving the hotel and speeding away.

"Are you going back to school... You don't talk about it much," Joanie asked softly, rubbing his hair as he lay next to her.

Chaucer was tired and just lay there quietly, feeling the warm night air.

"Not sure. I really miss being around my father, and I miss my sister too."

"Not your mother?"

"No, I don't," he said firmly. "She is just so different than my father. She just writes away her days with her made-up stories. She hardly paid attention to JOA and me after we moved to Vancouver, and now it is worse, since she bought her house with the barn." He hesitated. "Behind every successful author is an ignored and neglected family," he said with disgust in his voice.

"So what will you do? I'm leaving here next Saturday and I need to go to Long Island to be with my mother for a few weeks before I come back to Rochester for school."

"Maybe I'll go with you to Long Island," Chaucer said.

Without much hesitation Joanie replied, "No, that's not possible, I'm sorry, that is my time for my mother. She is having it very difficult with my asshole father. She needs my full attention, especially since I've been away for two months."

Chaucer thought for a moment. "Well, if I go back to Toronto, I could still come down to Rochester to see you on weekends or you could come to Toronto."

Joanie's mood had shifted to quiet anger after she mentioned her father. "Oh, Chaucer, this world is so screwed up. Why does it have to be this way? Why do people do such terrible things that hurt the ones they are supposed to love the most? My father, your mother, Tessa, and here we are now, after a beautiful summer together, about to say goodbye, why?"

"What do you mean, goodbye?" Chaucer looked puzzled and tired. "Why don't we just say we'll see each other in a month. We can do that, can't we?"

Joanie was silent. She reached over to Chaucer and hugged him. Maybe the talking was over for the night. The strong moonlight was still shining through the east window and a gentle breeze was rustling the leaves on the tree outside the south window. They fell asleep in each other's arms.

Chapter 19

The Western Light

JOANIE AND CHAUCER SAW EACH OTHER a couple of more times that next week, but it was not with the same excitement and passion. They both knew that their lives were not theirs and that other, much bigger, issues were now falling on them. For Joanie, it was taking care of her mother. For Chaucer, it was figuring out if he should return to college. Neither liked it but both were allowing their obligations to take over.

* * *

Joanie packed up her belongings when the Arts Academy's second session was over. She hugged her instructors and the school director. She made it a special day to have lunch with her landlord Emily Schoenfeld, the woman with whom she had hiked and who had become both her friend and her surrogate grandmother.

The morning that Joanie was leaving for Long Island, Chaucer drove to her place before going to the playhouse for work. When he pulled up to the barn, he saw her car was packed. He turned off the Renault and just sat looking at her car and the barn. He thought of all the nights that they had spent together that summer. He smiled to himself, happy to have met Joanie. He was not resentful; he was not feeling lonely or abandoned or sad, rather he felt thankful to have had such a special woman in his life. As he got out of his car, Joanie walked out the door, carrying a box of books.

"I was hoping you'd make it here before I had to leave," she said, smiling.

"Well, I wanted to take you to the Peace Maker Pool one last time before you left," Chaucer said with a big grin.

"You are such a nasty boy," she said, laughing out loud. "Yeah, that was a beautiful day for us, Chaucer. Let's always keep that day close to us, OK?"

Chaucer nodded, took the box from her, and put it in her car. He then looked at her, looked deeply into her eyes, saying nothing, and then put his arms around her, hugging her tight and kissed her.

Joanie accepted the kiss and then took his hands in her hands. "This is going to be hard now, you know. We need to say goodbye. Let's not make it harder than it is," and she hugged him again.

Soon, they broke apart, and Chaucer moved away. "I am going to miss you, Joanie," he said with a sad look.

"I am going to miss you, too, Chaucer." She reached out to him, kissed his cheek, and backed away. "I will call you tonight to let you know that I got there."

Chaucer nodded and watched her walk back into the barn. Then he got into the Renault and drove away.

*   *   *

Joanie drove back to Long Island to console her mother, who needed her more than ever. The legal fight with her husband was in full force, and her nerves were about spent down to little wires of no conductivity in the joys of life. Anyone who has ever been in such vicious family legal battles surely knows the price it extracts on the parties in the fight, and Joanie's mother was hurt and bruised and mostly one dimensional, and she was glad that her daughter had come home.

During her first week home, Joanie went out with her two best high school girl friends to their local bar in Port Jefferson. The joy of being able to throw back a couple of glasses of wine with her best and oldest girlfriends was therapy for Joanie. She was taking a few hours of liberty from home, and her mother's doomed Titanic ship of a marriage.

While sitting at an outside table with Betsy and Meredith, and in the middle of her second glass of wine, Joanie abruptly straightened her back so fast that Betsy asked, "What's wrong, Joanie?"

Joanie's old boyfriend Blair Griffith had just walked into the bar. Blair was her first serious love in high school, and after a couple years of dating it ended a year ago, when he had essentially stopped calling her. Blair was a good guy, so good that most girls wanted to know just how good he was, since his looks and posture were that of a secure man, not a wimpy guy like so many of the other guys at age 21. Blair had left Joanie for another girl, and she had felt hurt for a long time. Spending time with Chaucer had helped pull her back to joy again.

"I'm going in to see him," she said hurriedly to Betsy and Meredith. They both knew the whole story, and they looked at each other, both silently thinking, "This will be interesting." Joanie did a quick fix of her blouse and hair and walked into the bar, slowly, and up to Blair's side where he stood at the bar alone.

"Hey, Blair, I saw you walk in. How are you?"

"Wow, Joanie, really, I was just talking to Buster about you last night, wondering if I would see you before I went back to school. How are you? You look great! I heard you were out in the Finger Lakes at an arts school for the summer. How was it?"

Joanie gave a half grin. She knew. She knew by his eyes that he was really happy to see her, she could tell, so she remained calm on the outside but churning on the inside.

"It is so beautiful and serene up there. I had a great summer. The program gave me access to the best instructors on the East Coast. It was far more than I anticipated, Blair. I learned so much this summer…" Her voice trailed off.

Blair's eyes focused on Joanie's blue ones. "How was your summer?" she finally asked.

Blair did not want to talk. He would have rather just looked at Joanie's tanned face and her beautiful eyes. Then he said, "I did some summer school to catch up. I'm changing majors. I decided that I want to go to law school instead of being in the diplomatic service, so I had to take some additional courses. I just found out two weeks ago that my transfer has been approved, so I am going to Syracuse University for my senior year and hopefully into the law school there after graduation."

"Really, that is so great for you, Blair. I bet your dad will be happy. Maybe you can join his firm then."

"Maybe, but that's a long way from now. Look, it's really good to see you, Joanie. How about if we go over to the Frog Pond for an early dinner. My treat, OK?"

Joanie smiled broadly and she tried to control the fluttering in her stomach. When she saw Blair, she realized how much she had been hoping that he would want to see her again. She missed him. She had written an entire page of a love essay in his senior high school yearbook three years ago. She wanted him to be the one, and then he was gone. He was the one who she wanted to be with in her life, to have kids with, be strong and happy together. And now he might be back again. But she would take things slowly, she decided.

In the weeks ahead, Joanie and Blair started slowly, but then continued seeing each other almost every day. Because Blair had transferred to Syracuse University, Joanie and Blair knew that he could be in Rochester and at her school in an hour's drive, so that they would not be far apart at all. This helped Joanie realize that it was time to bring Blair back into her life, and he was very glad.

After Joanie had been home for two weeks, and she felt her time with Blair had been true and honest, she called Chaucer at the playhouse. She told Chaucer that he had been a loving and wonderfully romantic guy, and that she had never had a summer like she had spent with him, and it was the truth. Then she told him that she and her longtime boyfriend Blair had reconnected after she returned to Long Island. She explained it in enough detail that was necessary. She concluded that with her studies and schedule of new textile shows, plus seeing Blair, that she thought it best to not see him again.

"I don't want to hurt you, Chaucer. You were so very kind, gentle, and loving to me when I really needed a good friend. Getting back with Blair has nothing to do with what you did or did not do. It is just life, and life gets so complicated. Our summer was like a dream for me, a wonderful fantasy of fun, tenderness, good times, good music. I don't regret any of our time together, but things have changed for me now. I hope you can understand this." She realized then that she would not have been able to have this conversation face to face with Chaucer or put it into a letter. It would have been too hard. The phone was the only way. She could feel his disappointment in his silence, and it hurt her.

Chaucer mumbled just a couple "a huhs" while Joanie spoke. Her call was a shock. Their time together seemed so dreamlike. After Tessa, he needed a woman like Joanie. But now hearing from her that their time together was over felt overwhelming, like going over Niagara Falls and hitting the rocks below. Finally, he mustered some words, trying to hide his hurt and not wanting to sound like a tearful child. "I want you to be happy, Joanie. I know about parents getting divorced. It shakes you up so badly, so it is probably good that Blair has come back into your life. He's a very lucky guy. I hope he knows this. I will write you a letter. I want to tell you how much you made me happy this summer. Let me do that, OK?"

Joanie did not really want him to do this; she just wanted to move on. At the same time, she did not want to be cruel or unkind to this gentle and tender man. "OK, Chaucer, yes, please do that. I will want to read it." She paused for a few seconds. "You know, we can still be friends. We can do that, can't we?"

"Yes, I would like that Joanie, yes, I would really like that," Chaucer said, feeling a tad relieved that Joanie was not exiting his life completely. "You be good, stay happy, and if I ever meet Blair I will tell him how lucky he is to have a woman like you. And just so you know," he paused and swallowed hard, "I think I really did love you, and I will miss you, Joanie." He felt the tears coming and knew he couldn't hold on much longer. "Bye now," he said softly and hung up.

On the other end of the phone, tears filled Joanie's eyes. She realized how fortunate she had been to meet Chaucer at that time of her loneliness in the long days of summer, far from home, with her parents in a bitter divorce and her having no one to talk to about her emotions, her feelings. Chaucer had listened, and he was so damn handsome. She realized how her needs and emptiness had been filled by Chaucer, how he opened her to a month and a half of happiness and spinning romance. Yet she needed to close that chapter now and accept the coming year with Blair and her busy senior year. She knew that thoughts of Chaucer would bring her a soft smile for a very long time.

* * *

In the next week Chaucer finished his summer work at the Playhouse, turning down an offer to stay an extra month. He thanked Mrs. Thorsen and Jack Montgomery. It had been a good summer in Naples but he knew that he needed to move on. He felt beat up from his invigorating climb of the mountain with Joanie and then being thrown off a cliff. Plus he was still unsure if he would return to the University of Toronto. He just wanted to go home.

In Geneva, he began to pack and clean out his room at his aunt and uncle's house. It had been a good summer with them. The day before he was to leave to return to his father and JOA in Ottawa, he asked Kathleen if she would go down to the lake for a walk. She put some coffee in a thermos and off they went, a short drive to the park at the north end of Seneca Lake. They parked and walked for a while, then found a bench where they could sit and sip the coffee.

"Logan and I used to sit on this very bench and talk, just like we are," she said.

"Yeah, I wish I could have seen him." Chaucer said.

Kathleen smiled. "I'll fill him in on your summer with us. He'll be happy to know you were here."

Chaucer looked sad, almost lost. "Talk to me Chaucer, you have things to tell me, I know it, I can feel it," Kathleen coaxed.

Chaucer gave her a half smile, waited, then spoke: "OK, here it is," he said as he took a long deep breath. "This summer, in just three months, I got cheated on by my girlfriend after over a year and a half of investing in a relationship with her, then I fall magically in love with Joanie in Naples, and then she dumps me this week after she went home and started up with her old high school boyfriend. Plus my mother continues her games with JOA and me. I think that I am just coming unglued, Kathleen."

Kathleen put her hand on his, squeezed it, and smiled softly. "A lot of things are going on for you, Chaucer. Your world is spinning now, I can see it. I think it all started with your parents' divorce, and you and JOA having to leave Ottawa and our family there. Look, what your girlfriend did to you in New York City was totally wrong. She is very messed up. In fact she probably did you a favor because a woman who does what she did now would most likely do it another time anyway, so she probably saved you a lot of pain in the future."

Chaucer just stared out at the lake. Kathleen grabbed both his hands and held them tightly. She knew he was being so honest with her. His hurt was palpable, and she continued, "I think what you told me about Joanie makes sense to me. It probably does to you too if you think about it. You see women like me, my age, Joanie's age, if we love our mothers, and she apparently does, we feel their pain directly, so I think that Joanie was hurting badly because of what her father was doing to her mother; sort of like maybe what you feel for your father." She looked for Chaucer to acknowledge that she was right.

Chaucer nodded his head slowly. What Kathleen was saying made sense in a way that he hadn't thought about. Kathleen went on, "So Joanie comes up to Naples to spend the summer away from her home and realizes how lonely she really is. She meets you and shazam! You were in the right place to soothe her pain and her loneliness...and then she goes back home and shazam number two happens. She runs into her old boyfriend, her first real love, and the security of him wanting her now overwhelmed her, I think."

Chaucer followed along, seeing the wisdom of his cousin, learning things that he should have learned had he been paying attention the past weeks. Kathleen continued. "Joanie was kind enough and honest enough with you to tell you, and I respect her a lot for that Chaucer. She sounds like a good woman and you were right to fall for her, just at the wrong time, my dear cousin." She smiled at him.

Chaucer was now smiling a little, looking at Kathleen and appreciating his trusted cousin and friend. "Yeah, I was just lost in her company after Tessa. In Joanie's arms I felt whole again. I guess we both needed each other and used each other to get through our bad times. I can't blame her, I guess," he said, his voice trailing off. They got up and walked along the lake, slowly. They talked for a while more, about her brother Logan, and her teaching job, her new boyfriend too. Then she said suddenly, "I forgot to tell you that Jean Marc is coming home tomorrow, for a few days! Why don't you stay an extra night so you can see him tomorrow?"

Chaucer did stay an extra night, and even one more past that, because when he and Jean Marc got together, they conspired on a plan that would change Chaucer's life.

BOOK TWO
WANDERJAHR

Chapter 20

You'll Never Believe This, But Try

CHAUCER NEVER THOUGHT the Renault would make it to Los Angeles, at least not in its current condition. Jean Marc and he went to a local garage in Geneva that was owned by one of Le Guerrier's good friends. That day and the next, the mechanic replaced the head gasket that had been leaking oil, the water pump, all four tires, and the serpentine fan belt, and he installed new points and plugs. He also adjusted the headlights so they would shine on the road instead of in the drainage ditches. The car almost seemed new to Chaucer. He and Jean Marc left the following morning before daylight.

Jean Marc had heard through his entertainment industry connections that two temporary union jobs on the set of a movie in Los Angeles were available. So he made a couple phone calls and was told the jobs would be held for him and his cousin if they could get there quickly. Under the union contract, replacement workers could work for up to forty-five days before they had to join the union. One of the two guys who had left had been drafted by the U.S. Army, and the second guy had quit to work at another studio.

The production that Chaucer and Jean Marc would work on had been temporarily halted for a week by a disagreement between the director and the studio, and Canadian director Norman Jewison was replacing him. Jean Marc learned of this opportunity from a friend at New Paltz, who just so happened to be the son of the assistant director. John Marc would work in the costume department, and because Chaucer had experience on the Broadway production of *Superstar*, he would work on the set crew. The catch was that Jean Marc and Chaucer needed to be in Hollywood in five days when the production was set to resume.

The assistant director was a good man and told his son that the two boys could live in his pool house for free if they arrived on time, did their work well, and didn't make a mess of the pool area. And so the deal was made over the phone with Jean Marc in Geneva.

As for his studies at SUNY Purchase, Jean Marc got permission from the chairman of the theater department to miss the first month of class as long as his instructors signed off and Jean Marc made up class assignments. Jean Marc had little problem getting the necessary permissions since his reason for missing classes was a temp job in the real world of entertainment. Jean Marc had learned one important thing in the business already, and that was to have connections and be bold. This would serve him well in the years ahead in Hollywood.

Chaucer called Remy from Geneva and explained the situation to him. Remy understood and agreed to inform the University of Toronto that Chaucer wanted to take a semester off to take advantage of this unique opportunity in Hollywood. The provost granted permission.

* * *

With the Renault driving like it was practically new, Jean Marc and Chaucer drove west on the NYS Thruway to the Pennsylvania state line, then into Ohio where they picked up Interstate 70 in Columbus and took that to St. Louis where they jumped on the legendary Route 66. When Chaucer and Jean Marc were in junior high, they were enthralled by the television show *Route 66*, which featured two young guys (played by Marty Milner and George Maharis) driving around in their 1965 Corvette. Every young boy who ever watched it had his testosterone pumped up by a factor of 10, as the theme song by Nelson Riddle had been a staple on the radio for years.

The famous Route 66 highway carried Chaucer and Jean Marc through Oklahoma and the Texas panhandle onto Albuquerque and Las Vegas, and into Los Angeles. Being young and in a hurry, they drove about eighteen hours a day, sleeping in the car in truck stop rest areas and eating road food. They arrived at the assistant director's house in three days, leaving them a day to rest before he took them to the set where they started work at 6 a.m.

When the boys arrived, they vowed to drive back to New York slowly, stopping to see the Grand Canyon, Zion and Bryce National Parks, and some other sites that they both had read about. It gave them a plan for their return trip, something to look forward to in six weeks' time.

Once on the film lot in Hollywood, Chaucer and Jean Marc enjoyed the work and the people that they met. They worked twelve-hour days and sometimes more. The pay was very good, and the food on the set was free. At the end of their fourth week, they were invited to a cast party at the producer's house the next night. They were ready for some fun as their set building and costume work had been six or seven days a week and they had had only two days off in the past month. But they were happy just to have the opportunity to be actually working for pay in Hollywood.

They asked their manager if they had to "dress up" for the party because they had few nice clothes with them. Billy Sullivan replied, "Boys, just come showered up and bring an empty stomach and a good thirst, that will be fine. If you wear a jacket or a tie, the other guests might think you are tourists or sons of film executives. You want to stay away from that look." He paused. "And keep your traps shut too as some of the other guests will be the film execs and money men, and they mostly are bullies and ego schmucks. Another thing, be careful of the girls that you don't know because they'll be looking to hook up with the producer or his buddies for the 'weekend audition' and that's a big deal in this town, so don't get in their way, understand?" He winked at them.

Chaucer made big pie eyes and looked at Jean Marc, like "really?" Jean Marc just laughed and grinned ear to ear after Sullivan walked away. "What's so funny?" Chaucer asked. Jean Marc just smirked.

"Cuz, it's the same in New York City in the casting for new openings in Broadway. The guys with the money get the girls who want the jobs and the chance to make it big. It's basic sack-time casting. It happens all over. That's the reality, and I really don't like it myself, but I do understand it."

"Well, I don't like it. Guys using their power and money to abuse these girls. What's fair about that?"

Jean Marc looked at him straight. "Yeah, I totally agree with you; it's unethical, it's abusive, it's corrupt, and as I think you'll agree with me, it's sinful. But that is this business today, and if I get the chance, someday to be in a position to change it, you bet your ass I will, cousin. We wouldn't want Kathleen or JOA to be taken advantage of like that."

"You know, Jean Marc, I think of your brother Clint. I can imagine if some sleazy guy out here or in New York City ever did something like that to JOA or Kathleen, I think Clint would dismember him on the spot, kind of like a John Wayne movie with a better plot of justice!"

Jean Marc burst out laughing, laughing really hard. Probably his biggest laugh in weeks. "Oh my, now that could be a great screen play — Clint doing a John Wayne on a pompous producer or film exec. I'll keep that theme in mind for my screenwriting class this semester!" Chaucer laughed too. They were tight cousins and good friends too. So much in common, and so happy to be together again.

* * *

After Chaucer and Jean Marc had been at the party for about three or four beers and a couple of plates of good catered food, Jean Marc spotted a friend he knew from the Ithaca College film department. Jean Marc had attended IC before transferring to SUNY Purchase, so Jean Marc led Chaucer over to Jeff Magione and introduced them.

Jeff had been drafted before he could get accepted at Ithaca College and spent two years in the Army Supply Office at Fort Sill in Oklahoma before coming to school, so he was two years older than Jean Marc. The two of them had played baseball on the Ithaca College team their freshman year until Jean Marc blew out his pitching elbow in a game on a cold spring day.

"Hey, Jeff, it's good to see you. I heard from some of the guys that you had left school and moved out here. What are you doing now?"

"Film, baby, film! I was at an IC film seminar, and I was lucky to meet one of the presenters through my film professor. His name is John Gould, and he had been in the Army a few years before and then played baseball at UCLA, and now he is in the business here. We hit it off and stayed in touch. When his division of MGM made a deal to produce and market the next two films by a veteran screenwriting husband and wife team, they needed some people, and John called me, so here I am. I'll finish my degree at UCLA, but right now John has me heavily involved in his next film."

"Lucky you, old man, right place, right time, huh?" Jean Marc said, a touch wistfully.

"I'll say, you never know what is going to happen unless you jump in the water, I guess."

Chaucer found the conversation interesting and amusing for he clearly knew that Jean Marc was definitely a marketer, a networker, and a carnival barker all in one. He could talk shop with anyone and already knew plenty of people in the business through his networking.

"So what are you guys doing in L.A., and how'd you get in here at this big schmoozer?" Jeff asked.

"Well, I heard about this six-week gig from my friend at a workshop back in New York, and my cousin here and I decided to drive across country and work it, so here we are. This is our film boss's party."

Jeff stepped back a bit, looked at Jean Marc with a cocked head, and said, "Yeah, you'll do just fine."

Jean Marc looked puzzled but he smiled.

Then Jeff said, "We're doing a remake of Hemingway's *A Sun Also Rises*, and we start shooting in Spain in six weeks. We had a guy for the role of the friend of Pedro Romero, the bullfighter character who Lady Brett Ashley falls for. It's a small role requiring some dexterity, and the guy we had, a stunt man, just broke his leg finishing another film, so I need a guy who looks Spanish or French for the role. You have the black hair and the face we need; do you want to do it? You'll make some money and see Spain. We'll need you for three or four weeks."

While Jean Marc and Jeff were talking, Chaucer was looking at a young woman in a very short skirt with long dark hair, quietly talking to an older guy. She looked like Ali McGraw but wasn't. The guy had walked away and had been gone awhile, leaving her standing alone, so Chaucer walked over.

"Hi, can I get you a re-fill or a plate of hors d'oeuvres?" he said with his charming Chaucer smile. Chaucer was a handsome young man, but he did not market himself that way; he preferred just to establish some basic conversation, be polite, show some appropriate kindness for a situation, and see if that could get a discussion going. One would be accurate to say that Chaucer was "a good guy." JOA always had described her brother that way.

"Yes, that would be wonderful; a white wine would be great about now," the woman replied with a look of thanks that implied she had not seen a kind face all night.

"Great, I'll be right back." Chaucer excused himself and walked to one of the three small bars set up around the large swimming pool. In a moment he returned with a glass of chilled white wine. "I'm Chaucer. I'm here with my cousin Jean Marc. We work on the sets at the studio. Great party, isn't it?"

"Thanks." She took the drink, smiling at Chaucer. "My name is Morgan. My date walked away and has yet to bring me another drink so I really appreciate that I found at least one gentleman here tonight."

Chaucer gave Morgan his best "I've had three beers" grin. "Do you work in the front office in the studio? I don't remember seeing you on the sets."

"No, I'm a first-year grad student at the UCLA Film School," Morgan replied, giving Chaucer her full attention. "My boyfriend is an assistant producer of a few of the studio films that have been circulating the past year. I think the one that you may recognize is *A Separate Peace*, the film adaptation of the John Knowles book."

"Yes, actually, I saw it this summer when I was working in New York City. I thought it was well done — a good contrast of social and war-time issues." Chaucer quickly remembered not to appear too pedantic. "It showed the big difference from the times, of guys our age in the World War II era and our age now in the Vietnam era. I have three cousins in the Army now, in fact, they are the brothers of my cousin who is with me now."

"You didn't go then?" she asked.

"No, I'm Canadian. This is not our war." Chaucer replied in a low voice. Odd, he thought, but in the entire time that he had worked in New York City during the past summer, no one ever asked him this question. He pressed on. "Did your boyfriend serve? Is he a veteran?"

"No, that's not his thing; he fights his wars here in La-La Land," she said, snorting.

"Oh, I see. What are your thoughts on the war if I may ask?"

Morgan could sense Chaucer's decency and smiled at him. She liked his eyes and his politeness; she could easily tell that he was a rookie in the caustic sport of Hollywood. "My father and my two uncles were in World War II. They are real brave, quiet men, and I love them all. I think that they learned a lot about being a man during their time in the war."

"What do you think about Americans serving in Vietnam today?" he asked, looking at her intently, happy that he had engaged her.

"It's shameful. It's just so shameful that our guys have been there for seven years now," she said so passionately that it surprised Chaucer. "We were sold a bad war by Washington. I thought that President Nixon was going to end it but he's now part of the whole problem. My kid brother will be graduating high school this June, and I do not want him to be sent there, and neither does my father."

"Yes, I understand. My American cousins have had issues with the war as well." He stopped without going into further detail, and then resumed. "But we Canadians..."

In the middle of his sentence, Morgan's date walked up and stood between her and Chaucer with his back towards Chaucer.

"Come on, Morgan, let's go," he said in a bossy tone.

Chaucer did not like this rudeness; he did not like this guy just interrupting the conversation he was having. "Excuse me, but I was speaking with Morgan," he said in a polite tone.

The boyfriend, who appeared to be in his thirties, turned around and looked at Chaucer. With an amazingly condescending look, he said, "Buzz off, deck hand, this is not your party."

Morgan looked at her boyfriend with disgust and pity. "Jerry, I actually was having a very nice conversation with Chaucer, which you now have rudely interrupted."

Jerry persisted. "Morgan, I have another producer over here that I think it would be great for you to meet right now. I want to introduce you to him before he leaves."

"When I finish my discussion with Chaucer, we can see him," Morgan replied firmly.

Jerry grabbed her upper arm. "Come on, you might not get this chance again."

Morgan shook her head and stayed put.

Chaucer stepped a stride closer to Jerry. "Excuse me, but there are two things you need to hear." At this, Jerry turned to Chaucer. "I don't need to hear anything from you. Now buzz off like I said."

Chaucer grabbed Jerry's arm and turned him around and stood with his face about a foot from Jerry's. "Buddy, you are way out of line. Morgan and I are going to finish our conversation, and you are going to apologize to her for being rude."

Jerry laughed out loud. "You have no idea who I am, you fucking moron. Buzz off before I have you tossed out."

"OK, Jerry or is it Mary?" Chaucer said with a solid wide-eyed stare directly into Jerry's eyes. "You arrogant prick, not only do you owe Morgan an apology, you owe me an apology now," Chaucer said with the intensity of a guy about to drop his gloves in a hockey fight.

Jerry laughed in Chaucer's face and lifted both arms in an attempt to push Chaucer away. Chaucer knocked his arms away, which caused Jerry to throw a right-hand punch at Chaucer's head.

Instinctively, Chaucer blocked the punch with his left arm and threw a wicked right hand over the top where it landed directly on Jerry's nose, sending him to the ground with blood splattered all over his white suit jacket and pants.

Morgan shook her head and looked down at Jerry lying bleeding on the pool deck. "You deserved that, Jerry, you really did."

Two male guests walked over and helped Jerry up, handing him napkins to stop the blood. An older woman who was standing nearby and had witnessed it all said to Morgan, "Jerry deserved that; you are right."

Jerry staggered slowly into the house for some first aid. Morgan grabbed Chaucer's arm and led him over to the closest bar. Jean Marc, who had seen the event from afar, quickly walked over. Chaucer introduced him to Morgan. Morgan downed her drink and got another. "Jerry can be such an asshole. I'm sorry, Chaucer. Unfortunately, the guy you just decked is also a part of the producer team for this film, so he will certainly fire you tomorrow. Plus he may have a couple of his boys come to visit you, too, so I suggest that you think about getting out of town for a while. Did you get paid today?"

"No, they said we'd get paid on Monday because the party was tonight, and they had extra work to do."

"OK, here's what I will do. My mother's brother is Jerry's boss, he's part owner of the studio. So you meet me at the bursar's office at the studio at 10 a.m. on Monday and I will get you paid in cash, and then I suggest you leave for a while. Can you do that?"

Chaucer looked at Jean Marc, who nodded to him. "Yes, I'll be there then. I'm sorry Morgan. I couldn't help but defend you."

"Don't worry, Chaucer, you did the right thing given the circumstances. I think my uncle would be proud of you, he really doesn't like Jerry very much." They all smiled. Morgan shook Chaucer's hand, then Jean Marc's hand, turned and walked into the house to rescue Jerry from himself.

Chapter 21

Moon over Mexico

ON MONDAY, Chaucer collected all his earned wages from the payroll clerk in the bursar's office at the studio. Inside the big envelop was a smaller envelop. Inside that envelop was a note:
"It was good to meet you, Chaucer. You did to Jerry at the party what many others have wanted to do but were afraid to do because of the repercussions. I'm sure Jerry will send his two muscle men to visit you for payback, so it's best that you make yourself scarce for a while. I have enclosed the last two weeks of wages that you would have earned, plus a bonus. You acted from a deep sense of decency in defending me, and I truly respect and appreciate that. Perhaps our paths may cross again. In the meantime, thank you for being a gentleman. Regards, Morgan."

* * *

At a pizza place for dinner that Monday night, Jean Marc told Chaucer that he agreed with Morgan that he should leave town for two weeks. "Call me at the pool house. I'll have finished my work on the film set by then," Jean Marc told him. "We can drive the Renault back to New York together." Jean Marc wanted to work the remaining weeks as he was making great business contacts at the studio. He had been introduced to two young screenwriters who also knew a couple of Jean Marc's contacts in the theater business in New York City. Thinking of his future, Jean Marc wanted to get to know the screenwriters better while he was in Los Angeles.

Jean Marc told Chaucer about an interesting and inexpensive place in Mexico where Chaucer should think about hiding out for a couple of weeks. He could kick back and rest while Jean Marc finished his work on the movie set. The place in Mexico was known in L.A. as the "Catch 22 Beach" outside of Guaymas on the west coast of Sonora. It was a long one-day drive from L.A. The recent 1971 movie *Catch 22*, based on Richard Heller's book, had used the location for many scenes. The movie company had built a runway for the World War II B-25 planes for the film, with the Sonoran mountains in the background and the Gulf of Cortez in the foreground, great for cinematography. Jean Marc had learned about it from a set hand who had been there over the past summer. A small colony of Americans had started camping out near the runway. The area was beautiful and close to Guaymas for supplies. Plus, there were no Mexican police nearby to harass or extort money from the Americans, at least not yet, he was told.

Before sunrise Tuesday morning, with an escape and a new adventure in his mind, Chaucer tossed his backpack, a small suitcase, two bags of food and jugs of water into the Renault and headed towards the Mexican border. He took the interstate to Tucson and crossed into Mexico at Nogales and then headed south towards Hermosillo. From there it was an hour to Guaymas.

Chaucer arrived in town at dusk and found a bar off the central plaza; American music could be heard out of the open door. A large red-and-yellow sign nailed above the door announced "Cucarachas Borrachas." Inside a few Yankees were drinking bottles of beer. Chaucer asked them about the Catch 22 beach encampment. They said that they were staying there themselves and would take him when they went back later. One of the guys was named Ben, and he liked Chaucer right off. Being in Mexico, Chaucer told him to call him Pancho, a name he liked. "You don't look like no Pancho ta me," Ben said with a rough Texas drawl. "Where'd ya git that name?"

"My freshman year at college, I grew a big moustache, and my friends thought I looked like a photo of Pancho Villa, so I became Pancho to them."

"Ya fechen picked the right place to be then, Pancho," he said, semi-drunk and smiling like a mule. "Look, you better know there ain't any water to drink out at the camp, so if you need some, best get it in town now, and some tequila and cervezas, too."

"What are cervezas?" Chaucer asked.

"Beer, brother. Bring your own booze; there's nothing out there, Pancho."

"Where can I get some?" asked Chaucer.

"Come with me." Ben walked Chaucer out of the bar and pointed to a lit building across the town plaza. "Best git over there now. They close when they want to here."

"What's the name of this bar mean?" asked Chaucer with a grin.

"It means drunken cockroaches, that's what it means. Now off with you before they close that store," Ben said, amused by Chaucer's ignorance.

Chaucer hustled across the plaza, noticing a group of cute black-haired girls with some stocky boys. They paid him no attention as they talked boisterously in Spanish. He got to the store and bought a bottle of tequila, a bottle of mescal, some liter bottles of Carta Blanca, and some bags of rice and beans. He saw the water containers, but he had brought with him six gallons of water from Los Angeles in plastic containers because Jean Marc had warned him of the problems with the Mexican water supply.

He took his stash back to his car and locked it in the truck, then went back to the Cockroach bar to find Ben, who, luckily for Chaucer, was paying his tab with his two friends and was about to leave. "Oh, you came back?" said Ben.

"Well, yeah, I don't know where the beach is; I just know that's where I want to be."

"Brother Pancho, you just follow me in my pickup, 'cause that's where we're going now, and don't dilly dally cuz if you get lost out there, you'll never find it in the dark."

So Chaucer got in the Renault and followed Ben in his truck about ten miles out of town, down some back roads and then finally down an unpaved road. The stars shone bright, and a three-quarter moon lit the desert around them. About twenty minutes after leaving the town plaza, Chaucer saw campfires burning in the distance, so he knew he was getting close, and then they were there.

Chaucer saw pickup trucks, campers, about eight or nine trailers set up, a dozen or more tents and the campfires. He saw a few guys sitting on the beach strumming guitars, and a few girls singing and dancing near the fires. Was this Mexico or still California? he thought.

And so it was for his two weeks there. It was a campground of young Americans who could have been transported from Woodstock a couple of years earlier. Peace and joy were the currency. Everyone seemed kind, happy, communal in spirit. Meals were shared; beer, tequila and pot were passed around willingly. The days would be good here, he thought. "Thank you, Cousin Jean Marc," he said out loud.

On his first morning at the camp, Chaucer awakened from where he'd slept on the back seat of the Renault. He sat up, rubbed his eyes to wake up, and looked out the back window to the west. He had heard the sound of the waves hitting the beach in the dark, and he had seen the moonlight reflecting off the waves, yet in the morning he was able to see the vastness of the water in the Sea of Cortez, and then he looked east to see the beauty of the mountains. He quickly understood why these people had chosen this spot to camp.

That morning he met some of the campers whose tent was near where he had parked the Renault; he knew they were Canadians by their accents and choice of words. Then they pointed to the tent of another group of Canadians, so that first morning Chaucer met five people from Vancouver and two from Calgary. They had come for a week and stayed a month. They talked about Canada, Chaucer's life in Ottawa, and their towns in western Canada. They warned Chaucer about the rattlesnakes as the boys from Calgary had been surprised by one that had slithered under their truck to lie in the shade two days before.

On his first day in camp Chaucer remained quiet, because the campers were mostly quiet too. He slowly walked around, seeing a guy softly playing a guitar, some girls throwing a frisbee next to the water. He counted fifty-seven people and six dogs. He was tired from his long drive the day before, and he just wanted to rest. He missed Joanie and had dreamt about her during the night. He thought that he had allowed Joanie to own his heart because Tessa had owned his heart before. But now he had no woman in his heart, and the emptiness he did not like. Maybe this was from the absence of his mother in his life for so many years, or maybe his anger from it, as she never really had let him get too close. He had let go of Tessa from anger and then had fallen hard for Joanie. Mountain and valley, then mountain and now valley again. He had not protected himself. He thought that he needed to do better the next time.

Chaucer walked around the camp some more. The cars and trucks, most with campers on the back, had license plates from Oregon, California, British Columbia, Washington State, and the one truck from Alberta and one from Texas. The day was breezy and sunny. The heat would come soon. That was the weather there. No chance of rain as the camp was on the edge of a desert that came right up to the water. The continuous breeze off the water kept the bug population at bay for the most part. The daytime views of the water and mountains were just so beautiful that it inspired a calmness, a peaceful easy feeling in him. God's therapy, he thought.

I like the way your sparkling earrings lay
Against your skin, it's so brown
And I wanna sleep with you
In the desert tonight
With a billion stars all around
'Cause I gotta peaceful easy feeling
And I know you won't let me down
'Cause I'm already standing
On the ground

And I found out a long time ago
What a woman can do to your soul
Ah, but she can't take you anyway
You don't already know how to go
And I gotta peaceful, easy feeling
And I know you won't let me down
'Cause I'm already standing
On the ground

I get this feeling I may know you
As a lover and a friend
But this voice keeps whispering
In my other ear, tells me
I may never see you again
'Cause I get a peaceful, easy feeling
And I know you won't let me down
'Cause I'm already standing

I'm already standing
Yes I'm already standing
On the ground
Oh, oh

—Songwriter: Jack Tempchin,
The Eagles, circa 1972

Peaceful Easy Feeling (2013 Remaster) - YouTube

❊   ❊   ❊

On the third day at the beach camp, three young Mexicans rode up to the encampment on horseback. They had saddlebags, and the leader of the group was attempting to sell marijuana to campers. But soon Ben walked up to the Mexicans and spoke in fluent Spanish. They had an animated conversation, then Ben went to his truck and brought back a large cloth bag and pulled out three bottles of premium Tequila. He gave each Mexican a bottle and shook their hands. They all smiled, and then the Mexicans rode off as quickly as they had appeared.

Chaucer walked over to Ben. "What was that about, Ben?" asked Chaucer as he stood next to Ben and watched the horses gallop away.

"They know the police over in Guaymas, and we need to keep them happy. Had anyone bought any pot from those guys, later today or tomorrow, some local police would have driven up here and started searching the tents and campers. They would have found some or planted some, and then they would want to arrest whoever had it, unless we paid a bribe to forget about the arrest. Those guys coming here, which has happened before, was nothing but a setup."

"How long have you been here, Ben?"

Ben was older than many of the others, probably early 30s, and harder looking too. "I started coming here about a year ago. I come and go, you know, a causal thing for me depending on my business in L.A. How did you hear about this place?"

"My cousin and I were working on a movie set in L.A., and I got into a little trouble so I needed to get lost for a couple weeks," said Chaucer in his youthful, innocent way.

"Get caught selling weed, didja?" asked Ben with a big grin.

"No, not that kind of trouble…I punched out a guy at a studio party, and he happened to be a hot-shot young producer. I was told that he would send his boys to get me, so I needed to get lost. So that's how I met you at the bar in town; I had just driven in from L.A."

"OK, kid, as long as you are not a narco or a bail bondsman. A lot of people here would not like to have you around, understand?" Ben said.

"Hey, I'm just a Canadian who tangled with the wrong boyfriend at a party, that's all. I'll be gone in two weeks. I've got to get home soon."

"Don't worry, kid, I've smacked a few jerks in my day too. You'll be fine here. If you have any trouble with anyone in this camp, come to me before you start any trouble. We want to keep the local cops away from here, keep it peaceful. Ya got that?" said Ben confidently.

Chaucer smiled as he saw Ben as a decent, older guy. He was happy that Ben had taken a shine to him already. Chaucer was really starting to like the place now, after just a few days.

*   *   *

Later that afternoon, Chaucer decided to drive into Guaymas and see more of the town since he did not see much the night he arrived earlier in the week. He had made friends with a few other people in the camp, so he asked them if any of them needed to go into town for supplies. Stephanie and Sissy said yes, and just before they got in the Renault, Billy joined them too. Chaucer had been sleeping in the car with the windows down, which with the soft breeze of the water at night was actually a pleasure. The breeze kept the bugs away and the waves splashing on the beach created a tender background sound for sleeping, and for waking up in the mornings as well. So Chaucer had to tidy up his car before the others could find a seat.

Stephanie and Sissy had met Billy in Tucson, and the three of them decided to drive down the west coast of Mexico to see Mazatlán and then to Puerto Vallarta where the beaches were beautiful, and the dope was cheap and plentiful. Billy had quit school at the University of Arizona in Tucson after he received his Selective Service lottery number, which was a high number, so he knew he could not be drafted for Vietnam duty. He had not liked school very much anyway. He had been working in a bar in Tucson and playing music with some local guys in the small bars and cantinas when he had met the girls.

Stephanie and Sissy were traveling pals, high school friends from Connecticut who were working crappy jobs in Hartford. They had saved some money and decided to travel out west until the money ran out. Once they reached Tucson, they decided to go south into Mexico where they heard the living was cheap. After meeting Billy in a bar and telling him their plans, Billy asked if he could go with them. They readily agreed, thinking it was a good thing to have a guy along with them for security. Three weeks earlier the trio had crossed into Mexico at Nogales in Sissy's old Ford Mustang followed by Billy in his ten-year-old Ford pickup. South of the border, they had run into another guy from Tucson at a Pemex station in Hermosillo. He had just left the Catch 22 beach camp and told the three of them about it. He drew a crude map showing them the roads from Guaymas to the camp and told them to find it during the daylight so they did not get lost in the desert at night. They found the camp as the map had been true. Billie, Sissy, and Stephanie had not left the area to go further south yet as the camp was free, the people kind and peaceful, and they could score decent weed in nearby Guaymas in the local bars at night.

Once they got to Guaymas that day in Chaucer's Renault, Billy and Sissy headed off to the store, then to a bar for an anytime Happy Hour. Billy had come to like Sissy and could be seen glued to her at almost any time of day or night. Stephanie had been feeling like the odd gal out and was happy to meet Chaucer.

She liked him and called him Pancho, telling him that he would probably look funny in a Pancho Villa moustache but that the name was good for him in Mexico, and that is what she would call him. Chaucer just laughed. He liked Stephanie. She was nearly as tall as he was; she was lanky thin with long arms and long curly brown-reddish hair that she always tied back. Her face was friendly and mostly happy, and she had the genuine smile of a modest person.

The trip from Connecticut had been a real adventure for Stephanie. Her parents were separated, and her older brother was in the Navy, already serving for two years. She had lived with her mother until she and Sissy decided to find an apartment together. Her relationships with a few boyfriends did not work out for her, and after two years in the factory job, she and Sissy decided to make a break. She was now a year older than Chaucer and likely more pragmatic, coming from a working-class family in Hartford. When she was a teenager, her family life was seemingly normal, until her father moved to New Bedford to take a job on a fishing boat, as the pay was far better than his work in a warehouse. Unfortunately for Stephanie and her mother, her father took up with a woman in New Bedford. He never came home again and signed over the house to Stephanie's mother. He gave Stephanie his address in New Bedford but she never went to see him. Her mother said that he had been very difficult to live with over the years, and she was happy that he had left. She had a new guy in her life within a couple of months anyway. Legally she was still married but it meant nothing to her anymore.

Chaucer learned all this in the coming days as he and Stephanie quickly became a couple in the camp. Stephanie and Sissy shared a two-person tent just behind a sand dune away from the high tide level at the beach. Then Sissy decided to move into Billy's small camper on the back of his pickup.

One morning, Sissy announced: "Steph, Billy has asked me to join him in his camper. Do you mind if I leave you the tent for yourself?" she asked with the grin of a puppy who ate all his food and the cat's food too.

"No, honey, you really like Billy, and he treats you well. I don't want to stop you," Stephanie replied.

The day after Sissy moved to Billy's camper, Stephanie walked over to Chaucer where he was sitting alone on the beach, reading. "Pancho, I'm inviting you to dinner at the campfire next to my tent. Pasta and a little leftover chicken are on the menu, and I have a bottle of tequila too. Will you join me?"

Chaucer laughed out loud and smiled broadly. He thought to himself: "Where else am I going tonight?" so he replied, "Yes, I will come over, I'd love to," and he did.

It was another beautiful Mexican evening with the sun setting in the west over the Sea of Cortez. Stephanie boiled the sea water for the pasta. She tossed on the leftover chicken from her small camping cooler that she had buried up to the top in the sandy dirt in her tent. She added some onion and sprinkled olive oil on it all. It was a joyful meal on the edge of the desert, as the pair sat looking at the water. The breeze was slowing down as the sand cooled down with the sun setting.

After eating, Chaucer and Stephanie walked over to the big nightly fire where twenty or more people were congregating, some playing guitars, some singing, some laughing and even a few dancing to *Uncle John's Band* that the three guys with the guitars were now playing:

> *Oh the first days are the hardest days, don't you*
> *worry any more*
> *When life looks like Easy Street, there is danger at*
> *your door*
> *Think this through with me*
> *Let me know your mind, wo-oh, what I want to know*
> *is, are you kind?*
> —Songwriters: Jerry Garcia and Robert Hunter 1970

https://www.youtube.com/watch?v=TSlajKGHZRk

Chaucer and Stephanie stood there, looked at each other and smiled; it was where they both wanted to be at that moment. She put her arm around his waist and Chaucer did the same to her. Looking into her eyes, he felt a rush of blood so he gently kissed her. They stayed for a while, joining in the singing of some more songs, sipping their tequila in coffee cups. Then Stephanie took Chaucer's hand and led him back to her tent.

And so it was for the next ten days and nights. Chaucer moved into her tent and the two of them were together, a couple at the Catch 22 Beach in Guaymas, Mexico...

* * *

One night Billy and Sissy walked over to Stephanie's tent. Billy had bought some local peyote buttons in Guaymas the night before, and he wanted to share them. "How do you know this is any good?" Stephanie asked Billy.

"Well, these guys have been selling me some pot the past couple of weeks, and it has been fine, so why would they want to piss me off? Plus this area is ground zero for mescaline and peyote; this is the land of Don Juan Matus, the Yaqui shaman that Carlos Castaneda wrote about. Where you been, my beautiful sister? This is the stuff I came here for," he said with a wide grin.

"OK, just asking, Billy."

Billy opened his small leather pouch, pulled out a small pile of what looked to Chaucer like a mixture of brown weeds and horse manure. Billy used his Swiss Army knife to cut it into four pieces and handed a piece to the other three.

"OK, eat this, and let's make some tea. We'll be trippin, for hours, so enjoy it."

Chaucer looked at Stephanie. "You ever done this before?" he asked.

"Only here, the first week we arrived. It's different but OK, you'll like it."

So Chaucer did as instructed and ate his portion of the peyote button, as did the others.

Soon they were all sitting with their eyes closed, listening to the music coming from the crowd around the big fire. Then Chaucer stood up suddenly and put his head outside the tent and puked. It was a good puke as he saw the chewed peyote laying in the sand. His head was spinning in a way that he had not experienced before. The others hardly noticed him gone. Chaucer went to his Renault, found a jug of water in the truck, and drank a lot of it. He went back to the tent and peered in. The three of them were still sitting and looking half asleep, so Chaucer grabbed a beer from the cooler and a hunk of bread and walked over to the group by the big fire. Peyote was not for him. In a way, he was glad he had puked because he had to make a decision soon about when to leave the camp. He finished his beer, walked to his Renault and went to sleep — alone.

Chapter 22

Away on a Broken Wing

CHAUCER HAD NOW BEEN GONE from L.A. for over two weeks, and he realized that he and Jean Marc would need to get back to New York soon. He felt glad that he had taken off the fall semester, and now was unsure if he wanted to return to Toronto for school at all, but he knew that he should talk with his father about it. He decided to tell Stephanie that he would be leaving the next day and going back to the East. He hoped he could see her when she got back to Connecticut. He had really liked getting to know her and being with her. She had been very different from Tessa and Joanie. She was quieter, less expressive. Chaucer felt that she had a loneliness deep inside her. Perhaps it came from her parents splitting up, like Chaucer had experienced. He felt that she responded to his holding her, and that made him feel good. He knew that they both were unsure of their plans for the future, but she was a kind and gentle woman, and he liked that in her the best.

The next day, Stephanie slept until late in the morning. Chaucer had checked on her early but decided to let her sleep. About noon she came out of the tent and saw Chaucer sitting on the sand dune looking at the water, as the high tide was rushing in fast.

Chaucer greeted her. "Oh, hi, I wanted you to sleep. I thought that from last night you'd want to. How late did you all stay up?"

"Oh, Pancho, I was up most of the night it seemed before I could sleep. That peyote from Billy was wicked. I didn't even realize that you had left. I was fine for a while, and then I started to freak out. I had this hallucination. I saw my father on his fishing boat, and my brother and I were helping him with the nets. We were hauling them up on the deck, and they got really heavy so I called for my father to help me, and we pulled the net onto the open deck, and there was this really big fish in the netting so my father had to cut the net away to get the fish out, but it wasn't a fish, it was my mother...I woke up screaming, and I ran out of the tent. I went over to the big fire. Some people were still there so I sat with them and just stared into the fire, then I fell asleep, and someone put a blanket on me. When the sun came up, I walked back to the tent. Billy and Sissy were gone so I just crawled into my covers and went back to sleep." She paused, seeming to want to forget the whole night. "Hey, I made some fresh coffee, come have some."

Chaucer got up and went to the tent with her. She poured him some strong coffee and they sat back on the dune to watch the tide come in.

"Steph, you won't believe what I saw here before you came over!" He smiled. "The water washed up the biggest eel that I have ever seen. Seriously, it was black and must have been eight or nine feet long. I am glad I was not in the water, and then the tide took him back out in the undertow...I learned that the tribes in Vancouver believe that if you see a live eel, that your sexuality and fertility will grow and expand, and if you see a dead eel, you will become impotent. Fortunately for me, the eel was alive and well." He laughed, as did Stephanie.

She looked at him, with a tired but loving look. She looked so pretty that day; her unkept hair wrapping her cheeks and eyes. "So what shall we do today, my Canadian Pancho man?"

Chaucer hesitated and then began to talk slowly. "Well, I need to talk to you about me...us..."

Stephanie smiled a very tired grin. "That is an excellent idea, Pancho, let's talk, but I am exhausted so I will just listen."

"Well, here's the situation. My cousin is in L.A. and is about done with his work on this movie set, and I need to drive him back to New York very soon so he can finish his senior year at school. So tomorrow, very early I'm going to need to leave to get back to L.A." His voice trailed off.

She sat up very straight and stared at Chaucer for what seemed like eternity to him.

"Hold on, Pancho, are you telling me that you are leaving in the morning for L.A.? When will you come back?"

"I can't come back. I need to drive Jean Marc back to New York now. He needs to get back to school."

"Wait a holy minute now, Mister." Stephanie's face was turning red as she raised her voice. "You are leaving here *tomorrow*, just like that?" She was quiet for minute, trying to control her anger. "I invite you into my tent, and a week and a half later you are leaving, and not coming back, are you really serious?" she said staring at him. "So this is the end of us, just like that?"

"I'm sorry, Stephanie, I thought I told you the night we first met that I would be leaving in two weeks," Chaucer said a bit defensively, surprised at this reaction from Stephanie. "I'm certain I did."

"Well, if you did you either whispered it or thought you told me. I thought we were becoming a couple, that we would be together for, well, a while!" Her voice was getting loud.

"I am really sorry, Stephanie. I really like you, and if I didn't have to get Jean Marc home I would stay, don't you know that?"

"Oh shit, Pancho. I had some hopes for us, I really did... So the past two weeks of loving you was just a vacation treat for you, is that it? Really Pancho, how could you?" Stephanie stood up with her arms folded around her chest. Her eyes started to well up.

"I'm sorry. I didn't mean to hurt you or mislead you. Please don't be mad at me. I really like you, Stephanie, I really do."

Stephanie stared at the breaking waves, not looking at Chaucer. She started to cry softly. Chaucer stood up to move closer to her, to comfort her.

"Please get away, please," Stephanie gulped as the tears flowed down her cheeks.

"I'm really sorry, Stephanie. Maybe we could..."

She stopped him mid-sentence "Please go get your things out of my tent now, right now. Don't say anything else, please, just go and don't even think about saying goodbye when you leave." Stephanie wiped the tears from her cheeks with the palms of her hands, trying to recompose herself.

She turned away from Chaucer, left her coffee cup in the sand, and started walking down the beach. Chaucer watched her walk away, upset with himself at his forgetfulness and that he had inadvertently hurt her. Finally, he picked up the coffee cup and turned and walked to her tent.

Fifteen minutes later, Chaucer had moved all his things into his Renault. He sat on the car's hood and gazed at the water over the top of the dunes, thinking. It had been a good couple of weeks in Mexico. He had met many nice and kind people and he didn't want it to end this way. He really liked Stephanie, and they had been good together, almost too good perhaps, he thought, but he needed to get Jean Marc home and then he needed to get back to Ottawa and maybe to school himself. Knowing how upset Stephanie was, Chaucer decided trying to talk to her again was probably useless and might make things worse. It would be best for him to leave the camp that afternoon. It was difficult to have to leave this magical spot where Jean Marc had sent him, but he had to be true to his cousin and get him back to New York. On top of that, his mind said, "Chaucer, guess what? First Tessa, then Joanie, and now Stephanie, all in four months' time." He wanted to scream.

* * *

Chaucer remembered a campground on the southside of Tucson from his drive down now more than two weeks before. If he left the Catch 22 Beach now, he could make the Arizona campground before dark. That would also ensure that he could get to Jean Mark in L.A. by tomorrow afternoon as well.

Grabbing a pencil and a notebook out of the glove case of the Renault, Chaucer wrote a note and tore the page out. It read:

Dear Stephanie,

I am so sorry to have hurt you. I really like you very much and thought that perhaps we could find a way to be together for a longer time, either me coming back here or seeing you when you get back home. Thanks for being so kind and loving to me. You are a wonderful woman. Perhaps we can fix this later if we try.

With affection,
Chaucer (Pancho) Giroux

2110 Sixth Line Road
Ottawa, Ontario, Canada

Chaucer then walked around the camp area at Catch 22 Beach and said his farewells to some of the other travelers. He gave Ben a big bear hug and invited him to stay with him anytime he was in Ottawa or Toronto. Ben remembered that Chaucer had told him about the tough guys that Jerry, the assistant producer, might send after him, so he gave Chaucer the phone number of his cousin "Hoss" in L.A. Ben said to call him if he felt threatened and to tell Hoss that Ben said to take care of whatever the trouble was. Ben said Hoss was an officer in the East Los Angeles Chapter of Hell's Angels, and he'd be happy to help out Chaucer and Jean Marc if needed. Chaucer smiled big and hugged Ben. They had become like brothers in the past two weeks. Chaucer had liked that very much.

As he was walking back to his Renault, Chaucer spotted Sissy. "Hey Sissy, can I talk with you for a minute?"

"For you, cutie, I might have all day, but then Stephanie would beat on me," she said with a smile.

"Well, I think Stephanie is ready to beat on me, Sissy. You see, I need to get back to L.A. now, and Stephanie and I had a hard time saying goodbye earlier. I didn't mean to hurt her but I did. I'm really sorry, I hope you can believe me, Sissy."

"Well, Chaucer, she fell hard for you. She really likes you. She probably was not happy to learn that you were going, was she?"

Chaucer looked down at the sandy ground. "I really disappointed her; I know that now."

"Honey, look, a man sleeps with a woman for nearly two weeks straight, and then up and leaves, yes, that woman is going to be very pissed off at that man."

Then Sissy smiled. "Look, I will tell her that you were a good guy. You were very kind to both of us and Billy. She'll feel better in a couple of days. I'll help her out. I like you, Chaucer, and if I didn't like you I would tell you, but I do, so I will help her get through this, OK?'

"Thanks, Sissy. Do you know when you'll get back to Connecticut, you and Stephanie?"

She pursed her lips and shook her head gently. "We're just finding our way now. Could be in a week, a month, could be never, we're just letting go and seeing what happens. Like my older sister said when Steph and I left, we might never get this chance again, so Steph and I are going to let it all happen."

Chaucer nodded. "I understand that. I guess I am doing some of that too, Sissy."

He reached out to her, and she reached out to him, and they hugged for a minute. "I think she loves you, Pancho. I do."

Chaucer gently took Sissy's hand and put the note in her palm. "Please give this to her for me. I want her to have it, OK?"

Sissy smiled and kissed Chaucer's cheek. "Travel safe, Pancho. May God bless you."

Chaucer smiled and turned away, slowly walking to the Renault. He felt greatly confused from the emotion of the moment, and he breathed heavily. "What was going on these last few months? How has this roller coaster of women and emotions happened? Can't I get anything right anymore?" he asked himself. He kicked the sand, hit the hood of the Renault with his fist, and cursed. He found some tequila in his trunk and chugged it. Now he wanted to leave. In a few minutes he was off, down the unpaved road towards the mountains and the highway north to Arizona and L.A.

Chapter 23

West Coast Terminal

"Hey, cousin, I thought that I might see you today," said Jean Marc with a big grin when Chaucer walked into the pool house where Jean Marc was still staying. "How was the Mexican beach? I'm all packed. I got paid this morning, and I'm ready to roll east."

"It's a long story, and we've got plenty of road to make and time to kill, so let's split now. But I need some food first, and we need to gas up too," Chaucer said.

"Ah, OK, but we have one small, maybe big, problem to fix first," Jean Marc said, trying to smile and hide his anxiety. "Did you see the black Lincoln Continental in front of the house when you pulled in?"

"No, not really, why?"

"They were here last week for a while and here again this morning. The two guys in the car are probably the chumps that the arrogant producer Jerry sent to see us, or rather, you," Jean Marc said with a smile.

"Really? Are you joking me?" Chaucer said, staring at Jean Marc.

"No, I am not. Go take a look." Chaucer walked around the house and peaked through the bushes. Sure enough, there they were, two muscle men right out of central casting, sitting in the black Lincoln smoking and reading the newspaper.

Chaucer returned to the back of the house. "OK, I saw them. Now what?"

Jean Marc rubbed the stubble on his chin thoughtfully. "Well, I could call my brother Clint, but I think he's in Saigon right now," and then he laughed.

Chaucer laughed too as he knew his cousin Captain Clint Giroux was a legendary Army Special Forces Green Beret and a hard ass.

"Wait a minute!" Chaucer said suddenly. "I might have a way out of this. This guy I met in Mexico named Ben gave me the phone number for his cousin who is a Hell's Angel biker, and he said to call him if this very thing happened."

"Really, are you kidding?"

"Hell, no. I need to get to a phone and see if Ben's cousin might be able to fix this."

"Go knock on the backdoor of the house. The housekeeper will let you in, and you can use the phone in the kitchen. Go on now."

When Chaucer dialed the number that Ben had given him, a deep, gruff voice answered. "Is Hoss there?" The guy found Hoss and handed him the phone. Chaucer explained how he met Ben and told him the problem he now had.

"OK, I'll come take a look, gimme your address. Stay put until I get there," Hoss told him.

In about half an hour, three Harley Davidson hogs pulled up next to the Lincoln Continental. Chaucer and Jean Marc heard the loud motorcycles, so they walked to the front of the house that was located on a beautiful residential street off North Hillcrest Road. They couldn't believe their eyes. The three bikers and the two muscle men were laughing and hugging. Perhaps Chaucer was assuming too much, or was just stupid that day, but he walked up to the group and said loudly, "Hey, Hoss." A huge guy the size of a small bull, in a Hell's Angel leather vest, walked over and slapped Chaucer on the back.

"You're Ben's friend, I take it?"

Chaucer nodded.

"You a lucky guy, my friend, because these two boys are some of our boys too. They do work for us and vice versa. If they had gotten to you, your legs would have been broken."

Chaucer started to back away.

"It's OK. Come over here and meet these guys," Hoss said.

Jerome, one of the muscle guys, looked at Hoss and asked, "Is this the guy that decked Jerry?"

Hoss turned to Chaucer. "Did you?"

"Yes, he was rude to me and Morgan, and he swung first, so I hit him."

All five of the guys laughed really hard for a couple minutes.

When their laughter died down, Jerome said, "Congratulations, buddy, I've wanted to whack that prick myself. He's one rude bastard, but he pays us well." Jerome reached out and shook Chaucer's hand. Then he got in his big Lincoln, and he and his partner drove away, smiling and laughing.

The three biker guys laughed some more and started their hogs, but before they drove away, Hoss told Chaucer, "You are a hero to us now my, friend. None of us like that Jerry. He's just an asshole with money, so sometimes he pays some of us to teach guys a lesson. We don't like him so we're happy you busted his nose in public. Jerome is going to let Jerry know that they broke one of your legs, so you best not see Jerry for a while, or if you do, start limping." Hoss broke out with the biggest laugh. "Look, normally this kind of intervention from us costs you $300 bucks, but since you're a friend of Ben and you decked Jerry, this one is on the house. When you see Ben again, tell him I said hi." Then the three bikers drove away in a cloud of noise.

Jean Marc and Chaucer looked at each other and started laughing. Then Jean Marc said, "OK, Cuz, let's get out of Dodge now!"

*   *   *

It was a good drive back to New York. As they had promised each other, they stopped at the Grand Canyon, sleeping in their car in the National Park lodge parking lot that night. They were overwhelmed at the natural beauty and the ability to see the historical geology on the walls of the canyon. They also stopped to visit Bryce Canyon National Park the next day as Chaucer wanted to dance among the Hoodoos, and Jean Marc wanted to photograph him doing it. Late that afternoon they drove to Grand Junction, Colorado, and crashed at a Motel 6 so they could take showers and sleep in a bed for a night.

The next day they drove south to the Mesa Verde Cliff Dwellings, which both Chaucer and Jean Marc had read about. They wanted to see the amazing structures that were, according to different archaeologists, perhaps fifteen hundred years old. They were impressed at the ancient community they saw, as well as the rattlesnake that had camped out on the pavement under the Renault while they walked around in the midday heat.

The following day they drove to the U.S. Air Force Academy in Colorado Springs to see a high school friend of Jean Marc. Early the next morning they left for the long, straight drive from the eastern slope of the Rockies across the cattle range and flat farmland of eastern Colorado and Kansas. This gave them some quiet time to talk about the past month and the earlier days of summer.

"Rough summer for you, Cuz, fair to say, I guess," said Jean Marc with a caring smile as he watched the stretch of Colorado highway from behind the wheel.

Chaucer shook his head slowly, on the verge of a self-effacing grin. "Got that right," taking a deep breath and then giving a sigh of resignation. "It all began with my girlfriend Tessa in the city in early July, man. She just essentially kicked me down the road after over a year together. You know what happened; we talked about it on the drive out last month."

Jean Marc felt Chaucer's resignation. "Yeah, I can understand it. You pretty much freaked out. I remember the day it happened, and you stopped to see me in New Paltz. God, that seems like long ago now.

"I should have seen it coming. She was flirting all the time. I guess I wasn't paying all that much attention to us as a couple," Chaucer said. "But you know, after we broke up, I was OK, just mad more at myself than her. I guess it takes two people to make and keep a relationship, but at least I found out early, before we got super serious, you know. Your sister, Kathleen, told me that too."

Jean Marc smiled now. "That's the reason I am not chasing girls, at least not now. I've got a nice girl from Geneva, she's in school and serious about her education like I am, and we're waiting to see how our relationship develops. No hurry for either of us."

"Lucky you, I'd like to meet her sometime."

"You should; you'd like her. So what about that girl this summer in Naples, when you were living at our house? What was she like?"

"Luckily for me, she was kind, very cute, and most of all, she was honest with me, which after Tessa was a favor from God, I guess!"

"Yup, better to know than not to know, I would imagine," Jean Marc said.

"I sort of knew it was only a summer thing for us, but I kept things open and honest with her too. We really had a great summer together — music, hiking, talking late into the night. Heck, I think I spent more nights with Joanie that I did in my room in your house," he said with a Cheshire Cat grin.

Jean Marc laughed. "Yeah, I heard about your schedule from Kathleen. She said that she wanted to meet Joanie because she must be a wonderful woman for you to spend so much time with her."

"Yeah, she was, and so was Stephanie, the girl I just met in Mexico, just a different kind of woman, with a different past and thoughts about her future."

Jean Marc looked at him while also keeping an eye on the interstate highway. "Cousin, you are a real Romeo, aren't you?" He chuckled. "You need to control that little mule of yours."

Chaucer rolled his eyes. "Look, I really didn't plan any of it that way, it just happened."

"Bullshit, it takes two to dance, and I suspect that they didn't have to drag you off a chair in the dance hall."

Chaucer looked at his cousin and smiled, thinking of how Joanie had stripped down at the Peace Maker Pond and how Stephanie took his hand that night and led him into her tent.

"Well, I did my best to be a gentleman, I know that. Both Tessa and Joanie were college women, and Stephanie was not, not that she wasn't smart, just that her family was not pushing her or encouraging her to go to college. Plus her parents are separated, and her brother is in the Navy, so she only had her Mom to talk to and her Mom had no money to give her or any clue about college. Kind of sad to me, because even though Dad and my mother are divorced, they did help me plan and pay for school, which has been really important so far."

"So what happened with her in Mexico?" Jean Marc asked.

"Well, I met her and her traveling friend, Sissy. They both had quit their jobs in Hartford and decided to see the world, as she said. We all ended up at the Catch 22 Beach camp near Guaymas at the same time, and again, thanks for that referral to go there, the place is amazing, Jean Marc, you should go down there sometime to see it for yourself. It was so interesting there with all the different people, mostly Americans but a few Canadians too. We just talked and swam and played music and basically just lived. It was an amazing couple of weeks. I think I could have stayed another month, but some little prick in L.A. needed to get back to school in New York," Chaucer said with his biggest smile of the day.

"Yeah, yeah, yeah, blame your lost love life on me now. You're the biggest lothario I know, Cousin. This was your 'summer of love' from where I sit." Jean Marc chuckled.

Chaucer laughed. "Well perhaps it was, but I wished I could have planned it differently, I guess," shaking his head at the memories.

"Really?" replied Jean Marc. "How so? Your best chick dumps you, then you have two raging affairs with some great women, and when it's over, you can walk away with no complications, unless you knocked them up, of course."

"No, I DID NOT KNOCK THEM UP!" said Chaucer loudly and emphatically, not smiling or laughing. "I asked both Joanie and Stephanie about birth control, and they both were taking the pill, so they were fine with our time together. Plus I'm not a lothario, I want to be a gentleman, and if things go beyond that, I let it happen. I seriously need to know a woman and like her before I can get any more involved with her," he said.

Jean Marc smirked. "Yeah, right."

"No, really, I'm serious," Chaucer insisted.

Jean Marc smiled. "So you're telling me that you got to know Stephanie and learned to like her before you spent the night with her. That sounds like a really fast courtship, doesn't it?"

Chaucer laughed. "Well, I see your point, but Stephanie was very cute, and her voice had me at 'Hello!' "

"Ha, ha, ha," Jean Marc said sarcastically. "That's bunk to the non-lothario thesis you just spouted out. You're just kidding yourself, Cuz, you are just like all of us. Being horny at our age is like waking up. Do I need to tell you this, Cuz? I have to be very careful with myself, you know why?" Jean Marc said rhetorically. "Because I could easily be sidetracked from my studies and the career I want in the theater and film industry. It would be so easy because the women are all over, and so many are no different than us guys at our age, so it would be easy for me, really easy, to follow my little head instead of my big head and get tied up in a relationship and lose my initiative and drive to follow my first love, which is the theater and screen plays." He paused, trying to find the right words. "It is so easy to follow your heart, you know because you have done it, not that it is wrong, it is just wrong for me at this time in my life." Jean Marc then became quiet as he knew that he had been lecturing his cousin, and that was not what he wanted to do this day.

"Wow, you know when we have these conversations, I really realize that I have missed you. I wish that we had lived closer, Jean Marc, because I certainly could have used your thoughts and advice the last couple of years. I've sort of been lost between my parents' divorce, caring for JOA, and finding my way at school, so sometimes it was just easier to be with Tessa because she was comfortable and smart and kept me warm. I let my desires overcome my intellect, I guess."

"Look, we're not perfect, neither you nor me, so don't get that idea. We'll continue to make mistakes, both of us, but what is really important, as my mother always has said, is how you respond to a mistake. We can discuss this on the next few days of driving. It's a good thing for us to talk about, agreed?"

Chaucer smiled. "Yup, I need you to talk to me like this, Jean Marc. I really need you right now. Sometimes I feel so lost, and I'm really glad we can talk like this. I trust you, and you give me understanding and some hope that I can change and fix my messed-up parts."

"My mom has always said to me that God puts angels on our shoulders, and you only have to ask them for guidance. It's always worked for me, and it can work for you too, Chaucer. Look, I'll tell you what. When we get to Geneva, before I leave for school, I will take you to talk to Pastor Wagner. I know you've seen him when you attended services with my parents and Kathleen. He is a totally great guy. He helped my brother, Logan, in so many ways over the past few years. We'll talk to him together. He's very cool, and very focused in ways that help. Will you do that with me?"

Chaucer couldn't hide his surprise. "You're not joking with me now? Seriously, you want me to go with you to talk to a minister, what for?"

Jean Marc knew this question would be coming. "Because we, you and I, do not have all the answers that we need to keep us doing the best thing for ourselves, for others. It's like getting a tune-up, like you did for your car. You need to let somebody else take a look at some situations in your life to help you see your road ahead. Like I told you, Cuz, past performance is prelude to the future. Do this with me when we get to Geneva, it will be good for my lothario Canadian cousin."

When Chaucer replied, "OK, I guess so," Jean Marc's smile lasted for the next fifty miles.

* * *

That night they made it to Columbia, Missouri to visit an Ottawa friend of Chaucer's, Vinnie Belle Mare. His father was the managing editor at the Ottawa Citizen Daily, and Chaucer had known him since childhood. Vinnie was a senior in the School of Journalism at the university, and his father was holding a job for him in Ottawa. Vinnie showed them around campus and pointed out the two stone lions positioned at a tunnel next to the J-school. "Legend has it that they roar if a virgin walks through the tunnel," Vinnie said with a sly grin. Chaucer and Jean Marc broke out into a laugh. Then they walked over to Shakespeare's for pizza and beer before visiting a new bar just opened by a friend of Vinnie's named Dennis Harper. Dennis called the place Harpo's, and the boys had a great time talking about Ottawa and also the bitter NHL rivalry between Montreal and Toronto, especially the 1967 Stanley Cup finals that Toronto had won. There is no fence-sitting in eastern Canada: You either are a Maple Leaf or a Canadian Habs supporter. Jean Marc missed this sports talk from his days growing up with his brothers, so he was happy that night. It was a very good "guys night out" for the three of them, with beer and pizza thrown in for comfort.

In the morning the boys drove east to St. Louis as they both wanted to visit the magnificent Gateway Arch. The size and beauty of the creation by Eero Saarinen and Hannskari Bandel amazed Chaucer and Jean Marc. They rode the tram to the top and gazed out at the Mississippi River flowing as far as the eye could see on this sunny, clear day.

"Don't you wish we could see our lives like this, seeing our days far ahead into the future?" Chaucer asked.

Jean Marc softly shook his head. "No, not really," then he paused for a long time just staring out the observation window. "It would remove all the mystery for our lives. We'd lose our willingness to be creative, to bring our powers of love and reconciliation to bear on our future; our intellect would suffer...No, I like it just as it is now."

Chaucer looked with amazement at his cousin.

Jean Marc continued. "I believe that God loves us and guides us. He is in our heads and hearts, and he has given us those angels to sit on our shoulders. I feel that He has given us signposts along the roadway of life, and I really believe that He sometimes puts obstacles in our path just to see how we will respond, as a way of seeing if you have been paying attention to Him and his Son. That is what I believe because I learned much of it from our Grandmother Gillian in Ottawa and my Grandmother Abigail in Boston. They both told me essentially the same message."

Chaucer thought for a minute. "Yes, you are right. Grandma Gillian used to talk to me about our Christian life, our responsibilities. I guess that I have not thought about that in a long time, Jean Marc."

Jean Marc smiled. "It's not too late to start over, Cuz, you're still a young guy."

Chaucer nodded, then reached over and hugged his cousin.

* * *

Later that day they drove to visit another Canadian friend of Chaucer's at Heidelberg College, a small liberal arts school in Tiffin, Ohio, where they were able take showers and eat in the school cafeteria. It was a good night for them to all sit and talk about sports, the news, and how their faith had been growing or not, guiding them or not recently. Chaucer was learning much on this journey with Jean Marc, or maybe he was just paying closer attention to his cousin.

The next day, agreeing to make no more stops, Jean Marc and Chaucer were able to reach Geneva in the late afternoon. They had a wonderful dinner with Kathleen and her parents. The dinner conversation lasted for hours, filled with stories of L.A., Mexico, and their drive home. The next morning, Jean Marc called Pastor Wagner at his office in town. He answered the phone himself.

"Pastor Wagner, may I help you?"

"Hi, Pastor, this is Jean Marc Giroux, I am Logan Giroux's younger brother."

"Yes, yes, hello, Jean Marc, I remember you from the summer

camps when you'd come with Logan. How are you, young man?"

Jean Marc proceeded to tell him about his cousin Chaucer and what some of his issues were. Pastor Wagner said that he had some time after the lunch hour if that would be good for them, and they agreed that Jean Marc would bring Chaucer over to his office later.

Chapter 24

Lighten the Load, Brother

CHAUCER WALKED INTO PASTOR WAGNER'S OFFICE that afternoon. What he saw surprised him, for the walls had a simple painting of Jesus, like the painting that many people had in their homes, a medium-size crucifix, and six banners from Geneva High School: one from football, one from hockey, one each from boys and girls basketball, and one each from boys baseball and girls softball teams. He also had small plaques from boys and girls soccer, boys and girls swimming, boys lacrosse, and girls field hockey. Chaucer had never witnessed anything like this in a church building.

"Have a seat, Chaucer," Pastor Wagner said after shaking hands with him. Then he pointed to the walls, grinned widely and said, "Do you like my walls of fame?"

"Ah, well, yes, that is so cool that you like sports. What did you play before becoming a pastor?" Chaucer asked.

Pastor Wagner continued to smile. "Well, in high school and college, I played soccer and I ran track. I wasn't big enough to play contact sports like football or hockey, and I wasn't good enough to play baseball. I could never see the ball well enough to hit it." He chuckled.

"I have all these banners to remind me of all the children and students that have attended my summer camps, like your cousins Jean Marc and Logan did. So many of the kids from the camps went on to play for our high school teams and do really well. You see I believe that playing team sports helps young people develop so many of the skills that they will need in later life. Do you play on any teams, Chaucer?" Pastor Wagner thought that this question would break the ice and lead into more serious discussion.

"Yes, I've played hockey. It's a great game. It's fun and you make a lot of friends."

"So you still play then?"

"Well, I think that I will start playing again this winter, on the university club team where I played before."

"Why did you stop playing?"

"My girlfriend didn't like the game. She said my apartment always smelled like a locker room after a game because of my equipment bag, plus she always had things for me to do for her, so I stopped playing."

"And you'll start playing again this year?" asked Pastor Wagner.

"Yes. She and I don't go out anymore; she dumped me over the summer."

"Hmmm. So what else is going on, Chaucer? Your cousin seemed concerned about you; can you tell me?"

Chaucer hesitated and looked away from the clergyman.

"It's OK, there is no right or wrong answer to that question, son." Pastor Wagner showed Chaucer the smile that so endeared him to all his parishioners.

"Well, it seems to me like I get involved with women, really nice women, then something happens, and the relationship ends."

"OK, we can talk about that. What else is going on in your life that is important?

Chaucer took a deep breath. "Well, it's a lot of things now."

Pastor Wagner now knew that this would be a good session; that the Lord had brought this young man to him for a serious discussion, and it appeared that they might have it.

The pastor nodded. "Go on, I'm here to listen."

"Well, mostly it is the family things that have happened since my parents divorced, about my sister and her behavior, and what I need to do about my college studies, and especially why my relationships with women aren't working."

Chaucer found himself beginning to feel comfortable as Pastor Wagner's kind face looked at him intently.

"You certainly have many things on your mind, Chaucer, and the good news is that God is here to help you address each and every one of the things that you just told me. Tell me, do you read the Bible, particularly the Gospels?"

"Not in a long time. I just don't understand much of the old language, and besides, all that happened long ago. It's not really for these times. Life is all different now from back in the time of Jesus."

Pastor Wagner had heard all this many times. He smiled the comfortable smile of a secure adult who will help you, and not judge you, and this made Chaucer relax.

"Yes, that is true, the Gospels were written about 1900 years ago...but the good news for you is this...in the time of Jesus, as in the time of the Greek civilization hundreds of years before Jesus, and in the almost two thousand years since Jesus walked on the earth, human nature and human emotions have not really changed. Humanity had then, and we have now, love, jealousy, kindness, hatred, deception, false prophets, lying, cheating, power struggles, adultery, and more. Wouldn't you agree?"

"Well, we certainly have all that now," Chaucer said.

"And it has always existed, in every civilization over time. Do your research and it will be verified. You can trust me on this," the pastor said with confidence. Then he asked, "Chaucer, do you know who Saul was?"

"Yes, he owned a bookstore in our neighborhood in Ottawa. My dad and I often went there," Chaucer replied in all seriousness.

The pastor smiled. "No, not that Saul; the Saul in the Bible, you know him?"

"No, I don't."

"Do you know Paul in the New Testament?"

"Yes, I remember him. He was a good guy."

Pastor Wagner chuckled again. "Yes, Chaucer, he was a good guy. But Paul was Saul at one time, and that's what I want you to know more about him, and perhaps come to understand as well."

Chaucer sat up tall, listening with greater attention now.

"You see, Saul was a Roman soldier who was sent to arrest the followers of Jesus. Even though the Roman agent Pontius Pilate had Jesus crucified, he believed that the disciples of Jesus remained a real threat to his rule. However, while Saul was on his way to Damascus to arrest followers of Jesus, Saul had an intervention from the risen Jesus, and he was converted from a man who wanted to arrest Jesus's followers to the man who was the most important teacher and advocate of Christianity. Saul decided to change his name to Paul to better reach non-Jews, and he is the man who wrote many of the letters that are in the New Testament."

"What happened to Saul? What made him change so much, so soon?" Chaucer asked.

"He clearly had a life-changing event, didn't he?"

"Yeah, it sure seems that way," Chaucer replied.

"Perhaps we all have life-changing events, Chaucer. Don't you think that is possible?"

"Yes, I think it is possible."

"How do you think it starts for a person, Chaucer?"

Chaucer thought for a minute. "Like Saul, maybe with an experience?"

Pastor Wagner continued. "Yes, or maybe we all need to sit quietly, think, meditate, and ask ourselves: 'What is God's plan for me?' Do you think it could happen that way?"

Chaucer's eyes opened wide, and he looked around the office. His mind was clicking away, and Pastor Wagner could almost hear it. "Yes, it could; yes, I think it really could."

Pastor Wagner knew he had hit a home run at that point, and he smiled broadly at Chaucer. "I want to you think about that, Chaucer, and the more you think about it, the easier it will be for you to fix these family issues, and figure out how proceed with your education, and your relationships with young women. Son, the answers to these matters are within you, in your own heart and soul, and they will speak to you, they will speak to you as God has spoken to us all, all of us who listen. Can you do that for yourself and for me?"

Chaucer was silent as he thought about the pastor's words. He felt that the issues with JOA, his mother and father could be made better if he prayed on them, asking for help and guidance, and that his problems with women were likely because of his weaknesses rather than their actions towards him. This would take much thinking and listening for spiritual help, but it would be a start. Chaucer thought about the long conversations that he and Jean Marc had on the trip home, and how Jean Marc had such discipline and had set out his life goals. Chaucer wanted that. "Yes, that is a really great suggestion, Pastor; I can do that," he said with conviction. "I will be thinking about that: What does God want me to do with my life, and what is he telling me when I listen?"

"Your cousin Logan had similar questions before he left to fight in the Vietnam War. I encouraged him to listen to God and focus on God's plan for him. Just ask your cousin Jean Marc, he knows, he's a witness, and he can be your witness too. Chaucer, you can heal yourself by having a better understanding of what God's plan is for you, and you will find it inside yourself, so let it happen, let it come out, and once it does, lead that life to the fullest, and you will become one of the most joyful humans on the planet. Trust me in these words, Chaucer, and then trust yourself and trust in God's words, too."

Pastor Wagner stood up and smiled broadly. He knew that he had entered into Chaucer's mind the key question for him to answer. It might be weeks, or months or even years, but he knew the young man was now likely to begin a new journey and start a better way for him and the people in his life. He knew that the message and the answers were available to all who asked and listened. "The next time you are in Geneva to see your relatives, I would welcome your visit, and we can continue this discussion. Would you like to do that?"

"Yes...yes, Pastor Wagner, I would," Chaucer replied quietly as he stood up. "Thank you. Thank you so much for our discussion today. I will work on this, and I will send you a letter soon, and I'd like to come to see you again."

The pastor shook his hand firmly. "Thank God, Chaucer, and through God you will get the message. You take good care, and please tell your aunt and uncle and your cousins that I said hello." The pastor then handed Chaucer a note, and said, "Please keep this with you, my son, and remember these words."

Chaucer left the office and went back to the house to pick up Jean Marc for the drive to his college. While waiting for Jean Marc, Chaucer took the note from his pocket and read it:

Come unto me, all ye that labor and are heavy laden, and I will give you rest. Take my yoke upon you, and learn of me, for I am meek and lowly in heart, and ye shall find rest unto your souls. For my yoke is easy, and my burden is light.

—Matthew 11: 28-30

Chapter 25

Michael, Row the Boat Ashore

AND SO THE COUSINS had completed an adventurous time together. It had further bonded them in a way that only relatives can, being of the same blood and having a love for the family as they did.

Fortunately for Jean Marc, once he was back at school, he was able to use his recent work experience to write two papers for six credits of independent study. He also made up the work he'd missed in three other classes so he could complete his semester on time. He had always been a serious student.

The future developments for Chaucer were far different. Jean Marc was able to convince his L.A. film management friend Jeff Magione that although Jean Marc could not take the minor movie role in Spain, his cousin Chaucer could. Since Jeff had met Chaucer, and Chaucer looked much like Jean Marc, Jeff agreed that Chaucer would be fine in the film. The character that Chaucer was to portray had only a few brief lines. The studio allowed him to be hired. Because the movie was being filmed entirely in Spain, there was no need for Chaucer to get a Taft-Hartley union exemption from the Screen Actors Guild. Thus Chaucer was able to book his flight to Madrid and his hotels through the studio travel agent in New York City. Chaucer had to be in Madrid by November 1, and he would be finished with the filming in about four weeks.

After dropping off Jean Marc at college, Chaucer drove up I-87 to the Canadian border and then into Ottawa. He was excited to talk to his father about his upcoming trip to Spain. He was apprehensive about telling his father that he was also going to take a full-year leave of absence from the University too. He was unsure how his father would respond.

When Chaucer arrived, his father was in Miami on business for his shipping company, and JOA was back in Vancouver to finish her final year in high school there. He looked to see if he had any more letters from Bee Lawrence. He had a couple of envelopes and letters from the University of Toronto, but one immediately caught his eye. The return address was also Toronto but the sender's name was Tessa Fenholt.

Chaucer's first thought was that she had sent a letter of apology. He was so wrong.

He opened the letter. It was dated a month before — September 25, 1973.

Dear Chaucer,

Thank you for sending me the money for my Renault. You sent me more than it was worth but then that is who you are, a kind and generous man. I am sorry for what happened. I did not mean to hurt you then, and I miss you very much. Just so you know, Jack took advantage of me that day. We had smoked some, maybe drank too much. It was really stupid of me, and I am really sorry. I do not blame you for leaving as you did, and now I miss you very much, your touch, your smile, and your love.

Do you think we can try our relationship again? I really would like it if you'll let me back into your life. You see, Chaucer, I am pregnant, and the child is yours. The doctor I saw said I am at least three months along. I plan to finish the semester at school, then go home to have the baby. I will need your help and some financial support once I return home as I will be almost seven months along by then, and I will not be able to work.

Our relationship lasted over a year and a half, and I would like to get it back. You can be a good father to our child. So please write or preferably call me so we can talk. I want to hear your voice again. I miss you.

Love, Tessa

Chaucer stood in the living room, staring out the big bay window at the Ottawa River for what seemed a very long time. A million emotions and thoughts flashed through him: some of anger, some of disgust, some of humor, but mostly of disbelief. Tessa was lying to him, conning him, thinking she could continue to manipulate him, as he realized she had been doing the previous year. On reflection, he now was understanding that many times when he would object to something that she had wanted or had wanted him to do, she would use her sensuality and sexuality to placate him and get her way. And he realized that he always gave in to her when she did that. He felt like a puppy who got fed to just shut him up. He was now seeing this abundantly clear, and he was very mad at himself for being so shallow and unaware of the circumstances of their relationship. Being a year older, Tessa had easily made him acquiesce to her seniority in their relationship. "She just knows better," he always thought. He shook his head at his naiveté.

The next afternoon Remy arrived home from Miami. He looked tired. He carried his suitcase in the house, hugged Chaucer, and immediately called his golf club to make dinner reservations for the two of them.

Two hours later, sitting in the club dining room and sipping cocktails, Remy leaned back and looked at Chaucer, and gave him a tender, fatherly smile.

"Glad to have you home, Son. I missed you and your sister very much, so every day when you are home again is the best time for me."

Chaucer smiled back as this father.

"However, I do need to speak with you about the phone call I received last week," Remy said.

Chaucer looked at the waiter who was standing behind his father, and said, "Dad, behind you." Remy acknowledged the waiter, and both Chaucer and his father gave him their dinner order.

*   *   *

Remy Giroux had a million options available for his discussion with his son about Tessa. He chose the best one at the time for everyone.

"I saw a letter for you from Tessa. She called me, Son."

"What?" Chaucer's eyes widened and he leaned forward.

"Tessa hadn't heard from you so she called me last week. I remember her well from last Christmas when you brought her here to meet me. She told me about her situation, and she wanted to know if you were home, so I explained that you had been in Los Angeles with your cousin. She wanted to know if you would call her as soon as you got home."

"Dad, she broke up with me this past summer, when we were in New York City. You remember I told you that when I got home, and before I went to stay with Aunt Elizabeth and Uncle Jean Luc in Geneva."

"Yes, Son, I understand that, but now she says that she is pregnant and that you are the father."

"I didn't tell you about why Tessa and I broke up in July when I got home because it was too difficult, but now you need to know everything that I know." Chaucer swallowed to clear the lump in his throat, then began speaking. "She and I were living in a dumpy apartment in Greenwich Village so we could work on the *Jesus Christ Superstar* musical. She and I had a small room of our own. One day when I went to work early, they cancelled my shift so I went back to the apartment, and she was in our room doing it with another guy who I didn't know but who had been hanging around the apartment. He probably was a friend of one of the people who lived there with us; heck, we had eight other roommates. I was so shocked that all I wanted to do was get out of the apartment. So I grabbed Tessa's car keys, took her car, and came home. That was when I stopped to see Jean Marc, the day before I came home. So maybe the baby is not mine, maybe it's the other guy's or even somebody else's."

Remy waited, took a breath. "Chaucer, my dear son, this really is not as much about who the father is as who will care for this baby one day, isn't it?"

"But Dad, how does she know whether I'm the father or the other guy is?"

"Do you believe that the baby is asking that now? And besides, she believes the baby is yours...I think women know these things."

Chaucer looked around the dining room, with its dark wood panel walls, stone fireplace, and paintings of fox hunts, everything so orderly. He struggled to keep his composure on the outside but on his inside, he felt like he was tumbling. He couldn't speak for a few minutes. Remy waited patiently. Finally, Chaucer said, "I see your point, Dad, but what am I supposed to do now? I'm leaving for a movie job in Spain in a week."

"What movie job in Spain?" his father asked with a big smile.

"Well, I was going to tell you over dinner."

"So tell me now, we have all night."

And so Chaucer told his father all about his time with Jean Marc, the incident where he punched Jerry at the party, his weeks in Mexico and then their great sightseeing drive back to Geneva. He told his father how Jean Marc had gotten him a small role in the new remake of *The Sun Also Rises*, and how he was going to take a complete leave of absence from the University for the whole academic year, not just the current semester. He then learned that Remy had already contacted the university to advise them that Chaucer was taking a leave of absence for the current semester because the tuition bill had come due, and since Chaucer was off with Jean Marc, it was what a parent had to do.

Listening to Chaucer, Remy was impressed with the adventures of Chaucer and Jean Marc. It reminded him of how he and Jean Marc's father, Le Guerrier, would travel to Montreal and Quebec City in their youth to see the cities and enjoy a party or two, only Remy realized that Chaucer and Jean Marc were older now, and their journey had lasted six weeks and spanned the entire continent, not just a weekend and two hundred miles from home. "Chaucer, here is the point that I want to make, and I hope you will understand it, because it is probably the most important part of becoming a man, a responsible man. When you sleep with a woman, it is very possible that she could become pregnant. My own father, your grandfather, spoke about this with me and my brothers when we were young men too. Back then, the birth control options were very crude and limited. Today, women can use the new pill, and men can and should use condoms. " Remy looked at Chaucer, who was staring down at the table, looking somewhat embarrassed, Remy thought. But he continued.

"Tessa thought enough of you for a year to stay with you then, and she probably knows who the father is. We'll not know about this other guy, whether he was just a mistake or if she was with him many times before. The science of testing to determine the father is not very accurate although my attorney friends would argue differently, but we need to help Tessa and this child now. That is how I feel. A legal battle will not solve anything, and it will just complicate matters later as well."

"Dad, in her letter she said that she is staying in school until the end of this semester, then she wants to go to her parents' house and have the baby. She said she'll want me to send her some money until she can either go back to the university for her final semester or go to work."

"She's a senior, right?"

"Yes, she'll have one more semester after this one.""

"OK, that is good to know. I want us to help her with any medical costs, and I want us to send her some money after the baby is born. She might be able to finish her degree if she can attend the summer program. You and I want her to graduate. That will help her be a good parent and the baby will have a better life that way. Don't you agree, Son?"

"Dad, you make this sound so easy, really." Chaucer shook his head, wondering if Remy was being realistic. Remy didn't know Tessa like Chaucer did.

Remy looked very serious now. "When your Mother took you and JOA and moved to Vancouver back then, it broke my heart in two ways. I still loved your mother but I loved you kids even more, and when you all left, I felt like my entire life was gone. If I hadn't had the great business partners that I do, my good friends from my military days, I probably would have crashed and burned. As it was, I was not right for almost a year or so. I don't think that I ever told you this then, and I probably shouldn't have now either," he said with a sad face of resignation.

For the first time, Chaucer really understood just how devastated Remy had been when Olivia had moved herself, Chaucer and JOA all the way to Vancouver. Chaucer stood up and walked over to Remy and hugged him tightly "I love you, Dad. I always have, and JOA and I missed you so much when we left here. So many times I just wanted to get on a train and come back home."

Remy's eyes grew misty. He took out his handkerchief and wiped his nose. Then he smiled at Chaucer. "OK, let's do what we can to help this baby, Son. Will you do that for me and yourself and the child?"

Chaucer hesitated a long time. He thought of his recent discussion with Pastor Wagner in Geneva, and he took some deep breaths while staring at the table. Finally he looked at Remy. "OK, Dad, I will, I promise. I'm not going to worry about who the father is." But Chaucer knew in his heart that he would. Perhaps God would bring him answers to that question if he listened. Chaucer told himself that he would learn who is the father by seeing the baby in person. Regardless, the child would always know that Chaucer was the father in his or her life, and that Remy was the grandfather. Remy believed that they had settled the matter that night. Chaucer was not so sure.

* * *

A week later, Chaucer flew out of Montreal on Air Canada bound for Madrid. His travel package provided by the film company had him catching a train to Pamplona where the main scenes that he was to appear in would be filmed. It was the beautiful Plaza de Toros arena that Hemingway had written about that drew the movie company there, along with the cathedral and the access to the countryside. He would be there a month, and he planned to return to Ottawa for Christmas.

In the 1957 Darryl Zanuck original filming of *The Sun Also Rises*, the bull fighting scenes were shot in Mexico. The critics panned the film not only for that faux pau but also for some of the dialogue and the lackluster acting by the stars Ava Gardner, Tyrone Power, and others. Hemingway is said to have walked out of the theater after watching only twenty-five minutes of the movie version of his great novel. A new screenplay and better dialogue in the updated movie would be more true to the Hemingway novel, Chaucer was told. He had little interest in how the film would be received by critics as his role was small. His name would appear in the credits so he could always tell his relatives and friends, "I was in that movie." That was enough for him.

After Chaucer left Ottawa, Remy talked with Tessa twice by telephone. He wanted to reassure her that he would help her financially with any medical costs that her parents' health insurance would not cover, and he also wanted to give her the psychological comfort of knowing that he would help her and Chaucer should they decide to get married. Remy was an honest man, and helping those in trouble, especially Tessa who was quite possibly carrying his family genes, was the essence of his character. He did not need to be advised about right and wrong, love and charity, empathy and understanding. His parents had taught him well, and his success in business after World War II gave him the means to be generous. Tessa was happy to learn this from Remy. That week she composed a very personal and thankful letter to Remy, a letter from her heart that greatly pleased Remy when he read it.

Remy received a letter four weeks later from Chaucer telling him that he was enjoying the work in the movie and that he had made some new friends. Chaucer also wrote that rather than coming back home after the shooting, he wanted to stay in Spain and find work for the rest of the winter. Remy was disappointed when he read the letter. He was hoping that Chaucer would consider coming back, and perhaps work out a new relationship with Tessa. But that was not to be. Chaucer wrote his father that Tessa's behavior in New York City would probably only continue, and he was not going to marry her. Nevertheless, Remy decided that his initial decision to help Tessa would stand as he put the welfare of the child first.

Chapter 26

Wandering Days of Wonder

LUCK WAS WITH CHAUCER in Pamplona that November. After his scenes finished filming, he learned that the production company needed additional set assembly crew. He spoke to the production director, who had become friends with Chaucer during the prior month, and he immediately rehired Chaucer to work on the set for the remaining six weeks of the production. Chaucer could not have been happier as he had also become friends with a few of the other young men on the set, many of whom wanted to stay in Europe for a while after the end of the filming. "Why not?" Chaucer thought.

The shooting of the movie ended the week before Christmas. Chaucer reached his father in Ottawa by trans-Atlantic cable phone line.

"Buddy, so wonderful to hear your voice, Son. The operator said you are in Madrid. Tell me, how are you, how was the filming and movie project?"

"Hi, Dad. I'm glad you are home; I took a chance to call. So sorry to miss Christmas with you and JOA. Please hug her for me…Yeah, the movie project was fun. You'll see me on screen in early summer as long as the film editors in Hollywood don't cut my scenes." He laughed. "I was done with my part a month ago, and then they hired me to help with the set construction, like I had been doing last summer in Naples with the playhouse work."

"Very nice. I'm sure you had a good time and learned some things. You probably met some nice people too, right?"

"Yes to all of that, Dad. In fact there are three guys on the film crew who are going backpacking over here for a while, and I am going to go with them. I've wanted to do this and here is my chance. I made enough money on the film to do it, and we'll be staying at hostels and eating cheap."

"Well, that sounds like a good thing for you, Son." Remy hesitated, then spoke more slowly. "I have been in touch with Tessa. She is fine and seven months pregnant. She finished her last semester and is home now. She said her parents are being supportive. She invited me, and you, to come to Buffalo in the spring to meet the baby, and I told her that we would. That made her very happy. Will you do that with me when you get home?"

Chaucer was quiet for several seconds. "Can I think about it for awhile, Dad? I still have really bad feelings for her."

"Remember, Son, this is about the child now, not you or me. So I want you to think about that. The child will be part of us from now on, so let's plan to be happy with the situation as best as we can," Remy paused, "as best as you can, OK?"

"OK, Dad, I understand...We'll figure this out somehow, I'm sure."

"That's my lad, good. I'm counting on you, Chaucer. So how long are you going to be in Madrid?"

"I think the guys want to leave for Seville the day after tomorrow, so I'll be going then. I think they are talking about Tangier, Lisbon, the places down south where it is warmer now. Why?"

"Well, I want you to have some extra money in case anything happens. How long is your Eurail pass good for?"

"I got a ninety-day pass, and I just started it when we left Pamplona, so it is good until late March."

"OK, good. I want you to go to the American Express office in Madrid tomorrow as I will wire you 500 U.S. dollars this afternoon. It's on Calle de San Jeronimo, a few blocks from the Prado. I hope you'll visit the Prado before you leave; it's a magnificent museum."

"Yup, we're all going tomorrow, and we're planning to spend most of the day there. I'll go to the American Express office then."

"OK, good. Also, I may be coming to London for company business in mid-March, so perhaps you can meet up with me. I will be in Ottawa and Montreal for the next six weeks for sure, so call me collect every Sunday afternoon and let me know about your travels. Will you do that, please?"

"Yes, Dad, I'll call. Thanks for the extra money too. What do you hear from Mother, and how is JOA?"

Remy was silent for a bit. "You mother is fine. She sent me a letter last week. Her new book is finished, so she and her agent are flying to Los Angeles soon to negotiate a movie deal for the book. I never thought she'd ever leave her place in Victoria. But I am happy for her. Your sister is doing well in school, and she's behaving herself as best as I can determine. It was very important that she leave Vancouver and come back to be with us here last summer. She is doing quite well in school and seems happy. She's even writing letters to your mother, so I guess that is a good thing."

"That sounds good to me. Please tell her that I miss her. Well, it's been good to catch up with you, and thanks for the extra money. You're so good to me and JOA, Dad. I love you and I will start calling you on Sundays, I promise."

"Chaucer, that would be great, I love you too. Travel safe. Bye for now."

Chaucer hung up the phone and smiled. He understood that his father was a great dad, and how fortunate he and JOA were to have him as their dad. He was happy for his mother too. He only wished that she and Remy had been able to stay together. He felt a burst of sadness, and he sat down on a bench next to the phone booth. Being so far from home and hearing Remy's voice after so long and thinking of his mother and JOA had triggered his emotions. He surely missed his father and JOA, and he missed his family life in Ottawa. He thought of Tessa and the baby. This sobered him. He kept thinking of seeing Tessa naked in the apartment with that guy Jack and how upset he had been when it happened six months ago. But his father was right. This was not about him; it was really about the child that would be born soon.

Chaucer reached into his wallet and took out the note from Pastor Wagner with the quotation from Matthew's Gospel. He read it once, closed his eyes, then read it again. He realized his burden was light, and that he should embrace the child and all that was needed to be a father. He wanted to give his own father, Remy, the joy of having a grandchild as he knew that Remy would be so very happy.

"I'm not going to marry Tessa," he said softly, out loud to himself. "I'll only see her when I see the baby. I'll send her the money to help raise the baby, and I'll make sure to see the baby as often as I can. Maybe the child can even come to Ottawa for the summers." He stopped then. The future was a blur, and all he wanted to do now was to travel with his film friends and see some of the Iberian Peninsula and Morocco. He was just 22 years old; he wanted to just be a young guy for a while. He just wanted to live and be free while he could.

※ ※ ※

Two days later, the four young men boarded the train for Seville at the Madrid Estacion de Atocha. They had purchased sleeping bags, backpacks, and inflatable air mattresses from a British hiking store in Pamplona. They chipped in to add two pup tents for rainy nights. These three young Americans and a Canadian were ready for some fun and carefree weeks traveling the rails of Spain and Portugal. Their work had earned them the time and money, and this was their reward.

The Americans were all California guys; Ronnie and Seth had gone to high school together in Hermosa Beach, and Bryce was from San Diego. Ronnie and Seth had graduated from a community college and decided to get jobs on the movie sets with help from the father of a friend from high school. Bryce had been drafted out of high school, served two years in the U.S. Army with a year in Vietnam, then came home and just wanted to work for a while before going to college. He landed a job at the movie studio getting hired through the brother of a friend in the Army. The three Californians all liked Chaucer. He was different, with a gestalt unlike theirs. Plus, none of the Californians had any close Canadian friends, and they liked learning about Canada from him.

The boys arrived in Seville on a typical bright winter day in the Andalusia region of Spain. It was neither hot nor cold, just the right temperature for backpackers like them. They found the local pensione in the Santa Cruz old town area that an Englishman on the train had recommended. After checking in, they left their packs and immediately went out to find the closest tapas bars as they were famished and thirsty. That night they ate well. They all over-sampled the incredible sherries from the soleras of the nearby Jerez de la Frontera region. Walking back to the pensione, and to honor their Ottawa buddy, they broke out singing songs by Neil Young, a Canadian. Their singing was so bad and loud that various dogs were barking at them, and one woman even stepped out on her second-floor balcony and yelled, "Silencia, por favor, silencia!"

The next morning, nursing hangovers, they walked to the magnificent Seville Cathedral, which they located by finding the famous Giralda Tower. Inside they were amazed at the size of the church, the architecture, the coolness of the air, and the quietness of God. The space inside possessed a compelling sense of spiritual connection for any visitor open to the experience and a spiritual conversation. Few sacred places can overwhelm non-believers, but the Seville Cathedral is one of them. Chaucer found a bench and sat down quietly, bowing his head out of respect and humility, and perhaps to have a conversation with his spiritual father.

The other lads walked around quietly, respectfully, the rubber soles on their boots and shoes making no noise on the stone floor. They were in awe, in wonderment, in amazement of the beauty and history of the place. After about twenty minutes walking and gazing, Bryce came over to Chaucer and quietly said:

"We're going to get some coffee down the street from here; should we wait for you now?"

Chaucer looked up, as softly as a child, smiled, and said, "I'll find you guys in a little while."

"OK, the place is down the first street on the right off the plaza."

Chaucer nodded. He closed his eyes again. He thought about how he and Pastor Wagner had talked about listening for God. His breathing was slow and soft. He felt a stirring of another who was trying to speak to him. He whispered nearly inaudibly, "Speak to me. I am listening," but there was nothing. Chaucer waited, then softly said, "I am listening. I promise, I am listening." He continued waiting, his hands together as in prayer.

"Soon…soon," said the quiet voice in him.

"When?" whispered Chaucer.

"Soon…when you are ready to hear me."

"I am ready to listen, please speak to me."

But there was only silence.

After a few minutes, Chaucer stood up and left. He felt confused.

He had found a space that he had not anticipated finding, a sanctuary that had drawn him in, captured his focus, and removed his ambivalence over the guilt he was harboring about his decision not to reconcile with Tessa. The day before, while looking out the window on the train trip from Madrid to Seville, he kept replaying the conversation with his father about the child. He thought about how both he and his father would help care for the baby, and how the words "It's not about you, Son, it's about the child" kept coming back into his head the past two days.

He had decided that the cathedral was a good place to think about it, and when he did, he also felt the presence of God as a witness to his thinking. He wanted advice. He waited in silence for a word or a sign. He needed guidance, reassurance. It did not come to him that day.

*   *   *

The boys spent the next day walking around Seville, again suffering the consequences of the abundance of fine food and drink in the tapas bars near their albergue (hostel). They were able to get a tour of the historic bull ring Plaza de Toros de la Real Maestranza de Caballeria on the Paseo de Cristobal Colon next to the river. Inside they experienced a true museum of Andalusian culture and architecture, a ring of history and machismo extraordinaire. The plaza was more than 200 years old and a living testament to the regional machismo of Andalusia, and these boys loved it. Seth made a joke but the tour guide gave him a frown, so Bryce punched his arm and told him to shut up. Bryce knew that such things as the mystique of the matador, and the bull, in such an environment was not entertainment, but rather a deep part of the culture, and such things were never to be the subject of sophomoric American humor. Chaucer looked at Bryce and smiled, affirming his discipline of Seth at that moment.

The following day the boys left Seville on a local train for Huelva and the frontier, the town of Ayamonte on the Guadiana River, which separates Spain and Portugal. The boys thought it would be easy to cross to the Portuguese side, as they had decided that they wanted to see the beauty and history of the Algarve and Lisbon, but it was not. Spain remained under the rule of General Franco's regime, and the

Portuguese government was seeking to democratize after President Salazar, so the border frontier was actually a real frontier both in language and politics.

After their train arrived at the terminus station, the four boys and other travelers walked to the ferry landing to take the crossing boat for the ten-minute ride across the river into Portugal. The Portuguese customs officers, backed by armed police and some military, watched an orderly process of the twenty or so people depart the ferry boat and walk to the customs station. The American passports and Chaucer's Canadian passport were waved through after a perfunctory examination; however the police did quickly search their backpacks for any contraband. The boys then followed the others to the local train station to learn that the next train to Faro and the other Algarve towns was departing in ten minutes, leaving them just enough time to grab some lunch at the station's small food counter. One can't beat a Portuguese fish morsel on local crusty bread for the equivalent of 25 cents. They had two half-empty bottles of wine in their packs, enough for a glass each. The boys were happy.

They decided the destination for the day would be Faro since it was Saturday afternoon, and the town should have at least some night life on a November night. A friend of Bryce had recommended the Pension Lumena, run by a British guy who served good English beer at the bar in the hotel, so that was their destination. The train made it to Faro in less than two hours, which included many local stops on the rail link. From the Faro station, it was a 15-minute walk to the Lumena. As it was well past tourist and vacation season, there were rooms to be had at good prices, so the boys took two rooms, each with two beds per room.

Everyone took showers, hand washed some clothes and hung them to dry, then one by one they found their way to the pension's pub, a trellised outdoor bar called the Grapevine. Small and compact, there were a dozen locals sipping pints of Samuel Smith. Seth saw a jukebox and was amazed to see the selection of songs in this small out-of-the-way town. He dropped in a coin and pushed the buttons. In a few seconds, Frank Sinatra was singing "My Way." Seth smiled, walked over to Bryce and pretended to dance with him until Bryce pushed him away. "Get away, you idiot," he said, laughing.

About half an hour later, two young attractive girls walked into the Grapevine, bought drinks at the bar and sat at one of the tables.

Soon Bryce, Ronnie, Seth, and Chaucer were all sitting at the next table, smiling at them. The girls smiled back, but cautiously. Two women traveling alone in the Iberian Peninsula with its abundant machismo culture were sure to attract men. The girls expected it and were prepared for it.

"Hi, this is Seth, that's Ronnie, the ugly Canadian is Chaucer, and I am Bryce. Where are you young ladies from?"

"We're from Boston; we're Sisters in the Order of St. Teresa of Avila there. We're on our way to Santiago de Compostela in Spain from here. Are you gentlemen Catholics too?"

Hearing this news, the broad smiles of all four boys dropped a notch. "We've just finished working on a movie in Pamplona, and we're being tourists before we go home," Bryce replied. And so the conversation went, cordial and friendly until after another beer, Seth and Ronnie excused themselves to walk into town to look for more fun and available women.

Chaucer and Bryce stayed long enough to find out that the girls were cousins from Boston and not nuns at all, but students on a study break from a year abroad at Heidelberg University in Germany and on an actual trip to walk the Camino de Santiago. They were seeing the lower Iberian Peninsula first, then going north to walk the last 100 miles of the Camino before they would use their rail passes and return to Heidelberg.

"My name is Lisa, and this is my cousin Teresa. We get hustled all the time so we use different identities to keep the aggressive men away. See, it worked on your buddies," Lisa said laughing.

* * *

Late Sunday afternoon, Chaucer used the lobby phone at the Pension Lumena to try to reach Remy in Canada. It was noon in Ottawa, and Remy answered on the second ring.

"Hi, Dad. I'm calling to check in with you as I promised. How are you and JOA?"

"Hi, Son. It's good to hear your voice. Glad you called. We're both good; where are you now?"

Chaucer proceeded to tell him about Seville and Huelva and crossing into Portugal and arriving in Faro two days before. Remy said that his last conversation with Tessa a few days ago had gone well, and she was starting to accept that Chaucer had not expressed any interest in getting back together with her. Remy again reassured her that he would provide sufficient financial support as needed. He said that he hoped to visit Tessa and the baby in the spring. Tessa told him that she appreciated his kindness and would include Remy in the life and events of the baby. Remy had prayed for this to happen. He wanted to be part of the life of his grandchild. He had asked God in his prayers to grant both him and Tessa, her family and Chaucer, the kindness and love that the child would need. Remy's prayers were working, as Tessa seemed to have found the grace and love necessary to put the child first. That morning at his church's service in Ottawa, Remy had felt thankful, so very thankful.

"Good, Dad, I'm happy that she is OK with this, I really am. I want to see the baby one day and see if the child looks like us at all."

Remy was disappointed to hear this. "Son, by then it will not matter to me; it will only matter that the child has love and a good home. You need to make that important to you, too, OK?"

When Chaucer didn't answer, Remy paused, took a deep breath and then began, "Son, who is Stephanie Strowger?"

"Who?" Chaucer asked, unable to place the name immediately.

"Stephanie Strowger. She says she lives in Hartford, Connecticut," Remy replied.

"Oh, her. I met her in Mexico when Jean Marc and I were in Los Angeles. I went to Mexico for two weeks, which I can explain about later. Why are you asking about her, Dad?"

"You were in Mexico for two weeks? And you met this girl there?" his father repeated, now sounding annoyed with his son.

"Yes, Dad. I was staying at a beach camping ground in a town called Guaymas, and I met her and her friend Sissy there. How do you know about her?"

"How did she get my address here?" his father asked.

Chaucer was now shaking his head, thinking the situation was pretty ridiculous. "When I left Mexico to go back to L.A. to pick up Jean Marc, I left her our address in Ottawa. She was really mad that I was leaving, so I gave her our address so she could write me. I thought maybe I could see her again sometime, that's all."

"Well, she got our phone number and called this week. I was home so I spoke with her. She says that she was with you in Mexico in September and now she is pregnant."

"WHAT!" shouted Chaucer. "She said what?"

"She claims that you were sleeping with her while you were in Mexico, and now she is pregnant, and she wants money for an abortion. She said it will cost $1,200 in a clinic in San Francisco. She said she is there now with this other girl Sissy, and they have found a clinic that will perform an abortion, and the cost is $1,200. She only wants honest doctors, no underground fly-by-night doctors because she doesn't want to have medical problems from the abortion."

"Holy crap, Dad. I was only with her for a few days."

"Well, apparently you and her were right for each other because she tells me that you are the father. Look, Son, we need to verify all this to make sure that she and her friend are not trying to scam us."

"Well, Dad, for what it's worth, she is a really nice girl, and her family is messed up — her parents are separated —but I don't think she is devious. I liked her, and I was understanding of her need to get away from Hartford and travel with her friend Sissy. Heck, JOA and I felt the same when living with Mom in Vancouver and Victoria. We just wanted to get away, and that is how Stephanie felt."

"Oh, Jesus, save me. Son, you can't keep playing therapist to every pretty girl you meet."

"Dad," he replied loudly. "I asked her if she was using the pill and she said yes. What else was I supposed to do?"

"Well, how about starting with not sleeping with her. That is a perfect option for a gentleman."

Chaucer was silent. His father continued.

"Here is what I am going to do about this. Our company has a trusted agent in San Francisco, and I am going ask him to handle this for me. He is going to tell Stephanie that he will take her to a medical appointment with an OB/GYN physician that he knows and trusts. They will verify that she is pregnant and for how long to see if it matches the time you were with her in Mexico. If it does, then I will speak with her again. This will happen in the next week, so call me again next Sunday at the same time, and we will discuss this again. Also, I definitely will be coming to London in early March, so plan your travel to meet me there, got that?"

"Yes, Dad, I will be there. I'm sorry for all this trouble. I never meant for any of it to happen like this."

"Look, Son, life throws us curve balls, and how we respond is what defines us. Our faith and our God ask us to be good, honest, and kind people, and that is how we will manage this situation too. Now as your father, I want to tell you to keep your dick in your pants, understand that?!!" Remy raised his voice a notch. "In the war in Europe, my men and I all had times when we needed to remember that we had to keep ourselves safe. You have to understand that too; do you understand? All right then, I will speak with you next Sunday so please call as we just discussed. And one more thing, Chaucer. I love you and JOA very much, don't ever forget that, OK?"

"Love you too, Dad. I'm really sorry for all this mess...I will call you in a week. Bye for now."

Remy heard the profound resignation in his son's voice, and while he was angry about his son's poor behavior, he also immediately thought of the love and grace that Chaucer required at this time. Remy remembered being in the Navy in World War II, and the anxiety and loss of place that he had felt. Sure, that was war time, but the cause of such feelings do not mitigate the emotions in you. He knew his son was a good boy and had been an obedient boy, but was he now a good man? What had caused Chaucer to live a life, his romantic life, with such disregard for the women that he was or had been involved with? Remy would ponder that question now.

* * *

The next day after eating lunch, Remy called his pastor at his family's Presbyterian church, where he had been attending for decades. Pastor Leo Louden had been a long-time Giroux family friend and a personal friend to Remy. Remy asked for a few minutes of his time. The pastor said quietly, "Can you come over now, Remy? I can hear the need in your voice."

"Yes, I'll be there in twenty minutes. Thank you, Leo."

Chapter 27

The Wisdom of Solomon

IT WAS A CLOUDY, CHILLY MID-JANUARY afternoon when Remy drove to the church and met with Pastor Leo Louden in his office. The pastor had made a fresh pot of Remy's favorite Earl Grey Tea with added milk, which he poured into mugs, and they sat down in the old Morris chairs.

Remy proceeded to explain the situation about Chaucer and how there were two young women currently carry a child that they claimed to be Chaucer's. Remy said he was going to help with the financial issues that the two women faced. He explained what he was doing with Stephanie in San Francisco. Pastor Leo listened, then said, "Tell me more, Remy."

"She wants me to pay for an abortion, Leo, an abortion! Once my agent there verifies that the baby is within the time frame of her time with Chaucer, I am going to have my agent suggest that she go to work for him in our office in San Francisco. We'll have her doing whatever she can, even if it's just answering the phones. I want to support her until the baby is full term, and then I will ask her, as the grandfather, to sign over legal custody of the child to me." Remy spoke about some of the other legal issues that would likely be part of the negotiations with the mother.

Pastor Leo nodded and smiled. "You know, Remy, this does not surprise me about you. I sense, and I have felt this way since you and

Olivia split up, that you missed your family life a great deal. Perhaps that is why you travel for your business so frequently, to keep busy. Am I wrong?"

Remy thought for a moment, then quietly nodded. He knew Pastor Leo could read him, and he trusted and loved Pastor Leo like a brother, so he knew that he could open his inner feelings and not be vulnerable.

"Well, my friend, that plan could also be God's plan for the child too. God already knows this child and will be happy that you can intervene. I see much love and grace in this, Remy. How does Chaucer feel about this?"

"I haven't told him. He is in Portugal now, and I will see him in London in early March. I hope by then that this entire plan will be working. Also, by then, the baby with Tessa in Buffalo may be born too."

"And Tessa will keep the child, you say?"

"Yes, that is her plan as of a few weeks ago."

"And if she changes her mind, then what?" Pastor Leo asked.

"Then I will want to take that baby too, Leo. They will be my grandchildren, with Giroux blood. My own father would have done the same thing for me had I been as irresponsible as Chaucer!" he said emphatically, showing his displeasure with his son.

"Why do you think Chaucer has become this way? What is it about him that has changed, Remy? He was always a good lad, and you have not ever given me any serious reason before to doubt him. Your daughter, yes, but then you and I have worked with her over the past summers when she was here. Is she still taking care of herself and her schoolwork?"

"Yes, JOA is doing just fine now."

"Good. God has a plan for JOA, you know, but Chaucer, maybe God's plan for him is not yet complete. Tell me more about him."

Remy rubbed his chin thoughtfully and looked around the room. "I think that he is finally showing the resentment, the rebellion from the loss of the family that we have discussed. He seems untethered now, like a young man with no sense of direction. Perhaps the attachment to a woman is his anchor — these various young women — perhaps he needs more love than I can give him, Leo."

"Or perhaps he deeply misses his mother. I recall the strong influence that she had on both JOA and Chaucer when you were married. You were away a lot, working on building your business so you could provide for your family, being a fine, supporting father, doing all the best things for your family."

Remy sighed. "Oh, Leo, I wish I could do it all over again. I would not have been away so much; perhaps then Olivia would not have left me and taken the children." Remy stopped, overtaken by a burst of remorse.

"Come, come, Remy, you did the best you could at the time. God does not guarantee perfection, or a perfect world, he only gives us a tool kit to fix and maintain ourselves, to give help and grace to others, to love others as he loved his son. Our faith is a path, a journey, and our God is with us all on that journey. God is within us all; if we pay attention, we can find God, hear our Father speak to us, which is why we pray — to open that book of goodness and grace we have in us. I know you understand that, and I have faith that you believe it as well." Pastor Leo smiled at Remy and continued. "Here's what I will venture, Remy, more as a lay counselor than as a pastor. Chaucer, by his actions, seems like he both misses his mother and her love, and at the same time without knowing, subconsciously wants to hurt the women who show him kindness and love, and walking away from them at a time when his seed is growing in them is likely the time that would hurt the most. I don't think your son would do this on purpose, not the lad that I have known, but perhaps, just perhaps, the loss of his family life here in Ottawa, and the things that have happened with JOA and Olivia in Vancouver, have pushed him away from his innate kindness. Perhaps his joy in life has been damaged so that he cannot see the joy that others have, or that he sees it and does not see how he can ever be that joyful again."

Remy was silent for a while. Pastor Leo sipped his tea and waited.

"You may be right, Leo." Remy looked at Pastor Leo, their eyes met, and the pastor nodded that he understood.

"Leo, can we pray together? Can we pray for clarity in the days ahead, for the clarity for Chaucer in his decisions, and for clarity and grace for the two women?"

"Remy, please know that I have never had clarity or certitude. I only have trust. So I can pray for you to have faith and trust in God and in your son and that the grace and wisdom of Solomon will find you and shine on you both, and on the two women as well, that is what I can pray."

Remy and Pastor Leo both bowed their heads and prayed quietly for a time, then the pastor stood up, walked to Remy in his chair and put his hand on Remy's shoulder. "Dear Lord, may you grant this son of yours the continued peace, grace, and love that he will need in the coming days, and I pray that the winds of your benevolent wisdom will fill his sails and guide him and his son, Chaucer, to carry forth your word and your peace, in the name of your son, Jesus Christ our Lord. Amen."

With that, Remy stood up and hugged Pastor Leo, and shook his hand tightly. Pastor Leo could see soft tears of God's presence in Remy's eyes. It had been a good meeting among the three of them that afternoon.

Chapter 28

Rode Hard and Hung Up Wet

CHAUCER WAS VERY UPSET after his call with Remy. He could not believe that this girl, Stephanie, was pregnant too. He had not thought about her in months, and he struggled to replay the events of those two weeks in Mexico. He was sure he had asked her about precautions the night she invited him to stay in her tent. Chaucer had condoms with him but she insisted she was taking the pill. Yes, they had been together many times while he was there. He liked her, and she liked him, but Chaucer remembered that he had not spoken of staying long, or that there might be a longer connection between them other than maybe he might make a visit to Hartford to see her at some time if she ever even went back to Hartford. Just when he thought that the mess with Tessa was resolved, now this.

He tried to push all of this out of his mind. He went for a long walk around Faro that afternoon, hoping to settle himself. When he returned to the pensione hours later, he needed food and company at that moment. That night, he, Bryce, Lisa, and Teresa walked down to the edge of the water to have a dinner at the Fin del Mundo Café, a place recommended by Ray Tomison, the owner of the Pensione Lumena. For two dollars (US), you got a huge piece of fresh local fish, potatoes, and green beans, and for another dollar you got a liter carafe of the local white wine. So the four of them ate, drank, and talked for hours, laughing so loudly that the owner came to the table and asked them to quiet down. Chaucer got a three-hour reprieve from his troubles.

* * *

Two days later, Bryce, Seth, and Ronnie took the train west to Albufeira, then to Sagres. They wanted to hike down to Point Sagres, the end of Portugal on the southwest coast. They wanted to jump into the ocean, off the very tip of Europe, just to tell their friends in California that they had done it. Then they were going north to Lisbon and the Oporto wine region for a week or so, and then take a one-way flight to Rome. Chaucer hugged them all, as soon he needed to start his way to London to see Remy, and they made plans to see each other again in California one day, or if they ever came to Montreal, Toronto, or Ottawa. It was a good farewell for them, with hugs and exchanges of addresses. The boys had become close from working on the movie set and through their travels together. Friends made on the road are the best, Chaucer thought. No prior background or history together, just real times in the present. Those times can bond people like no other.

That night, Lisa, Teresa, and Chaucer went to the Fin Del Mundo again for dinner. They talked about their plans for the coming days.

"When are you leaving for your Camino walk?" Chaucer asked.

"Well, we're thinking about going to see Gibraltar while we are here, then maybe take the ferry to Tangiers. Have you been there?" Lisa asked.

"Nope, but I haven't been thinking straight the last two days since I spoke with my dad on Sunday."

"Trouble?" Teresa asked.

"Oh yeah, my trouble, big stuff, I'm freaking out about it right now," Chaucer replied.

"What is it? We'll listen," Lisa said, leaning forward toward Chaucer.

Chaucer shook his head. "Thanks, but not now," and he pounded down half a glass of wine as if it were water.

The girls looked each other and sighed. "Maybe another time, Chaucer," said Teresa, looking directly at Lisa as their eyes grew larger.

* * *

The next day Chaucer spent time in the small library at the Pensione Lumena. He found a copy of the novel To Kill a Mockingbird, and having not read it, he sat on the sofa and read 100 pages before he looked up and saw Lisa standing in front of him. She was very pretty with long, dark hair and a smile that could set a room on fire.

"You'll like that story, Chaucer," she said quietly. "Atticus is an amazing man. I love that book."

"You're right about that, but I want to date Scout when she gets older," Chaucer replied with a big grin.

Lisa smiled broadly. "You're such an ass, Chaucer," and they both laughed.

"Teresa and I were talking this morning, and we'd really like it if you would come with us to Gibraltar."

Chaucer put a bookmark in the book, closed it, and set it on the sofa next to him. "Really, when are you leaving?"

"Well, maybe tomorrow, maybe the next day. We need to be back to Heidelberg in about three weeks, so we want to go south, then back to do the Camino de Santiago pilgrim's walk, then we'll take about three or four days to get to Germany. We want to be back by February 15."

"OK, let me think it over. Are you and Teresa going to Fin del Mundo again tonight?"

"Does a wild bear shit in the woods?" she replied with a wide grin.

"OK, I'll go with you guys to dinner; we can talk then. Say 7 p.m.?"

"Yup," Lisa replied with a smile and walked out of the library room, and Chaucer went back to Harper Lee's book.

* * *

That night they all walked to the Fin del Mundo café as a brisk, cold wind came off the Atlantic. The weather was changing so they agreed it was a good time to leave Faro. They settled on a travel plan. They would leave Faro for Gibraltar the next day. Chaucer felt the need to get moving again. After finishing the book about Atticus Finch, Chaucer was motivated to move on, make plans, fix his life, take charge.

These young women from Boston were kind souls, and he really felt comfortable with them. Lisa and Teresa believed Chaucer to be a gentleman; they had liked him from the first night at the Pensione Lumena. He was a warm and funny guy, and they wanted to hear him out about his troubles. Kind women are like that, at least the women who had good mothers and grandmothers who raised them with kindness.

That night, Chaucer was on the verge of telling his female friends about Tessa and Stephanie, but he clammed up just before his words were about to come out. He could not yet bring himself to reveal his problem. Perhaps he was realizing that he had not yet decided what to do, or perhaps he was once again hesitating on accepting his role as a father. Whatever the reason, he didn't talk about it that night. He thought that another time might be better for him, which was the male way of saying, "I haven't figured this out yet."

* * *

On a rainy and cold Wednesday morning, Chaucer, Lisa, and Teresa boarded an east-bound train for the Spanish frontier. At the border they walked a couple blocks to board the river ferry at noon. Once across the river, they were lucky to catch an immediate local train for Huelva, arriving just in time to get some lunch before the two-hour siesta shut down everything. Then they boarded a southbound train and arrived in Algeciras about an hour before dark. By then, the rain had stopped. As they walked out of the terminal station with their backpacks, they saw what they had come for: Gibraltar in all its magnificence.

Docked at the waterfront was the ferry to Ceuta, the Spanish enclave in Africa. It was a busy site, with passengers, cars, and trucks waiting in line to board. Close by there were a few small parks and parking lots for the cars of the short-term travelers to Ceuta.

It was the dinner hour, so they found a tapas bar across from a park, and they left their packs locked together against a wall in the bar. They grabbed some bar stools and ordered tapas and bottles of cervesa. Sitting next to them were an English couple who appeared to be in their late twenties or thirties. They had been to Tangier for a couple of days, so they talked about things to do and hostel locations. Chaucer, Lisa, and Teresa knew this was a good way to get insider information. Travelers always love to tell other sojourners about good places to eat and sleep and things to see, because that is a way for the traveler to confirm their choices and validate their trip.

"Where do you plan to go after Tangier?" asked Arthur, as he and Sybil were finishing their second glass of wine.

"We're not really sure; maybe Fez, maybe Marrakech," said Chaucer as he looked at Lisa and Teresa, who both shrugged. "Where were you guys?"

Arthur winked at Sybil. "We went to Marrakech for the hashish. You can get a kilo there for eighty quid, if you know where to go."

"Why would you want a kilo of that stuff?" asked Lisa, abundantly naive.

Sybil smiled at Arthur, who laughed. "Just part of a business deal for us. You like hashish?"

Lisa answered in a serious tone. "I've heard about it, but no, I don't know much about it."

Chaucer stepped in to change the subject. "Can you recommend a hostel or hotel in Tangier?"

And so they talked more, until Arthur and Sybil finished their bottle of wine. Before they left the bar they told Chaucer, Lisa, and Teresa about a campground about a mile up the coastal road where they could stay overnight. It would not be crowded at this time of year like it would be during the summer months. Arthur said that he had stayed there once a few years ago, and you could see the lights of Gibraltar across the water.

Arthur also told them that their plan to visit Gibraltar in the next few days was a "no go" unless they entered from the sea. Chaucer, Lisa, and Teresa did not know that the Franco government in Spain had completely closed the border, and thus there was no access to Gibraltar from Spain. The only way in was by air or boat now. Chaucer and the girls told Arthur and Sybil that they would take their advice about the campground for the night. Arthur winked and said, "Good choice; you can catch the Ceuta ferry here in the port. Look, we'll give you all a lift up the road to the campground. We're leaving now."

Arthur and Sybil dropped off the girls and Chaucer a mile up the coastal road near a sign that said Campground de Algeciras. It was early evening and the sun was bouncing off Gibraltar, one of the Pillars of Hercules at the west end of the Mediterranean Sea, the gateway to the Atlantic. They thanked Arthur and Sybil for their kindness and the ride, grabbed their backpacks, and walked into the campground. The office was already closed, so they simply found a nice spot to camp for a few days.

With the daylight receding quickly, Chaucer found some wood and built a small campfire. The girls unrolled their sleeping bags in the tent and brought out a bottle of red wine that Lisa had bought at the bar. As the twilight turned to darkness, the lights of Gibraltar shone bright across the Bay of Algeciras. The crown of the Rock, 1,400 feet above the Mediterranean, appeared magical in the night. While five miles separated them, it made it all the more mystical with the sun now gone.

They drank the wine straight from the bottle, passing it back and forth. After many sips, Chaucer looked at the fire that lit the faces of Lisa and Teresa. He pulled out a very small piece of aluminum foil and opened it to reveal a small chunk of hashish. "Surprise, this is from Arthur and Sybil!"

"Is that what I think it is?" Lisa asked.

"Yup, he told me to share it with you tonight; it's his gift for us 'North American colonists and members of the Commonwealth,' as he called us." They all laughed. Arthur also had included a small ceramic pipe.

Chaucer looked around. There was no one else camping within 200 feet of them that night, so he broke up the hashish, put it in the pipe and asked, "Ready?" The girls laughed. "Sure, I'll try it," said Teresa, but Lisa shook her head. She looked at Chaucer and with a kind face said, "My father is a policeman back home, and my brother and sister and I all swore to him when we started high school that we would never use or experiment with drugs of any kind."

She looked at Teresa with a hawk-eye look of "you know better, too." Teresa nodded and said, "Yes, you're right" to Lisa, and then she smiled at Chaucer.

Chaucer reassured them. "Hey, no problem with me. I understand what you are saying. My dad is the same way about any drugs, but my mom is almost the opposite in her free thinking, probably one of the reasons they got divorced when I was a kid," he said with a frown. "Anyway, I smoked some of this stuff at school last year, and then again in New York City last summer so I'm going to have a little unless it will be offensive to you," he said, looking at Lisa. She smiled gently and shook her head. "No, Chaucer, I'm not offended. You do as you wish; it's your life, your decision, it's just not for us, thanks for understanding and respecting us."

Chaucer used his knife to shave off a bit of the small block, then put it into the pipe and lit it. He smoked it for a minute, then got up and walked over to the nearest trash barrel and tossed the pipe and the rest of the hashish away. When he came back and sat down with the cousins, he smiled, feeling high. "It would be selfish and impolite to keep smoking that in front of you. I just wanted to be able to say that at one time I actually smoked real Moroccan hashish, just to be able to have done it. Kind of like if I was from Boston, to be able to say that one time, just once, I had skated in a pickup hockey game with Bobby Orr or Phil Esposito, or took some shots on Gerry Cheevers in net, that is all that was about. Just a guy having a one-time experience." He laughed the high-pitched, stoned-boy hashish laugh.

Lisa and Teresa smiled broadly at Chaucer. They saw their polite and gentle guy, and they were happy to be with him. They understood what he had said about the experience thing, as both their fathers had played hockey as young men, and Lisa and Teresa and their cousins had been to Bruins games at Boston Gardens. They loved the Bruins, especially Derrick Sanderson, the long-haired wild player who often winked at girls during warmups. They knew that if their dads had met Bobby Orr or Phil Esposito or Gerry Cheevers somewhere in Boston, that they too would be talking about it. They understood Chaucer and had reached a smooth rapprochement with him about this one-time hashish fling. They all could move on and laugh about it. And they did.

Over the next hour, they finished their wine with some bags of peanuts that Lisa had bought. Chaucer added some more wood to the fire and the night passed with them talking about the journey from the morning in Faro to the view of the silhouetted Gibraltar at night, right across the water from them now. It all seemed dream-like — new experiences for them. They had become a good team together; Chaucer and Sister Lisa and Sister Teresa, the temporary Sisters of Teresa de Avila.

They soon grew tired as it had been a long day of travel. The girls eventually crawled into their sleeping bags in the tent, and Chaucer rolled his bag on a tarp next to the tent. Within a few minutes Lisa poked her head outside the tent. The temperature had dropped, and there was a chill in the night. "Chaucer, come inside, there is room for you in here. It will be too cold for you to be outside tonight. Just don't snore!" Chaucer laughed and picked up his sleeping bag and positioned it against the wall of the tent. It was a tight fit but acceptable and warmer than being outside. They had a cozy night, all sleeping soundly, although as Lisa found out in the morning from Chaucer, it was she who was the snoring one.

Chapter 29

To Leo the Lion Again

A Noiseless Patient Spider

A noiseless patient spider,
I mark'd where on a little promontory it stood isolated,
Mark'd how to explore the vacant vast surrounding,
It launch'd fort filament, filament, filament, out of itself,
Ever unreeling them, ever tirelessly speeding them.

And you O my soul where you stand,
Surrounded, detached, in measureless oceans of space,
Ceaselessly musing, venturing, throwing, seeking the spheres to connect them,
Till the bridge you will need be form'd, till the ductile anchor hold,
Till the gossamer thread you fling catch somewhere,
O my soul.

—Walt Whitman (1872)

CHAUCER FOUND COMFORT AND KINDNESS in these two cousins from Boston. They were smart and loved the joy of travel. Traveling with them was easy and the conversation light-hearted. Both were pretty, young women, and Chaucer was learning to appreciate them as fine, new friends. Too often in the past he seemed to want to be in love with a woman, and when he wasn't, he felt alone. It was not that his loneliness was based on a need to be controlled or control another, but more like filling the void from a loss. It was a feeling that he could not shake off.

Back in Ottawa, Remy was sleeping alone that night. He had met with Pastor Leo two days before to discuss the situation with Chaucer again. Remy's love for his son knew no bounds yet that did not prevent Remy from discussing Chaucer with Pastor Leo on their regular monthly lunches. Pastor Leo very much enjoyed Remy's company. He had learned much from Remy about the business of international shipping and trade. Pastor Leo, when joking with Remy, would call him the "Saint Paul of the shipping business" for all his travels and his friendships in the port cities of Europe and the Mediterranean.

That night, after finally falling to sleep, Remy had a detailed dream about his last meeting with Pastor Leo. In the dream, Remy and Pastor Leo were sitting at the bar at the Golf Club. Pastor Leo asked about Chaucer. Remy explained that he would see Chaucer in London soon, and as Pastor Leo knew, Remy had the important topic of the babies to discuss.

"As I have thought about this Remy, I believe that Chaucer really loves you, and knowing that you miss the family, Chaucer will be impregnating five or six more girls this year. I think he wants to fill your house with babies so that you will be very happy! Isn't he a thoughtful son; wouldn't you agree?"

"Yes, that seems true, Leo. I think that Chaucer wants our family to be big and joyful. He can even have six boys and make his own hockey team here."

Pastor Leo was smiling now. "If that happens, then I want to coach them, and you can too. I think that we should ask Chaucer to have twelve more sons just like Jesus had twelve apostles, and then both of us can have a team too. And if JOA has six boys then we can have four teams, and we'll have our own league. What fun, The Giroux Family Hockey League!"

And then Pastor Leo ordered an entire bottle of wine. He told the bartender named Manny to put the cost of the wine on God's tab. "Manny, you know God? He's in here a lot," Pastor Leo said, and Manny replied, "Yes, he is, I'll put it on his bill," and he uncorked the bottle of an expensive Châteauneuf du Pape. Then Manny said,

"But wait, you're not a priest, and this is the wine of the Popes." Pastor Leo winked at Manny and said, "Martin Luther and the Pope are friends tonight, we're celebrating our reconciliation. Just put it on his tab, please." Pastor Leo looked at Remy with a confident smile. "Remember, Remy, God blesses us with the children and tells us to care for them, to love them, so that they may love God and his son whom he sent into the world, and God loves hockey too."

Remy grinned and nodded in agreement. Both men agreed that Remy should act to help all the mothers, and if necessary, as the grandfather, Remy should take the children into his care. Pastor Leo said that his ministry in Ottawa had taken in many orphaned children over the decades, but he could not remember another situation like this one with Chaucer who would have twenty sons and six more nephews, and he poured more wine for him and Remy.

"I've had many parishioners over the years confide in me, ask me about guidance with an unplanned pregnancy, but never twenty at once, not like this, Remy. Your son, our son, has created quite a new chapter for us, don't you think?"

Remy smiled and chuckled softly. "Yes, Leo, he has, but think, all the more children to baptize and more children to fill the chairs in the Sunday School too." Pastor Leo laughed. "The Lord works in mysterious ways," said Remy, smiling at Pastor Leo.

Pastor Leo shook Remy's hand. "Peace be with you, my fine friend. See you on Sunday."

Remy woke up, looked at the clock, smiled, and rolled over to return to sleep.

Chapter 30

The Pillars of Hercules

AFTER A DAY OF WALKING around Algeciras, Chaucer and the cousins decided to take the Spanish ferry to Ceuta. It was an inexpensive ticket and just a two-hour ride across to Africa. The ferry direct to Tangier through Gibraltar was far more expensive, and it took more time, so they opted for the Ceuta boat.

The day could not have been more perfect for the voyage, with bright sun and a mild breeze. The three of them stood in the bow of the ferry with the wind blowing their hair.

Chaucer asked: "Do you know the Pillars of Hercules?" as he looked at the cousins.

Teresa said, "Is it a movie?" and Chaucer smiled as Remy had told him about the Pillars of Hercules when he was a boy.

He grinned. "Good guess. No, it's Gibraltar and that peak over there" as he pointed to the Jebel Musa in Morocco, straight ahead. "Those are the two pillars. I was told that the ancients in the Mediterranean believed that the world was flat, and if you left the Mediterranean and sailed or rowed west that you could fall off the earth out in the sea somewhere, so the ancient mariners back then rarely went past Gibraltar and the Jebel Musa for fear of never to return." Chaucer smiled broadly, knowing that the cousins were duly impressed with his knowledge of ancient folklore. But of course, Lisa could not let that settle, so she said, "So do you know the myth of the civilized Canadian bear who didn't shit in the woods?" Chaucer just grinned, laughed, and replied, "Yes, that's me!" and he hugged them both.

*   *   *

Like the British and Spanish bickered about Gibralter, the Spanish and the Moroccan leaders could not seem to resolve and coordinate their governmental relations over Ceuta, and so the tourists and the locals paid the price every day. Perhaps the conflict was spurred from the days when the Moors from north Africa occupied much of the Iberian Peninsula or maybe it came from recent issues of the world wars of that century, but the Spanish Catholic toehold of Ceuta in Africa, rather than Tangier, was where many people first set foot on the Islamic dominated north coast of Africa.

Chaucer and the cousins departed the ferry and walked to the Moroccan frontier where they cleared Moroccan customs, then boarded a local bus to Tangier. Ceuta was not a nice-looking area — too many fences and barricades and not enough palm trees to excite the imagination. They discussed their thoughts about the next few days, and the cousins decided that they did not want to be in Morocco without Chaucer given the dominate male paternalism of the Islamic culture. Chaucer agreed with them. So they planned to spend a night in Tangier and then catch a train to Marrakech to see the magical city. They hoped to be back in Ceuta to catch the return ferry in three or four days.

When they boarded the bus bound for Tangier, they placed their three backpacks on the far back seat of the bus, piled on each other. Then they sat on available seats further up in the bus, and as the bus rolled on, they talked about finding a place to eat lunch in Tangier. With no particular impulse, Lisa turned to look behind her on the bus and saw a man who had been in a seat behind them going through their backpacks. She screamed, "Hey, stop that!"

Chaucer leaped out of his seat to confront the thief. The bus was just in the process of coming to a stop to pick up more passengers, and the driver had opened both doors on the bus.

The thief had something concealed in his hand when Chaucer confronted him. The thief turned to Chaucer and pointed a big, curved jambiya knife at him. Chaucer backed up, slowly and calmly.

The thief bounded past Chaucer and was about to descend down the steps to exit the bus, but Lisa stuck her foot out and tripped the thief, which caused him to smash his head on the metal frame of the seat next to the stairs, drop the knife and the bag he was holding.

Teresa, who was sitting across from Lisa, stepped hard on the wrist of the thief, and he shouted in pain. Chaucer charged him but the thief rolled down the steps and ran off rapidly. He had been holding Chaucer's toiletry bag from his backpack, apparently thinking it was valuable, so Chaucer picked it up off the floor and brushed the dirt off it. He smiled at Lisa. Teresa, her eyes as big as saucers from watching this, rolled her eyes. Chaucer also picked up the jambiya knife and put it in his backpack, a souvenir of the crime scene. The other bus passengers, three women in hijabs and two in burqas, chattered in Arabic, amazed at the toughness and quickness of the Boston women, something that they would likely never see again in their lifetime in Morocco.

In about half an hour, the bus entered Tangier from the coastal road. Chaucer and the cousins got off with their packs near the port area. After the incident on the bus, they were glad that they had decided to just stay the one night in Tangier and catch a train to Marrakech the next morning. Asking around to others they learned that the train terminal was just a block away, so they walked there to look at the schedule and buy tickets.

It was not tourist season, so the streets were mainly filled with locals walking, scooters, buses, small autos, and a few camels loaded with packs and being led by hand. When Chaucer, Lisa, and Teresa got to the train terminal, it was empty of passengers. There were no trains moving and few employees around. They saw a man in a western suit who looked English or French, so they stopped him.

"Hi, excuse me, do you speak English?" Chaucer asked.

"Aye lad, I'm Seamus Kinney from Dublin. You're an American, I see."

"Actually, Canadian." Chaucer gave a smile that was quickly returned by the Irishman. "My friends and I are going to Marrakech. Do you know anything about this train system? It looks closed or something."

"Well, lad, it is for now," Seamus said.

"Closed! Really, it's closed? Do you know why?"

Seamus continued smiling his big Irish grin. "Just the way this place works; it's not Toronto or London here, you see." He laughed.

By this time, the cousins had walked over to listen to Seamus; they had been walking around the terminal making observations and trying to figure out the wall signs in Arabic and French.

"This is what I heard in my office in town about an hour ago. King Hassan has shut down the railroads and put-up roadblocks. It seems some Army unit is causing trouble in Casablanca now, wanting to start a rebellion or some such nonsense," Seamus explained. "This happens a couple of times a year it seems, at least since I have been here."

Chaucer and the cousins looked at each other in disbelief.

Seamus continued. "Yes, about four years ago they had a big coup attempt, but the King found out early and executed about 150 of the insurrectionists and threw a bunch of others in prison. In Morocco, they all pretend to love Allah and pray half the day, then in the other half of the day they try to kill each other or steal from each other. Strange land it is, you see." Seamus just smiled at the three of them. "You can still probably find a bus to Marrakech if you really want to go there. The trains could be down for days or be running in a couple of hours. The King never tells any of us locals."

They all giggled and shook their heads. After a huddle and some discussion, the twins and Chaucer decided to stay the night in a nearby hostel and then leave on the ferry back to Spain the next day. In their brief time in Morocco, they had seen and experienced enough to have formed an opinion. Such is the beauty of travel, they agreed.

The rest of their time in Tangier was not exciting for them; the Kasbah that afternoon proved to be dirty, very crowded, and uninviting, and none of the three liked the food they saw or ate in their couple of meals. The allure of an exotic non-western culture in Morocco had interested them but they now learned that not all illusions are the reality. While some visitors like Arthur and Sybil came to score cheap hashish, Chaucer and the cousins had no compelling interest in the hashish craze of the hippie world. They were just fine with some great sunsets, decent wine, and good friends. They were learning that less could be more when traveling.

* * *

The morning sun the next day soon took the winter chill out of the Tangier air. After a non-eventful bus ride back to Ceuta, Chaucer and the cousins bought their tickets and boarded the late morning boat for Algeciras. It appeared that it would be another beautiful day trip across the strait. But soon after they left the harbor, the chilly morning mist over the warm Mediterranean turned into a thick fog, obscuring the beautiful views that the travelers had experienced on the trip over the day before. The air grew chilly as well, so the three travelers left the bow rail and went below, sitting at a table by a window, but the fog left them with no view. It seemed like a good time to talk as the boat was absent of many travelers that morning.

"You seem awfully quiet today, Pancho," Lisa said, using the nickname that Chaucer had let slip out the day before.

Chaucer gave a half smile. "A lot on my mind today; I had some spooky dreams last night, I guess."

"Wanna share? Boston women are usually pretty polite listeners, you know," Teresa said.

So on this chilly day, with time to spare and worries abounding, over the next hour, Chaucer told the cousins about Tessa and Stephanie, little by little. He did it with enough detail so it helped the cousins better understand why Chaucer had not made any romantic moves on either of them, which the two had discussed in private over the last week. They could see the struggle that he was having, surely the biggest tumult of his young life.

Because Chaucer had earlier mentioned his parents and the divorce, Teresa asked him about his father, about his mother. Perhaps that was the wrong thing to ask, or perhaps it was the perfect question.

"My mother took my sister and me with her to Vancouver when they divorced. JOA was almost 12 and I was 14. I don't think either of us wanted to leave Dad or Ottawa then, but my Dad was still traveling all over for his business, and my mother insisted we go with her."

"Your sister's name is JOA?" Teresa asked.

"My mother named her for Joan of Arc, so we call her JOA." Chaucer smiled, hoping this revelation would give them a clue about his mother.

Lisa looked at him with serious eyes. "JOA, really? Hmmm. So what happened when you all left for Vancouver, you didn't like it?"

"I wish it had been easy, Lisa. It was a very complicated time, you know, leaving our dad whom we loved, leaving our friends and schools in Ottawa, having no experience with Western Canada." He paused, looking at the table. "And then our mother seemed to change overnight. She became completely involved in her writing, almost becoming a different person to us, and within a year she moved us to Victoria on Vancouver Island. We were both in private boarding schools, which we really disliked." He shook his head and paused, and looked at them with resignation, as a young puppy who was lonely in a new home.

"Well, for me, I just felt abandoned. My dad would come to visit a lot , and then I started going back to Ottawa for the summers. In a way I felt like I had lost both my parents. I felt on my own, which in a way was OK, but I had really loved my family in Ottawa, and overnight it seemed to have been taken away...disappeared...so I withdrew from things I guess. I lost my joy along the way, but for my sister it was worse, and she rebelled by smoking pot and drinking alcohol at school and not even wanting to come home on weekends or holidays. At the same time, our mother was writing more, and her books were selling well, and she would almost lock herself in her writing room and hardly pay us any attention, at least not like she had done at home in Ottawa. JOA and I call it 'the years of our emotional wasteland' now. "

Lisa looked at Teresa with the look of "ah ha, now we know" and Teresa nodded in agreement. They seemed to understand Chaucer better now. Both Teresa and Lisa had benefitted greatly from having a good family life in Boston. Sure, it was not perfect, but their lives had been good enough to develop them into emotionally mature young women, and this gift had provided them with the ability to listen, understand, and give a hand and a heart of sympathy to those, like Chaucer, who were still working out the problems of their lives. It was such empathy that Lisa and Teresa had in abundance. And that morning, on that boat, with this young man who was their new friend, they did just that.

The cousins were able to surmise that Chaucer, the gentle man they now knew, had been denied the love of a mother, and he sought it from his relationships with women. But then when those women needed to lean on him for his love and support, he denied it to them, perhaps as a way of getting back at his own mother for divorcing his father, and subsequently withdrawing from her emotional attachment to him and his sister. It was speculation by Lisa and Teresa but likely a valid theory of human responses in such situations. This was the diagnosis they made of Chaucer that day.

Of course, they did not posit that with Chaucer at that time, rather they discussed it over the next few days in their private moments. They observed him more, questioned him over the week that followed. Their theory became more and more validated. In her journal, Lisa wrote, "Human psychology seems universal; the parts of life that drive human behavior are always the same: love, greed, jealousy, hate, dominance, loneliness, fraternity; they are at play every day in every human. Chaucer is no different."

* * *

In the next days, the cousins traveled with Chaucer by train to Granada to visit the beautiful Alhambra. This 1,200-year-old fort and palace had roots to the Romans, and the existing buildings constructed by the Arab Islamists and the Spanish Christians. The cousins were students of evolutionary religion, and this visit was essential for them, and interesting for Chaucer to explore as well. They had booked two nights in a local hostel, which turned out to be a fortuitous decision, because on the afternoon of their day-long visit inside the Alhambra, while walking and talking in the adjacent magnificent gardens, they drank water from a garden hose that had been set out and used by the staff. They soon found out that the water supply was not potable water, and that night after dinner they all had serious gastrointestinal issues, or as visitors to Mexico have appropriately named the condition, "Montezuma's Revenge." Thus they needed another day to recover. Twenty-four hours later they were in a tapas bar in Granada eating well, although sparing the wine that night.

Over the following three days, the travelers returned to Madrid and eventually ended up in the northwest town of Leon, where they planned to part. Chaucer and the cousins wanted to see the architecture of the magnificent Leon Cathedral and the Convent of San Marcos. Lisa and Teresa had studied the Spanish Civil War at Boston College, and they were very interested in the convent because it had been turned into a prison and a dungeon during the Civil War.

Thousands of opponents to the regime were sent there, and many died within the walls of this beautiful structure. They explained this history to Chaucer. He had not known just how brutal the Spanish Civil War had been, and it had happened only forty years before.

Lisa and Teresa also explained to Chaucer that from Leon, they would hike the remaining 100-plus miles to Santiago to the west. They told Chaucer about their History of the Saints class taught by Father Leary at Boston College. Father Leary had done his theology doctoral research and project on Saint James, who was buried in the Cathedral of Santiago de Compostela. They had really enjoyed the class and the relationship that they had developed with Father Leary on campus. They wanted to honor him, and also explore their Catholic faith by walking a major part of the Camino de Santiago. The plan was to walk fifteen miles per day and arrive in about eight to ten days, depending on the weather and soreness of their feet. The walk would end with a mass at the cathedral, a fitting end to their pilgrimage.

Chaucer was in awe when they explained this to him. They had not mentioned these details over the last two weeks, when they had talked about their education at Boston College. In their conversation this day, they even showed Chaucer a map of the trail (Camino) so he could see the location.

As the three of them sat on a park bench near the Leon Cathedral, Lisa and Teresa both reached into their backpacks to retrieve a small box wrapped in decorative paper. They smiled at each other, then looked at Chaucer.

Teresa said, "Our mothers are sisters, as we mentioned to you, and before we left Boston for this journey, they each gave us a box knowing that we would be making the walk to Santiago. They said not to open the boxes until we reached Leon, so today is that day." The two women looked so happy and excited. Chaucer just grinned. He had grown very fond of both of them, and he felt sad, realizing that he was going to be lonely traveling without them.

They slowly unwrapped each box at the same time and lifted the lids. "Oh my God, these are beautiful!" they said.

"What is it?" Chaucer asked.

"They are identical silver scallop necklaces. I can't believe this!" said Lisa as she squeezed Teresa's arm.

Chaucer peered down at the open boxes and smiled, feeling happy for the girls. The necklaces were quite beautiful. "Why scallops?" he asked.

Lisa grabbed his hand. "It's the symbol of St. James," she explained. "His body was being brought back to Santiago from Jerusalem where he had been killed, and before the boat landed, a storm came, and his body was washed overboard. A few days later, the tide brought his body to the northwest coast near Santiago, and it was covered with scallop shells. So the scallop shell has come to be identified with St. James, Santiago, and the Camino walk for believers like us." She felt so excited to hold the silver scallop shell. She wiped tears from her eyes, overwhelmed with love for her mother and Teresa's mother.

Chaucer could only look in awe at her joy. He was seeing his friends incredibly happy in their beliefs, their family, their coming pilgrimage. He thought of his father, his mother, and his sister, and he wanted all this same joy to be in his family again; everyone all together like his life had been before, when he had known happiness like this. He realized how long it had been since he felt as happy as Lisa and Teresa did at this moment. Had God put him in this very place to be a witness to the joy of Lisa and Teresa, to ask him to remember his happy days, to challenge him to find that happiness again. He thought about it all that day, and the next and the next, and it would become an ever-present question for him in the days ahead.

That night Chaucer, Lisa, and Teresa planned to have their last dinner together. The cousins would be off early on the Camino walk, and Chaucer was going east to Bordeaux, then to Mont-Saint-Michel in Normandy before taking the channel ferry to Portsmouth and a train to London to meet his father in ten days. He was sorry to leave them. They had become good friends, perhaps true friends.

Another traveler that they met at the Leon hostel that afternoon suggested a small local restaurant near the hostel, so at 8 p.m. they walked a few blocks, located the restaurant and found a table inside. They sat quietly; they all knew that next morning they would be saying goodbye. The girls felt the joy of starting the pilgrimage but the sadness of saying good bye to Chaucer, and it weighed on them at the table. Chaucer understood, but said little, preferring to drink the Spanish red wine from the carafe that they had ordered. During dinner, they reminisced about their meeting in Faro, the camping near Gibraltar, the thief on the bus in Morocco, and the beauty of the Alhambra. It had been a special time for them, weeks that they would treasure in their memories and likely never forget.

"Teresa and I have really enjoyed our time with you, Chaucer," Lisa said after they finished sharing the highlights of their time together. "We will miss your smile and your company," she paused, "and while we still have some time, we decided that we wanted to tell you that you have become our new brother! You're now part of our family; you OK with that?"

Chaucer smiled broadly, nodding his head. At first, he didn't want to say too much; he was happy to have their confidence and friendship. Yet he knew; he knew that they probably had the answer to the question burning inside him. He could just sense it in them. His expression turned serious as he asked, "What should I do about the situation with Tessa and Stephanie? I really want to know your thoughts."

Lisa smiled, as did Teresa. Teresa replied, "Funny you should ask, because we wanted to talk with you about that before we left you. So this will be an open discussion, an honest talk with your new sisters." She smiled and poured more wine into each of the three glasses.

The cousins proceeded to tell Chaucer that they had women friends who had taken the abortion option. They discussed one good friend who kept her baby, finished college and started a career, all with the help of her parents in Boston. They had also known others who, after learning of their pregnancy, had gotten married young and were raising the babies with success. They knew how important it was for the families of their friends to help out, and they had seen it happen in their Commonwealth Avenue neighborhood in Newton. (Lisa and Teresa had lived close by each other all their lives, and both had commuted to Boston College and lived at home.)

The cousins did not like the idea of getting an abortion as the easy option, but they also understood that the circumstance of each situation was different. They would not criticize a woman who had used abortion as a choice to end an unexpected pregnancy. Still, they did not like the termination of an unborn child to be the answer as it was against all their spiritual beliefs and against Catholic church doctrine. Lisa said that every person had to answer to God for their decisions as St. Peter had written in his letters, and it was not her role to be judgmental as she was not the one who was pregnant and not married. Teresa agreed. She said a friend in that situation needed understanding and compassion, not criticism or shame directed at them.

"Your father seems like a great man, Chaucer," Lisa said. "Not many parents or men I know would do what your father is doing. I think both Tessa and Stephanie are very lucky women." She stopped and looked directly in Chaucer's eyes. "So are you going to walk away?"

Chaucer's face fell, and he squirmed uncomfortably. Perhaps he should not have even discussed this with them at all. Perhaps he should get away from them now, leave the table, and go for a walk alone.

Then he remembered his meeting with Pastor Wagner and how the pastor had told him he needed to listen for the word from Heaven. Perhaps Lisa and Teresa were really angels sent to guide Chaucer. Imagine that, he thought, and he smiled. Besides, even if they weren't heavenly angels, he liked and trusted them both, and this would be as good a time as any to hear them. And so, he stayed and he talked. He told them the full story about his dislike for Tessa and how she cheated on him, and how he liked Stephanie yet did not ever expect to be in a long-term relationship with her, given her discussions about wanting to travel with Sissy around the country and never go back to Hartford.

Lisa could see the conflict, the hurt in Chaucer's face. She leaned across the table and took his hand in hers. Softly, she said, "Chaucer, this is not a decision for just this month, or this year. It is a decision that you will carry your entire life. So think big and think long term. It is likely that you have two little babies growing in Tessa and Stephanie right now. Let's assume that they are your children. Do you want to someday look back and say that you failed them? You are 22 years old now, old enough to be a father, smart enough to be a father. Teresa and I want to encourage you to be brave enough to make sure that these babies are born and will be cared for. We hope that you don't run away, and we don't think that you will run away, not from what we have seen of you in the past weeks." As Lisa smiled, looking deep into Chaucer's eyes, she reminded him of JOA and the deep bond he felt with his sister. If JOA were here right now, Chaucer could imagine her saying the same words. Perhaps even cousin Kathleen would, too.

Chaucer stayed silent, consumed in thinking, unable to form the right words to respond.

Teresa smiled at him. "God is with you, Chaucer; he will give you the strength to make the right decision. His love and mercy will never leave you, so be happy knowing that, OK?" and she stopped as the waiter delivered the plates of rice and beef. "You don't have to make up your mind now, but you will soon. Lisa and I will be at Heidelberg University for the coming semester, and we'll be home in Boston by June. We'll give you our addresses in Boston and our address in Heidelberg, so write us and tell us what you decide. We'll be supportive of you as sisters should be."

Chaucer nodded his head and drank some more wine. Then the table got quiet. Chaucer thought and ate, and the cousins did too.

After a good ten minutes of silence at their table in the noisy restaurant, Chaucer said softly, "I won't hurt those babies."

"Sorry, I couldn't hear you," said Lisa, with hope bright in her eyes.

"I won't let those babies be harmed. I will protect them; I want them to live," he said a bit louder, with the words getting stronger as he spoke to them. He looked at both women, giving them a small but firm nod.

The cousins smiled, even while chewing. Then they stood up and both went to Chaucer's side of the table and hugged him while he sat. Lisa said gently, "You'll be a fine brother for us both. We'll always be with you in spirit. You're a good person, Chaucer, and God's grace and mercy will be with you always. We love you." With that, they both kissed him on the cheek.

Well I had a lover,
I don't _think_ I'll risk _another_ these days
These days I seem to be afraid
To live the life that I have made in song

But it's just that I have been losing
For so long...My friend

Please don't confront me with my failures
I have not forgotten them...

— Jackson Browne

https://www.youtube.com/watch?v=X9bcztN7NmA

Chapter 31

Angels Fly On

EARLY THE NEXT MORNING after coffee, apples, bread, and cheese, Lisa and Teresa planned to leave for their long walk to Santiago and their anticipated reunion with St. James. Chaucer was to board the 8:10 a.m. train destined for Bilbao on the north coast, then travel on to San Sebastian where he hoped to spend the night before crossing the border to Bordeaux the next day.

The Boston cousins walked Chaucer to the train station. It was a bittersweet departure for him, as he had learned much from them. They had restored his faith and comfort in women. They had showed to him happiness, kindness, and grace of spirit that he had not had in his relationship with any woman except his Grandmother Giroux, cousin Kathleen, and JOA. When he first met Lisa and Teresa three weeks earlier, he decided just to be joyful in their mutual happiness as cousins. They had proved in only a few weeks that they could be as trusting and loyal as any male friend that he had ever had. He very much enjoyed watching them, their fundamental joy and trust in being together, free of all worldly encumbrances except their backpacks. They had offered their gift of faith as an example to Chaucer of their friendship, asking for nothing from Chaucer but giving him much. He was going to miss them for a long time. Later on the train that day, he would miss them dearly.

At the train station they said their farewells. First Lisa hugged Chaucer tightly and kissed him on the cheek, and then it was Teresa's turn. Then they both stood facing Chaucer, and each took one of Chaucer's hands and held it with a tenderness of a mother.

Lisa smiled. "You have much to do, work to start, lives to protect. We know you will succeed, Chaucer; you have the strength and the brains to carry on. And we hope we will see you when we all are back home. You will find us, or we will find you. That is for certain, agreed?"

"Agreed." Chaucer grinned.

Teresa covered Chaucer's right hand with both her hands and looked deeply into his eyes. "I had a dream in the night about you and these two babies. You had them in your arms, and you were holding them tight, and they were smiling and cooing. Your father was standing next to you, and he was smiling too. He said to me, 'Teresa, these are my grandchildren, and my son is a good father. Our family is very proud of him.' Then I woke up. I think it was not a dream, Chaucer. I believe it was a prophesy sent to you through me. I believe with all my heart that this is your mission. I, we, believe in you." Teresa hugged him again.

As she turned, a tear dripped down her cheek, which she quickly wiped away and laughed, embarrassed. Then she and Lisa were gone, walking down the Camino de Santiago with the beautiful angels of God on their shoulders helping to lift their full backpacks.

Lisa had placed a small note in Chaucer's hand as she had held it. He decided to put it in his pocket and read it later on the train. So off he walked, going into the terminal in time to catch the 8:10 train to Bilbao by way of Oviedo.

After transferring to a different train later that morning in Oviedo, he found an empty cabin, so he stretched out on the bench seat. He took out the note from Lisa and unfolded it. It was in her handwriting, the gentle script of a young woman:

Dear Chaucer,

Teresa and I wanted to leave you with these words from the Book of 1 John 3:18 "My little children, let us not love in word or with tongue, but in deed and truth." You will be a good father in deed and truth, we know this because we have seen you as the kind and loving man who you are. It will be a great adventure for you, and you will do just fine.

Remember to look us up in the coming year when we are all home again.

You can reach us through Boston College Student Affairs, or these are our addresses: Lisa O'Conner, 3448 Ellis Rd., Newton, MA

Teresa Colby, 82 Paulson Rd., Newton, MA

Remember to carry the grace and mercy of God with you each day.

With love, Lisa O'Conner

BOOK THREE: CONVICTION

Chapter 32

St. Émilion

THE TRAIN ARRIVED LATE into Bordeaux after being held up at the crossing into France. The Civilian Guards (Guardia Civil) of the Franco government were anxiously searching for some Basque separatists who had attacked a convoy of government vehicles the day before outside of San Sebastian. They were interviewing every man and woman who were attempting to cross into France. Chaucer's Canadian passport gave him no advantage that day. With his longer hair, grown out over his time in Spain, he now looked like any suspect for any police purpose. After waiting an hour, then being searched and questioned by a brutish policeman in broken English, he was allowed to leave Spain.

With that matter solved, Chaucer felt happy to be only a week or so away from meeting his father in London. He missed Remy greatly, and he felt pleased, knowing that he would tell Remy about his decision about the babies. His decision created a new truth in him. He would be the father, and he would care for the children. His doubt was erased. He would be the giver of love and comfort to these children. He boarded the train for Bordeaux, thinking all these good thoughts now.

Arriving in Bordeaux, Chaucer found a hostel near the train station, and after walking around the city for a few hours, he stopped for dinner and returned early to his bed. He liked Bordeaux. It had a soft joyful happiness to it, maybe because it was the wine capital of France or just maybe because he now had an inner happiness and new resolve within him.

The next morning he boarded a bus for St. Émilion, a village about twenty miles east. His father's favorite wine, for any special occasion or meal in Ottawa, was always bottle or two of St. Émilion Chateau Ausone. He had many bottles in his wine cellar. Remy could discuss the vintage and the St. Émilion classic blend of Merlot and Cabernet Franc with any epicurean or oenologist. He learned about the wine during his time in the war and defended his beloved St. Émilion against any bottle of Medoc, Pomerol, or Paulillac challenger. Besides wanting to bring a couple bottles of Chateau Ausone to Remy in London, Chaucer was also on his way to pay his respects to an old friend of his father's in St. Émilion, that is if he could find him.

It was a warm winter morning when the bus unloaded passengers in the center of St. Émilion. Traces of snow remained from a storm a week before. Chaucer walked a few blocks to the Eglise Monolithe de St. Émilion, having seen the massive bell tower hovering over the village. The ancient and massive church, about 800 years old, had the biggest underground catacombs in Europe and attracted Christians and historians and tourists from all over the world.

Yet that imposing site was not why Chaucer had wanted to come to St. Émilion. Yes, it was about the wines that his father loved, but it was also to see if he could find a priest named Étienne DuBois. Father DuBois and Remy, along with his American and Royal Canadian Naval colleagues and the deceased French resistance fighter Jacque DuValle, had conducted a secret mission against the Nazi and Vichy forces in 1944 in support of the Allied invasion in the south of France, coinciding with the D-Day invasion in Normandy. They had stored weapons in the catacombs of the Eglise for distribution to the various French Resistance groups.

When Remy and his colleagues served as Royal Naval intelligence officers, they were tasked with getting the weapons off-loaded from a compromised neutral Brazilian ship along the coast near

Bordeaux. Because the Allied planes could not reach St. Émilion to airdrop the weapons and munitions and return to base given the distance and weight of the loads, the Allied command arranged for delivery by sea. Remy and his team were charged with the delivery and coordinating with the American OSS and British SOE agents already there. The clandestine operation was a keen part of the war history in St. Émilion that had survived to be told in the local schools and taverns.

When Chaucer reached the Eglise, he walked to the adjacent rectory to ask about Father DuBois. Chaucer knocked on the thick wooden door. A few minutes later, it opened and a stately white-haired man in a black cassock smiled and said, "Bonjour."

"Bonjour. I'm Chaucer Giroux from Ottawa, Canada, and I'm looking for Father DuBois."

The priest peered closely at him for a few seconds, almost as if he wanted to make sure he had heard correctly. "You are the son of Lt. Remy Giroux from Canada?" Father DuBois said softly in English with a heavily French accent.

Chaucer grinned, realizing he was talking to the legendary Father DuBois. "Yes, Father. Are you Father DuBois?" The priest nodded. "My father sends his greetings to you."

And so it was, that Chaucer's father had been at this very church in 1944. Father DuBois was a young priest then. He loved his native France and disliked the Vichy collaborators who had sucked up to the Nazis, but he had to co-exist with them at the directive of the Vatican. In the early autumn of 1944, as the Allies were overwhelming the Nazi forces and word was out that Father DuBois had spoken against Vichy, the Gestapo put him on a train for Germany destined for a work camp because he was young and strong. Before the train could reach the border though, the Allies bombed the rail line and stopped the train, rescuing all the prisoners, including Father DuBois.

By the time he was able to return to St. Émilion, Remy Giroux and the joint Canadian-American special team was gone. After the war, the church reassigned Father DuBois to new locations and other work in the French colonies of Senegal in West Africa, and then Mauritius in the Indian Ocean. He did not return to St. Émilion, his hometown, until 1970. It was then he learned that in 1955 Remy Giroux had visited St. Émilion in search of him while Remy was in Bordeaux on business. As the years went by, Father DuBois and Remy had exchanged letters but had not as yet been able to see each other in person. So Father DuBois was overjoyed to meet and shake hands with Chaucer, who bore a striking resemblance to the young Remy the priest remembered.

 Father DuBois gave Chaucer a complete tour of the Eglise, and from there they walked to a little tavern to meet a few of the other locals who remembered Remy and the events of 1944. Chaucer was overwhelmed by the hospitality of the villagers and the staff at the Eglise. The villagers relayed story after story about the war in heavily accented English, or Father DuBois translated for those who spoke in French. At Father Dubois' insistence, Chaucer readily agreed to spend two nights rather than leave the next day. Father DuBois showed Chaucer the actual small room in the Eglise where Remy had stayed during his time in St. Émilion. He insisted that Chaucer sleep in the very bed that Remy had slept in thirty years before. Chaucer made notes in his journal of all that happened as he wanted to share it with JOA and his father once he was home.

 The night before Chaucer was to leave for Mont St. Michel in Normandy, he and Father DuBois shared a simple dinner in the rectory. They also shared a bottle of Chateau Ausone, which Father DuBois had in his cellar (the owner of the vineyard was a parishioner and donated wines to the Eglise for the personal use of the clergy). Chaucer told the priest that Remy had remembered drinking some Chateau Ausone in 1944 with Father DuBois, and that Remy still considered it his favorite red wine.

 Chaucer had something else to talk about with Father DuBois but before he could bring it up, the thoughtful priest said, "My son, I have noticed a trouble in you the last two days. Am I correct?"

 Chaucer nodded in agreement.

 "Shall we talk about this? I believe that God has put us together these two days. Perhaps I can help you."

 So Chaucer proceeded to explain to Father DuBois his dilemma with Tessa and Stephanie and the babies. He told him that he had made his decision, the same decision that he had discussed with Lisa and Teresa a few days before.

 The priest sipped his wine. "My son, the biggest trouble was for you to get the devil out of your head. You see, when we pray, whether you sit in silence or whether you are walking in a park, God will come to you with answers. But first he has to help you get the evil out, and when that is done, then your goodness, grace, and true spirit can emerge."

He paused, observing Chaucer, then drank more wine, wiping his beard on his sleeve.

"You are the son of my friend, a friend of France, and a friend of the people of France. We make friends with those who we love, those who have offered us their service in the time of our greatest need. We witnessed the man of God who your father is. Are you not like him, my son? Are you not like your father, having lived in the same house with this great man?"

Chaucer's eyes dropped and he grew quiet. The priest sensed that perhaps he had said something wrong; he paused and waited.

Again, as before at times, Chaucer spoke in a voice so soft and quiet that it was barely audible.

The priest leaned in. "Tell me again my son, my old ears are weak."

So Chaucer told him about the family breakup, the divorce, and the separation from his father for five years. The priest nodded and drank more wine.

"That father of yours, like the heavenly Father, teaches us great lessons, lessons that we always keep inside of us, and when we need them, we open them. Our heavenly Father, your father, Remy, do not need to be with us then, for they have blessed us with a great strength to sustain us." He paused. "Blessed are they who hunger and thirst for righteousness, for they will be satisfied. Blessed are the merciful, for they will be shown mercy."

Chaucer listened, thought for a few minutes, and then smiled. He knew that the heavenly Father and his father, Remy, had given him the strength and the lessons to be the father to the children. And Father DuBois was kind enough to reaffirm that for him that day. Perhaps the bottle of Chateau Ausone had helped with the lesson.

Chapter 33

To Normandy

THE TRAINS TO THE NORMANDY COAST from St. Émilion could get there without going through Paris, but it was a near two-day trip given the number of transfers. Chaucer boarded in St. Émilion, then changed trains in Périgueux, then Limoges and then onto the Loire town of Saumur where Chaucer spent the night. The next day, the train from Saumur took Chaucer to Angers, where he switched and boarded a train to Rennes, finally arriving in St. Malo on the coast after dark. The weather had changed, and the cold winter winds were blowing in from the Atlantic and down the English Channel, creating a big chop even inside the St. Malo harbor area. Chaucer was able to find an inexpensive hotel near the train station, and in the early morning he took a bus along the coast to Mont-Saint-Michel. He planned his timing to catch the low tide so he could walk the road out to the historic rock and spend the day, leaving with the later low tide. The late bus then would then take him to Cherbourg where he planned to take the overnight ferry across the channel to Portsmouth.

The low tide at Mont-Saint-Michel peaked at 8:45 a.m. that day, and his bus dropped him at 9:30 a.m., so he hustled down the road, watching the incoming water beginning to fill the marshes. During winter, the visitors and tourists were sparse, and it was joyful for him to walk the mostly empty narrow streets in Mont-Saint-Michel, visiting the few shops and galleries that were open and stopping for coffee and lunch. His bus to Cherbourg would depart at 4 p.m., so he had to mind his time and not get caught on the rock when the road was flooded over.

At mid-day, with much of his walking around the small streets completed, he hiked to the top of the pathway, to the cathedral where the small group of Benedictine monks lived in seclusion. The church was open, and he walked into the cloisters that looked down on the Channel waters. It was a sunny day, but again windy and cold, and he could see the outline of Jersey Island forty miles to the north. Chaucer had dressed in a heavy sweater, scarf, and jacket, and he needed the warmth that day. But he had come for the views, a plan that he had made long ago so nothing the weather could throw at him could deter him. Now he had an additional and different focus for being in this most holy location. He wanted to cauterize his decision about the babies into his heart and mind, into his very soul. It was a life-changing decision for them all.

The cold wind blew into his face as he stared out into the rough Channel waters far below. Today there were no boats; the sea was too rough and too cold. But he saw hope, he saw a chance to become a man in the eyes of his father, and that meant everything to him. Remy had never told him all the details about this mission to St. Émilion during the war. Father DuBois had now done that for him. As it would be unlikely that Chaucer would ever become a soldier, he still wanted his dad to know that he could also be true and responsible. He thought that he did not want these babies to grow up wondering about their father. Who was he, what kind of a man was he? Was he honorable and kind? Chaucer decided that those questions would not be necessary for these babies, his babies. He thought that those questions should not apply to any babies in the world. God did not want it that way, he believed. It was a fundamental law of humanity, and of God. Fathers need to stay and take care of their children. The more he thought about it, the more he understood it. Some species could create and leave, but not humans. God had not created humanity to be that way. Chaucer smiled as he knew that he had purged the devil from his head.

Chaucer believed that Father DuBois was right. He was right about Remy's character. It was the character of his father that Chaucer had seen all his life. Chaucer had not believed that he could be that good, that just and honest, yet somehow the priest believed it.

Perhaps it was Father DuBois's connection to the Holy Spirit, or perhaps it really was something so simple that Chaucer looked like his father, his voice was lately sounding like his father, and perhaps the priest just knew the son of the brave Remy would be like him too. Regardless, the priest knew; he knew.

※   ※   ※

The next day in the local bus station, Chaucer saw the sign for Villedieu-les-Poeles, a small town about fifteen miles to the east, but his bus would not be passing through it. He remembered how his mother, Olivia, had often talked about the copper pans that her own mother had acquired on her trips to France, how she would always visit this town Villedieu-les-Poeles, the place where they made the copper cookware. Olivia had numerous large and small copper pans and kettles, beautiful and shiny, which her mother had given Olivia over the years. Olivia actually loathed cooking (she would say it was the work of old women, not her generation who were trying to free themselves from the kitchen, the washroom, and the nursery) yet she displayed the shiny copper cookware in her Ottawa kitchen for her friends to envy. Chaucer thought about how his mother had freed herself from so much of these traditional roles of the women. Yet in doing this, she had simultaneously cut the bonds that mothers have with their children. Chaucer still had the emotional bloodstains from how she had cut her motherly relationship with him. He saw those bloodstains all over JOA as well.

So on this day, he would make no effort to find time to visit the town of Villedieu les Poeles and search for the perfect copper cookware for his mother, or his grandmother Photina, who likewise he had never really understood. It was a day like this that had him thinking about his mother and how she had left so much undone, so much abandoned, so much that both JOA and Chaucer had left behind when she took them west to Vancouver.

He remembered the nights in his boyhood room in Vancouver and Victoria, missing his father and the home in Ottawa. He remembered thinking in those days and nights that in time when he had his own children, that he would not do these things to them. Thinking of these memories this day on the bus to Cherbourg made Chaucer very confident that his thinking about the babies had been the right decision. He was feeling that he could become a mature man now, like Remy. The weight of his decision was feeling much lighter by the day. He was feeling good about being right.

*   *   *

The ferry to Portsmouth departed just before midnight. Chaucer boarded about 10:30 p.m. He quickly found a passenger lounge chair, which he moved to a spot behind the main bulkhead on the stern of the top deck. It would be a cold night for the crossing but he loved sleeping outside under the stars, which were bountiful this night. With lounge chair and foot rest sheltered in the stern, the wind from the passage and the diesel smoke from the engine stack would blow over him, yet he would be able to see the sky, and rock gently with the motion of the big boat. He purchased the biggest cup of tea and bag of tarts that he could find inside at the food counter, then rolled out his sleeping bag on his chair, ready for the overnight ride.

When the ferry left port and cleared the breakwater, the Channel was calmer than the prior day. Chaucer lay back in his chair, drinking his tea. As he looked through the stern rails, he saw the lights of Cherbourg harbor slowly fade into the darkness. He felt a heavy load being lifted from him. He felt the closing of a chaotic part of his young life, and he believed that the seed of the good and just man that his father Remy was, was also growing in him. His life could now be different. He would make it different. He knew that he had to let go of his hurt. All these things that had occupied his mind every day had stolen his energy and blocked the kindness and mercy that could have healed him. He hoped now, on this night, as the ferry moved across the waters of the English Channel, that these bad things had not sailed with him from Cherbourg. He knew it was time to let it all go. He prayed that he could.

As he lay back, he watched the stars sparkle. The slow rolling of the ship, and the darkness and the stars above gave him the idea that he was in a womb, as a baby would be. As his babies were now, he thought. He wondered if they were thinking about him as he was imagining them comfortable inside their mothers at this moment. He felt their darkness but also their security, as he was warm and tight in his sleeping bag. He would embrace the love and kindness and mercy of his father, the man he loved, and who had never left him as a father. He could be this kind of father, like Remy.

Chapter 34

The Bear

WHEN THE BOAT ARRIVED IN PORTSMOUTH in the early morning, it was a cold, damp English winter day. He found a phone booth and called the London office of his father's firm. The manager told Chaucer that his father had gone to Maidenhead, about 20 kilometers southwest of London, and he wanted Chaucer to meet him at the Bear Hotel in town. So Chaucer caught a local train and upon arriving in Maidenhead, he walked to the Bear Hotel to find his father. At the front desk, the day manager gave Chaucer a room key and said his father was expected in the afternoon. Chaucer went to the hotel restaurant, had a hearty breakfast, then decided to go to the room, take a much-needed hot shower, and wait for his father to arrive.

When Remy walked into the room later, Chaucer was sound asleep on one of the beds, so he put his bag down quietly, left a note on the table, and went to the pub for a drink. Remy had not seen Chaucer in eight months. He looked at him sleeping and smiled broadly. He remembered Chaucer as a boy, sleeping like this in his Ottawa bedroom. He loved his son very much and was looking forward to being with him in the days ahead.

* * *

"Hi, Dad," said Chaucer as he walked up to Remy in the hotel bar. They hugged mightily; Remy kissed his son's cheek and rubbed his hand through his long hair. After Remy released Chaucer from the bear hug, Chaucer spoke first. "I thought I was to meet you in London, Dad?"

"Well," Remy began, smiling broadly, "during the war, I was stationed with our small Canadian Naval intelligence unit here in Maidenhead for a month as the invasion was being planned. I have not been back in all these years, and I thought it would be a good place for us to first meet up. It is a small and quiet town; I think we need that, don't you?" he said smiling.

Chaucer agreed and sipped the beer that his father had bought for him. "How's JOA? Is she doing well in school? What do you hear from Mom?"

"JOA is doing very good progressing towards her graduation," Remy said smiling. "I don't hear much news from your mother," he continued with a grin of firm resignation. He grabbed his pint glass, lifted it to Chaucer, and looked at his son. "Here's a toast to our family, and the great joy of seeing you again. We have much to talk about the next few days." Chaucer nodded and affirmed with a smile. It was time, it was the right time.

After they finished their beer, Remy said, "Come on, Son, I want to go for a walk and show you something in town." They left the Bear Hotel and walked the quiet streets of Maidenhead and talked. Remy took Chaucer to the big field at the edge of town where he and the Canadians and Yanks had bivouacked in their large tents. Perhaps two thousand men had camped there in the months prior to the invasion on D-Day in 1944. Remy had a few photos of all the tents and jeeps in an album in Ottawa that he had shown his children years ago. Now he and his son walked on the grass that was in those photos.

"What was it like then, waiting for the invasion?" Chaucer asked.

"The funny thing was, we knew we would be going but just not when. My unit, we had prepared our reports from our earlier missions, and we were not sure how we would be used after that, until a month before the actual invasion, then our commander assigned our group to a new mission. We were sent to the coast, actually to Portsmouth where your ferry came in. They had prepared us for a special mission near Bordeaux. It was me and the other three guys in my Recon unit. It was long ago but being back here in Maidenhead now it all seems like last month."

Chaucer smiled broadly and said, "Dad, Father DuBois said to say hello to you!"

Remy laughed loudly. "Did you really see him?"

"Yes, a week ago I stopped in St. Émilion, and he was at the Eglise. He was so happy to see me. I told him I would be seeing you soon and he was delighted. He showed me all around, and he even put me up for a couple of nights. He actually had me sleep in the bed where you had slept twenty-eight years ago. "

"I am so happy that you were able to see him. I really need to get down there myself soon. Better yet, we'll go together. I'll review my travel plans, and we'll do it together, maybe even bring JOA, too."

"That would be great, Dad... Oh, I have something for you that he gave me before I left."

Remy smiled. "And what would that be?"

"I told him that your favorite wine was Chateau Ausone, so before I left he took me into the wine cellar at the Eglise, and he gave me a bottle of the 1945 Ausone. He said you would appreciate it," Chaucer said.

Remy burst out, "Oh my God, he really gave you a '45 Ausone, seriously?"

"Yup, he said he wanted to imagine the two of us drinking it together."

"Chaucer, the '45 vintage was one of the best years ever for all of Bordeaux." He paused, smiled, then added, "Maybe God made it that way for the suffering that the French had to endure for all the war years."

"I have it in my backpack in the room."

"Well, we'll bring it into the restaurant tonight and have it with our meal. I can't think of a better way to honor Father DuBois and celebrate that I have gotten to see my son again!"

And so they did. They toasted Father Dubois, JOA, Canada, the Queen, and even the Montreal Canadians hockey team. It was a glorious reunion dinner for Remy and Chaucer.

* * *

The next day, Chaucer shared with his father the changes in his thinking that had come to him, and how he viewed his responsibility as the father of the two babies. He mentioned meeting the cousins Lisa and Teresa from Boston and how they helped him better understand his situation. Remy was so proud of his son, and he smiled in recognition. He had prayed for this moment.

At dinner the second night Remy decided that he would ask Chaucer if he was ready to join his company. He knew it would have to be a decision that his son made voluntarily, and not forced on him if it was to be successful for the two of them and for the company. Remy opened the discussion, saying, "Our senior manager from our U.S. Gulf Coast operations has been transferred to London and his work has expanded greatly, so we need someone to help him over the next four to five months until we can get our man from Suez up to London permanently. I think that it would be a good time for you to think about joining the company permanently too. This short-term work will give you a good feel for the business, and it will allow things with the babies to stabilize. What do you think?"

Chaucer was not surprised by this. His intuition had been that his father was going to ask him about working for the company. Chaucer felt ready, and he happily agreed. He was glad that Remy had presented it. The timing seemed right.

Remy and Chaucer spoke in earnest about the job and the babies. Tessa would be having her baby in a month in Buffalo. Remy had already been sending her money for medical appointments and baby things. Tessa had been grateful and had promised to allow Remy and Chaucer to be a part of the baby's life, especially when she returned to school to finish her degree. Stephanie and Sissy were working in San Francisco at the company office, and Remy was also paying the rent on their apartment. The talk of an abortion was over, and Stephanie was going to have the baby. Remy was hoping that he could adopt the child because Stephanie was, as she had said to Remy, "not ready to settle down yet." At least the rough outline of a life for the babies was now in place, and both Remy and Chaucer were pleased with this. It seemed to be a good start.

Chapter 35

London

"JASPER, THIS IS MY SON, Chaucer," Remy said, standing in his London office. Jasper and Chaucer shook hands. "As we discussed, he will be assisting you for the next four or five months until we can get Walid here from Egypt." Jasper Grandemaison was Remy's valued senior manager. Jasper had been with Remy for more than 20 years and had set up the operations in Houston, New Orleans, Tampa, and Miami for him. He was bringing his experience to London as Remy and his partners had recently bought a competitor who was retiring, and they needed a trusted, experienced manager to take over the new acquisition. Jasper was a native of New Orleans, and like Remy, his family had an old French colonial heritage. But Jasper's relatives had left Canada long ago and had migrated west, then down the Mississippi to settle in the French town of New Orleans, Louisiana (NOLA).

Jasper and his wife, Margola, who was a well-connected antiques dealer in New Orleans, had been successful and had invested wisely. Their oldest daughter, Bridgette, and their youngest daughter, Magnolia (Maggie) had graduated from Tulane University, and the middle daughter, Suzette, had graduated magna cum laude from Louisiana State University in Baton Rouge. Margola was happy to try London for a year as their three daughters had all finished their undergraduate degrees, and their big house in the garden district was lonely for them, so when the opportunity was presented to Jasper, she agreed to go. Besides, any intelligent antique dealer like Margola knew that she would love to be in London, home of the best auction houses in the world. Maggie was also coming to London for a semester that was part of her master of social work degree at Tulane.

Within a week of arriving, Margola found a wonderful rental unit in the Mayfair district of London for her and Jasper, near where Remy had a small flat that he or others from the company would use while in London. It was there that Chaucer would now live while in London on his temporary assignment with the company.

*   *   *

Once Remy had set Jasper and Chaucer up with the work as office director and temporary assistant director for the new operations in the acquired company, he was going to Glasgow and then home. He was pleased with the way that Jasper and Chaucer had connected during his two weeks working with them. But he had other company business in Glasgow, and then he needed to return to Ottawa.

The night before his train trip to Glasgow, he and Chaucer went out for a celebratory dinner. Sipping his champagne, Remy said, "I'm very pleased that you and Jasper are going to be working together for the next few months. When Walid comes from the Suez, I want you and Jasper to brief him on all the things that you have done. Then, I would like you to come to Ottawa and finish your last year at Carleton and get your degree. They also have a fine one-year MBA program through which you'll be able to earn credits for the work that you are doing here. How does that sound to you?"

Chaucer smiled. He had not felt this settled in a long time. Finally, he seemed that he could see his future amid all the confusion and craziness of the past year. "Thanks, Dad, I would really like that. I'll want to go to Buffalo and see Tessa and our child. Will you come with me the first time I go?"

Remy wrinkled his eyebrows and hesitated. "Son, no, I believe that this is best to begin just between you and Tessa. Perhaps she has changed, maybe the two of you can talk about a life together. It's your responsibility to construct a new relationship with Tessa, and whether you remain separate or get back together, I want that decision to be yours." Then he smiled a confident smile, a smile that was seen by Chaucer as his father being the kindest man he had ever known. Chaucer acknowledged his father with a nod, said, "I understand," and then poured them both a second glass of bubbly.

*   *   *

Thus, to Glasgow Remy Giroux went. Although Remy rarely mentioned the office there to Chaucer, Remy seemed to be very fond of going there on all his trips to Europe. Each trip either started in Glasgow or ended in Glasgow, Chaucer recalled. Now immersed in the company business and affairs, he became curious of this. Perhaps it was Remy's work with the Royal Navy, and it involved a national security matter is what Chaucer guessed.

Jasper himself had not been to the Glasgow office so he could not provide any inside information to Chaucer. After a few days, Chaucer became so busy with sorting ship manifests and insurance coverage issues that he forgot about the question of the Glasgow office.

*   *   *

In the second month of his work in London, Chaucer met Magnolia, Jasper's youngest daughter. She had arrived a few days before from New Orleans where she was working on her graduate degree. Her program at King's College in London was to begin the following week.

One afternoon when Chaucer was in his dress shirt and tie, on the phone with his Lloyd's of London agent, he noticed a confident-looking, young and pretty woman come in the office door, looking for someone or something. He felt an attraction to her immediately, as she had long black hair pulled back and piled on her head, like so many of the Englishwomen wore their hair. She was neither short nor tall, large nor small. Her body just seemed to fit her perfectly. She looked curiously at Chaucer, as a teacher would look at a sixth-grader who was not seated when the bell sounded for the start of class. Chaucer seemed a touch embarrassed, but he then noticed a soft grin below her dark eyebrows, her black eyes perfectly set in a subtle beauty that was a face of purpose and poise.

"Hello, you must be, Chaucer," she said firmly, then paused. "My father has spoken so kindly of you." She extended her hand, a hand that was warm and firm to him.

"Yes, hello. And you must be Jasper's daughter Magnolia."

"I am. Please call me Maggie. I am sure we will be friends soon, and I prefer Maggie," she said with a nod.

"Your father has just stepped out and should be back in a moment or two. Can I get you a tea or a coffee?"

* * *

When Jasper returned to the office, he invited Chaucer to his flat as Margola had planned a special New Orleans dinner for the four of them — a favorite Beef Burgundy and a New Orleans-styled soufflé of onion, young potatoes, and cheese. They started the evening with fresh oysters just in from the French coast that afternoon. Paired with a bottle of Moet Champagne, it was the perfect combination to begin the meal and start the conversations.

The long dinner conversation was a great introduction for Chaucer and Maggie, who appeared to have much in common despite being from different countries, of different religions, and of different academic experiences. Being at the table with Maggie's affable parents seemed to help those differences evaporate. It seemed like a magical evening for Chaucer, as he was missing the company of Remy in London.

They proceeded to enjoy three hours of interesting talk, lubricated with two bottles of Bordeaux Claret. The evening ended with coffee after 10 p.m. and made Chaucer's walk to his flat a pleasant end to a special evening. He had enjoyed the company of Jasper and Margola very much, and he believed that he had made a good connection with Maggie. Chaucer was greatly charmed and impressed with Maggie's intelligence, smile, and maturity. He could not remember ever feeling this sense of amazement and awe about a woman after only being in her presence for just one day, not even the night that he had first met Joanie in Naples. But he did not want to be in love again, as least not right now. He had so many thoughts of the babies, Tessa, Stephanie, and even Joanie still in his mind; how could he have room for another relationship?

That evening when he laid on his bed, the food and wine comforting him well, he went to sleep and dreamed of a new life. The vision was of him, an older Chaucer, being in a fine house somewhere with a breeze softly blowing in the French doors of a room, the curtains moving gently, and some young children playing on the lawn outside, their voices carrying into the room where he was sitting. A voice came from another room, quietly singing an Edith Piaf song in French, and he was at perfect ease with it all. Was it really happening or was he dreaming it?

She then walked into the room with glasses of red wine, one of which she handed to Chaucer. The woman was Maggie. She looked at him directly, with a loving face, and her lips said, "This is what you wanted isn't it, Chaucer? This is what I saw in your face that first afternoon we met. I could see it in your eyes; I could see the hollowness and loneliness in your face. You wanted this to be your life."

And then he woke up. It was still the middle of the night. He drank some water from a glass on the nightstand. He was happy about his dream, and he wanted to go back to sleep to continue the dream, but he couldn't now. He just kept thinking about Maggie and the things that they had talked about at dinner. He laid in bed, the streetlamps sending in light that made shadows on the wall. He kept thinking about Maggie, and then when he awoke again it was 6 a.m., and he had to be at the office in two hours.

* * *

In the next weeks, Chaucer learned that Maggie had a boyfriend in London. He was another graduate student from Tulane who was also taking a semester in London, studying the law in the English courts and clerking for a magistrate who oversaw commercial bankruptcies. Chaucer would see Maggie and her boyfriend together occasionally at his favorite coffee shop or at a pub in Mayfair where many students congregated after hours. Chaucer met a couple of local English women his age but his urge for love was vacant; his desires were muted for the time. His work with Jasper was not intellectually difficult but it was a very precise type of work that required his concentration. The ships that the company either owned or leased, or leased to others, had to have proper maritime insurance for each journey, for both cargo and crew. Booking and scheduling of loading and unloading had to be targeted, and with the often-unpredictable ocean weather and other delays at sea, every ship in the organization needed oversight. There was little margin for error.

The new office in London had to manage all the systems and ensure that they were in synch with the rest of the company's large fleet. The company was nearing the end of its third decade in business. Chaucer enjoyed the work, and he proved quite up to the confidence that his father had put in him. Jasper reported to Remy that his son was working out very well.

In his third month in the job, Chaucer was feeling confident in his work and in his relationship with Jasper and the four clerical staff members in the office. One day he received a phone call from Maggie. She invited him to meet her after work for a drink at The Cumberland Station, a local pub near where they both lived. He agreed. He was curious as to the basis for the call as he had not seen Maggie in about three weeks. It was a mid-May evening, and the springtime daylight was stretching out nearly to 10 p.m. The trees were full of green leaves, and the smell of spring flowers was penetrating even the ubiquitous smell of diesel in the London streets. Chaucer was delighted to be walking to see Maggie.

"Hi, it's been a while. How are your studies going?" he said to Maggie as he came to the table carrying a pint of Samuel Smith ale and a Sancerre wine for Maggie, her favorite.

"Thanks for coming," she said with her beautiful New Orleans smile. Her southern accent was subtle, just enough to be noticed, and Chaucer loved to hear her voice and listen to her speak.

"How's Richard?" he asked.

"He's gone back to New Orleans, a week ago. He finished his work here and needed to get back for the start of summer classes. He wants to take the bar exam in a year, so he is pushing himself to finish and be ready."

"Seems like a nice guy," Chaucer said.

She looked around the room, then at Chaucer. "He is, he is a good man, but we have decided to go in different directions now. One of his old girlfriends started writing him while he was here, so he told me that he was going to see her when he got home."

"Oh, I see; how do you feel about that?" Chaucer said with a look of concern.

"OK, I guess. I mean we were good together but not in love as I found out. His studies and ideas about work as a government lawyer were his most important plans, which was fine, but I just wanted him to be honest with me, and I learned that he was not," she said.

"Oh, yeah, I guess it is hard to be trusting when you feel that the other person is not confiding in you and being honest." Chaucer took a deep breath, puffing his cheeks and exhaling slowly. He thought of Tessa.

Maggie smiled, then giggled softly. "It seems that you know what I mean, yes?" she asked.

Chaucer smiled, then laughed. They had touched each other like kids who are both eating really good chocolate ice cream at the same time, and then smiling at each other knowing that the other kid is having as much joy eating the same ice cream as you are. Communal joy.

That night for over two hours they talked and drank beer and wine and split a big plate of a comforting Shepard's Pie from the bar. They talked about past boyfriends and girlfriends and how things had not worked out or had worked out then didn't later. Chaucer, knowing that honesty with Maggie was the only currency, told her about Tessa, Joanie, and Stephanie. He told her most everything, except about the coming child with Stephanie and the baby boy that Tessa had delivered. That was a bridge too far that night.

Maggie told Chaucer about her previous boyfriends and how each of them had started out sincere and loving but then devolved into either an uncaring, egotistical person or a person who had not been honest with her, or both. She was not put off by what Chaucer told her about his life the past year, and even held his hand near the end of night, knowing that it had been difficult for both of them to speak of all these matters. She looked into his eyes and saw the hurt he had as he spoke about it. Perhaps it was her social worker training that allowed her to do this, or perhaps it was that she was gravitating to Chaucer for being Remy's son, or maybe it was both those feelings and others that she had yet to understand in herself. Whatever it was, by the end of the evening, they both felt a strong bond with each other. Before they left the pub, Chaucer asked Maggie if she would like to attend church with him at Westminster Abbey on Sunday. He had been going there because he liked the minister and being in the Abbey with all the surrounding history, its dead poets, and literary giants.

"You know that I am a Catholic, right?" she said.

"Yes, your father told me, but God doesn't care how you believe, just if, and the Anglicans allow all Christians to take communion if you'd like to take it."

Maggie smiled. "OK, it's a deal. What time?"

"How about I meet you at your flat about 9, is that OK?"

Her smile was broad and genuine. This made Chaucer quite happy.

Chapter 36

And Mother Dear

When Chaucer returned to the company flat that night, there was a letter from California waiting for him in the post box. It was from his mother and dated three weeks before:

> Dear Chaucer,
>
> I trust this letter finds you well in London. I am glad you have been enjoying working with your father's company. I am sure he is quite happy about that.
>
> Thank you for your letters from Spain, Portugal, and St. Émilion. They have been forwarded to me here in Los Angeles. Your travels have been interesting, and I am sure that you have had some great experiences and met many fine people.
>
> I have been in Los Angeles for three months. Perhaps JOA has written to tell you. She visited me here once but did not like it so she returned to Victoria to check on the house before going back to Ottawa. Her college days are very good for her, and her health and happiness are fine. My time here has been spent with a film producer, Jacob Rosensteen, and his team of screenwriters. Jacob's company purchased the film rights to my second book, and

he then hired me to assist with the screenplay. He is from South Africa, and he owns a big vineyard there and other land. I have fallen in love with him, and he has now asked me to move into his home here while we work on the project. He is a sailor, and he has taken me sailing, which I truly enjoyed. I wanted you to know this about Jacob and me because I have not mentioned it to JOA or your father yet, but I will soon.

If the screenplay is finished on schedule, I should be back to Victoria in two to three months. If you or JOA or your father have any need to stay at the house there, please use it.

I never thought that I would ever leave Victoria for any length of time but after my first week in Los Angeles with my agent, and meeting Jacob, things changed in a way that I never imagined they would. I am happy here, and I want to share these things with you.

I will write again soon and send my future letters to Ottawa as you father tells me (we still call each other) that you will likely be back there for your final year in university.

Please know that I am happy, and that I miss you. I hope this movie project is successful, but I dreadfully miss my quiet days in Victoria and writing in my loft.

Much love,
Mother

    Chaucer laughed and lay the letter on the table. He was happy to get the letter and know that his mother was happy. His laughter was predicated on learning that his mother actually had left Victoria for some new experiences. He smiled when he thought of this man Jacob Rosensteen because he knew what a case his mother could be, and that Jacob likely had not yet seen that demanding, self-isolating side of his mother. He, JOA, and Remy had learned the hard way, and it had not been easy for them. But those days for the three of them were over; they were free of mother bird now. It would be Jacob's turn, his test. Chaucer smiled.

    That night in bed, Chaucer lay thinking about Maggie. He liked her very much and admired her independence greatly. He was hoping to be able to spend more time with her. He told himself that he had no illusions of anything beyond a new friendship, but the Devil in him just laughed at that.

"Are you joking, Chaucer? You really want to be in love with her. You really get excited just being around her, just like that first meeting with her, stop kidding yourself, you dummy. But you didn't tell her the whole truth, did you, Chaucer?" asked the Devil and then the Devil laughed very, very hard.

"No, really, I just want to be friends. She is so relaxed, very confident. I need to absorb some of that from her. Bug off, leave me alone. We'll be friends, Maggie and me. Just watch me, I'll prove it to you," Chaucer thought. He set his alarm for 7 a.m., rolled over and went to sleep.

*   *   *

Sunday was a damp day, but the London rains that had threatened never came. Chaucer met Maggie at her flat where they chatted with Jasper and Margola, then they walked to Westminster Abbey for the 10:15 a.m. service. It was not far from the Mayfair flat on Clarges Street.

As they walked, Chaucer told Maggie that he had been coming to the service at Westminster almost every Sunday since he had been working with her father.

"Did you attend with regularity in Ottawa as well?" she asked, as she was a Catholic who tried to attend weekly mass whether in New Orleans or London.

"No, I didn't," he said, "but during the last months I have started to go again. I find that I am better at understanding myself when I spend time in a church. I even will stop in Westminster on my way back from the company office. It is a great building, far more than a church for me."

"How so?" she asked with an inquisitive look.

"Well, I love Poet's Corner and all the history of the place," and then he stopped, turned his back to Maggie, cleared his throat with a loud "Ah hum."

Maggie giggled. "What are you doing, you silly boy?"

Chaucer spun around with a most austere and somber look and proceeded in a profound voice, as would an old professor:

> *Of old the bard who struck the noblest strains*
> *Great Geoffrey Chaucer, now this tomb retains.*
> *If for the period of his life you call,*
> *the signs are under that will note you all.*
> *In the year of our Lord 1400, on the 25th day of October.*
> *Death is the repose of cares.*
>
> *N. Brigham charged himself with these in the name of the Muses 1556*

When he finished, Maggie smiled, laughed, and clapped. "Bravo, bravo," she cheered.

Chaucer put his left hand on his stomach, waved his right hand in the air and bowed an acknowledgement to Maggie, and they both laughed loudly.

"My mother made me memorize that as a boy," Chaucer explained. "She said if I am Chaucer Giroux, I must know the words on the tombstone of my namesake in Westminster Abbey, and so by age 6 or 7 she would call me into her parties or gatherings at home and introduce me to the guests. 'Gentlemen and ladies, here is our son, Chaucer, to recite blah, blah, blah' and the guests would clap when I finished, and I would bow and run off for my reward — a big bowl of ice cream."

"I'm sure that grew old for you after a time," Maggie said with a touch of sympathy.

"Well, I do like ice cream, so I tolerated it." Chaucer grinned. "She wanted me to recite more Chaucer, but my father put an end to it after a couple of years. He said it was not good for me and embarrassing for him, and so she stopped it."

Maggie was properly impressed, and the remaining conversation walking to Westminster was warm and happy.

When they arrived, they found seats in the center of the massive cathedral. Maggie whispered that after the service she wanted to see the Geoffrey Chaucer tomb, and he nodded.

The service began and the Anglican priest spoke that day of St. Joseph and his devotion to Mother Mary, his love of Jesus, and his family. Maggie absorbed it all, having heard a similar message many times before. But Chaucer sat motionless and silent. He heard the priest talk about how important it was to have strong fathers in each family, and Chaucer thought about Remy and how he had been that for him. And then he realized that he himself was anything but a St. Joseph. His pride and arrogance had engulfed him. He had walked away from his babies. He had made excuses, and he had made self-satisfying reasons to ignore fatherhood. His relationship with these women had never been conducted with the idea of having babies with them, as least not while he was so young. He had his life to lead. He could not be forced to be a father.

Maggie looked to Chaucer because he was quiet and motionless. His face was like stone and she was startled to see that his eyes were moist. She reached over and put her hand on his, and he acknowledged it with a small nod. Maggie sensed a deepness of thought in him, but she did not yet know all his troubles, although she could see his troubles were not buried like Geoffrey Chaucer was, not far from where they were seated.

* * *

In the following weeks, Chaucer and Maggie saw each other almost every other day. By the end of the second week, Chaucer knew that he had to tell her about the babies. He knew that if he kept it from her any longer that she would surely question his trust and truthfulness. Yet he remained hesitant.

Over morning tea at the neighborhood bakery in the third week of their meetings, Chaucer decided to take the plunge.

"It's time to tell you everything about Tessa and Stephanie, the two women I spoke to you about, do you remember?" he said, biting his lip, a little tense.

"Yes, I remember. Why, weren't you honest with me the first time?" she said, her face serious.

"I was honest, but not complete. There is more to the story, more that I must tell, and I hope you will understand." Chaucer was scared now, so he waited, took a deep breath, and then started, speaking slowly and deliberately.

"OK, you know that I was seeing Tessa for well over a year at the university, and that I believed we were dating just each other the entire time, and then I told you what happened in New York City last summer, right?"

Maggie nodded, her face expressionless.

"And I told you about how I met Stephanie in Mexico during my two weeks there, right?"

Maggie nodded again.

"Well, this is the rest of both situations. My father knows about everything, and he is completely supportive of me, so this is not a family crisis for me, nor I have tried to hide this. I just didn't know how far you and I might progress, and now that I feel we have something to build on, well, I want you to know the rest."

Maggie wrinkled her forehead, waiting for more.

"OK, I found out last fall that Tessa was pregnant. She delivered a baby boy last month in Buffalo, New York. She and I will not be married, now or ever, but I will support her and the child. My father is helping, and he wants this baby to be his grandchild very much. He has spoken to Tessa, and a plan is being worked out so she can finish her degree at the university this year. That's the rest of the story."

Maggie sat quietly, thinking. "OK, hmmm, and what about Stephanie?"

"Well, even though I was with her in Mexico for just a few nights, she is pregnant now. She wanted me to pay for her to get an abortion in California."

Maggie remained quiet. Chaucer was surprised that she had not gotten up and walked away yet. But she sat and stayed calm. "OK, I can understand how you would not want to tell me all this a few weeks ago. Go on, finish about Stephanie, please."

Chaucer could feel sweat running down his back, thinking that he was blowing his chance to ever have a relationship with Maggie.

"Well, my father convinced her not to have an abortion," he said.

"And how did he do that?" she asked, wondering if this whole matter was real.

"Our company has an office in San Francisco, and that's where Stephanie is now with her roommate Sissy. Dad hired them both to work in the office and is paying for her medical care and the rent on their apartment. Stephanie has agreed to allow my father to legally adopt the baby, his grandchild."

"And you and Stephanie are not going to get married either?" she asked.

Chaucer gulped, feeling like he was in need of oxygen. "Well, when I met her in Mexico, I told her I was going back to L.A. in two weeks. We got together while I was in the beach camp. She invited me into her tent a few nights after I met her. I know this sounds crazy but it's true. Then when I told her I had to get back home with my cousin Jean Marc, well, she lost it. She walked away, and then she wouldn't even say goodbye. So I left her a note with my address in Ottawa, and then I drove back to Los Angeles to get Jean Marc. I had no idea that she would get pregnant because she told me that she was taking birth control pills."

"And you believed her?" she said.

"Of course, I believed her. I didn't want her to get in trouble. Heck, we had just met, and she asked me into her tent. I never suggested it or forced her."

"You had plans to marry Tessa, did you?"

"Well, we never even talked about that. We were just trying to finish our degrees, and then sometime after graduation we might have discussed that. Plus she was a year older than me so I thought that she would be moving to New York City for work so the idea of marriage was pretty remote. I really didn't have thoughts about marriage a year ago."

Maggie continued to sit expressionless, thinking. They were silent for a while.

Finally, she spoke. "OK, let me respond as a social worker first and as a Catholic second...It seems that both mothers are being cared for in your plans with medical care, education, and employment, at least for now. That is good. As a Catholic, I am very pleased that neither woman decided to have an abortion. These children are God's gift, and no parent, or couple, should ever abort a baby that they created through the abundant grace of God." She said this firmly and with conviction looking Chaucer in the eye. "So here's my other concern about you. Is it your style to just sleep around with any girl that says, 'Hey, buddy, come into my tent?'" she said with a degree of sarcasm.

Chaucer took a deep breath and looked at the ceiling. He knew Maggie was right; his behavior had been poor and not the best to define who he was, or how he wanted to be. "Maggie, I'm almost 23 years old, and I have had exactly four intimate relationships in my life — a very short one for a week at school in Vancouver, then Tessa in Toronto, and then Joanie and Stephanie, which just happened last summer and in October. All four of them dumped me — all of them.

"Why, are you creepy or weird or something?" Maggie asked, not at all attempting any humor.

"Hey, wait a minute, that's not fair. I have told you all the details. You don't have to hit me below the belt like that, you know plenty of who I am already." Chaucer was starting to get angry.

"OK, I'm sorry, that was not nice. I apologize, please don't be mad," Maggie said, looking forlorn. "I am just trying to absorb all of this. It's a bit much, you know?"

"I know," Chaucer said, changing his tone. "Maggie, I really like you, and I want our relationship to be honest and kind, so I had to tell you all this. Had you met me a year ago at this time, none of this would have happened, and we would not be having this discussion like this. The last nine months as I sorted all this through have been the second most miserable time in my life. Sometimes I seriously cannot believe what has happened."

"Yeah, I guess it has been a bad time for you," Maggie said, looking sympathetically at Chaucer. "So what was the first most miserable time in your life then?'

Chaucer cringed and looked away for a moment, reluctant to dredge up the old feelings. "Well, when I was fourteen, my parents divorced, and my mother took me and my sister to Vancouver. You know, I have told you some of this already. JOA and I had to leave our father, our friends, our relatives, schools, leave everything to go with her. I hated it, and so did JOA but we had no choice, we were just kids. I have come to resent my mother for that now that I am older. It just was a really bad time for JOA and me. You and your sisters are so fortunate to have had a home in one place with your parents for your entire life. You have been very fortunate, you know."

Maggie nodded and delivered a soft smile of gratitude. Chaucer held off, then finally smiled back. An understanding between the two of them seemed to have begun.

* * *

Over the next couple of weeks Chaucer and Maggie talked everything over and through and under and sideways. It created a trusting, beautiful bond between them that was starting to grow into

And Mother Dear

more than that.

They continued to talk about many issues besides his concerns for his need to become an involved father to the babies when he got back to Ottawa. Maggie talked about her sister Suzette, who had two small children and a troubled husband who gambled. She said that he was always in debt, and Suzette was borrowing money from her parents more and more to support the family. Maggie was worried about Suzette, who had been an academic star at LSU but married a handsome man that was not very smart or very moral as it turned out.

Chaucer told her about his mother's strange English family, the evolution of her writing life, and now, her venture into perhaps successful screenwriting too.

As the picture of Chaucer's past life started to be filled in, Maggie grew more confident in spending time with him, as she was learning that he was not the spoiled son of one of the company owners. Chaucer indeed had a difficult history, but she saw in him a man who was kind, polite, intelligent, and working on developing his emotional maturity. She saw in him a transcending arc of empathy and love. The good life she had in her family, her studies in social work, and her deep faith in God had given her a heart and a brain that placed her (at this point in her young life) far above most others in her ability to sort out honesty from the common ego-driven bragging of too many of the people she had met. Her comfort with Chaucer was growing. She was pleased.

Chaucer and Maggie also had many discussions about beliefs and religion. Chaucer felt that his introspection of his spiritual nature or lack of it had been evolving in him. He talked about his meetings with Pastor Wagner, his time with Jean Marc, his days with Father DuBois, and his time on the road with the Boston cousins Lisa and Teresa in Portugal and Spain. He told her about the great happiness that faith and belief in God had brought to Lisa and Teresa. Chaucer knew that he needed to understand more, much more but he had made a start. He was pursuing a faith that was incomplete, with too many questions and not enough answers yet. This was another of the reasons that he was so very attracted to Maggie, for she had a deep faith, and she too continued to seek a greater understanding of it. Chaucer wanted to do the same. He wanted and needed the mercy and understanding of a life cloaked in a deeper spiritual faith. It was like a hunger in him, and he needed this faith as food to feed his starving soul. He knew this now as the events of the past year had forced him to look inside himself, and he had realized that he was hollow and wanting in faith. He was tired of hearing the whispers of the devil in his head.

And so Maggie and Chaucer talked not only about themselves and their families as they grew to know each other more, but they expanded their discussions more and more to matters of faith and spirituality. This grew from the confidence and trust that each was developing in the other, as all meaningful relationships eventually do. If not, they are ended, or sometimes just tucked away as an experience. Without this trust and mutual confidence, relationships simply collapse from a lack of foundation, as exemplified by Chaucer's experience with Tessa and Maggie's relationship with her former boyfriend, Richard. This was not going to happen with Maggie and Chaucer, as week by week they were building a good foundation, and they both felt it.

Chapter 37

To Pamplona

IN THE FOLLOWING TWO MONTHS while Maggie was finishing her studies in London and Chaucer was winding down his time working with Jasper at the London office, their relationship seemed to move quickly into one of confident intimacy, the first step to it being called love. They rushed nothing. They both took little steps, Maggie more so than Chaucer, to ensure that what was developing was real and not just a relationship of place or convenience or mere circumstances.

Jasper and Margola approved. Chaucer had been a good employee at the shipping office. He had learned much and had been a great assistant for Jasper. He had earned Jasper's respect, and Jasper had made that known to Remy as the weeks, then months went on. Maggie's parents were almost in awe at how she spoke about Chaucer, which she had done in a fashion that they knew that he was good for her. She said that he was a gentleman in his behaviors. Her parents had seen a London crawling with young, troubled souls who seemed lost and hopeless with drug and alcohol use. England was finally emerging from the tremors, destruction, and rationing of World War II. England also was trying so hard to let go of the two tragic wars of the past two generations but the culture was cracking in places from the new forces of a more modern time. This was obvious to Jasper and Margola.

Soon Maggie's parents learned that she and Chaucer were planning a trip as a way to reward themselves for the successful past months of work for Chaucer, study for Maggie, and the relationship that they were building for themselves. At a causal dinner in the Cumberland Pub, Maggie and Chaucer announced that they would be leaving soon for a few weeks in Spain. Chaucer wanted to return to Pamplona for the San Fermin Festival (the Running of the Bulls), and Maggie wanted to explore her faith more by walking a portion of the Camino de Santiago. "I'm 23 now, and we'll be safe traveling together, and we will have separate rooms, too," she told her parents confidently. After some questions and discussion, Jasper and Margola smiled. Each reached out to touch the hands of both Maggie and Chaucer as a way of affirming their approval of the trip. Maggie had confided previously in her mother that she and Chaucer had agreed to separate rooms during the trip. Margola had expected to be informed of that matter without having to ask Maggie, so confident was she of the upbringing that Jasper and she had provided their daughters

"Chaucer, we have faith in you, that you will watch out for yourself and Maggie," Jasper said. "Our daughters mean everything to us, and we want Maggie and you to be safe." He nodded at both of them.

Margola smiled and agreed. "When you return, we'll want to learn about your travels. So take care of each other. We will pray for your safe travels and return to us. When will you be leaving?"

"We will take a British Airways flight from Gatwick to Bordeaux next week, then take the trains to Pamplona where we'll stay for a few days," Chaucer explained as he smiled and winked at Jasper and Margola. "Then we'll take a train to Leon, and we plan to walk the last 120 odd miles to Santiago."

Maggie chimed in. "We hope to be back here in less than three weeks as I want to get back to New Orleans for a few weeks before my last exams. I'll be done with my master's degree program then," she said with a big smile.

"I've talked with my father, and he is happy that I will be taking a few weeks off too, now that Walid is here from the Suez office. I'll be starting my last year of college after I get back," Chaucer explained. Jasper and Margola continued to smile. They had a sense that Maggie and Chaucer were falling in love, but they did not say anything that night, and neither had Maggie told them about Chaucer's babies in New York and San Francisco.

*   *   *

Pamplona was packed with Americans, Brits, and Canadians in the second week of July for the Running of the Bulls. Most all had read Hemingway in high school or college and were living out a dream. People were camping all over town in parks and vacant fields. Fortunately for Chaucer, he had contacted his friend Felipe Samatos who was the manager of the Hotel Yoldi where he and the movie company had stayed last November while they were filming the movie. Felipe did some maneuvering of reservations and was able to get Chaucer a small room with two single beds for three nights.

Chaucer thanked Felipe and did not tell him that the two single beds were perfect for him and Maggie. In the prior months, the intimacy level of their relationship had significantly evolved, but not to the level of sleeping together. Chaucer was fine with that as he already had plenty of women problems back home and sleeping with another woman was not going to make his situation better, not that he would have been opposed to be sleeping with Maggie. He still had the one angel on his shoulder, too — the one that kept reminding him of the strong admonishment from Remy about his role to be a gentleman around women.

Maggie for her part was very comfortable just kissing and talking with Chaucer for now. She too understood his situation and did not want to be just another temporary woman in his life. She saw some honorable options for them in the future that she did not want to compromise on. She was smart enough to know that love evolves over time, and she really liked Chaucer. His inner conflicts were simmering, and their conversations were very indicative of his need to grow emotionally and spiritually. Maggie wanted the next few weeks to be their time together to see if they could be a real, honest viable team in life. She would be patient. She was making this journey a test for Chaucer.

*   *   *

When Maggie and Chaucer arrived in Pamplona, the Running of the Bulls for that day was over. Each day of the San Fermin Festival, the bulls are let go from a coral at the end of Calle Santo Domingo. The sound of a large rocket launched from the coral alerts the runners and revelers that the bulls are coming. Most of the runners likely have been up all night, caught in the joy of the annual festival. The runners, most dressed in the white and red colors of San Fermin, can then estimate the time it will take for the bulls to arrive where they are standing along the route. Hours before, the large street barriers have been erected along Calle de la Estafeta and the other streets to keep the bulls on a path to the Callejon and the Plaza del Toros. There, the true runners and the many drunks must run by the Hemingway statue and into the ring to play matador for a while until they stumble and leave or the bulls are taken out by the dobladores.

After checking into the hotel, Maggie and Chaucer strolled to the Café Iruna on the Plaza del Castillo, the town square, just blocks from the Plaza del Toros. They each wore their red panuelos that Chaucer had gotten from Felipe at the front desk at the hotel. Chaucer and his movie friends had made the Café Iruna their hangout after the filming each day.

"Café Iruna, what does Iruna mean in Spanish?" asked Maggie.

"It's the Basque name for Pamplona. This is Basque country Maggie, not Spain," he said with a coyness of a know-it-all.

"Please explain, Mr. Canada, who knows everything," she retorted with a cute look.

"The people here want their own land and language and country; they don't feel like a part of Spain, especially since the Civil War. Franco and the fascists bombed them; they destroyed the town of Guernica, only fifty miles north of here. My friend Chaco explained it to me last year when I was here." Chaucer thought for a moment. "It's sort of like where I live in Ottawa. Some of the Quebecois in Montreal and Quebec City would rather have a French-speaking country of their own rather than being a province in Canada, so I can understand what the Basque people want too."

Maggie nodded thoughtfully. "The Cajuns in Louisiana sometimes talk like that, but it is only when joking. They have their own part of Louisiana and pretty much control it anyway. It's kind of funny how people are so tribal, isn't it; that must have evolved from the biblical times and the tribes of Israel," she said.

Chaucer looked puzzled and not wanting to appear dweebish or ignorant, replied, "Sounds about right to me."

When Chaucer and Maggie walked into the Café Iruna, it was busy and noisy. The older bartender Chaco was at the end of the bar. When he saw Chaucer enter, he shouted to him, "Comandante Chaucer, hola, mi amigo" with his big toothy smile under his bushy moustache. Chaucer walked quickly to him, and they shook hands and hugged. Even though the place was very crowded and noisy, Chaco still took time to greet his friend. Maggie was impressed. Chaco got them a table and made sure that they got their food and drinks quickly. When he brought the tray of food and drink to them, he looked at Chaucer.

"Your woman is very beautiful, my friend, you are lucky," Chaco said with the smile of a happy old man, glad to see his young friend again. Chaucer smiled and nodded to Chaco.

"Si, ella es hermosa y muy inteligente tambien," said Chaucer in his best Spanish with his best semi-Castilian accent.

Chaco looked at Maggie, smiled, took her hand and kissed it as many old Spanish gentlemen would do. "Your friend, this man, he is very kind and has a big heart. You are very lucky, Senorita," Chaco said in broken English. He then turned and walked slowly back to the bar.

After their day of travel, they enjoyed the food and drink, and their walk around the streets of Pamplona. Maggie and Chaucer were tired, so they went back to their hotel a few blocks away, where they took a siesta. With the nice overhead fan keeping the room cool, they slept for an hour or so despite the noise of the people dancing and drinking in the streets below their window.

Maggie awoke first. She lay in bed watching the fan whirl, thinking of Chaucer and the days ahead. She had missed Richard hardly at all since he had left London and returned to New Orleans, walking out on her as he did. She realized that she had been emotionally chasing him, which Chaucer did not make her do at all. He was always available, and their talks were deep and getting deeper as the days went on. She liked that her father, Jasper, had spoken so well of Chaucer's father, Remy, complimenting him as a smart businessman and an honorable man. Now she was seeing some of these things in Chaucer too. It seemed that although he had been separated from his father for many years while living in Vancouver with his mother, he loved and admired his father greatly, and in his own way aspired to be like him. Yet the abandonment of the two women who carried his babies still was a big question for her, a very big question. She believed that she needed to find out more, and the sooner the better.

※　※　※

That afternoon after their siesta, Chaucer led Maggie again around Pamplona to show her the town and the places where they had been filming in the previous November. Many of the festival tourists were now resting and recovering from the hangovers of the previous night. The streets were less busy and crowded, at least until the Parade of the Giants took over. Later, Chaucer took Maggie to the bull ring where they would go the next morning to watch the runners. They walked the length of Calle Estafeta to find a good spot to see the bulls and the runners in the morning.

"Will you run tomorrow, Chaucer?" Maggie asked.

Chaucer laughed out loud. "My ego and vanity tells me to run; my brain is telling me to watch and enjoy it." He hesitated and then spoke. "And you see, I have the babies to consider now. It would not be fair to them if I was injured or even killed here, would it?" he said very seriously.

Maggie smiled outwardly and nodded her approval as his words pleased her greatly. Inwardly she knew that Chaucer was going to take care of his responsibilities as a father, and this pleased her. She prayed that he would have the mercy and grace of the Lord and St. Joseph. She knew this was to be true because she had prayed for him for so many days in the past month. She knew that her faith was strong, and that she had sought the intervention of God into the life of Chaucer and the babies. She believed that her faith and her prayers gave her hope. She had not prayed to find love for him or for him to love her; she prayed only for the children and for Chaucer, asking for mercy and understanding. Now she believed that she was experiencing a growing love for him, as both a man of responsibility and a man for her to love. She was not so sure of precisely when this feeling had first begun for her, but she felt it growing in her now. It felt good to her. It was happening for a reason, she thought.

As the darkness approached and the street noise and revelers increased, Maggie and Chaucer went back into the Café Iruna. It was packed, barely a place to stand. Chaco was not working now. Chaucer elbowed his way to the bar and ordered four bottles of El

Lion beer, paid for them, and brought them back to where Maggie was standing by the door. They stepped outside into the warm twilight and sat on the steps drinking their beers and watching the people in the plaza.

Eventually, as the darkness engulfed the plaza, they walked over to the gazebo in the center and joined in a group of young people singing. Americans, Canadians, and British people were singing loudly as three guys were strumming guitars in the center of the Gazebo. Some Beatles, some Simon and Garfunkel, and some Gordon Lightfoot songs made up the repertoire.

"I saw a guitar in your flat a few weeks ago, do you play much?" Maggie asked Chaucer, who just laughed.

"Yeah, I know about four songs, and they all have the same chords," he said, looking a little embarrassed.

"Play one for me now. I am an unapologetic romantic in situations like this. Win my heart, Chaucer. Sing me a song," Maggie said with a romantic look of purpose.

Chaucer looked at Maggie, saw her firm lovely face, and accepted the challenge. "OK, watch me now." He handed her his bottle of beer and walked between the onlookers by the gazebo. The three guys playing guitar had just finished a song. Chaucer approached a lanky, dark-haired man who looked to be about Chaucer's age. "Mate, can I borrow your guitar? My girlfriend wants me to play a special song."

The guy looked closely at him. "Hey, are you Canadian?"

"From Ottawa," Chaucer replied, surprised. "You?"

The guy smiled. "I thought I heard an accent. Yeah, I'm from Toronto, so are these guys. We all came to play here for the week. Going to London to play next week." He handed Chaucer his guitar. "Go easy on it, mate. I'm running low on strings."

Chaucer thanked him and started to remember the song by putting his hand on the strings to form the chords he needed.

And then he turned to the people watching, saw Maggie, and with a stoic face, started playing the music for the recent hit song "Heart of Gold" sung by fellow Canadian Neil Young. And then Chaucer let go with singing the words:

Neil Young - Heart Of Gold - YouTube

I want to live, I want to give

I've been a miner for a heart of gold
It's these expressions, I never give
That keep me searching for a heart of gold

At this point, the other two on the stage joined with Chaucer on their guitars as they both knew and loved the song too. The people watching all started singing gustily. Maggie stood and started dancing, swinging her arms and hips, smiling so big.

I've been to Hollywood, I've been to Redwood
I crossed the ocean for a heart of gold
I've been in my mind, It's such a fine line
That keeps me searching for a heart of gold

Chaucer looked out and found Maggie's smiling face in the crowd, and she blew him a kiss. He sang even louder, his deep happiness reflected in his energetic singing. To the delight of the crowd, the four Canadian boys sang the entire song a second time. The audience clapped and cheered when the guys finished with a flourish. Chaucer stepped down, handing the guitar to his new Toronto friend.

"Good work, mate! Come back again for another song when you can," the guy said.

When Chaucer got back to Maggie, she put her arms around him and kissed him. "Have you found your heart of gold across the ocean that you were looking for?" she asked him.

He smiled, put both arms around her, squeezed her and they held another kiss a long time. "I think that I am getting really close, don't you?" he said to Maggie.

She smiled softly. "I think we're working on it."

They walked away from the gazebo and wandered the crowded, noisy streets of Pamplona that night, eventually going back to their room about 1 a.m. They wanted to be back at the street barriers early in the morning to get a good spot to see the bulls and the runners. They fell asleep easily, each in their own bed.

* * *

A big full sun greeted Maggie and Chaucer the next morning. Many of the turistas who stood on the wooden barriers at Calle Estafeta with Chaucer and Maggie smelled of alcohol and tobacco and marijuana. Most looked sleepy from the all-nighter they just pulled off. This was the fourth day of the bulls running. So far only one runner had been killed. He was an Irishman who had stumbled and been gored badly in the neck and bled out before the medical team could save him. About four or five others had been gored each day, but none resulted in deaths that were reported. Many of the drunken runners were hurt from falling or stumbling on the stone street rather than by the bulls.

Close to 8 a.m., the rocket launch announced that the bulls had been let loose. According to prior estimates, the first bulls would be within sight of where Chaucer and Maggie were standing in about two minutes. And they were. Six ugly young bulls were chasing six steers with bells on their necks. In front of the steers were fifty to sixty runners who were just a few yards in front of the steers and bulls, with plenty more runners well ahead, who by their positioning, were risking nothing it seemed.

By coincidence and just prior to the rocket launch, Chaucer saw Chaco wearing his Red Cross vest and standing in the space between the two sets of barriers. He shouted to Chaco who immediately walked over to him and told the local policeman who was standing nearby that Chaucer was his amigo, so the policeman allowed the couple to crawl through the first barrier and into the space with Chaco.

"Mi amigo, these bulls are bad ones, mean ones, watch them closely," Chaco said as he motioned both Chaucer and Maggie close to the second barrier.

As the group of bulls were approaching where Chaucer and Maggie stood up at the inside fence, a chubby runner stumbled and fell just ten yards from them. As the bulls were about on him, he jumped up and tried to frantically climb up the fence just feet from where Chaucer was. With the runner's hands on the top rail of the barrier and his feet frantically trying to climb up, the bull who had marked him gored him in the buttocks. The sound of the puncture was like the sound of a knife going into a plump summer tomato, and then blood spurted out.

Chaucer grimaced. Maggie screamed. The runner let go of the fence and lay below Chaucer, bleeding. Other runners and bulls ignored him and kept running down the street to the bull ring a few blocks away. Two pastores realized that the attacking bull was now a suelto separated from the pack, and they came to the aid of the prone, bleeding runner. They used their long, hard willow sticks to beat the suelto bull viciously enough that he ran down the street after the others. Eventually, the first aid medical crew, which included Chaco, came to the bleeding man, and he was placed on a stretcher and taken away.

The Running of the Bulls was now over for that day, all over in less than ten minutes. The festival men came along and quickly pulled the barriers out of their holes in the cobblestone street. People dispersed, some going to the Plaza del Castillo, some going to their hotels to sleep, and many, including Chaucer and Maggie, going to the arena, the Plaza de Toros, to watch the brave drunks play matador with the bulls. Chaucer and Maggie stayed for a while until the excitement was no more. They had seen enough for one day. They would stay one more night, watch the bulls again the next morning, and then take the train for Leon to start the walk to Santiago.

Chapter 38

There Was a Gentle Whisper

"WHY ARE YOU DOING THIS WITH ME?" Maggie asked, as she and Chaucer sat comfortably across from each other in an empty cabin on the local train to Leon. Chaucer looked up from reading Walter Starkie's book *The Road to Santiago: Pilgrims of St. James*.

"Because I believe that I am falling in love with you," he said, grinning like a boy eating his favorite dessert, "and because I want to sort out my reasons for agreeing to accept my fatherhood for the children, and because I want to learn about the history of this walk first hand, not just read about it in this book." The sunlight bathed Maggie's face, and Chaucer thought how much she looked like an angel that late morning, her dimples indented as she smiled at him, her black hair hanging on her shoulders.

"I thought that you had that all worked out from your discussion with your father."

"I did," he said, "but that was only half of it. I said I would do it because it is the right thing to do, the moral thing for me, but I also want to believe that I really mean it, that I feel it too." Chaucer made the face of an uncertain buyer.

Maggie put her *International Herald Tribune* newspaper down on her lap. "Are you looking for a sign from God, maybe?" she asked.

"In a way, yes. I think the spirit of life and love will let me know, and I think that this coming week as we walk the trail that I might be able to receive it if I stay silent and listen, if I am ready to see it, hear it, feel it. Does that make sense to you, Maggie?" he asked in a loving tone.

She grinned at him, got up and moved across the coach to his bench and sat next to him, holding his hand and putting her head on his shoulder.

"You are a sweetheart, Chaucer.... I think you just might learn about the grace of God this week if you are open to it." She kissed his cheek, and he put his arm around her. Soon they were both napping to the rhythm of the train's motion and the sound of the steel wheels on the rails.

* * *

They awoke as the train made a stop to discharge and load passengers in Miranda de Ebro. They took some apples, bread, cheese, and water out of their packs to eat lunch. Maggie wanted to talk more about the week ahead. For her, this would be the culmination of her adventurous semester studying in Europe. To end it with a spiritual event like the walk to the Cathedral at Santiago was ideal for her. Her parents, observant Catholics, had been very happy to learn that she would be walking for a week on the Camino de Santiago. They were even happier when she told them that by walking from Leon, she would earn enough pilgrimage stamps in her credential (proof) form that when presented to Oficina de Peregrino (Pilgrim Office) in Santiago, that she would be awarded an official Compostela from the church. They were also happy that Chaucer would be with her all the way on the journey as they didn't relish the thought of their daughter walking alone for a week, even on a holy pilgrimage. There had been reports of some pilgrims being robbed on the Camino, perhaps by thieves who lacked spirituality and hoped to steal that from their victims as well as their money.

Sitting in the coach car, Maggie was mostly quiet. "I'm thinking that tomorrow after we get our credential from the office in Leon, that we should probably be as silent as we can during our walk," she said in a soft voice to Chaucer.

"You think?" he asked, surprised at hearing this.

"It seems to me that if God will be talking to us, and if we're praying as we walk, that being as silent as we can, would increase our, your, opportunity to receive the spiritual message that we hope to find this week." She paused. "What do you think?" she asked earnestly.

Chaucer rubbed his chin, thinking. He looked at her without an expression. "Well, can I give you hand signals if I need some water or I have to pee?"

She laughed and slapped his thigh. "Yes, yes, we can talk but we should try to focus, don't you think? The week is going to go by quickly, and soon we'll be on a plane back to London."

"OK, I see your point, and I agree. We can call it the University of Silence." He stopped, trying to decide whether to voice a question that had been in the back of his mind for several days. He decided to take the plunge. "Soooo, what happens to us when we get back to London? Are we going our separate ways, like it's been nice, see ya?" Chaucer was not smiling but serious. He had a flashback to Joanie from the previous summer in Naples when she told him their relationship was over.

"You could come visit me in New Orleans, and we can see where we want to take this thing that we have worked on. What do you think?" Maggie sounded relaxed and optimistic.

Chaucer looked directly into Maggie's eyes. "Yes, I would like that very much, Maggie. Look, I know that I come with a lot of baggage that I created for myself, but I am going to manage it, and I think that we could really be a good couple together. I don't want you to bail out on us, do you?" he said.

"No, I think you know that I don't want to, but I also have some important career things that I need to finish up at Tulane in the coming months, and then I to need start my working life, my career, and I hope that you will understand that and maybe be with me while I do it. What do you think?" she was grinning, looking deeply into his eyes.

"I think, yes," he said with a big smile, crossing his fingers and his toes.

It was close to dark when the train pulled into Leon. Walking out of the station, they were able to locate their hostel within ten minutes. They dropped off their backpacks and went to find a tapas bar (called a pintxos bar in the Basque region) where they ate and drank local beer, talking into the night.

The next morning for breakfast they stopped at a local market for more bread, cheese, and fruit, buying as much as they could carry as they did not know what lay ahead in the small villages and towns on the Camino. Maggie and Chaucer had their physical bags packed and ready for the pilgrimage. They were still thinking and preparing for the days of silence and meditation to come. It would be good to see the beauty of the Camino, the fields and hills as they walked to the resting place of Saint James. This pilgrimage was a serious event for Maggie; walking the Camino was a major spiritual undertaking for Catholics like her, a time for her faith to grow and a time for her to receive God's word. In her prayers now, she was asking for Chaucer to experience the same.

Maggie had made a mental list of her needs on the pilgrimage. She wanted atonement for her sometimes abruptness, her selfishness, her not having a life equal to the calling of her faith. She had read about St. James and his counsel that believers should match their faith with their actions in life, which was probably the reason that she had decided to be a social worker for a career. A talented social worker with the Christian conscience of St. James could help many and be her way of living the Beatitudes of Christ.

Chaucer was also thinking about his mission in the coming week. He was hoping for a time of expiation for his mistakes, perhaps his selfishness and his initial response to the knowledge that both Tessa and Stephanie were pregnant with his child. Surely it was needing to be that. Even though he had settled the matter with his father months before, he still had his recurring doubts. He knew the bad wolf was still walking inside him. He wanted that demon out of his brain and his soul. This was the time to purge that bad wolf once and for all time.

He was glad he had read Walter Starkie's book *The Road to Santiago*. One passage that kept coming back to him were these words, this parable:

> It is a pilgrimage towards the other world, in the summer months under a star-studded sky, with the luminous track of the Milky Way to guide the wanderer westward to Compostela. A ghost-accompanied pilgrimage, moreover, for even after death myriads of souls make their way to the Shrine of Saint James, as we are told in a lovely local

Asturian folk legend, which describes how on a gloomy night, when not a star was shining, a forlorn pilgrim soul lost its way…then a knight came to the pilgrim and said, "If thou art the devil I conjure thee to depart; if thou be of this world tell me what thou dost need." The pilgrim then answered: "I am a sinful soul journeying to Compostela, but there is a deep river in front of me and I cannot pass."

"Trust to the rosaries thou didst say in thy life," answered the knight.

"Alas, woe is me, for I said none," said the pilgrim.

"Trust to the fasts or to the alms thou didst give," said the knight.

"Alas, I gave none," said the pilgrim.

But the knight was charitable, and he pitied the soul, so he lit the sacred candles for him, and the lost soul crossed the river and went on. That same night the soul returned from the holy pilgrimage singing, "Blessed be the Knight who by saving my soul, saved his own soul as well."

* * *

In the next days on the Camino, Maggie and Chaucer spoke very little. Their mouths were small, their ears and eyes large, their hearts open. The weather held steady, with little rain and warm summer temperatures modified by a ubiquitous breeze from the prevailing ocean winds off Galicia. Their shoes and feet tolerated the many hours each day of walking the trail. By the third night, after walking almost sixty miles, they were tired. They realized that they still had to cover about seventy more miles to reach the cathedral in Santiago, so they decided to slow the pace to fifteen miles a day, and to add an additional day to their pilgrimage.

That night, at a small hostel in the town of Molinaseca, they decided to go into the old church of San Nicolas, where it was cool and quiet. It was a time to sit and reflect, to pray quietly after three days on the Camino. Chaucer sat in a different pew than did Maggie. As he sat with bowed head, he saw a handwritten note on the bench. It was written in English and apparently left for others to read. Chaucer picked it up.

Before a new chapter is begun, the old one has to be finished.

Stop being who you were and change into who you are.

Signed, Sean from County Cork

He held the paper in his hand and thought, "Was this meant for me? Does Sean know me?" His sunburnt face grew a smile and he paused to look around the church. "Was Sean watching me or was this what I came on the Camino to find?" Chaucer had an overwhelming sense of satisfaction at that moment. And then suddenly Maggie was next to him, grabbing his hand.

"Ready?" she said, and he nodded with a confident grin.

As they started to leave the church, a middle-aged man with a floppy hat, long beard and a backpack at his feet was standing there, looking at them like he knew them.

"I've seen you the last two days. Everything OK?" he said.

Neither Maggie nor Chaucer said anything at first. Finally, Maggie spoke. "Did we see you yesterday at the watering place in Astorga?"

"Yes, I was there," he replied.

"Now I know, we saw you the day before too, on the trail."

"Yes, perhaps you did. My name is Reuter Steenluger. I'm German and going your way to Santiago. Please call me Rudy," he said with a broad grin, the face of a happy and confident man.

They learned that Rudy had started his pilgrimage twenty-eight days before, at the very start of the traditional Camino in St. Jean Pied de Port in France, a few miles from the Spanish border. He said he was taking thirty-three days for his walk, one day for each year that Christ was on earth. He wore a large wooden cross on his chest, hung by thick rawhide around his neck.

"I was born in Mansfeld in Saxony, where Martin Luther lived. My parents and all my ancestors were good Lutherans, as am I. We all accept and believe in Christ and understand that our salvation comes from the grace of God, not from the things we do or say or don't say or don't do. Had Pope Leo accepted these truths 450 years ago, I'd be a Catholic today," he said with a joyful laugh at the irony of his words.

Maggie also laughed. "Yes, you are probably close to right, Rudy. As a Catholic, I know we have made a few mistakes in our religion over the centuries, so we are happy to give you the forgiveness of your theology errors and welcome you back now."

Chaucer laughed out loud, extended his hand to Rudy, and said, "Well, I'm a Presbyterian and a neutral party in this discussion," at which point they all smiled and embraced.

They spent some time discussing the past weeks of Rudy's journey. He spoke about his love of St. Paul and the disciple's years of wandering and teaching the word of Jesus.

Knowing that Rudy had traveled alone, Chaucer asked, "Has your silence been rewarded?"

"It always rewards us if we pray. We need to ask the right questions for our life and wait and listen for God to guide us. What are you finding in your days on the Camino?" Rudy asked.

Chaucer and Maggie looked at each other and smiled. She said, "I have been hearing the whispers of the Lord. The spirit is active for me, but more so in the past few days than ever," and she nodded to Chaucer.

He looked at Maggie and Rudy, thinking them better Christians than himself. "I have so much to learn to make up for my years of not really listening. My joy is that I am also beginning to hear the whispers; yet I am praying for more and praying for the wisdom to ask the important questions. That is all I can offer now. Perhaps in five more days if we see you in Santiago I can tell you more." With that, Chaucer shook Rudy's hand again and slowly turned back toward the hostel, as he was tired and wanted to meditate and rest.

Maggie watched him walk away, and she looked at Rudy with a smile of understanding. "He is a good man, a very fine man, and his needs now are great. I pray for him every hour on our walk. I hope that he will receive the rectitude from the voice of God and understand that his new chosen path is also God's path for him. I am happy that he is now hearing the whispers of our Lord."

Rudy reached out to Maggie and held her hands gently in his two large paws. "You are a good woman, I can tell. You will help guide your friend; I can see that in your eyes. May God bless you both. I will see you at Portico de Gloria at the cathedral in five days' time. I will stay there until you come. Go with God, my friend," and with that, Rudy turned, headed out of the church, and started walking west on the trail, not saying where he would sleep that night, or even if he would sleep.

https://www.youtube.com/watch?v=PZ59spYH9mk

— "Into the Mystic", Van Morrison

* * *

In the middle of the night, at the hostel where Maggie and Chaucer had taken their single beds, there was a soft knocking sound on the front door. After a few minutes, the awakened hospitalero (manager) came to the door in his sleeping clothes. He saw Rudy, holding a lit candle, standing quietly.

"What is it you seek?" the hospitalero asked Rudy.

"There is a young man inside. He needs God's help, and I was sent to speak to him."

"Come back in the morning, please, everyone is asleep," the hospitalero said.

"His name is Chaucer. He is with Maggie, and I must see him now, for it is God's wish."

The hospitalero relented, knowing that he was on the Camino de Santiago and things like this often happened with the pilgrims. He went to the room where Chaucer was sleeping and awakened him gently.

In a few minutes, Chaucer came to the door and saw Rudy standing with the lighted candle in the dark night.

"Rudy, what it is it? Did something happen to you? Are you OK?" he asked, concerned and rubbing the sleep out of his eyes.

"God spoke to me on the trail as I walked in the night, after I had left you earlier. He told me that you needed guidance and that I should see you this very night. He said you have a trouble that is inside you, and you are confused, that I should listen to you. Come sit with me on this bench and tell me this thing that is inside you, my friend." Rudy had the look of a man who was serious and showed a quiet determination that Chaucer knew would not be deterred.

And so Chaucer went back inside, put on his pants and shirt, and then walked over to the nearby bench where Rudy was sitting, still holding the candle. With coaxing from Rudy, over the next hour, he explained to him his situation with Tessa, Stephanie, the babies, Remy, and his new relationship with Maggie.

Rudy said little, letting Chaucer talk quietly in the warm darkness. After a while, with the first rays of light coming faintly over the hill to the east, Rudy started to speak quietly, almost at a whisper.

"In the Gospel, Matthew told us of how in the early morning, just like this, an angel of the Lord came to Mary Magdalene at the tomb and told her about Jesus, coming to life again, how Jesus gathered the disciples and told them to go in the lands and baptize the people into the commands of his teaching, and that he would be with them always, to the end of the world, and Paul wrote to the Romans that the Holy Spirit tells us that we are all his children and shall share in his treasures, and that even as Christians, while we have the Holy Spirit inside us, we also groan to be released from our pain and suffering. Paul told the Galatians, 'We are God's own sons and everything that he has also belongs to us, for that is how he planned it, and we shall call him Abba, our Abba, our Father.' "

Chaucer, still feeling sleepy, had trouble taking in all that Rudy was saying. "I'm not sure I know what you are saying, Rudy; tell me more, please."

Rudy was calm, as a good teacher and shepherd always is. "I am here with the same message as the angel gave, early in the morning, explaining to you that you are being reborn now, Chaucer. You have these children, and you must share with them your treasures, what you can bring to them, to baptize and educate them, giving them all you have, now and forever, and these children and others that come into the rest of your life shall call you Abba, Abba their father. That is what I am saying, that you have a mission now, a calling. The foghorn is sounding, and you have heard it. It is your mission, your calling, to deliver the teaching of Jesus with these children, if you accept it as your role as a Christian man, if you accept this calling. Or you can reject this, as a man of free will who decides to walk away from the love that God wants you to give to these and other children. Perhaps that is your reason for being on the Camino with Maggie, to make this decision. Or perhaps it is not. I cannot answer that for you, my friend; I can only hold the candle out for you to see in the dark, until the morning light of God can shine in your face.

That is all I was sent here to do for you."

And with that, Rudy stood up, took Chaucer's hands into his hands, and whispered to him softly. "This is what God has asked me to say to you this night, and now I must return to the Camino. I shall see you in five days at the cathedral, my friend. Keep this note in your pocket." Rudy handed Chaucer a small piece of paper, then turned, picked up his backpack, and walked west as the daylight climbed over the eastern hills behind him.

Chaucer went back into the hostel and opened the paper under a dim light. It read:

I still have many things to say to you,

But you cannot bear them now,

When the Spirit of truth comes,

He will guide you into all truth

— John 16:12-13

Chapter 39

The Mystical Days of the Camino

THROUGHOUT THE NEXT DAYS on the trail, Maggie and Chaucer spoke very little. She had been in a deep sleep that late night when Rudy had returned to speak to Chaucer, and Chaucer, for reasons only he would know, never mentioned his nighttime candle-lit discussion with Rudy. Chaucer realized that he had been touched by the hand and whisper of God that early morning, and if it had all been a dream, then it was still the God in him that had spoken to him. What Chaucer needed to do was what most other pilgrims do who come to seek expiation and wisdom on the Camino; they need to listen quietly and contemplate in silence. Thus he wanted to think clearly and deeply about what Rudy had spoken about. Each of the next four days, Chaucer prayed for more answers, asking God to help him understand what was being asked of him now.

Maggie also prayed — at night, and while walking, and while resting to eat during the day. Some of her prayers were about her evolving love for Chaucer and his coming to terms with his fatherhood. But most of her prayers were for guidance on her coming days as a social worker. She had long ago been given the word from God that she would do her best work in the world, not as a religious sister, but as a lay person who would work with physicians, nurses, social service agencies, psychologists, employment services, the courts, and the legal profession to help the needy people of New Orleans with their family and individual problems. Her prayers now were about finding guidance on how to best start this work. As a woman of conviction she was not yet pointed in the best direction on how to begin to apply her education, training, and Christian energy to the people whom she could best help. She believed that her days on the Camino could provide this guidance before she returned to New Orleans and completed her work at Tulane University.

* * *

The Spanish rains finally came, and Maggie and Chaucer walked in wet weather that week, and it slowed them down. They saw others under their rain ponchos on the Camino, and mostly gave them just a simple polite greeting and kept going. They barely spoke to each other as they wanted it that way. On various times during the day, they smiled at each other, and even held hands for long periods, but otherwise they were quiet, thinking, praying, and listening. Their sore feet and hunger pangs were of little concern, for their attention was directed elsewhere.

Over the next three days, they walked through the towns of O Cebreiro, Tricastela, Sarria, Palas de Rei and stopped late into the day, just before dark, in Arzúa, which left them with thirty-five miles to reach Santiago in two more days if the weather cooperated. They knew at their current pace that on the second day they would arrive too late in Santiago to attend the noon mass at the cathedral, which Maggie very much wanted to experience. So they decided that on the second day they would complete the walk to Santiago, stay the night, and the next morning go to the Oficina del Perregrino (Pilgrim Office) on Rua Vilar to obtain their Compostela, which would allow them to sit in special seats at the noon mass that day. Maggie was intent on being a witness to the swinging of the giant silver Botafumeiro (incense burner) during the mass, which her parish priest in New Orleans had told her to be sure to witness.

They left Arzúa before sunrise on their second-to-the-last day on the Camino and walked at a faster pace. On their final day they arrived at San Paio, just seven miles from Santiago, at about two hours before sunset. They stopped only for water, bread, and cheese, and kept going to Santiago, where they arrived with some remaining daylight. They immediately found beds in a hostel about a half mile from the cathedral. They left their packs and walked, very tired but holding hands, down to the Pazo do Xelmirez Archway and on to the Praza Obradoiro in front of the Cathedral of Santiago de Compostela. The brilliant setting sun was shining on the cathedral spires. The long walk seemed worth it, if just to see this amazing sunset where St. James lay.

Maggie and Chaucer smiled at the other pilgrims who were sitting on the steps of the great church. They were silent and in awe. They had made it — exhausted physically, enriched spiritually.

Like the other pilgrims, Maggie and Chaucer were in a state of amazement as they gazed upon the beautiful cathedral. They had completed their now nine-day long journey of solitude, listening, and contemplation.

"It's still open, Maggie, let's go inside," Chaucer said.

Up the steps they walked and entered the imposing and silent cathedral. It was a cavern of humanity's honor and respect for God and the patron St. James, more dramatic and enormous in size than they had expected, compared to the size of the other churches that they had seen on the trail since leaving Leon. They looked up and saw the sunlight streaming through the windows facing west. The sunlight illuminated the stained-glass art of St. James, Jesus, and the scallop of the Camino, which had shown them the entire way on the path to Santiago. They squeezed hands tightly, with a sense of accomplishment. Chaucer kissed Maggie, and they hugged. No words were spoken, only the firmness of the hug in two people who did not need words to express their feelings. They had done what they set out to complete.

At that moment, Maggie smiled knowing that in her days of walking, she had accepted her calling as a social worker who would focus on working with the poor and the needy, in guidance from the priests and deacons and sisters in the New Orleans Parrish. She had learned over the past days that surely was to be her purpose in life. She believed this calling from God to be real.

Chaucer had finally released any reservations and committed himself to being the legal and spiritual father of his babies. He would do all the things required to support and love them. He had set behind him his reluctance and now understood that his calling from God was to be the Abba that God had been to him, and that Remy had been to him in this world. Whatever sacrifices he had to make, he was now going to accept with a spirit of joy and maturity. There would be no more doubts for him. He had the note from Pastor Wagner in his wallet. He took it out and asked Maggie to read it with him. They whispered the words:

> Come unto me, all ye that labor and are heavy laden, and I will give you rest. Take my yoke upon you, and learn of me, for I am meek and lowly in heart, and ye shall find rest unto your souls. For my yoke is easy, and my burden is light.
> —Matthew 11: 28-30

* * *

That night, as the receding sun had turned Santiago into a dark quiet town, they walked back to their hostel from the cathedral. They were tired and hungry and stopped in a small restaurant where the menu board showed modest prices. Inside over food and local wine, they started to speak softly, likely exchanging more words at the table than in the past week. Their togetherness was clear.

"I'm going to work for the diocese in New Orleans, if they will have me," Maggie told Chaucer. "I know now that is my calling, to be a good Catholic and help those in the diocese that need my help. This is the least I can do to live my faith. I understand that better now, from this pilgrimage," she said with a loving smile, staring into Chaucer's attentive eyes.

"I am so very happy for you," Chaucer said, "and this has been the experience that I truly needed to understand my life, too." He looked tired but more whole in spirit than ever.

"What was your special moment this week or was it a series of moments for you?" Maggie inquired.

"I believe it was both one thing and many things, Maggie. It was evolving in me and then I met a man, perhaps a patron, with a candle. He came in the night, and he spoke to me, and that moved my understanding ahead, like a new wind that fills the sails of a boat adrift, because in the last few days, I kept hearing the voices of little children in my head, calling Abba, Abba, and I believe that they were calling me to be the father that they need. So the line that had been crooked became straight, and I can see me as their father forever now, and maybe the father of others when I get married."

"Will you marry someone one day, Chaucer?" Maggie asked, not coyly or rhetorically.

He looked at her straight away. "No, not someone, and not someday." Maggie looked at him oddly, with a minor degree of confusion.

He softly whispered to her. "I want to marry you, Maggie. I think we have what it takes to have a good life together. You are that someone, and this is the one day." It was the perfect time for him to propose — a small restaurant in Santiago, after nine days of walking the Camino and both having learned what the Spirit had guided them to do with their lives.

"Will you, Maggie?"

She did not answer but looked down at the table. He said nothing, just remained quiet as he had learned to do these past weeks in her presence.

When she lifted her head, she looked at him, her beautiful dark eyes melting him in his chair. "I must live in New Orleans, Chaucer. I will be working for the church, I hope. My family is there, and you are from Ottawa, and you have two little babies. I'm confused by this."

Chaucer nodded his head, not saying or expressing anything except patience.

"Would you move to New Orleans and be happy?" she asked.

"I could if I had the right purpose," he said, again exhibiting the ultimate patience.

"And you'll always be the father for the two babies?" she asked. He nodded with confidence. "And we would have our own babies too?" she continued.

"Yes, if that is our plan, and God agrees."

Again, Maggie looked down at the table, her hair now falling over her cheeks.

Chaucer still remained silent and patient.

After what seemed to him like an hour as he sat looking at this most incredible woman across the table from him, Maggie raised her head, and tears were dripping down her cheeks.

Chaucer did not touch her; now was not the time. He just sat and looked and waited.

She reached out to him, put both her hands on his and squeezed them, then looked him in the eyes. "Yes, I will," she paused, "but not now."

Chaucer, not smiling or dancing or whistling as much as he wanted to, quietly asked, "When?"

Again, she hesitated. "I need to finish school in the next few months and negotiate a position with the diocese. You'll need to complete your plans for the care of the babies during that time," she said.

"And then?" he said.

"And then, yes, I will have you for my husband, that is my answer," she responded, her face breaking into a smile.

With this, Chaucer reached into his jeans pocket and pulled out a small envelop. He took out a small ring decorated with a scallop shell of silver. Her eyes grew large, and she smiled.

"I bought this yesterday at the small store we stopped at for our food. If you said yes tonight, I wanted to have something to give you, and this seemed the best I could find for now. Let's call it our Camino of Santiago St. James engagement ring. I can get you a better one soon, OK?"

She just smiled and said, "This will be just fine for me."

* * *

After dinner, they walked the lonely and dark streets of Santiago, arm in arm, and eventually made it back to the hostel just before the hospitelaro locked the door. Inside, they kissed passionately and then went to their beds in rooms separated by gender, full of excitement and hope, sleeping well and dreaming good dreams.

In the morning after they both obtained a Compostela at the appropriate office, they went to the cathedral hoping to find Rudy as they had promised. They arrived about an hour before the noon mass, and Maggie was excited about the prospect of witnessing the tiraboleiros swing the large silver Botafumeiro filled with incense. As they crossed the plaza, they saw Rudy sitting on a bench smoking a long clay pipe and reading a Herman Hesse book.

Approaching him, Chaucer said, "Guten Morgen, mein Professor." Rudy looked up and smiled, responding "Guten Morgen, mein gutter schuler und sein schooner." (Good morning, my fine student and his beautiful friend.) Chaucer translated for Maggie, and she grinned.

"I had faith I would see you this morning. Did you have faith that we would meet here, too?" Rudy asked them.

"Yes, we knew you would be here," Chaucer replied.

"Good, then your pilgrimage has served you well. Shall we go to the Tree of Jesse together?" Rudy asked, and the three of them walked up the steps to the Portico de Gloria. There they saw the beauty of the carved art, some 750 years old, with the Christ and the apostles, with St. James sitting below. Rudy looked at them and said, "Let us all touch it together, for Isaiah said, 'There shall come forth a shoot from the stump of Jesse, and a branch shall grow out of his roots.' That Jesse was the father of King David, and this was the prophecy of the coming of Jesus the Messiah. This was confirmed for us in the Gospels of Matthew and Luke."

Chaucer and Maggie looked at each other and then placed their hands over Rudy's hand that he had already placed on the carving. Rudy closed his eyes and quietly prayed aloud: "Lord, please grant us humble pilgrims a life of service to others, and bring kindness and peace to those we encounter, and Lord, please grant your son Chaucer his role as Abba, the father Joseph, and Maggie, her needed role as Mother Mary in her life of service. I ask this in the name of your son and our savior, Jesus Christ." All three in unison affirmed the prayer with "Amen."

Before they could step away, Chaucer, still holding the hands of the three of them to the carving, prayed, "Lord, thank you for sending to Maggie and me the light and the whispers on this journey, and for sending us your good servant Rudy to guide us, in the name of your son, Jesus Christ, Amen," to which Rudy and Maggie replied, "Amen."

As they walked into the cathedral, they were all in a state of joy and contentment. They had made their journey; they had heard the whispers; and Chaucer had seen the light that Rudy had symbolized with his candle that night on the Camino. Chaucer told Rudy that he and Maggie would be married in the coming year, and she showed him her silver scallop ring, which drew a broad smile from Rudy and strong pats on the back for both, including a bear hug for Maggie and a strong handshake with Chaucer.

Prior to the start of the mass, Rudy took a small pad and pen from his pack and recorded the full names and addresses of Chaucer and Maggie, and then gave them his address in Germany. He invited them to visit him should they ever be nearby, and he said that he would be in touch with them to see how their marriage and family life were going.

They all sat through the mass, singing the hymns in their best Spanish. Maggie took communion while the men, non-Catholics, sat in silent prayer, as the Catholic church did not permit communion for them. As Maggie walked toward the altar, Rudy quietly said to Chaucer, "See my friend, Martin Luther was correct, they still don't get it after 450 years." Chaucer smiled.

With the mass over, Rudy and Chaucer and Maggie stood in the plaza and said their goodbyes. Rudy was continuing his pilgrimage out to Cape Finisterre, another three-day walk. The Camino officially ends there at the Ara Solis (altar to the sun) and the lighthouse, where the body of St. James was brought ashore in the first century and from there taken to Santiago.

They wished each other luck and departed with more hugs. Maggie had to get to a phone to call her parents in London to find out about her open flight to Heathrow from Madrid. Chaucer planned to fly to Montreal, so they both needed to get to the Santiago station to catch a train to the Madrid airport.

BOOK FOUR: APPLICATIONS

Chapter 40

Suzette

AMERICAN EXPRESS HAD RECENTLY ESTABLISHED a small office in Santiago at the best hotel in town on the Plaza Galicia. Maggie and Chaucer knew that she would be able to call London from there. Once they found the AmEx office, they had to wait until it opened at 2:30 p.m., as this was Spain, not London, and the lunchtime siesta was two hours and thirty minutes.

Once they got access to a phone, Maggie placed the call to Jasper's office, and he answered immediately.

"Hello, Father, it's Maggie, and I'm with Chaucer in Santiago," Maggie began. "We're calling about our flights to New Orleans and Montreal tomorrow."

"Oh God, Maggie, we have been waiting for you to call us," Jasper responded quickly. "There has been a terrible accident back home." He paused for several seconds. "Suzette was hit by a speeding car on Magazine Street, and she is in Tulane Medical Center. Your mother flew out yesterday to be with her. She is hurt badly, and we need to get home immediately."

"Father, how bad is she? Are the kids and Rufus OK?" Maggie could feel her chest tightening as she pictured her sister lying in a hospital bed.

"They weren't in the car; they were home. It's bad, darling, she's in intensive care. That's why Mom left right away. Also we need Chaucer back in the London office immediately to take over for me. We're flying out tomorrow, so you and I will be on the same plane. My flight from London stops in Madrid at 2 p.m., and you'll join me on the plane, which will take us to Miami, then to New Orleans. Remy booked a flight for Chaucer from Madrid to London at 3:30 p.m. tomorrow. Tell Chaucer it's on British Air and booked under his name. His father wants him back here until we can bring in a new person from New York early next week, then he said Chaucer should go back to Ottawa."

"So am I on Pan Am for the 2 o'clock flight?" Maggie asked, confused and trying to comprehend these events.

"Yes, please get to Madrid as soon as you both can and don't miss the flights. I will see you tomorrow, darling, and please pray for your sister. Pray deeply for her, Maggie, we don't want to lose her." Jasper hung up. Maggie could not remember ever hearing her father's voice so trembling and anxious.

Maggie hung up and quickly explained to Chaucer all she knew about Suzette and the accident. Suzette and Rufus had two little kids and had just bought a small home in New Orleans. She was a great mother to the kids and a wonderful sister to Maggie and Bridgette. Maggie's great happiness of becoming engaged to Chaucer had been body-slammed by this news.

Chaucer then used the AmEx phone to reach Remy in the company office in Montreal.

"Dad, I just learned about Jasper's daughter in New Orleans. Maggie and I finished our pilgrimage this morning, and she just got off the phone with Jasper in London. Can you fill me in on any more news?

"Well, it's not good, Son. Jasper told me that her car was broadsided by a criminal the police were chasing. He ran a red light and hit her car on the driver side. The fire department had to cut her out of the car. Jasper said she was going to a pharmacy to pick up some medicine for their son who was sick, and her husband stayed home with the kids while she went out. Her mother flew out as soon as she learned about the accident, and Jasper agreed to stay in London until he heard from Maggie so they could fly home together."

"We were two days late getting here to Santiago so that's why Maggie just called her father. You want me to go to the London office for now, right?"

"Yes, we really need you there as we are very busy right now, and I can't fly there because of my work here, so I am sending over Mick Hardy from the New York City office in a week. You know the London operations well, so we need you to be there with Walid until Mick can get there. I'm counting on you, Son."

"Don't worry, Dad, I'll be able to handle it. I want to tell you something really important…I proposed to Maggie yesterday, and she agreed, so we are engaged and hope to get married in New Orleans within a year, maybe even next April or May, and I want you and JOA to be there for us."

Remy's voice reflected his happiness. "Well, that is great news. I am very happy for you both, Son."

"And, Dad, I will be taking care of the babies like you asked of me. I want to go over some things with you when I get back home. Can I come home after Mick Hardy gets to London?"

"Yes, that is a good plan. We'll discuss it all then. Please make sure you are on that flight to London tomorrow, Chaucer. Walid needs you at the office. Please call me when you get there. We'll hopefully know more about Maggie's sister then as well. I love you, Chaucer, and I am very pleased about your plans with Maggie. She is a fine woman from a good family. Bye for now."

"Thanks, Dad. I love you too. Bye."

With that call completed, Maggie and Chaucer strapped on their backpacks and walked hand in hand the ten blocks to the station to catch the 4 p.m. train to Madrid, which would be arriving at 11 p.m. Due to the late arrival in Madrid, and knowing that the hostels all would be closed for the night, Remy had asked the AmEx office in Santiago to book two rooms for Maggie and Chaucer at a small hotel he was familiar with, located next to the Madrid airport, to ensure that they would make their flights the next day.

"Chaucer, I'm scared, this must be really serious if both Mom and Dad are going home."

Chaucer held her hand tightly. "We can manage whatever needs to be done, Maggie. You'll be there to help, and I'll take some of the work off Walid until we get more help. I'm sure your father will have some better information tomorrow," he said in a comforting voice, sparing Maggie the details about the seriousness of the accident that his father had told him.

The next day Maggie and Chaucer sat quietly in the Pan Am waiting area at the airport. The arrival and departure information board showed that Maggie's flight, carrying her father, would land on time, and boarding would begin in an hour. Chaucer held Maggie's hand as they sat next to each other, sipping coffee. Both had checked their backpacks already and were just waiting.

"I'm going to discuss with my father a good plan for the babies, Maggie. I don't want anything to get in the way of us now, I promise you," he said with as serious a face as she had ever seen on him. "I've messed this up, but the mess is over. I will fix it and make you proud of me."

She stroked his hand with hers, smiling softly. "Darling Chaucer, I want you to be proud of yourself and think of yourself as a father now. I will come to know these babies, and maybe they will come to know our babies, but we have to make sure that they are well cared for, and that you know that God is pleased, for if God is pleased, then you, I, and the babies will be pleased."

"Yes, I understand, Maggie, I really do. Our pilgrimage was right for us. We have a good path now, sort of like the path that the scallop signs of St. James showed us on the Camino."

Maggie smiled. "Yes, that is a very good way to think of that. We were shown the way, and we received the message. I am very happy for us, Chaucer. We will be great as a team. I am glad you asked me to be your wife. We will have a good life together."

In a few minutes, the announcement to board the Pan Am flight to Miami connecting to New Orleans was made. They got up hand in hand and walked to the gate.

"We have to believe that she will live, Chaucer, we just have too," Maggie said as she squeezed his hands tightly, and a tear dripped down her cheek.

"Yes, we have to believe, and continue to pray for her. Please call me at the London office tomorrow after you see your mother and your sister at the hospital. I want to know what's going on, OK?"

"Yes, I will. I will miss you, Chaucer. I know we will get through this. I will speak with you as soon as I have any information, I promise."

Chaucer grinned confidently. "Now go home and comfort your mother; she will want to see you. You and your father have much to discuss on your flight."

Maggie put her arms around Chaucer and hugged him tightly, and then they kissed deeply, not caring who was watching. "I do love you, Chaucer," she said as she stared into his eyes.

And with that, she turned and walked quickly to the Pan Am flight attendant at the passageway who marked her boarding pass. She then turned and smiled again at Chaucer, and they blew kisses to each other, and then she was gone.

Chapter 41

Running on Empty

CHAUCER WALKED THROUGH THE TERMINAL to a bar and sat alone, just staring out the window at a runway. He sat frozen, rigid even, missing Maggie already. He had been with her every day for the last month. She had to get back to her family, to help them with this crisis, and to finish her studies at Tulane. She owed the Social Work Department her final paper as well as an evaluation of her foreign study program. Chaucer had to let her get on that plane, but he did not want her to go. They needed each other right now. It was a hurt that he had known before, but it was a good hurt this time, a hurt with a future, not someone leaving him and not caring, but someone leaving him and loving him at the same time. He was starting to understand the difference.

An hour later after sipping a beer, Chaucer returned to the waiting area and sat in a chair listening for the announcement for his flight to London. He was sleepy and closed his eyes; he fell asleep and began to dream. He dreamt that Maggie had found him sleeping and had sat down next him. She kissed his forehead and hugged him; he felt her warmth and smelled her hair, then felt her hand on his cheek, and then he woke up. She was not there. But he smiled because she had been there and would be there. He thought of the other women whom he had liked and dated and were now gone, all gone except Maggie, The Mag of NOLA. No more pretending or diving deeply into emotions with other women anymore; that was over. Maggie had come into his life and would stay. And then he heard the boarding call for his flight.

*   *   *

On the plane, Chaucer thought of his father. He missed him too. His father's voice, like Maggie's voice, was comforting. He felt so lucky to have Remy as his dad. It had been almost nine years since his mother had left Ottawa. His father had not remarried, perhaps would never remarry. Sometimes when Chaucer was home, and he watched his father closely, he could see in him a vacant loneliness in his face, his eyes, the way he was quiet, and now, as Chaucer was feeling the absence of Maggie, he was beginning to understand just a little bit of what his father had been living with for all these years.

"Do you ever miss Mom?" Chaucer would occasionally ask Remy when he was staying in the Ottawa house.

"No, Son. That was a long time ago. We each have our peace, and our separate lives now" is how Remy would usually respond. But Chaucer knew that Remy was lying to him. Chaucer knew that he kept a special photo of Olivia on the dresser in his bedroom, and he knew that some nights, when his father was sitting by the fire reading a book, sipping his glass of port, that he longed to hear his wife's voice or footsteps in the house. His father had loved his mother so well, he thought.

"Why did she go?" he asked himself. Chaucer knew it was not because his mother had met another man, and his father had also been faithful to his mother, Chaucer believed. His parents would only tell Chaucer and JOA that they had come to have separate lives — hers taken up with her research and writing, his with his shipping company and the travel it required. They both were strong-willed people who were intensely driven by their work. So intensely driven that they drove each other away. How sad, Chaucer felt. How very sad for them, but also for JOA and him as well.

When Chaucer landed at Gatwick that night, he took a cab to the apartment and soon was asleep. It had been a long travel day and a physically exhausting nine days on the Camino trail.

The next day he rose early and after making coffee, he went for a walk in Mayfair to settle him. He did not want to go to the shipping office first thing. He had called Walid and explained his weariness from traveling and that he would not be in until tomorrow, and Walid agreed.

An hour later, feeling scattered in place and person, he walked to Westminster Abbey for some peace. Chaucer longed to hear Maggie's voice. He walked around inside the abbey, gazing at its beauty and thinking of Maggie. He came to Poet's Corner and sat; he did nothing except just be, sitting and dreaming. He felt at home in that spot, with his personal family history of Poet's Corner with Geoffrey Chaucer in his tomb. His maternal family had a bunch of DNA interned in that stone box. Odd but comforting to him.

By late morning, he had been wandering in the abbey for hours. He realized that all day he had not eaten more than an apple that he had in his satchel. His mind was dizzy from missing Maggie and reading everything he could at Westminster Abbey. He decided to leave and walk outside for fresh air. He found a bench in Victoria Gardens Park, sat down, and laid his head softly on his satchel and looked at the scattered white clouds. He soon fell asleep.

And so he dreamt, and it was about Maggie, and she was sitting across from him at a table, he thought it was at Mandina's, the New Orleans restaurant that she loved, and they were eating crawfish and drinking Dixie Beer, and laughing. She was rubbing her foot on his leg under the table, and he was smiling. He reached across the table to her, and she took his hand. "You do things to me, Maggie. I get feelings like I never have had."

She smiled and nodded. "What kind of feelings, Chaucer?" He smiled back but didn't say anything because he couldn't talk, he was just staring at her, but he could feel her hand in his hand in the dream. And then the noise on Abingdon Street woke him. But he did not sit up. He just lay there; he was still holding Maggie's hand and he was smiling because he could feel her hand, its softness, and her voice was still in his head. He lay for a long time there on the bench. He wanted to get back to her in the dream, he wanted to be with her now.

Whippoorwill's singing
Soft summer breeze
Makes me think of my baby
I left down in New Orleans

I left down in New Orleans
Magnolia, you sweet thing

You're driving me mad
Got to get back to you babe
You're the best I ever had
You're the best I ever had
You whisper, "Good morning"
So gently in my ear
I'm coming home to you babe

I'll soon be there
I'll soon be there

Magnolia, you sweet thing
You're driving me mad
Got to get back to you babe
You're the best I ever had
You're the best I ever had
You're the best I ever had
You're the best I ever had

—Written by J.J. Cale
Guitar and Voice by John Mayer

https://www.youtube.com/watch?v=GjlFzh_FnP0

Chaucer knew that Maggie was to call him in London later that day. It would be a late call, probably dinner time in New Orleans and close to midnight in London. Chaucer went to a grocery store to buy food for the apartment. For the rest of this day he would write about the journey on the Camino de Santiago in his journal. It would keep his mind on Maggie — her beautiful smile, the way she walked, the excitement of her touch, the security of her voice. He knew that she had been so very good for him. It scared him but also gave him a sense of not being alone anymore, of being with someone that he could trust. That was it! He knew he could trust her. With her good family, her chosen career to be a social worker, her abundant spirituality and decency. Yes, if he couldn't trust Maggie then he was out of answers, and that was not the world that Chaucer wanted to live in ever again.

* * *

The weeks that followed were filled with anxiety and sadness for Maggie and her family. After a week in intensive care, Suzette died. Maggie, her parents, Maggie's other sister, Bridgette, and Suzette's husband, Rufus, were at her bedside in the hospital room. The medical team had advised her parents that morning that her vital signs were showing a decline and to prepare for the worse, so they summoned their parish priest, Father Altobello, to come to the hospital and administer the last rites. Suzette's injuries had been extensive, and she soon was unable to breathe on her own, and after seven days she was gone. Suzette was now with God.

The wake and funeral were large family gatherings and noticeably somber compared to the usual New Orleans traditions. Chaucer was unable to be there as his work in London had been extended due to a major shipping incident in the North Sea. One of the company's fleet ships had run into a Norwegian Oil Rig at night, causing the death of four oil workers and major damage to the rig and to the ship that struck it. Walid had to immediately travel to Goteborg, Sweden, where the company's ship had been sent for repairs and an investigation of the accident, thus leaving Chaucer as the London office manager until Walid could return. Chaucer needed to secure information required by Lloyd's to begin the insurance claim and to mitigate the damages and losses. Remy had given Chaucer a list of the records and information that the company would need going forward in the insurance claim and the litigation that would certainly follow. This could not have happened at a worse time for Chaucer.

Chaucer spoke with Maggie on the phone almost every day. He tried to comfort her but her sorrow was too large. She and Bridgette needed to focus on their parents, especially her mother who was beyond grief stricken. Chaucer did his best, given his distance from the family. Maggie understood.

Remy too was heartbroken, wanting Chaucer to be with Maggie during this time. Remy had known the family well as Jasper had been with the company for many years. So Remy caught a flight to New Orleans to represent the company and his family. Chaucer was grateful for his father's thoughtfulness. At the wake, Jasper and Margola hugged Remy and thanked him for coming. His presence was comforting to them.

Rufus, Maggie's brother-in-law, was especially overwhelmed with grief and sadness. The night of the accident, he had come home drunk and had failed to stop at the pharmacy for the medicine that his son needed for his ear infection. Suzette was angry with him and took the car to drive to the pharmacy before it closed, and that was when the accident happened. The family did not know about the condition that Rufus was in before the accident as he never revealed it, although later, his daughter Lyla who was four, said things to her grandparents and Maggie that led them to believe that her father's condition was the reason her mother had driven to the pharmacy.

Everyone in Maggie's family was in a state of depression. So many things had changed in the matter of a few seconds at the intersection of Magazine and Julia streets. To carry on now, especially for the care of the two children, would take all the energy that Maggie, her parents and her sister, Bridgette, could muster. Rufus was becoming less and less helpful as the days passed. His life was unraveling, and Maggie and her family were learning more and more about what the real Rufus was like.

Chapter 42

The Stephanie and Tessa Book of Children

IT WAS THREE WEEKS BEFORE Mick Hardy was able to come from the New York City office and relieve Chaucer in London. The time had allowed Chaucer to better understand the loss of Maggie's sister. Even though he had never met Suzette, he knew how much she meant to Maggie and her family in New Orleans, the family that he would join upon his marriage to Maggie in the coming year.

Chaucer wanted to get back to Ottawa as soon as possible. He wanted time with his father to sort matters out about the babies and talk to Remy about his future with the company. Chaucer and Maggie had talked about having their wedding in New Orleans in May, and that they would live there when married. How that would impact his education and where he would work were big questions to discuss with Remy.

After Chaucer arrived in Ottawa, he and Remy had many good and detailed conversations. Remy was also clearly exuberant about the engagement of his son and Maggie, as Remy admired Jasper, his wife, and his family. Remy was happy that the two families would be bound by this marriage in the future, and he hoped that this family linkage would also help in some small way to ameliorate the sorrow of the loss of Suzette.

Remy and Chaucer decided to call Olivia in Victoria to give her the happy news about the engagement and the sad news about Maggie's sister. Olivia had just returned from Mexico with her boyfriend, Jacob Rosensteen. They had been there to look at locations for a new film that he would be producing. Olivia's voice sounded joyful when she heard the news. "I'm very happy for you and Maggie; she sounds to me to be an intelligent woman with much to bring into a good marriage. I am sorry to learn about her sister, what a terrible accident. Please give her and her family all the help and comfort you can. I will try to arrange my schedule so that I can attend the wedding in New Orleans, so please give me as much advance notice once you set the date." Chaucer agreed, but he actually did not care if his mother attended the wedding for his sake, but he did want Maggie and her family to meet his eccentric mother. Chaucer felt no remorse in his thoughts about this; he wanted any remorse to be gone from his history and eliminated from his future. The Camino journey had fixed this in his mind.

JOA, who was living in a house near the University in Ottawa, was in her second academic year there. When Chaucer arrived from London, he called her to tell her about his engagement to Maggie and the details of the wedding. Her immediate response was to drive over to see her father and brother. When she arrived, she ran up to Chaucer, whom she had not seen in almost nine months, and hugged and kissed him on the cheek with great vigor. She wanted to see a photo of Maggie, her future sister-in-law. "Oh, Chaucer, she is beautiful, how did you manage that one!!!" she said with great laughter. Remy and Chaucer just smiled broadly.

"We hope you'll be able to be in the wedding, JOA; Maggie can't wait to meet you, too." JOA was so very happy to be asked and screamed, "Of course I want to be in the wedding! Who's going to keep an eye on you that day if not me?" she shouted. Remy and Chaucer loved seeing this genuine excitement in JOA for it reminded them of her as a child, and that was a fine memory for them.

The three of them then spent the dinner hour talking about Chaucer's time away, JOA's studies at school, and the possible timing of the wedding the following May. JOA was in great sympathy for Chaucer and Maggie about the accident in New Orleans and offered to help in any way, which Chaucer was grateful for. He told her that he hoped to be going to New Orleans soon, and then he would let

JOA know how she could help.

Later that night after JOA had gone back to her University house, Remy poured a glass of port, lit a Cuban cigar, and asked Chaucer if he wanted either (Chaucer took the port and declined the cigar). They walked out on the porch overlooking the Ottawa River. It was time — time for Remy to let Chaucer in on the news.

About two months ago, Remy had flown to San Francisco to visit the company office and see Stephanie. He spent two evenings at dinner with her to discuss the future of his grandchild and the future of Stephanie, who at this time was almost eight months pregnant. Stephanie and her roommate, Sissy, were still working in clerical jobs at the company office there. Now Remy needed to have Stephanie come to terms with her future and the future of the child.

The discussions were amicable as Remy represented the sympathetic father figure that had been so missing in Stephanie's life. Remy was as kind and loving to her as he could be, and they reached a verbal agreement, which would soon be set down in writing. Stephanie had come to understand over the past six months that she was not ready to be a mother, to raise a child, to settle down. Her wanderlust still needed to be satisfied, and she and Sissy had talked of continuing their travels. They both wanted to go to Hawaii, Australia, and Europe while they were young and not married. Stephanie was quite happy that Remy had hired her and would be the grandfather of her baby, as her own parents were not together, unreliable, and financially poor.

She decided to agree with what Remy proposed: permit Remy to legally adopt the baby as the grandparent and have full custody. Stephanie would retain very liberal visitation rights as well. Further, Remy would give her and Sissy one-way tickets to Sydney, Australia two months after the birth of the baby, and he would hire both Stephanie and Sissy for a six-month period for clerical work in the company office there. In addition, he would give Stephanie $5,000 (U.S.) after the baby was born. The baby would have the Giroux name and reside in Ottawa with Remy, JOA, and a nanny that he would hire.

Stephanie believed that this agreement was in the best interests of the baby, Remy, and her. She had come to better understand herself and what she wanted from life while in San Francisco. She also had learned to trust Remy, likely the first male adult in her life that she had come to respect and trust. He had done everything that he had said he would do for her. Furthermore, and of real fundamental importance to Stephanie, Remy was the real blood grandfather of the baby. This all led her to feel comfortable and quite grateful. She realized that no man had ever treated her with such great respect and honor, certainly not her own father. She also knew that she would not want to marry Chaucer or be in a romantic relationship with him, so this agreement would preserve her as the mother and keep her and Remy as family and friends. It all made sense to her, so she agreed and expressed her satisfaction at the dinner table on the second night. Remy was pleased. Sissy agreed with the deal between Remy and Stephanie, and in her own way, she had a crush on Remy as being that handsome and respectful male that had also been absent in her life in Connecticut as well.

While in San Francisco, Remy made arrangements with the office of the local ob-gyn where Stephanie was a patient and with the hospital where she would deliver. Once the baby was old enough to fly, and Stephanie had recovered, he would fly them both to Ottawa so she could see his home and where the baby would live, meet the nanny, and feel reassured that the baby would be raised well. She could not believe her good fortune and how the craziness and panic of the first months of her pregnancy had turned out like this. Her sense of trust in Remy continued to grow with his continued honesty and kindness. She was beginning to believe in miracles, and she had even taken up offering prayers of thankfulness, which she had never done before.

As Chaucer listened to all this from Remy, it occurred to him that the baby would be born any day now. He knew that the whispers from his pilgrimage of atonement and expiation had been a prophecy for him. He sat quietly with his father and thanked God for his father, his wisdom, love, and kindness. He knew that the world was a better place for having a man like Remy in it. Still, Chaucer needed to reconcile his plan of living in New Orleans and the baby being in Ottawa. He hoped that Remy would have some ideas on that.

Remy left the porch for a few minutes, and when he returned, he handed Chaucer a copy of the agreement that he had signed with Stephanie. It outlined the matter of dual Canadian and American citizenship for the baby, and all the other issues. The lawyers had been able to construct a document that granted dual citizenship for the baby because Chaucer was the father and a Canadian and Stephanie was the mother and an American. The magistrate in Ottawa had approved the agreement forthwith. Here it was, in black and white. Chaucer read it, got up, and hugged his father. "Thank you, Dad. You are so amazing; this means so much for me and Maggie." Remy just grinned. He knew that he had done the best for all of them. He was a very happy man again after all the years without his own children as now his grandchild would live with him, although he and Chaucer needed to agree to that.

"OK, that is the plan with Stephanie," Remy said. "Now I'll tell you about my discussions with Tessa." Chaucer had little indication about what his father was about to tell him.

"We have firmly established that her baby son, whom she named McCarthy, is your child. Agreed?" Remy said as he looked at his son. Chaucer, without expression, softly nodded.

"He was born while you were away. He is five months old, happy, and healthy. She named him for U.S. Sen. Eugene McCarthy, who was the first to speak out against the Vietnam war and against the policies of President Johnson. She said that she even sent Senator McCarthy a photo of the baby telling him that she named the child after him because of what he did to challenge the President. The senator sent her a signed letter of appreciation and a certificate making the baby an "official" citizen of Minnesota. I have a copy of that letter in my office to show you. Tessa is a strong-willed woman, Chaucer. She reminds me of your mother in some ways." Chaucer made a face and shook his head ruefully at the thought.

Remy continued. "Tessa and I met in Buffalo in May when the baby was ten weeks old. He looks like both of you; he's adorable. Tessa is living with her parents, whom I met. Her father worked in the Lackawanna Steel Mill for thirty-five years, and he is not well. He has emphysema from the toxic materials at the mill and smoking cigarettes. He carries an oxygen tank around when he leaves the house, Tessa said. Her mother is very heavy and has diabetes and other issues." Remy's voice sounded sad. "They do not seem to have the energy or the means to bring up a grandchild, and they did not express an interest in having the baby live with them forever," Remy said calmly.

"Tessa will be returning to school in Toronto later next month as she needs only one more semester for her degree. She was quite friendly and helpful in discussing options for the baby. We agreed on this plan." Remy stopped and took a breath. "She will bring the baby here when the semester starts." Chaucer stared intently at his father while he spoke. "My lawyer will prepare an agreement where I will be, as paternal grandfather, in joint custody of McCarthy, and he will also have joint Canadian-American citizenship. Tessa and I have agreed to discuss and negotiate living arrangements for the baby given her circumstances of being at the University of Toronto, and the need for her to finish her degree. We also agreed that Canadian provincial family law will govern our agreement. Her parents agreed to this as well, trusting me as the other grandparent. Our mission, that of her parents and me, was to keep everything honest and amicable for the sake of Tessa and McCarthy.

"My nanny will live here full time, and JOA will help out on weekends. Tessa will come here to pick up the baby and take him to Buffalo for school breaks. I will pay her gas and food money whenever she needs to come here and return to Buffalo. Like Stephanie, she is glad that I am the biological grandfather. She and her parents are very comfortable with this arrangement, as am I," Remy paused and looked directly at Chaucer, "and as I hope you are too."

Chaucer nodded, speechless at this turn of events. Perhaps the spirit of God had been at work with Remy long ago because his kindness and generosity was clearly manifest over his lifetime as far as Chaucer could determine. He thought of his Giroux grandparents and about his uncle in Geneva. This all made sense to Chaucer. He was from an honorable and kind family, and he realized he was a blessed man.

Remy continued, "After we receive Stephanie's baby, we will reassess the need for a second nanny, either full or part time. Right now, I have my eyes on two sisters here in town — Roisin O'Rourke, the one who has agreed to be a live-in nanny here, and her older sister, Ciara, who is a retired nurse, who may agree to help her out. All of this is to be determined as the circumstances develop. So that is where we are...I like this arrangement, and I believe it should work. I also have had a discussion with a friend at the Golf Club whose brother is a local pediatrician, and his practice will be happy to accept the babies once everything is in place."

With all this said, Remy stood up and walked to the railing, taking a large puff of his cigar. "Two last things, Chaucer, just so you know now. First, Tessa has started to break the ice about her post-graduate work. It seems that she will want to follow her opportunities in the arts, meaning her musical and singing career. She and I both agreed that could put her in a situation where the baby stays here in Ottawa for extended periods of time. I told her the same thing that I recently explained to Stephanie, and that is I may want to have primary custody rights of the child if her career takes her all over the country or beyond. Again, she seemed OK with that as long as she could have extended visitation and temporary custody when she was in Buffalo or wherever she might call home. I agreed to that, although she and I have not signed any papers as I have done with Stephanie. I guess we will need to see how it goes with Roisin in the coming months, but everything we do must be in the best interest of the babies, and the conversations with their mothers must always be based on mutual trust and complete honesty. Don't you agree?"

Chaucer nodded and smiled lovingly at Remy. He looked to the sky and thought, "God, you surely created a special human in my father. Please make many more like him."

"OK, the last thing is about you. Where do you, as the father, fit into all this? Well, that is what we need to discuss now." Remy stopped to sip his glass of port. "I am very pleased for you and Maggie, as I have said. I know that chances are that you will end up living in New Orleans after you get married, and I doubt that Maggie wants to move here, based on what you told me about her career goals. So assuming you are away much of the time leaving me, JOA, and the nanny with the children, I will need you to come home five or six times a year to help out, especially when I am away in Scotland or at our other offices. Also, when the babies are older, in a couple of years, you know, walking, talking, toilet trained, etc., then you should expect to have them come to stay with you for lengthy visits, so they can know you and Maggie, and to give me and JOA, assuming she stays in Ottawa, and Roisin a rest or a vacation. That is what I will need from you if we are going to make this right for the children and our family. And look, your mother seems to have little interest in much of these developments other than to know what my, our, basic plans are. So we need to write her off. She now appears to have a Hollywood boyfriend who is taking her all over and getting deals for her books and making deals for her to help with screenwriting, so I am happy for her but I am not expecting anything from her." Remy was finished, and he looked at his son with a sense of accomplishment on his face.

"Well, Dad, this all sounds fine and logical. To answer your questions, yes, I want to be involved with the babies. I want to be the father, as I should be. You see my pilgrimage on the Camino has removed any doubts that I had, and you need to know that now. But what about my work or school? I still need another year for my degree, and do you want me to still work for the company?" he asked, needing to put his questions into the conversation.

His father puffed on his cigar and paced the porch floor, hands now behind his back. He cleared his throat.

"Chaucer, more port?" he offered, and Chaucer agreed, holding his glass out as Remy poured. He knew from his years with Remy, that the "Father Moment" was about happen.

"Son, you are aware that almost all our major actions as men have major consequences, yes?" Chaucer nodded his head in agreement.

"Your actions with these two women have put you into a new set of circumstances, responsible circumstances and you are at an age where you must now accept the consequences of your prior actions," Remy said as he slowly paced the floor, "which means that you will now have two children to raise, which I am pleased to help with, but I have determined that you are going to have to take a major role in the business now. Here is how I see this. At some point in about ten years or so, my partners and I expect to begin to retire or reduce our commitment. We have talked about putting you in charge of some major North American operations of our company, maybe even as director. You have done great work so far, we all have agreed on that, including your soon to be father-in-law, Jasper, who speaks so highly of you."

Chaucer sipped his port and listened intently.

"You have a career path now, and you do not need a university degree to proceed in our company. You just have to work hard and produce results, so going back to the university for another year should now be out as an option. And since you will likely be living in New Orleans, and we have offices there, and in Houston, Tampa, Miami, and Charleston, I want you to start to assume more work and responsibility in our Southern Group. We will be promoting Jasper to North American senior vice president as soon as Malcolm

Whittingham retires in a few months, and we want you to be his executive assistant in the New Orleans office. That will give you time to learn what you will need to learn to take over for Jasper when he retires, probably in ten years or sooner," he said looking directly at Chaucer.

"Your family responsibilities are now laid out for you, and while you may have wanted to pursue another career, you now have children and a soon-to-be wife to account for, and this is an option that makes the most sense for you, for me as your father, and for our company."

Chaucer grimaced, seeing his life options just disappear with his father's tidy plan. He got up and walked to the railing near his father. He stood quietly for a few minutes, looking out at the Ottawa River. As he did, a fishing boat motored past their house, and a beam of sunlight reflected off the metal hull of the boat, making Chaucer blink. He heard a whisper that said "Abba, Abba, Abba" and it made him smile. He thought of Rudy on the Camino with his light and the words he spoke. Suddenly Chaucer's concerns just melted away. He knew that if he trusted in God, and with Maggie at his side, "all would be well and all manner of things will be well," as he remembered this saying from the writings of Julian of Norwich, a Christian mystic in the Middle Ages whom he had read about.

Chaucer took another sip of his port, smiled, and turned to look at his father face to face. "Dad, that is a wonderful idea and plan. I could not ask for or expect more. Like I said, JOA and I are very fortunate to have you as our Abba."

"Your what?" Remy asked.

"Our father, Dad, our Abba, we are very blessed." Chaucer's face was solid, with no hesitation or uncertainty. Chaucer felt very calm inside now.

Chapter 43

Six Weeks Later—Early September

OVER THE NEXT TWO WEEKS, Chaucer had plenty to do. The first thing he did was visit his old family barber in town. Remy did not demand that Chaucer get a more business appropriate haircut, but he strongly suggested it to his son. Chaucer had over time let his hair grow quite long, which was fine for a music career or a professional hockey player, but not all that appealing for his expanding role in the company. When he returned home that afternoon, Remy looked at Chaucer, nodded his approval, and said, "Good decision, Son." Chaucer smiled, knowing that his family and his work would now be his most important focus.

Chaucer spent his mornings with Remy reviewing the entire business operation with a special focus on the U.S. southern ports. In the afternoons, he helped JOA with some big repairs to her apartment, prior to the semester beginning at the university. Remy then took Chaucer to Montreal where they met with the senior partners for three days to affirm that Chaucer would be going to New Orleans to work with Jasper there. Chaucer had known almost all the senior partners since he was a little boy in Ottawa, and as Remy's son, they had kept tabs on him over the years, hoping that a fine lad like Chaucer might one day join the company that his father had started almost thirty years before.

On the drive home to Ottawa, Remy and Chaucer spoke less

about the company and more about Chaucer's coming role as a father. Remy could tell that Chaucer was still in awe over his new responsibilities. As they drove along the highway, they exchanged many words.

"Son, I have spoken to Pastor Leo about you and about how you have been coming to your decision. We had a very good discussion. He reminded me of some spiritual matters that are important for you to understand at a time like this, so I hope you will call him and set a time to visit him at the church. I know you want to get down to New Orleans as soon as you can, but I believe that a little tune-up with Pastor Leo now would be very good for you. After all, he has known you all your life. What do you say?"

Chaucer softly grinned. "Yup, he has, he's known me all these years. Yes, I think that is a good idea, Dad. I'll call him when we get home, thanks for thinking of that."

Remy smiled, happy that Chaucer was so open to his suggestion.

"One other thing, Dad, can we work out my schedule with the company and plan a date when I can go see Maggie?"

Remy nodded. "Sure, let's get out our calendars and discuss this at dinner. You do need to be with her now. She needs you, Chaucer. Yes, I agree, you need to go soon."

* * *

Two days later Pastor Leo gave Chaucer a big hug when he walked into his office at the church. It was a good hug, for both.

"The good Lord has truly blessed my day. Chaucer, you look well. I was very happy to get your call yesterday. Dad OK? Mom and JOA?" he asked as they both sat down in his office. The pastor had photos of his boys and grandsons wearing hockey and soccer sweaters on his wall, along with pictures of various religious figures, and of course, his large artwork of Jesus from the Sermon on the Mount.

They discussed Chaucer's family and his recent months in Europe, including his time on the Camino de Santiago with Maggie and his engagement to Maggie. Pastor Leo was delighted to be with Remy's son and learn about his current situation and travels. He remembered Chaucer sitting in that very chair years ago when he was about to leave for Vancouver with his mother and JOA. He

Six Weeks Later—Early September

remembered the anguish in the boy, with the pending loss of his relationship with his father. Pastor Leo recalled that day well.

Chaucer began, "I have never been so quiet in all my life as I was walking the Camino. It was just incredible for me, and for Maggie. We met an older guy from Germany, his name was Rudy. It was like magic, how he found us and what he said to me."

"Magic, in what way, Chaucer?" the pastor asked, knowing so well that what is often perceived as magic, or as a magical moment, is usually a time when a person's soul is touched by their thoughts and/or deeds, and that the spirit of God and voice of God inside them has spoken.

"Well, he came at a critical time in our pilgrimage, just when I thought that I would have heard more from God, as I was wondering if it was just a beautiful scenic walk or was it really a spiritual pilgrimage."

"Go on."

"The more I think of that first day when we met Rudy, and then the night when Rudy came for me when I was sleeping, I think it was on purpose. I think that God sent him to me, to get me to listen even better, you know, my need to understand my role as a father. I thought I had been listening, but Rudy was the messenger sent to get me to focus." Chaucer looked at Pastor Leo. "Do you think he could have been the messenger for my spiritual forgiveness?"

"What do you think, my son?" the pastor asked.

"Well, yes, it just had to be that, Pastor Leo, didn't it?"

"God works in mysterious ways, Chaucer, you know that. He gives us a good brain to think about these things and then sends us little notes to get us to understand ourselves better, which is to understand God's voice within us, that's what I think." He smiled gently.

Chaucer smiled back, comfortable in Pastor Leo's presence, at peace with himself about the babies now. He was happy to have this time with his old friend, spiritual mentor, and coach.

"I spoke to your father about the role of St. Joseph in the life of Jesus, and how that could be a lesson for you. Did he mention our conversation to you?" Pastor Leo asked.

"Well, he started to talk about that a few days ago but we were also in the middle of some meetings in Montreal at the company office, and he never finished," Chaucer said.

"OK, I'll let your father have that discussion with you so I will only say that Joseph is the patron saint of fathers and families. Just remember what he did for Mary and Jesus. Think of the love and kindness in his heart. St. Joseph listened to the voice of God, just like you have done. I also suggested that your father take you to the St. Joseph's Oratory in Montreal as well, to pray there and open your hearts — I mean open your heart, Chaucer — to the life of St. Joseph."

Chaucer looked at him, puzzled, thinking, "Why did he say 'your hearts,' then change it to just mine" but Chaucer let the thought slip. "Yes, we should have done that when we were in Montreal a few days ago. I'll ask him to go with me before I leave for New Orleans."

Pastor Leo smiled. His mission with Chaucer was accomplished that day.

*   *   *

That night at dinner, Remy and Chaucer discussed his transition from Ottawa to New Orleans. Chaucer's bigger role in the company, with the pending marriage to Maggie, left them with much to organize and plan. Chaucer was pleased that his father was so very thorough in his thinking about his new life in New Orleans.

They also talked about the babies. Tessa's baby boy, McCarthy, was now almost six months old and doing just fine. Remy suggested that they both go to Buffalo to see the baby, yet while Chaucer was ready to be the father in absentia, he was still not ready to see Tessa. His forgiveness for her was in his mind, not yet totally in his heart, and he knew that he must remedy that soon. "Dad, I do want to see McCarthy very much, but I'm still not all in on seeing Tessa right now."

Remy looked at his son. "Well, that is good about seeing the boy, and soon you'll have to see Tessa if this whole plan is to work out for everyone. Remember, this is about the child, not about you and Tessa or me. We need to think about the child now and going forward, don't you agree?"

Chaucer looked at his father. "My mind and heart are with Maggie now. Our lives are going to be merging, so I am thinking about us."

"That's not good enough, not big enough for what is happening now. I strongly suggest that you rethink what you just said because it was about you and not about your son; do you understand that?"

Chaucer shrunk back and looked defeated. "You're right, Dad, I am an abba, and I need to be better and bigger in my thinking. Actually, I can hear Maggie saying the same thing if she were here right now."

Remy smiled broadly. "Well, I am glad you are seeing this moment for what it is, and I can't wait for Maggie to join this family. She and I together will be able to manage you just fine, I see."

And with that, Chaucer laughed and hugged his father. "OK, let's plan a visit for us both to see Tessa and McCarthy; it is time."

Remy let out a small sigh of relief, knowing that his son was growing up to assume his obligations. H was a very happy man.

* * *

Stephanie's baby boy, named Mickey, was now more than two months old and healthy. She was recovering well in San Francisco, and she would be coming soon to Ottawa with the baby to visit Remy and see the house where the baby would live, and to meet JOA and the nanny, Roisin O'Rourke, whom Remy had indeed hired.

Stephanie had always loved baseball. Her maternal grandparents had occasionally taken her as a child to see the Yankees play in the Bronx. She had loved the handsome Mickey Mantle and had a crush on him as a little girl, so she wanted to give the boy a name that meant something to her. The legal adoption of Mickey was on schedule for November.

Remy and Chaucer also made time to drive to Montreal to the St. Joseph Oratory site where they sat and talked, prayed and meditated. JOA accompanied them, and in the short road journey she learned much about the last year and a half in Chaucer's life. Even though her father had kept her informed about Chaucer, she could hardly believe that her big brother was now the father of two children, and he would be moving to New Orleans to get married, all happening so soon.

Rather than laugh or be sarcastic to his situation, JOA felt completely happy and joyful for her brother. She loved the thought of having two nephews and being their aunt. She knew how much he had missed their father and how their mother had treated them as baggage to be stored in a closet. JOA had been there; she was his witness. Her affection for her mother was nearly non-existent, just the opposite of what she felt for Remy and Chaucer. They were a family again, her family. JOA felt that Olivia was the mother of Chaucer and herself essentially in name only.

On the return trip to Ottawa that afternoon, the words of Pastor Leo in their meeting two days before came back to Chaucer. Why had he said "your hearts" when he meant just "my heart?" Chaucer couldn't get that off his mind.

Chapter 44

More Questions

IN NEW ORLEANS, the death of Suzette had thrown the family headlong into anger, grief, and confusion. Prior to Suzette marrying Rufus, Jasper and Margola had liked Rufus very much, but over the past eight years since the couple married, their view of him had gradually changed. When Suzette and the children came for Sunday dinners, often Rufus failed to attend. His business seemed to be intact for a while, yet Suzette often asked her parents for loans to "tide them over until the clients of Rufus would pay their bills." Suzette never told her parents what the problem was, but Rufus had been gambling over the years, and little by little the old friends that his wife and family knew were gradually being replaced by new friends, many who were previously unknown and seemed unsavory.

Rufus's father, Jean-Baptiste, lived in Houma in the bayou area southwest of New Orleans. Jean-Baptiste owned a fleet of six helicopters that serviced the oil rigs owned by the smaller drilling companies. He and his wife had sent Rufus to college to be the first in either of their families to go to LSU. That was where Rufus met Suzette, and they married after they graduated. Rufus had started a small remodeling/design company whose clients were area contractors, but after a few years, the business slumped and many of his clients quit, forcing Rufus to close down his business and thus making Suzette the sole supporter of the family. The salary that Suzette made in banking was good but not enough to make up for the loss of income from Rufus's business. Rufus told Suzette's family that he had picked up some private, individual clients. He worked out of their house, thus making day care easier for him and Suzette. Cash flow was unpredictable but they had enough money to allow them to buy a small home. Jasper had provided the funds for the down payment, so the couple could get a bank to approve a mortgage. Yet Jasper never felt comfortable with Rufus after his business failed.

One afternoon two weeks after Suzette's funeral, Jasper drove to Houma to visit with Jean-Baptiste. He wanted to have a father-to-father chat about Rufus. With Rufus having two children to care for alone, Jasper and Margola wanted to have greater assurance that Rufus was not suffering from an illness or another issue that was being kept quiet from them. The two men had a good, hour-long conversation about Rufus. Jean-Baptiste had only revealed that Rufus had come to him to borrow some modest sums of money since his business had failed, and this did not seem unusual to Jean-Baptiste given the circumstances, although Rufus had not repaid his father for any of the loans so far.

After their discussion, Jean-Baptiste took Jasper to his favorite Cajun club for fried catfish and golden moonshine. About an hour before dark, Jasper and Jean-Baptiste toasted to their children, hugged, and Jasper arrived back home as the sun was setting. Jasper had learned nothing significantly new about Rufus during the visit. He was still not at ease; his instincts told him something was awry. Perhaps it was the voodoo in the Cajun swamps west of New Orleans, or perhaps it was just nothing at all. Whatever the cause, Jasper was not all good with his son-in-law. Given the circumstances of the death of his daughter, Jasper remained skeptical of Rufus.

In the first weeks after the accident, Jasper and Margola had Rufus and the two children over for dinner with Maggie and Bridgette every night. Rufus and the kids were subdued and the dinners were rather somber affairs. Nothing seemed to work to ease their pain: not hugs, prayers, special foods, etc. The joy in life was gone for them, but especially for the kids as their mother's death had left a large void in their lives, one that would last forever.

* * *

The fall of 1972 was a time of slow recovery for Maggie and her family. Jasper and Margola gradually resumed their working lives. Maggie finished her Master of Social Work graduate program at Tulane and graduated in December. Bridgette took a leave of absence from her job, and she and Maggie were omnipresent at Rufus's home caring for the children. Lyla was almost five years old and Jackson was nearly three.

Chaucer spent months working with Remy and company managers preparing for him to move to New Orleans and coordinate the company offices in the southern states. Most of this training was accomplished at the company headquarters in Montreal. He had not seen Maggie in months but Christmas was coming, and they would be together then. They both had decided that being apart was best for them for now. They spent much time on the phone together planning the May wedding and reviewing possible living locations and options in New Orleans.

Remy had been to Glasgow once each month for the past year working on the United Kingdom special projects, some of which were now top secret as they coordinated with the Royal Navy Command. His visits to Glasgow had been many over the past years, and he wanted Chaucer to accompany him on a trip there soon.

Chaucer and Remy were also learning to be a father and grandfather to McCarthy (Mac) and Mickey (Mick) who were now living at the Ottawa house with them. Remy had hired two sisters to be nannies for the boys. He had known Ciara O'Rourke, who was a retired nurse, and her younger sister, Roisin, through their brother, Donal, from golf club events over the years. Roisin lived in Remy's house with the boys, and Ciara came to help out for a few hours most days. JOA also helped some nights and on weekends, especially if Remy and Chaucer were away on company business.

Chaucer was introduced to fatherhood quickly as Roisin had instructed him on feeding and changing diapers. At first, he resisted but soon his paternal instincts prevailed, and he was all in on the caregiving. As Remy watched Chaucer and JOA take care of and play with the boys, he would get sentimental thinking about himself doing these very tasks for them years ago. Remy was so happy that he helped Tessa and Stephanie. He had earned his money by hard work, and to spend his resources on his family was his honor, his privilege, and his Christian duty, he believed. Remy never had second thoughts about his actions to protect and embrace these little children.

During the visits to Ottawa by Tessa, which occurred every month or so, Chaucer was conveniently in Montreal at the company headquarters. He wanted it that way, and Tessa seemed pleased by that as well.

When JOA and Roisin met Tessa for the first time, they all smiled and were joyful together. Roisin was in her early fifties and knew how to manage people and babies, having herself grown up in a family of nine in County Cork, Ireland. She was a happy woman, and she knew how to spread happiness in any room. Remy had made an excellent choice in hiring her.

Chapter 45

Glasgow

IN LATE NOVEMBER Remy had pressing European business in the London office and particularly in Glasgow. Over dinner one night in Ottawa, he spoke to Chaucer about his upcoming trip.

"I'll be in London on the Royal Navy project for three days, then I'll go to Glasgow for three more days. I would like it if you would fly to Glasgow and meet me, so please arrange your schedule through the travel agency. It will be in two weeks. Can you do this for us?"

"Sure, Dad. What is the work about in Glasgow?" asked a curious Chaucer.

"Well, it's part of the project with the Navy and part personal, too," Remy replied with a twinkle in his eye. Chaucer saw his father's look and filed it away.

After dinner, they both played with the children. Mac was now seven months old, smiling, starting to crawl and making funny baby sounds while Mick was four months old and joyful and curious too. Chaucer had seen the chaos of the previous year turn into a new, wonderful family life almost overnight. His conversion to the committed Abba was manifest in the Ottawa house. Remy, JOA, and Roisin often smiled at each other watching Chaucer sit on the floor with the two boys and playing with little cars and stuffed animals. His happiness radiated, his laughter making the children smile broadly. The struggles and hurt that Chaucer had once carried were tucked away. His heavenly Father and his earthly father had helped him do this. The role of Abba was real for Chaucer now. He seemed to love it.

* * *

Chaucer was preparing for a weeklong visit to New Orleans to see Maggie, which would start the week after he returned from Glasgow with Remy. The engaged couple had much to do, wedding plans to confirm.

"You'll arrive on the 21st, is that the plan?" Maggie asked on the phone.

"Yes, is that OK with you and your family?" Chaucer asked.

"Dad said you can have the third-floor guest room for the entire week. He and Mother and I have most of the wedding plans thought out, and we want to review them with you."

"Sure, but if you think that everything is good then I'll be happy with that, OK?" said a confident Chaucer.

"How are the boys doing?" she asked, and Chaucer proudly shared the new things that Mac and Mick were doing and how much fun it was to watch them develop week by week.

"So will we be looking at places for us to live during my visit?" he asked. Maggie assured him that she already had some locations scouted out to show him. "Are you all set to start work for the diocese after Christmas?" he inquired.

"Yes," Maggie replied confidently. "They wanted me to start now but I explained our need for time to plan the wedding, plus the time that I have been spending with Suzette's children, so Father Altobello was OK with my starting after the New Year. He said that I will have my plate full with the problems created during Mardi Gras in February, so he wants me ready for that."

Chaucer chuckled. "Is it really that bad, Maggie?"

"You'll see for yourself soon enough. It's like two weeks of New Year's Eve with the big Krewes having their best events and floats the last five days. It looks crazy to the outsider, but it is well planned. It gets really rowdy here, which is why I will be working during the entire event. People just drink too much, and then conflicts erupt, etc. I just know that I will be very busy, Chaucer."

"OK, I understand, it's probably like a night when the Montreal Canadians win the Stanley Cup, and Montreal breaks out into a big celebration, but in your town it's for two weeks."

"Yes, that's a good comparison," Maggie replied with a little laugh.

*   *   *

Two weeks later Chaucer took a flight out of Montreal to Glasgow. He caught a shuttle bus to the hotel where the company employees stayed when in town. Remy met him in the lobby.

"Good flight, Son?" he asked.

"Yes, very nice, Dad. What are our plans for the next couple of days?"

"Tomorrow and Thursday, you and I will be at our office at the docks. We have some engineers to meet with and review some ship surveys that they have done for us. We're likely to buy three new container ships for our work with the Royal Navy. The Navy is sending an officer to sit in the meeting with you, me, and Malcolm Buchanan tomorrow and Thursday. I believe that the U.S. Navy is also sending an officer."

"Dad, this sounds like a big project for the company," Chaucer said, with a bit of awe in his voice.

"Yes, it could just be the start. We'll take it slow and see if it fits in with our business. You know that the government agencies are notorious for not paying their bills on time, and if we do this, that will need to change. That is why we are starting slow as a test, sort of a pilot project for us and them."

"OK, I understand, Dad. That sounds like a good plan," said Chaucer, realizing that his father had him involved for a reason, and now he understood that better.

For the next two days, Remy, Chaucer, and Malcolm Buchanan, the director of the Glasgow office, met and negotiated with the engineers and the Royal Navy representative while the U.S. Navy officer observed. They reached some agreements about the ships and established a critical path management chart for the next six months to move the project to the next phase. Everyone was happy as the two-day meeting ended.

On the way back to the hotel, Remy looked at Chaucer with a

happy and confident smile.

"Son, we are going to dinner tonight at the home of a local scientist, Dr. Teasag Fraser. She teaches at the University of Glasgow here, and she is an expert in evolutionary biology. She studies and does research in Australia, New Zealand, and Costa Rica. I am sure that you will find her very interesting and pleasant. What do you say?"

"Sure, sounds like fun. That is what JOA's degree will be in. I remember you got her interested in it, and she loves it," said Chaucer, smiling.

Remy suggested that they briefly retire to the hotel bar for a post-meeting, pre-dinner cocktail, so he led Chaucer into the barroom, and they sat in a booth by a window overlooking the River Clyde. They could see the company docks in the distance.

The waiter brought their drinks, and Remy proposed a toast: "Here's to our new agreement with the government and Royal Navy," he said as they both smiled, "and here's to our expanding family." They clinked glasses and sipped their drinks. Chaucer sat relaxed and content.

"So tonight, you will meet Professor Teasag Fraser and her 6-year-old son, Jockie," Remy said, calmly smiling. He paused and leaned over toward Chaucer. "Chaucer, Jockie Fraser is your brother," Remy announced and sat back.

Chaucer almost choked on his drink. He stared at his father. "What? What do you mean, he is my brother?"

"This is the other reason that I wanted you to come to Glasgow with me," Remy said as he smiled confidently, took a deep breath, and sat back against the wall of the leather booth.

Chaucer, obviously confused by this announcement, looked nervously at Remy's face. Instantly his mind flashed back to the conversation that he had had a few weeks ago with Pastor Leo when the pastor used the words "open *your* hearts to Joseph." Now he knew that he was speaking about both Chaucer and Remy. Pastor Leo knew about the child in Glasgow. Voila!

When Chaucer didn't speak, Remy continued. "After your mother and I divorced years ago, I was depressed and a bit angry, and I missed you and JOA and our family life. A couple of years later after Monica and I stopped seeing each other, and while I was here on company business, I was introduced to Teasag at a dinner party.

We took a liking to each other. She too had been divorced so we had a similar psychology at that time. She was very easy to be with. She didn't have children, and mine were gone. About two months after we first meet, she had an academic conference at McGill in Montreal, and she contacted me at our office. We had dinner again, and that was when we started dating. I would see her when I was here in Glasgow, and she came back to McGill for another meeting the next year."

Chaucer smiled because he now understood why his father had made so many trips to Glasgow over the years. Chaucer was making sense of it all now.

"Well, after about a year of seeing Teasag, she was pregnant with our baby."

"Oh my God, Dad!" Chaucer blurted out. "So it happened to you too?" he said smiling as large as he could, shaking his head, and trying not to laugh.

"Yes, it did. It wasn't planned but after long discussions on my next visit here we both decided that having the child would be the right thing to do, for the child and for us too. We wanted to have the child. Money was not an issue as we both have our careers, and Teasag and I decided to have a child to share between us."

Chaucer felt so happy, sort of like he had just been voted into an elite college fraternity. He and his father were peers. Perhaps that is the reason that his father had been so supportive of him with the babies the past year, he thought.

"Dad, it is so amazing to learn this about you. I can't wait to tell JOA and Maggie!"

Remy's face turned serious, and he looked sternly at Chaucer. "You and I will talk to JOA about this together, and not a word before then, understood? And say nothing about this to Maggie or her parents until after you, me, Maggie, and perhaps her parents are together, and I can share this with them. Agreed?"

"Why?" Chaucer asked, puzzled because he did not like the idea of keeping a secret from Maggie.

"Because your sister is still young, and she needs to hear and understand the full story about Jockie. I don't want her thinking that our circumstances, yours and mine, are the new standard, or worse, that her family has no morality." Chaucer nodded his concurrence. Remy continued, "I know Maggie's parents well. They are practicing Catholics. I would like to explain the circumstances, so her parents understand. And once you, Maggie, and I are together, I want to be able to discuss Jockie with her and you. There is a much bigger issue here, and I want to make sure she hears it directly from me. OK? Are we in agreement on this, Son?"

Chaucer thought about the love that Remy had shown for him since the divorce and while Chaucer had sorted out becoming a father himself. Chaucer felt a swell of emotions at that moment at the table.

"Yes, Dad, you have my word on this. We'll do it together as you want; that is the best way." He reached across the table and put his hand on his father's arm and squeezed it. Remy smiled.

"Good, thank you, Son. OK, let's go meet Teasag and Jockie and have a family dinner," and they both smiled broadly.

*   *   *

The dinner at Teasag's house went well. She loved meeting Chaucer. His politeness and Giroux charm impressed her. Remy was happy that the two of them hit it off so well, and that Jockie took to Chaucer right away.

As soon as Remy and Chaucer arrived that night, Jockie ran up to Remy and hugged him tight as Remy bent down to embrace the six-year-old. Jockie bore a strong resemblance to Remy.

"Dad, Mom and I missed you. Did you bring me anything from Ottawa like always?" he asked.

"Yes, I did, but first I want you to meet your older brother, Chaucer." Remy stood and turned to Chaucer. "Chaucer, this is Jockie. He is six years old."

Chaucer, excited to meet the lad, squatted down, shook Jockie's hand, and Jockie instinctively hugged him with both arms. Teasag and Remy smiled at each other, and then embraced and kissed. They were so very happy to have the boys finally meet and show affection for each other.

With that Remy reached into his jacket pocket and retrieved a small box. He got down on one knee and said, "I think you'll like this, Son. I gave your brother, Chaucer, the same gift when he was your age."

Jockie took the box, looked apprehensive, then opened it. His face exploded into a wide smile. A wristwatch! Just what he had wanted.

"You'll have all the other boys in school jealous of you, Jockie," Teasag said as the three males smiled.

The rest of the evening was just like the first few minutes. The love and affection between Remy and Teasag set the merry tone of the dinner. Chaucer had rarely seen his father this joyful since the divorce. He wanted him to be this way always. He loved his father so much. It was the one certain truth in Chaucer's life when so much of the rest of his life had confused and hurt him.

* * *

Before the night was over, Chaucer learned even more surprising family news. Teasag, her teaching assistant, and four graduate students were leaving Glasgow for six months to conduct field research in Australia and New Zealand. They were to depart the first week of January. The University Research Foundation and the government science committees in Canberra and Wellington had approved their grant request. They would be studying the impact of agricultural chemicals on frogs and other lamp post aquatic species. It was a seminal evolutionary study that Teasag had worked on for years.

Because Teasag would be gone for at least six months, Remy and she had agreed that he would take Jockie to Ottawa for that time. Chaucer was overwhelmed with surprise and joy. He thought of so many things at that moment. He thought of his joy in being an abba and now a big brother to Jockie. Chaucer believed that God had showered him with three children to love and protect. He felt so very fortunate, so very blessed. His happiness that night was beyond measurement.

Chapter 46

Naked on the Naked Earth: St. Francis of Assisi

CHAUCER ARRIVED IN NEW ORLEANS four days before Christmas. He and Maggie spent their days planning the wedding, set for May 15, 1973. They walked the streets of the Garden District and looked at apartment options. Jasper and Margola treated them to lunch a couple of times at Commander's Palace on Washington Avenue.

The Christmas holiday was celebrated with mass in the morning at the St. Stephen's Catholic Church followed by a beautiful dinner that Jasper and Margola had planned and executed to perfection. Rufus, the children, Bridgette and her boyfriend, Charles, all joined them for mass and dinner.

When the family sat down for dinner, the tone turned somber as they couldn't help but feel the absence of Suzette. Jasper remembered the birth of Christ to Mary and Joseph, and he prayed that God would care for Suzette and all the family. He asked for the forgiveness of past sins and guidance for the new year. Maggie cried softly, and Chaucer held her hand tightly. The children looked sad, but Jasper stood behind them at the dinner table during the prayer and placed one hand on the shoulder of each of them. Rufus sat silent, looking remorseful. Chaucer just watched quietly as the family struggled to manage their feelings of loss. Once Jasper finished the prayer, the adults did their best to lighten the atmosphere, chatting with the children about the gifts they had received from Santa and making plans to take them on outings during the holiday week.

* * *

Three days after Christmas, Rufus called and spoke to Chaucer. He asked him to meet him at a bar in Algiers for a drink that night. Chaucer agreed, but when he told Maggie about the call, she said that the waterfront bar that Rufus suggested was in a bad part of Algiers, and that if Chaucer was going to go then she was going to go as well, so Chaucer would not get lost in an unsafe area. He agreed, acknowledging that he did not know New Orleans yet like Maggie did.

At 8 o'clock that chilly late December night, Chaucer and Maggie drove her car across the Crescent City bridge to Algiers and found the Shipping News Tavern on Patterson Road. As Maggie already knew, it was a rough part of Algiers. As they pulled up in front of the tavern to park, Rufus was standing outside, leaning against the front of the tavern and smoking a cigarette.

"Hi, Rufus," Chaucer said as he and Maggie walked up.

"I thought you were going to come alone," Rufus replied, clearly annoyed.

"I didn't want him to get lost over here, Rufus, you should know that," Maggie said in a less than pleasant voice. "Where are the children tonight, Rufus?"

"Come on, let's have a drink," Rufus replied. "The kids are at Bridgette's." He turned and they followed him inside. It was a tavern with all sorts of clientele — some older neighborhood folk, some dock workers, and a few biker types playing pool in the back near the restrooms.

Rufus got drinks at the bar and carried them to a table against the far wall. After a few minutes, Rufus asked Maggie to excuse him and Chaucer for a few minutes. Rufus took Chaucer up to the corner of the bar to talk.

"I don't want to involve Maggie and her family in this, Chaucer, but I'm in some trouble right now," he said looking a little drunk and nervous. "I understand that your family has money, and I need to borrow some tonight. I'm in trouble, and I need at least $1,500. Can you help me out? I'll pay you back next week."

Chaucer was shocked. He barely knew Rufus; he had just meet him for the first time a week ago, and Chaucer thought that his demand was crazy.

"Rufus, my father owns the company that Jasper works for but I don't get paid that kind of money, and besides, I would never carry it on me even if I had it. What's going on with you anyway?"

"Look, I made some bets last week on boxing, and I lost. Plus, I owe these guys more than I lost on those bets. They are meeting me here tonight, and I need to give them something so they'll back off," he said, his eyes bulging now.

"Well, I have $80 on me, and Maggie probably has some cash that we can loan you now. I could ask my father to wire me more tomorrow. Will that help?" he asked.

Rufus just shook his head. "Not even close, I need more right now. Never mind, sorry to get you involved. Go back to Maggie, I need to talk to a guy in the back."

Chaucer walked back to the table and sat with Maggie, who began asking him about his conversation at the bar.

Less than a minute after Chaucer sat down, two big guys in leather jackets walked in the front door. They looked around and saw Rufus at the back bar and went directly to see him. The three of them walked out the front door but within a minute Rufus walked back in and right up to the table to Chaucer and Maggie.

"I think I'll be OK, let me have that $100 now. I'm talking to them, and I'll be back in a few minutes," he said still carrying his bottle of beer in one hand, another cigarette in the other.

Chaucer nodded and looked at Maggie. They pulled out the cash they had, handing Rufus $100. He grabbed it without even saying thanks and walked quickly out the door.

Chaucer shook his head, clearly worried. "He's in trouble Maggie. He wants to borrow $1,500 from me right now, but I told him I didn't have that kind of money but that I could probably get it tomorrow by having my father wire it to me."

"My father told us recently that he believes that Rufus has a bad gambling problem, and he is very concerned about it. He said that he even spoke to Rufus's father, and his own father didn't know about it. I bet those guys that he is with outside are trying to collect from him. I hope that he can talk his way out of this. They didn't look like nice guys to me."

Chaucer and Maggie sat and waited for Rufus to come back inside. Ten minutes later, after they had finished their drinks, they decided to leave, not knowing where Rufus had disappeared to and not feeling comfortable in the tavern.

Chaucer took the empty glasses to the bar and left four quarters for the bartender, who nodded a thank you.

They left through the front door, and not seeing Rufus, they walked to their car just a few parking spaces from the front door. As they got to the car, Chaucer saw blood on the sidewalk and then heard a grown. He looked in the direction of the sound and saw Rufus laying between their car and the one parked in front of it.

"Rufus, Rufus!" he shouted. "What happened?" Maggie looked down and saw Rufus and screamed. Chaucer knelt down next to Rufus.

"Did those two guys do this, did they do this?" Chaucer shouted.

"Oh Christ, I'm hurt. Get me to a hospital," Rufus moaned.

"Maggie, stay with him for now. I'm going inside to call for help!" Chaucer ran into the tavern and up to the bartender. "Call an ambulance and the police!" Chaucer shouted. "My friend has been stabbed and he's lying on the sidewalk bleeding." The bartender grabbed the phone from under the bar and made the call.

Chaucer remembered his first aid training from when he played hockey. He asked the bartender for a towel, got it and ran outside. He knelt next to Rufus and put the towel tight to his stab wounds on his stomach and applied pressure to stem the bleeding. Maggie took off her sweater, rolled it up and put it under Rufus's head. They waited, exchanging desperate looks, as Rufus continued to moan softly.

Within a few minutes, they heard sirens, and a police cruiser and an ambulance arrived. The ambulance crew quickly took over, loaded Rufus on a stretcher and drove away. Two police officers took statements from Maggie and Chaucer and a few others who had seen the two men in leather jackets. When the police were finished about forty-five minutes later, Chaucer and Maggie drove to the hospital where Rufus had been transported. Just a few minutes after arriving, they learned that Rufus had lost too much blood and had died on the operating table. He was just 29 years old.

Earlier, Maggie and Chaucer had called Jasper and Margola from the bar after the police had interviewed them. Jasper then called Bridgette and relayed the shocking news about the attack. Bridgette brought Lyla and Jackson over to Jasper's house. Later, from the hospital, Maggie called her parents to tell them that Rufus had died. It seemed like a replay of the night that Suzette had been in the auto accident just months before. Margola called the parish priest, Father Altobello, and he drove immediately to the house. Jasper called Rufus's father, Jean-Baptiste, in Houma and told him his son was dead. Shocked, Jean-Baptiste said he would drive immediately to the hospital to collect Rufus's personal property and make arrangements for the body. By the time Jean-Baptiste arrived at the hospital, he learned that Rufus' body had been taken to the county morgue for the medical examiner to conduct a criminal autopsy. It was a chaotic scene for all. Both little Lyla and Jackson's parents were gone in one season; how unfair it seemed to Maggie and her family. The family felt weighed down in their mourning, yet Maggie, her parents, and Bridgette tried to console the children as best they could.

In the coming weeks, Jasper and Margola, along with Rufus's father and mother, emptied out the small house where Rufus and Suzette and the children had lived. The two sets of grandparents agreed that Lyla and Jackson would live with Jasper and Margola, who had a large home. Lyla could attend her same school and keep her friends. Rufus's parents agreed to come to mass and dinner each Sunday so that the children would have as much family and continuity as possible. The adults all met with Father Altobello and Maggie to work out a plan to make sure that the children were involved in as many activities as possible to keep them occupied. The four grandparents agreed that the children would be told that Rufus died as the result of a ruptured blood vessel in his brain, and that his death was immediate. They wanted to shelter them as much as possible for now.

Chapter 47

Spring Comes to Despair

THE TRAGIC EVENTS, the losses in the five months of the prior year were to be replaced by the happiness of the marriage of Maggie Grandemaison and Chaucer Giroux on May 15, 1973 in St. Stephen's Catholic Church in New Orleans. Remy, JOA, and Jockie came from Ottawa. (Remy had flown into New Orleans the week after the murder of Rufus to discuss business and family matters with Jasper, Margola, and Maggie. He told them about Teasag and Jockie at that time. They were understanding and supportive.) At the wedding, the Giroux family from Geneva, New York, were represented by Elizabeth, Le Guerrier, Kathleen, and Jean Marc. At the last-minute Olivia came with her boyfriend, Jacob, as they flew in from Mexico City where MGM Studios were filming Olivia's screenplay. After meeting Olivia, Maggie now felt more informed about her. Seeing Olivia in person helped Maggie to understand Chaucer's feelings of parental betrayal and loss. Olivia had not altered her sense of detachment from her children even at the wedding, and Maggie witnessed it.

Olivia's writing fame and now screenwriting success were growing in film and literary circles. She had even permitted herself to be interviewed on radio and television in Canada and the United States. After more than a decade of emotional separation from Chaucer and JOA, her obliviousness to her children was manifestly apparent in her behavior. Whenever Chaucer and JOA were together in the same space with their mother, they were always silently communicating with their eyes and tiny smiles. They saw the humor in it all.

    JOA and Maggie became fast friends in the three days of wedding events. This pleased Chaucer as much as anything that week. Before his eyes he was watching the two women that he loved the most bond as only such women in these circumstances can: by their smiles, their hugs, and the aura that emanates from their friendship and collaborative kindness to those around them. For Chaucer, the joy of watching JOA and Maggie forming a sisterly, family bond was the reward after seeing JOA lost and miserable for those years in Vancouver.

    And then it happened — a magnificent wedding on a beautiful spring day in New Orleans with the crepe myrtle in full bloom. The large families of both Jasper and Margola were present, making up about two-thirds of the guest list. A Grandemaison family-favorite Cajun band played at the reception late into the night. It was the consummation of the past year of courtship for Maggie and Chaucer. Their romance would be permanent as would their spiritual faith, which seemed to go hand-in-glove for them. Jasper, Margola, and Bridgette all saw this connection that day, and for a time it eased the pain of the loss of Suzette and Rufus. At the reception dinner, Maggie stood and gave a beautiful toast to Suzette, leaving few dry eyes.

    Standing with her parents off the dance floor, Bridgette looked at her sister. "I wish Suzette could see how happy Maggie is today." Jasper nodded slowly. Margola glanced out the nearby large window and said softly, "She does."

Chapter 48

FAMILY MATTERS

*Come what sorrow can, it cannot countervail the exchange
of joy, that one short minute gives me in her sight*
—Romeo in *Romeo and Juliet*

I stumbled when I saw
—Gloucester in *King Lear*

THE NEXT DAY MAGGIE AND CHAUCER flew to Miami and spent the night in a suite in an airport hotel before flying to Madrid the next day. Jasper had asked his parish priest in New Orleans to make the connection with the clergy at the Cathedral of Santiago de Compostela so that the priest there could bless their marriage in the church that had been the catalyst that bonded Maggie and Chaucer the previous year. Because Chaucer was not Catholic, the Bishop of New Orleans had to make a special request directly to the Vatican to get permission for this to occur. It was approved because of the background report that had been researched. Since neither Maggie nor Chaucer had been married before, and they had both gotten their Compostela certificates from their pilgrimage on the Camino de Santiago the previous summer, the Vatican approved the request. The second blessing at the Cathedral of Santiago de Compostela by Father DiGregorio meant everything to both Maggie and Chaucer. It seemed that God had put them together for a reason, and the blessing that day confirmed it to them.

During the honeymoon in Santiago and Madrid, Maggie and Chaucer had plenty of time to think and dream together about their vision for their married life. Maggie was a couple of months into her new position as deputy director of social ministry in the Diocese of New Orleans. Chaucer would soon become the third in command of the southern division of the company. They also were the father and stepmother of two baby boys who lived a long distance from New Orleans. They realized how blessed they were with their work and responsibilities in their life together.

Waking before sunrise on the third day in Santiago, Chaucer felt a need to think and be alone. Maggie was sound asleep, softly breathing. Chaucer quietly slipped on his clothes, scribbled a short note that he put on his pillow, and left the room. He wanted to walk as he had something deep in him that was calling "talk to me." He got a coffee at the hotel café and walked in the darkness to the plaza at the cathedral. He was alone, it was quiet, and the first rays of light were coming up in the eastern sky. He found the bench where he remembered seeing Rudy sitting the previous summer, so he sat there and sipped his coffee. It was the kind of quiet that he was hoping for.

He started to deconstruct the events of the past year in the calmness. He thought about how Rudy had helped him, the love Remy had always bestowed upon him, how Maggie had showed him real romantic love and attention and grace in her demeanor to him. He closed his eyes and he prayed, "Dear God, why did this happiness take so long to find me?" He thought of his passive anger at his mother for her years of ignoring him and JOA; he thought of his pseudo love of Tessa and her betrayal, his falling so hard for Joanie, and his own betrayal of leaving Stephanie and playing with her emotions. He thought of Lisa and Teresa, the wonderful cousins from Boston who educated him on so much in just a few weeks of travel in Portugal and Spain with them the previous year. And he thought about Maggie, still sleeping now, and how their love had evolved over time, through experiences and truth. His prayer continued, "Forgive me for my sins, Father. I was selfish to others who hurt me. I wish to forgive them, and I ask for your forgiveness of me. Thank you for sending Lisa and Teresa and my German mentor, Rudy, into my life at the time that I needed them most. And Father, thank you for sending me Maggie for I will give her all the love and grace that I can, and together we will try to carry out your work on earth, as your Son taught us." Chaucer then recited the Lord's Prayer. "Amen."

When he opened his eyes, the plaza was getting light. He felt happy that he had come to this bench to be quiet and pray. He heard footsteps approaching. He looked up and saw it was Maggie. She sat next to him, putting her arm around his shoulders.

"I heard the door closing, and I saw your note. I had the feeling that you would be coming to this bench where we sat last summer. Are you OK?" She kissed his cheek and felt the moisture of his tears that had fallen in the early light.

"I am," he said as he hugged her. "I woke up and just needed to be alone in the quiet and to be here. This spot, where so much of what made us complete, it happened here, it's a special place for me — for us."

"Yes, it is," Maggie said softly.

"I needed to thank God for our blessings and ask forgiveness this morning. I let the hurt of my parent's divorce consume me for a long time, in ways that I didn't know until I had worked my way out of it, through prayer and with your love, Maggie."

"I think I understand. I could see you changing, and it warmed me because I do not think we could have married had you not fixed it inside of you. You opened yourself, and God showed you the way. I believe that with all my heart, Chaucer."

Chaucer hugged Maggie tight. This catharsis of his past pain had been a long time coming. Maggie held him and stroked his hair.

"We're going to be just fine, darling," she reassured him in a quiet voice. "You have come a long way for this happiness. Your father loves you, JOA loves you, I love you. Most of all God loves you. We are going to be just fine."

Chaucer kissed her cheek. "I love you so much, Maggie. We are going to have a good life together. I will not let you or the kids down."

"I know you won't; your heart is a good one and your soul is healing. We'll be fine. Now let's walk some more and then get some breakfast, OK?"

* * *

On the third day of the trip, sitting at an outdoor restaurant in Santiago, they talked about their coming days. They had two little boys in Ottawa, a new little brother in Ottawa by way of Glasgow, new jobs, and a marriage to manage.

"Maggie, we'll have our hands full once we get back home, but I know we'll be able to take care of it all," Chaucer said confidently.

Maggie smiled. "True, yes, we'll have each other. We are together for some reasons that we have yet to understand. I think God put us together for many things, especially to take care of Mac and Mickey."

Chaucer nodded in agreement. He looked up at the steeple of the cathedral, which he could see from where they were sitting. He thought back to his pilgrimage walk with Maggie and the days since they had been in Santiago. He felt a surge of joy and confidence. "Yes, we need to be a team to help others who need us. I think we have enough love to share with others, don't you?" he said with confidence.

Maggie smiled softly in acknowledgment. She knew what he said was true. She felt it and reached over the table and put her soft hand on his. Chaucer smiled back; no words were necessary then. They were sharing a communal moment in their new marriage and words could only dilute the feeling they both were having.

Then the bells of the cathedral tower rang eleven times for the morning hour. Maggie looked at Chaucer for several seconds and then said, "I think that we should adopt Suzette's children," and she looked him in the eye for his reaction.

Chaucer wasn't surprised to hear Maggie express this. He knew how fond she was of Lyla and Jackson, and he had been expecting this matter to be discussed in the coming days. Now was a good time.

"Well, your parents are in their 60s and your dad is hoping to retire in a few years. I know they adore Lyla and Jackson but becoming full-time parents to them is a lot to ask. Bridgette is not married so being the mom of two kids without a husband would be hard for her, so we're the right people to be their parents, plus you are their mother's sister, which makes it even better for them. You're serious about this, right?"

"Oh yes. I've been thinking about this for months. I spoke to Bridgette about it but I wanted to wait to talk about it with you until after our wedding. It would be a big responsibility for us, you know," she said.

Chaucer grinned. "You accepted my little boys into our life, right? Now this is perhaps my test. Can I, or we, accept Lyla and Jackson into our life too? Having four small kids in a new marriage? That's not a small challenge is it?" he paused, looked at his new wife and thought what a strong, emotionally solid woman she was. "Yeah, I think we can, we'll just have to structure our marriage to make it work. And we probably should plan to defer having our own child for a few years too, don't you think?" he said.

Maggie looked confident and joyful after hearing this. "Yes, and yes! Yes, we can do it and yes, we'll have to wait to have our own child if we take Lyla and Jackson, plus have the boys in Ottawa too." Maggie giggled. "I may be the first woman to have four kids in the first week of marriage!" They both laughed, their hands still clasped tightly together.

* * *

Maggie and Chaucer flew to Ottawa at the end of the honeymoon. Maggie wanted to meet Mac and Mickey and see Jockie again, and she wanted to thank Remy for all the help that he had given them.

JOA answered the door as the cab arrived from the airport. She hugged her brother and Maggie and immediately introduced Maggie to Roisin, who, as a Catholic like Maggie, embraced her and immediately said a prayer out loud thanking God for bringing Maggie into the family.

Roisin had a fine lunch planned so they all sat at the table with the three boys (two in high chairs) to eat and talk.

Maggie liked Jockie very much. He was polite, talkative, and very cute with a Giroux smile and his curly reddish-brown hair that he inherited from his mother. Maggie learned that Jockie in Gaelic means "God is gracious." "How special,' she thought. "Yes, God is gracious," she said to herself, looking around the table, seeing two small boys, a now seven-year-old Scottish lad, JOA and Chaucer from a broken marriage, and the lovely Roisin who had such special grace to share. Indeed, from the ashes of life God was so gracious as to give them all Remy as their earthly father and grandfather and employer. Maggie's heart was full; she felt overwhelmed at that moment. "Could all this be happening to me?" she thought, and then she softly bowed her head and silently said a prayer of thanks.

Maggie proceeded to tell JOA, Jockie, and Roisin that she and Chaucer were also going to adopt her late sister's children. JOA and Roisin looked at each other with big smiles out of both surprise and admiration. Jockie was happy that he would now have an American niece and nephew, whom he had met in New Orleans at the wedding. He was now a wee lad in a much bigger family than he had known just a year before.

Remy learned about the planned adoption of Suzette's children in New Orleans when he arrived home from work that night. His joy was great, his love and admiration for Chaucer and Maggie even greater than before. It had occurred to him that this scenario could happen when he first learned that Rufus had been murdered in December. His thoughts then were of the children, and he was confident that Jasper and Margola would take care of them. Now his son and wife would become the parents. He thought of Teasag at that moment too and how happy that she would be for the grace of Chaucer and Maggie. He also smiled thinking of Jockie and his name: "God is gracious."

* * *

The plane landed in a light rain at New Orleans airport on a Saturday afternoon, and Jasper was there to pick up the honeymooners and bring them to his house for a family dinner with Bridgette, Lyla, and Jackson. He, Margola, and Bridgette learned that night that Chaucer and Maggie wanted to legally adopt the children. The family wanted to know more, so Bridgette took the children into the livingroom to watch a movie on TV and then came back to the table.

Jasper looked over the top of his glasses at Margola and said, "Well, since Suzette has been gone, we have discussed the future of Lyla and Jackson, and now that Rufus is gone, too and the two of you are married, this is a good time for this discussion, don't you think?" Everyone nodded.

Jasper continued. "So what are your thoughts on an adoption?"

Maggie looked at Chaucer, who nodded for her to speak for the two of them.

"We have discussed this over the last week, and here are the things that we think would make this work for the children, and for all of us. First, we will be living in New Orleans for the foreseeable future, and that will give Lyla and Jackson stability, as they will be near their grandparents too." Maggie paused and looked at the others; they were listening closely.

"Our other children are in Ottawa, and that is where they will be for the next few years, with JOA and Chaucer's father, and Jockie will also be visiting them, so that situation is stable. Chaucer and I will find a house nearby so you (she looked at her parents and sister) will be able to see them as much as you want, and they can stay overnight sometimes with you. And lastly" — she knew this was the most important and sensitive part because of Chaucer's previous unwillingness to act as the father to McCarthy and Mick —"when Chaucer and I were on our pilgrimage to Santiago, he received his calling from God to become a good father."

Chaucer smiled and nodded firmly, saying, "We all want what is best for the children, and between the five of us, we can give them stability and a good life here in New Orleans. I believe that Suzette would want that, and Maggie and I are committed to that, as we believe the three of you are as well." He looked for and saw heads nodding in agreement.

Jasper looked at everyone, smiled, and sat back in his chair. "This appears to be a good plan for you two. Let's all sleep on this for a few days, have another discussion, and then make a decision as a family, as you'll have to start looking for a home nearby soon. We have a friend who practices family law here, and we could get him to prepare the adoption papers to submit to the court. And lastly, let's all ask Lyla and Jackson what they think. Let's do this individually so it's not a ganging up on them. Let's feel them out. I think that we owe them this." With that, Jasper put his napkin on the table, got up, and went to pour himself a glass of port.

Over the next few days, most of the concerns of Jasper and Margola disappeared as they thought and talked it over. They came to believe that this newly married couple would be able to manage this added responsibility as well as the responsibility of the boys in Ottawa.

The plan that evolved was for the children to stay with Jasper and Margola for the time being to give Maggie and Chaucer time to find a large enough home near the elementary school that Lyla attended, and where Jackson would start in a preschool program. The children would then move into the new home with Maggie and Chaucer. In the end, the five adults all agreed this was the best course of action for the children.

* * *

A month after Chaucer started work at the company office in New Orleans, Remy asked him to come to Ottawa for company business but also to spend time with Mac and Mickey. Maggie decided to take vacation time from her job to join him. They were to stay for two weeks, then return to New Orleans.

As fate would have it, Olivia had informed Remy and JOA that she was coming to visit them and her mother in Ottawa for a week when Chaucer would be there too. Olivia would meet Mac and Mickey for the first time, and see Jockie again, having met him at the wedding in New Orleans. This would be only her second visit to Ottawa since she, Chaucer, and JOA had left for Vancouver more than ten years ago. JOA and Chaucer felt somewhat conflicted about seeing Olivia again in their childhood home where they had all lived years before. On the other hand, Remy found the situation rather humorous; the thought of seeing Olivia's face as she encountered the three boys now living at her former home made Remy smile. It was going to be an odd couple of days, he thought.

"What do you think Mom's reaction is going to be, Dad?" Chaucer asked.

"Well, she will likely be polite and mildly amused and start taking vigorous notes in her head to use in one of her next books. That's what I think," Remy said with a confident smirk and a chuckle.

JOA and Chaucer relaxed and chuckled too.

* * *

After Olivia had been in Ottawa for a few days and had met the three boys, Remy hosted a welcoming reception for Olivia; her mother, Photina; Olivia's new boyfriend, Abraham Pearlman; Pastor Leo and his wife; JOA, Chaucer, and Maggie on the back patio overlooking the river. Remy served drinks to the adults and ice cream for the boys, with Roisin helping with the children.

Olivia was as kind and pleasant as Remy, JOA, and Chaucer could have wished for. Abraham seemed to be a fine gentleman. Olivia surveyed the patio and the children and walked over to Chaucer and took her son's hands in her hands. "You have yourself a beautiful family, and your father tells me that you and Maggie will be adopting her niece and nephew in New Orleans as well," she said as she smiled. For a moment, she stared deeply into Chaucer's eyes, admiring the man that he had become. Chaucer noticed a brief sadness in her, perhaps a little watering of her eyes. Olivia coughed, and then asked Abraham to come over to where she was standing with Chaucer. Maggie stood at Chaucer's side, quiet.

"Abraham, my son will have four little children in his family soon, and I am so happy for him."

Abraham nodded and reached out to Chaucer to shake his hand. "Quite a beginning for you and your new wife," he said with a sincere smile. "I wish you patience and happiness."

Chaucer replied, "Thank you, I appreciate that, but" and he stopped in mid-sentence as Maggie gave him a subtle bump in his back with her hidden hand. "And I am happy that you could meet the little guys today. They are great boys."

Abraham smiled. "And I see that your father has also been busy," at which point Chaucer laughed, and Olivia squeezed Abraham's arm to stop him from continuing.

Both men wanted to say more, some humorous and some perhaps less than kind, but the two women held them in check as they understood that the less said the better at a time like this.

On the patio that night, Olivia quietly shared with Remy, JOA, Chaucer, and Maggie that her long relationship with Jacob Rosensteen had ended after Olivia heard of multiple trysts that he had had with young actresses half his age. She laughed about it as she talked, also saying that the Hollywood immorality was not her way of life, and she would not accept having a gigolo as a companion. Olivia opted to leave out a few details, mainly that after the abrupt termination of her relationship with Rosensteen, which Olivia did with dignity, she then networked with her female friends who were filmmakers and writers in Hollywood to have them spread the word around Hollywood circles that Rosensteen had a limited libido and a small penis. It worked because soon after the gossip spread, Rosensteen tried to get a restraining order from the Los Angeles County Court to prevent Olivia from talking about him. Olivia's attorney reported back to her that the female judge on the case dismissed the request with a great deal of laughter, reportedly stating from the bench that no evidence had been submitted by the plaintiff in scientific or photographic form that she could examine. Even the bailiffs in court that day laughed with the judge.

Olivia explained to Remy, JOA, Chaucer, and Maggie how she had met Abraham. After Olivia had left Rosensteen and returned to the quietness and seclusion of her beloved writing studio-barn, she agreed to meet with another producer and studio executive at a waterfront hotel in Victoria. His name was Abraham Pearlman, and he admired the books and screenplays that Olivia had written. He also was a native of Vancouver Island, so his trip to Victoria was of a dual purpose: to see his relatives and friends and meet with Olivia about potentially producing some of her new work.

They liked each other from the start. Abraham reminded Olivia of Remy's politeness and dignity and how Remy had behaved when he had first met her years ago. Abraham and Olivia's relationship began strictly as a business friendship but gradually they spent more time together in Victoria and Los Angeles. Abraham owned a small house in Empire Landing on Santa Catalina Island, so whenever Olivia was in Hollywood on extended business, she and Abraham took the ferry over for a few days of hiking and meeting up with other movie business friends. This was a good relationship for both of them because of their mutual love of Vancouver Island and their work in Los Angeles.

A few nights before Olivia and Abraham were to leave Ottawa, Remy arranged for dinner with them, JOA, Chaucer, and Maggie at the golf club. They took a large booth in the corner of the dining room for privacy.

During dinner Olivia, sipping her omnipresent flute of champagne, asked Chaucer about his plans for the four children. He thought of his understanding of his abba role but he didn't mention that to his mother because of her skepticism of religion. Instead he said he and Maggie felt a strong moral commitment to all the children, and that they were hoping to be the best possible parents to all the children.

"Mother, every child needs to be loved, and Maggie and I are going to love these four kids, and any that we may be blessed to have between us," Chaucer explained. "We want to give them as much love and happiness as we can." He knew that saying this to his mother was his way of telling her that she had not done that for him and JOA. JOA, who was sitting next to Chaucer, softly kicked him under the table in lieu of smiling broadly, which surely would have annoyed Olivia, who continued sipping her drink, purposely ignoring the dig from Chaucer.

But Chaucer didn't stop there. "Actually, Mother, I would love to start a big school, a residential program to adopt as many children as I could to give them a place to live, to go to school, to have a chance to live a good life, what our gracious God wants, and what we all want for all his children."

Olivia looked down her nose at Chaucer and said with half a smile and a hint of sarcasm, "Great idea, and while you are doing this, also ask God for the money you'll need to do this too."

Chaucer realized that he had gone too far, even though in his heart he meant it. But he also knew that insulting his own mother was ungodly, so he softly said, "I'm sorry Mother, I did not mean to upset you in any way. It's just that I see situations all over where kids are not cared for, or put in foster care or worse, are aborted and never even get the chance to live. This is very hurting to me." JOA reached below the table and grabbed and squeezed Chaucer's hand.

Remy, Olivia, and Abraham could all hear Chaucer's sincerity in his voice and see it in his face.

His mother's face softened. "That is a really good and important feeling to have, Chaucer. It is who you were as a boy, and I am glad to see you are still that same son now." Olivia was oblivious of the pain that Chaucer had lived through until he met Maggie.

Abraham, who was listening and watching all this very carefully, then said, "So if you had the time and money, what would you do with it, Chaucer?"

Everyone looked at Abraham inquisitively.

"What do you mean, Abraham?" Chaucer asked.

Abraham looked kindly at Chaucer. "If a foundation were to give you funding to create such a program, would you do it? Would you develop it?"

Chaucer smiled at Maggie, thinking he would play along with

this. "Sure, I would do it both here in Ottawa and in New Orleans. I'm sure that it can be done," he said. "Why do you ask?" He expected Abraham to say something trivial and move on to a new topic about Hollywood or entertainment.

Abraham called over the waiter and ordered another martini. Olivia and the others joined in for a second round.

Abraham looked at Olivia, grinned, then began: "Chaucer, Maggie, Remy, JOA, let me tell you something about me so that you'll better understand what I am about to say. While my name would make it appear that I am Jewish, that is not my entire history. You see, I am half Hebrew and half native Salishan from Vancouver Island. My father I have never known. He was a forest management scientist from back east working for a summer at the logging company property near the reserve where my mother and her family lived. I learned that her husband had died, and she met my father at a music club off the reserve that summer. My mother got pregnant with me, and because she already had four other children, she put me in an orphanage in Vancouver that was run by the Catholic church. My father did one good thing before he vanished; he gave the orphanage money to care for me provided that they gave me his family name, and they did. Was Pearlman my father's real name? Probably, because through the years at the Catholic orphanage, the priests told me that they received more money donated by him, but he never left any address or contact information. The priests and the school did a fine job of educating and caring for me. At age 18, I traveled to Seattle and joined the U.S. Marine Corps and fought in the Pacific during the war, and that got me U.S. citizenship."

By this time Remy was staring at Olivia with a look of "Did you know all of this?"

Abraham continued. "After the war, I moved to Los Angeles with two of my Marine Corps friends who grew up there. They got me a job at Paramount Studios, and soon I went from driving a truck to managing the transportation department to working for one of the older executives who heard about the Indian-Canadian-Marine named Abraham Pearlman. Over the years I have taken over for him, produced some good movies, and made money. In the last couple of years, I have joined up with some of the other studio executives to create the Hollywood Studios Charitable Foundation. We help out people in need and get pretty good publicity too, which helps us with our movie business. So now you know." He hesitated and looked at everyone around the table. "I could take your idea and present it to our board and suggest some funding for you. So, think about it, and let's discuss it before I leave for Los Angeles."

Maggie and Chaucer had a hard time closing their mouths as their jaws had dropped so much listening to Abraham. Remy sat back, happy and smiling, as did Olivia. JOA was quiet, just listening very carefully, taking it all in.

Chapter 49

To the Drawing Board

BY THE TIME THAT OLIVIA AND ABRAHAM left for their homes on the West Coast two days later, Abraham, Chaucer, and Maggie had decided that the newlyweds would create a plan for developing a residential school and home for orphans and services for expectant women in need. There would be one in Ottawa and one in New Orleans. They would obtain local partners, develop budgets, staffing and operational plans, and then submit the entire proposal to the Hollywood Studios Charitable Foundation (HSCF) for consideration and possible funding. Abraham recommended that they submit their proposal within six months. As a member of the Finance Committee, he was aware that funds for the current HSCF fiscal year would be ample given that two other proposed projects had never been approved, and if those reserved funds were not allocated by year's end, they could not be rolled over to the next fiscal year and thus be unavailable.

Soon the wheels were in motion. Maggie called her boss at the diocese and asked for his help in setting up a meeting the following week with the archbishop of New Orleans to discuss having the Catholic diocese become the sponsor of the program in New Orleans. Remy met with Chaucer and Pastor Leo in Ottawa three days later. Pastor Leo liked the plan, and he proposed that the Presbyterian churches of the federal district become the sponsors in Ottawa.

Maggie returned to New Orleans and Chaucer remained in Ottawa as they met with the church leadership groups in both cities to brainstorm ideas and review available sites and capacity. Whether these services and programs were needed was never in question. The Roe v. Wade decision in the U.S. in January 1973 and the liberalization of the Canadian abortion laws in the late 1960s had caused churches great concern with advocating for and protecting the right to life for the unborn. They wanted to offer as many alternatives to abortion as possible. In the next few weeks, Maggie and Chaucer prepared a draft organizational and operation plan, and the two sponsoring church organizations reviewed them. If HSCF approved the grant, then the churches would move forward with raising additional funds locally.

When the plan was completed and ready for transmitting to Abraham and the HSCF in Los Angeles, the North American Children's Benevolent Program, Inc., submitted it. NACBP was a 501(c)(3) religious charitable organization under the U.S. tax laws with the board of directors being a combination of the senior clergy from New Orleans and Ottawa. The listed officers were Remy as president, Jasper as vice president, Maggie as treasurer, and Chaucer as secretary. Olivia, Margola, Teasag, and JOA were all listed as board members. For once, everyone had come together for the sake of protecting the unborn and the orphaned children. Maggie and Chaucer developed the preamble to the charter for the organization, which read in part:

"We serve as a Christian organization dedicated to the needs of children and the protection of the unborn. We offer alternatives to abortion for expectant mothers and act as a beacon for the love, protection, and education of and for children who are in need. We provide health care, educational programs, job training, temporary residential units, and social services support to expectant women that require or request it. We provide legal services for adoptive parents at no cost to them. As Saint Teresa of Avila said, 'Christ has no body now on earth but yours. No hands but yours. No feet but yours. Yours are the eyes through which the compassion of Christ must look out on this world.' Our mission is to provide these services for any expectant women and/or orphaned children in the geographic areas that we serve."

The Catholic Church in New Orleans undertook this joint

venture as a path to implementing the visions of the Second Vatican Council in Rome in the early 1960s which had been called by Pope John XXIII. The constitution of *Gaudium et spes (The Modern World)* was a primary guide for the leadership, and the abundant needs of the citizens of New Orleans and Ottawa would help meet that dictum.

The Presbyterian leadership in Ottawa was pleased to help but made it clear that their role was not to be constricted by any requirement or mandate by their Catholic partners in New Orleans. This was included in the proposal for funding to HSCF. A controversial element of the program was the payment of $1000 to each client who successfully completed the program, whether or not she kept her baby. The program was to preserve the life of the baby so if they had to pay the mother not to turn to abortion, so be it. Chaucer and Maggie felt that God was agreeing with this, and so it was included in the plan.

In just a few short months Maggie and Chaucer had embarked on a journey that would inspire them, their families, and the communities in which they served. Their marriage would be a very busy life of service, trust, and love. They never doubted that they would be successful...not them.

* * *

Abraham was good on his word. Within two months of submitting the plan to the HSCF Finance Committee, Abraham called Remy and Jasper to congratulate them on a successful application for funding the program. He explained that the HSCF board had approved three years of funding at $125,000 for each year for both locations. The funding was contingent on each location also raising the same amount locally for a matching of the HSCF grant because the HSCF board wanted to make sure that the communities involved had an equal interest in the programs. The HSCF board would give the local communities six months to establish the matching funds.

Soon after the approval, the HSCF public relations director sent an announcement extolling the awards to the Hollywood press, explaining how important it was for these programs to help women. Concurrently, several studios issued press releases announcing new film projects in development that mimicked sentimental films such as

Boys Town (which starred Spencer Tracy) and/or featured dramatic plots of orphans achieving greatness in adulthood. This was precisely what the studios wanted their HSCF program to accomplish: show the public that the studios had compassion and then turn that into financial success. One studio already had a trailer released of a movie with Sophia Loren starring as a nun in an Italian orphanage.

Remy and Jasper were overwhelmed by this development. They immediately called for a strategy meeting of both families a week later in Ottawa. Meanwhile Remy called Olivia; she called him back two days later from her house in Victoria.

"So, I imagine you know the good news about Chaucer and Maggie's orphanage program?' Remy asked.

"What about it, Remy? What are you talking about?"

"The program that we all discussed with Abraham at the golf club when you were here!" Remy had a hard time hiding his impatience.

"Oh yes, that program. You'll have to excuse me, Remy, but I have been locked up in my writing room in the barn revising a screen play that Abraham and three other producers need finished in two weeks. It's what I do best now, and it is work that I get lost in so you'll need to forgive me for my loss of memory on this," she said casually.

"Well, the kids are really excited, Olivia, and they are so very appreciative of the support from the Hollywood Foundation. Please tell Abraham, or better yet, do you have his personal phone number? I would like to thank him myself."

She gave Remy the unlisted phone number for Abraham in Los Angeles. "You should know that this was a done deal the day that he told Chaucer and Maggie to submit their proposal to the foundation."

"What do you mean, in what way?" Remy asked.

"Abraham controls the foundation, Remy. It's basically his hobby to find good things to spend all their money on," Olivia replied. "Remember he was brought up in an orphanage himself and knowing that Chaucer is my, our, son, and that he is a bright and honest young man whom you can trust, well, Abraham was excited about funding it, but please don't tell that to Chaucer and Maggie. They need to get out and raise the other money for these orphanages. Don't you agree?"

"Yes, I do agree. Jasper and I will make the calls to get it started. My company will start with a $10,000 donation for each location."

"Well, that is good. OK, nice to hear your voice but I must get back to work now, Abraham is a hard movie executive to work with even though I sleep with him occasionally," Olivia said with a little chuckle. "Oh, and by the way, your son Jockie is adorable. I hope to meet his mother one day too."

* * *

Remy and the others soon learned that three different Hollywood studios were working on new movies about the care of children without parents. They calculated that this would help their fundraising efforts because they also knew the influence that Hollywood had on the culture in the United States and Canada. Remy also called and spoke to Abraham directly, thanking him for funding the programs. Abraham confirmed that some of his studio colleagues were in fact now working on movies that would present the virtues of good care for orphans, and how it could result in other young people overcoming their loss of a parent or parents to be successful in life. Remy thus recognized this entire scenario for what it was: Hollywood money invested so Hollywood would look good and make more money from movies. This was fine for Remy because he understood the business world. He and Jasper discussed this business aspect of the funding with Chaucer and Maggie. They wanted them to understand the HSCF motivation for being so generous. It is what good fathers do.

Chapter 50

The Beginning

I was a stranger and you welcomed me.
—Matthew 25:35

EARLY ONE MORNING over strong chicory coffee, Margola announced to Jasper: "We need to speak with Father Brennan." Jasper agreed. "We need to explore our concerns with him right from the start, and we should have Maggie and Chaucer with us in that meeting."

Jasper and Margola, natives of New Orleans and lifelong active members of their Catholic church, were well aware of the controversies that the Catholic Church had suffered in the past with regard to their prior effort and experience in operating orphanages. They remembered the fiasco of the 1950s when the church was found to be almost enslaving young unmarried pregnant girls to work in the churches and at Catholic schools as cleaners and cooks while they were pregnant, and then taking their babies into the orphanages while asking the sinful mothers to go away and repent.

Investigative reporting in both the *Times-Picayune* and the *Catholic Action of the South* newspapers finally uncovered the scandal. Reporters exposed the practices of the church, which led to major reforms, including priests and religious sisters being transferred to other locations, the hiring of a secular director of the orphanages, and the creation of an oversight board. Over the next few years, the diocese changed its practices, and the scandal was lost from the headlines much to the joy of the church leadership. Eventually the orphanages were shuttered as the social realities of the New Orleans area continued to evolve. With abortion now legal, pregnant girls and young women were not going to the church for help and their babies were being aborted. Many people of faith and many with no faith saw this new abortion culture as murder of the unborn and a bad turn in the collective compassion of the society. "Were the unborn just an inconvenience from the sexual freedom of the times?" was the question being posed in commentary. Jasper and Margola certainly wanted this new program to be a viable, responsible alternative to abortion for women.

* * *

A few days later Chaucer, Maggie, and her parents met with a chancellor in the diocese to discuss the operations of the program. They had many details to discuss and resolve to meet the grant's requirements.

The archbishop had appointed Father Brennan to be the liaison for the planning of the new orphanage. The big question was where it would be housed. Fortunately, Father Brennan had a facility in mind, and he had invited Sister Mary Joseph, head of a local order of religious sisters, to attend the meeting. It turned out that the sisters occupied only half of their historic convent that had been built in the 1880s and was located on property adjacent to the diocesan campus.

Sister Mary Joseph was thrilled to hear about the plans to offer an alternative to abortion. "Over half of our convent is empty now," Sister Mary Joseph explained. "We're just not getting the number of interested girls and women anymore; young women have so many more options with careers these days. We could possibly make that space available to your program. Come on, I'll show you the rooms."

Sister Mary Joseph led the tour and showed them the twelve empty bedrooms and the four common areas that were no longer being used. They were spartan and clean, just vacant. The other half of the building was in use but most of the sisters were at the school next door, teaching classes, so the entire facility seemed empty.

Maggie, her parents and Chaucer, seeing the vacant space, looked pleased. Maggie was already envisioning cheerful paint colors and comfortable furniture, shelves of engaging books, and bins full of toys.

Maggie smiled. "Father Brennan and Sister Mary Joseph, I have researched the licensing requirements of the State of Louisiana, and I believe that this facility would meet them. Our program would request a license for twenty-four children at first, and if it goes well, then perhaps we could add to our capacity for more children depending on how much additional space that the sisters could provide. Our program will be hiring six or seven caregivers and a cook. We would supply the equipment, like cribs, changing tables, toys, playpens, etc. We could pay for a few of the sisters to help out if you think that would be OK, and that they would agree."

Sister Mary Joseph was beaming. "I think this is a wonderful idea. Of course, I would have to discuss it with the other sisters, but I think having the children and expectant women here would bring new life, in more ways than one, into our convent."

Jasper and Margola were so proud of their daughter. She seemed to have such great enthusiasm for the program, and her willingness to adopt Suzette's children gave Jasper and Margola complete faith that she and Chaucer would find a way to make the orphanage program work.

For weeks, Jasper had been speaking to his long-time business friends about supporting the program, and his efforts were starting to see pledges being made in various amounts and with various stipulations. Progress in the program would trigger the release of even more cash from the donors. Likewise, Margola was tapping clients of her long-established antiques business and socially-conscious friends for funds and pledges of funding. Soon the local media began contacting Jasper and Margola for interviews. Both were experienced enough to understand the value of publicity via talk on the radio, news on TV, and articles in the *Times-Picayune*.

Within the six months that Abraham and HSCF grant had stipulated that the matching funding had to be secured, Abraham received the call from Jasper that the money had been raised. Jasper had wisely sought the help of his long-time friend and local banker LeBoutillier de'Carvier as the trustee and fiduciary for the funds that were raised and pledged. Mr. de'Carvier (who went by the nickname

"Tools" to his intimates) was from an old New Orleans family with a stellar reputation for honesty, so the donors were more than pleased to see his involvement with the orphanage. The path looked promising for Maggie and Chaucer in New Orleans.

Chapter 51

Ottawa Jumps

UNLIKE THE CONTROVERSIAL EXPERIENCE of the prior Catholic orphanages in a large old city like New Orleans, Ottawa had two small orphanages with a good track record. Perhaps it was due to the reasonably good funding history from the federal and provincial governments, and perhaps it was because Ottawa was a much smaller and more homogeneous community. However in the past few years since the abortion laws had been amended via court cases and regulation reform, there had been a drop in the need for orphanage beds. Remy learned this from his discussions with Pastor Leo.

"Remy, I do not like the way our culture is turning," Pastor Leo told him one day during their monthly lunch meeting. "Our youth seem to want to follow the Americans in so much, and now I have learned from my medical friends and parishioners that the number of abortions in Ontario and Quebec is increasing rapidly since Trudeau had the criminal code amended six years ago. And even though it takes a 'committee of doctors' to approve an abortion now, the Morgentaler case angered plenty of young doctors, and these committees are essentially just a rubber stamp now," Pastor Leo paused, with a look of disgust and helplessness. "Look, if it was up to me, I would find the money and build the best and biggest orphanage here in town. God loves all these unborn babies and has a plan for all of them, but man is taking them away. Men, women, they're playing God with the lives of these helpless little children in utero, and it makes me disgusted. I get physically ill when I think of what they do to abort a child, especially when the mother is four or five months along. The babies are really little kids then, wanting to grow, wanting to join us and become our little brothers and sisters." Pastor Leo looked sad and on the verge of tears as Remy watched him speak. He was just the man that Remy needed, and wanted, to be his partner in the development of the Ottawa orphanage.

Remy let him settle a bit before he spoke, putting his arm around Paster Leo and giving him a hug like old friends do when it is needed. "Well, perhaps God has put you and me in this room today to begin to do something about this. I have discussed with you this grant from the Hollywood people so you know about it, but now I am about to embark on a big fund-raising effort in town, and I am hoping you can help me in two ways," Remy said with the confident smile that friends give to one another. Pastor Leo returned the smile and continued listening.

"First, I will give you the details so you can discuss it with our congregation and with your clergy friends here, and second, I have set up a foundation with my business partners to channel funds from my company to help fund the orphanage. I do this for two reasons; first, to make sure that the matching funds for the Hollywood grant are there and an accounting firm can verify it, and second, to reduce our taxable corporate income so the Trudeau administration can't keep using our company like his personal bank. My American partners have educated me on these matters in ways that I had paid little attention to, believing that our government was doing good work for all Canadians, but I do not approve of many of the things that Trudeau is doing anymore." Pastor Leo smiled and nodded in agreement.

"The other thing that I would like you to consider," Remy said looking at the pastor, "is that I think we need to start speaking out more about the need to offer alternatives to abortion. You know our program can help these women bring these babies into the world. We can raise them and find them good homes. I want to pay for any legal costs that adoptive parents may face, too. Maybe even help these women, mostly young women, to rethink their decision, help them with employment, education, and housing. There is so much we can do and I want to use my company's profits to help them."

Pastor Leo could see the passion in Remy as he spoke. It was a moment that such friends could experience only by knowing, trusting, and respecting each other for many years, for they knew the mind and truths in one another.

Chapter 52

St. Jerome's Shadow

As the weeks passed in New Orleans, the Catholic church officials along with Sister Mary Joseph were being increasingly receptive and helpful to the plan that Jasper, Margola, Maggie, and Chaucer were discussing. The plan had been presented to the archbishop of the Diocese, and his concerns would need to be addressed if the project was to advance.

Father Brennan met with Maggie and Chaucer in early November for lunch at Mandina's on North Canal Street. Maggie and her family had known the priest for many years, and he was like an uncle to her.

"The archbishop is comfortable with this project, Maggie, but he also wants to leave his stamp on it too. He believes that it will be doing the work of God, but it also has to have a name that will resonate, a name that he can discuss with others in the church, our civic leaders, and the news media people too." He looked at Maggie and Chaucer with wide eyes. "We're happy that it appears that Sister Mary Joseph will consent to you using half of the convent for your program, and as it expands, we are sure that other church resources will be available."

Maggie nodded, while Chaucer sat eating an oyster, just listening. "We really had not thought of a name for the program, Father. We actually were hoping that you would suggest something. The important matter to us is that it must be identified as funded in part by the Hollywood Studios Charitable Foundation since that is their requirement."

Father Brennen smiled. "Well, Hollywood and the church usually are not in agreement with much, although the archbishop did show us the movie *The Exorcist* a few months ago at a retreat. Seems he and Father William O'Malley who played in the movie were classmates and good friends at Holy Cross University decades ago. Father O'Malley was an advisor to the movie and also played a priest in the film. Many thought that the movie was exploitative of the church, but not the archbishop. He has used it as a teaching tool and as an instrument of fundraising too. Getting the Hollywood Foundation the appropriate funding credit should not be an issue."

Maggie and Chaucer smiled with relief.

Father Brennen continued. "However the archbishop wants to name the project 'The Saint Jerome Catholic Charitable Children's Home.' How does that sound to you?" he said with a smile.

"Why that name, Father?" Chaucer asked.

"Well, Saint Jerome Emiliani was canonized in 1767, and in 1928 Pope Pius XI named him the patron of orphans and abandoned children. This seems perfect for this project, don't you think?" he said as he handed Maggie a one-page history of the life of Jerome Emiliani.

"Please take this and review with it your parents. I think you'll be fine with it, my children," he said as he looked confidently at Maggie and Chaucer. "Let's talk more about this next Monday when I meet with you both and your parents. We have a detailed budget to review then if we want to get this program going accordingly to your schedule. Please excuse me now as I must get back to the diocese for some meetings. Thank you for the fine lunch." He stood up, smiled at them, shook hands with Chaucer, and kissed Maggie on the cheek and left.

"That went well," Chaucer said with a grin.

"Yes! Here, let's read this together" she said, so Chaucer shifted his chair around to Maggie, and they read the history of Saint Jerome together.

Maggie smiled broadly and looked at Chaucer like a big sister would. "Seems like you are a lot like Saint Jerome, my dear," she said to Chaucer as he peered down at the history of Saint Jerome which read:

A careless and irreligious soldier for the city-state of Venice, Jerome was captured and chained in a dungeon, where he had time to think, and he learned how to pray. When he escaped, he returned to Venice where he took charge of the education of his nephews and began his own studies for the priesthood. In the years after ordination, events called Jerome to a decision and new life. While serving the sick and the poor, he soon resolved to devote himself and his property solely to others, particularly to abandoned children. He founded three orphanages, a shelter for penitent prostitutes, and a hospital. On reflection, very often in our lives it seems to take some kind of 'imprisonment' to free us from the shackles of our self-centeredness. When we are trapped in some situation we don't want to be in, we finally come to know the liberating power of Another (God). Only then can we become another for the troubled and the orphaned all around us.

http://dayofwrathdiesirae.blogspot.com/

Chaucer looked solemn as he thought about these words. After a moment, he nodded to Maggie. "Yes, that was me, wasn't it? I guess it took our pilgrimage on the Camino, and meeting Rudy that night...and our talks to help me understand and change...to open up myself to the word of God...to help me change my life...Yes, that was me," and he leaned over and kissed her softly on the cheek.

The next day Maggie and Chaucer told her parents about their meeting with Father Brennen. Maggie and Chaucer both endorsed the use of the name Saint Jerome for the program. Jasper and Margola agreed, especially after Chaucer explained his reasons for agreeing.

Chapter 53

The Final Phase for Saint Jerome's

IN THE ENSUING WEEKS, the fundraising continued with various meetings and cocktail parties with wealthy friends and business associates and customers of Jasper and Margola. Maggie solicited support from her young adult friends, and alumni, faculty, and staff of the Tulane social work program from which she had graduated. She also held a couple of tea and coffee sessions with the many friends of Suzette and Bridgette. These meetings were not only to raise money for the St. Jerome program but also to help her recruit staffing and volunteers for St. Jerome's.

Soon, the lease for the building was completed with the Catholic sisters. Insurance was acquired and used furniture was located and moved into the facility. Concurrently, Jasper and Margola were using their influence as respected members of the New Orleans inner social, political, and business circles to have discussions with the medical community and the media to inform the local physicians and reporters about St. Jerome's program. It did not take more than two weeks before the intake volunteer director had received four requests from pregnant young women who wanted to come to live at the program facility until the babies were born. Maggie successfully recruited a female friend who was an ob-gyn physician from the Tulane University Medical School to volunteer her time for a weekly visit to the facility to tend to clients' medical needs.

The final service that Maggie engaged in was to find a way to provide legal services to prospective adoptive parents. She called a good friend of her parents who taught at the Tulane Law School and explained the program to him in detail. She asked if he had any ideas on how best to provide legal services to any couple that wished to adopt a child. After some discussion, he said he would pitch to the law school dean the idea of creating a program where students could receive credit for providing pro bono legal assistance during the adoption process.

Maggie could not have been happier when two weeks later, the dean of the law school approved the pilot program. New Orleans was coming to help. Jasper and Margola called their friend at the law school and thanked him profusely.

Chaucer helped with the facility's setup, specifically a library and TV room. He convinced local bookshops to donate books and promised to give them credit through signs in the facility's library. A friend of Margola's who was a real estate agent had a house listing where the owner was going to throw away his old TV, so Margola arranged for Chaucer to pick it up. He also created, with the advice of Maggie and Margola, a beautiful meditation and counseling room where family members and clergy could come to speak with the young clients to help them with their decisions about the life of the child to be born. He worked hard at his tasks, seemingly driven by his faith, but also by his own sense of guilt for his prior poor behavior. He was proving to himself that he was a changed man.

*   *   *

Over dinner one night, Maggie and Chaucer had a revealing conversation. Chaucer had been working full time in his job, going to meetings in Houston, Mobile, and Tampa, and the rest of his time was completely spent with Maggie and getting the St. Jerome's program ready.

"I never thought that I could be so busy yet so happy," he said to Maggie, as she sipped her glass of wine.

"Me too, it seems that every day we are building another part of the program, meeting with volunteers, talking to friends and others about donations. I really never believed that I would ever feel comfortable asking people for money, but for this program and for these women and children, it is joyful and fun. It's sort of like my calling to do this, and that makes it fun and satisfying. Don't you feel the same way, darling?" she said with a loving and warm face, staring into Chaucer's eyes in a way that only a person in love can do.

"Yep, it's crazy good, almost unbelievable that we are doing this, Maggie, and now is a good time to talk about the call I got from my father late this afternoon. He, JOA, and Pastor Leo would like me to come back to Ottawa for a couple of weeks."

"Why? Are there problems with the program getting started there?" she asked.

"Well, not big problems, but enough things that need to be worked on that he thinks it would be good to have me help, plus he will be going to Italy and Spain on business and stopping in Glasgow on the way home. He said he would be gone for almost three weeks." Chaucer looked concerned. "Plus, I need to see the boys, too."

"OK, I understand. Mom, Dad, and I have things going well here, so you should go. We want these two programs to be successful, don't we?" she said with her beautiful smile. "I want you to know that in my outreach work this week, I met the woman who runs a food bank in the Desire neighborhood. I was in a meeting with Father Brennan, and he asked me to talk about our program to the people there who all run various agencies. This nice woman came up to me after the meeting. Her name is Melba Jacobs, and she said that she has a niece who is pregnant and wants to get an abortion, but Melba is trying to talk her into having the baby. So, I want to meet with her and talk more about our program. Her niece could be another client."

Chaucer reached over and touched Maggie's hand. Their love for each other was so obvious, that any person seeing them together would notice, and perhaps smile at them for their abundant happiness.

"Good, let's do all we can to help anyone who we can. We need to save these babies, Maggie. They need us to act for them, just like Melba Jacobs is doing. I'd like to meet her when I get back from Ottawa."

That night Chaucer packed a suitcase and his briefcase with his files. In the morning, Maggie dropped him at the airport for his flight to Ottawa. JOA would pick him up that afternoon.

Chapter 54

Melba Jacobs

ONE MORNING A FEW DAYS LATER Maggie drove to the Desire Food Bank to meet with Melba. Maggie wanted to answer more of Melba's questions about the program and recruit her to be an ambassador for the program in her neighborhood, one of the poorest parts of New Orleans.

Over coffee in Melba's small office, they talked. Melba was a friendly looking black woman about mid 50's in age. She had a smile as wide as Canal Street when she used it. She had moved to New Orleans from Baton Rouge with her husband, who was a chef. He had drowned a decade ago in a fishing accident on a day off from the restaurant. Melba had one son who had attended LSU and played football but had gotten injured, then left college to take a position with the Baton Rouge Police Department based on a recommendation from one of his coaches at LSU. Melba had joined the St. Mary of the Angels Catholic Church in the nearby New Orleans neighborhood called the Florida area. Over time she was recruited by the food bank to manage their programs in various needy neighborhoods. Melba was a serious manager and a strong Christian with an abundance of faith.

"I'm glad that you could come visit me, Maggie. I've met your mother at some church events, and when I met you last week, I knew that we could have a good talk," Melba smiled a half smile. "I don't like abortion one bit, and my niece in Baton Rouge seems to think it's the answer to her problem now."

Maggie just listened attentively, drinking her coffee.

"Sheila says she is too young to be a mother, and her boyfriend got drafted by the Army, and he is gone now. My husband's nasty brother and his wife want to kick her out, and she says she has no other way to deal with her condition. The other thing you should know, Maggie, is that she probably wouldn't come to your program because she doesn't trust the Catholic church, and she and her parents don't trust white people," Melba said.

Maggie nodded, knowing full well that many blacks in Louisiana, especially those in the rural areas, had been treated very poorly, or even terrorized in the past by the whites where they lived. She knew this from growing up in New Orleans. She knew that the new South was trying hard to be a better, different South but that many blacks had a much different life experience than she had had over the past twenty-five years. That recognition, along with discussions with her parents and sisters over her early years, had been her motivation to choose a career in social work and stay in New Orleans to attend Tulane. Maggie loved New Orleans and Louisiana, and she wanted to make a difference, make a mark as a Catholic and a social worker.

Maggie looked at Melba with an open heart and said, "Maybe Sheila just hasn't met the right white people," and she said no more at that moment.

Melba sat back in her chair and looked closely at Maggie, wondering if she had heard her correctly. She waited for Maggie to speak again but Maggie did not, she sat with her hands folded together on the table.

Melba had waited because she knew that most white people loved to talk and explain away anything that a black person would raise any question with. She had seen it all her life, especially the wealthy white women who had never experienced these troubles, these acts of cruel and unkind behavior directed to blacks and poor whites too. So, she waited.

Maggie just sat thinking, wanting to hear more from Melba. Maggie remembered that when she was a teenager, her grandfather Mael Grandemaison told her in his deep, crackling voice some good advice: "Maggie darling, when you are talking to someone about something important and trying to win them over to your side, you need to listen carefully and not talk." She recalled asking him, "Why, Grandpa? Why shouldn't I tell them what I know so they will want to join me and be on my side?" She remembered his most important words that day. "Maggie, if you start explaining things, then you are losing. Folks want to be heard, listened too, not be fed a line, so just listen, you'll hear plenty, and then you'll know what to do." Maggie remembered her grandfather smiling and hugging her that day.

Finally, after a few more minutes, Melba asked with a stern face, "So, who are the right white people then? Who is going to take care of Sheila and then a little black baby in seven months from now? Is your program at the church going to do this?"

"Do you think she will want to keep the baby?" Maggie asked.

"Lord, child, we be getting in this deep now," Melba replied, shaking her head.

Maggie continued to sit quietly.

"I want her to keep this child. She made it with that rascal, and now she need to keep the child. God would be angry with her if she didn't," Melba said.

"Melba, I don't think God is angry with anyone, just disappointed."

Melba thought for a moment. "Honey, you got that right, mighty right. Now what's this program you got, tell me now," said Melba, comfortable that Maggie was truly listening.

Maggie cleared her throat with a soft cough and began, "We have rented some vacant space in the convent on Napoleon Avenue. We have recruited a doctor and a nurse for medical services for the women and the babies. We have a kitchen to prepare meals. We have a library, and we will be providing education classes for the women too." Maggie hesitated and looked at Melba.

Melba smiled and nodded. "Go on," she said.

Maggie continued, "Like you, our board would like the mothers to keep the children, and we can provide some funds and other incentives to help them."

Melba looked at her. "And what if they won't keep the babies, then what?"

Maggie said. "Then we'll keep them until we can find a family to adopt them, a good family."

Melba nodded. "Who's gonna adopt these little black babies in

New Orleans? We got plenty of them already."

"Then we will raise them in our orphanage as long as they need a home," Maggie said.

"Who be payin' for all this girl?" Melba said with a condescending tone. "You got all this money, do ya?"

Maggie slowed down and waited before speaking. She smiled and leaned across the desk toward Melba. "Melba, we do have good funding, and we will continue to have the money needed to protect these babies and the mothers that decide to keep the babies."

Melba was impressed with Maggie and her confidence. Maggie had convinced Melba that she was real and not just a "white do good-er" who comes in with all kinds of promises and then disappears. Plus, Melba knew Maggie's mother and trusted her.

"OK," Melba nodded. "Let me talk to Sheila about this. If she's interested, I'll bring her to the place, and you can talk with her, show her around, give her some knowledge. You OK with that?"

"Yes," said Maggie, knowing in her heart that Melba was honest and true.

* * *

Melba was true to her word. The following week Sheila drove down from Baton Rouge and she and Melba met with Maggie at the facility, now officially named St Jerome's, and they had a tour and a long discussion. Melba and Sheila seemed happy when they left, and the following day, Melba called Maggie and told her that Sheila wanted to have the baby and stay at St. Jerome's, but she did not want to keep the child. She preferred to let the baby stay at the orphanage until an adoption could be arranged. Maggie agreed, and thus Sheila would become one of the first clients of the St. Jerome's program.

As the weeks passed, Melba joined the board of directors of the St. Jerome's program and began a series of meetings with other community groups and churches in the black neighborhoods of New Orleans. Maggie also recruited other trusted women to reach out to the rural Cajun towns and the lower income white neighborhoods. Within three months of going active, Maggie had six women volunteering as outreach program recruiters and educators in the greater New Orleans area.

The program itself had a capacity of twenty-four clients given its available space on the St. Jerome's campus. At the end of the first three months, Maggie already had seventeen spaces accounted for. Eleven young pregnant women were in residence and six more would be moving in soon. The volunteer ob-gyn physician and nurse were making weekly visits to see the clients. The Tulane Department of Social Work and the School of Education were both sending student interns to the program to work with the clients. Two of the clients even enrolled for classes at Tulane despite their pregnancy status, and they were welcomed at the university in part because of the good work that Maggie had done to form the partnership with her alma mater.

Jasper and Margola continued to raise money and draw support to the program. The one problem that Maggie had was finding time to spend with Suzette's children, who were not yet legally adopted. Bridgette and Margola helped enormously as did Rufus's parents, who often took the children for entire weekends. It seemed like God, through family, had stepped in and helped Maggie and Chaucer. Chaucer had his plate full between the program in New Orleans, helping with the program in Ottawa, and still working for Remy as his assistant for the southern region in the shipping company. It seemed both their lives were as busy as could be.

Chapter 55

Ottawa Redux

WHEN REMY HAD CALLED CHAUCER back to Ottawa, it had been for more reasons than he had explained on the phone call. While the ability to rent appropriate space and raise funds for the program had not been the concern, the ability to convince referral partners in the Ottawa area was. In Ottawa, some referral sources that worked well in New Orleans would not see the new program as essential due to the existence of some Canadian government programs already funded by the federal and the provincial authorities. In addition, many in the Ottawa area did not want to be seen or labeled as anti-abortion. Thus, Remy and Pastor Leo had to revise the original plan.

The start of this new plan involved a meeting that Remy had in Montreal at his company's headquarters. One of his senior employees from the Mediterranean division was an Israeli national named Shlomo Benjamin. Over lunch and social talk, Remy told Shlomo about the orphanage program he was creating in Ottawa. Shlomo listened carefully and then told Remy that his uncle, Laslo Heitman, was a rabbi in Montreal who could likely help with recruitment from the large Jewish-Canadian communities in Montreal and Toronto. Benjamin set up a dinner meeting for the three of them for two nights later.

The meeting proved quite productive for Remy and Rabbi

Heitman. The rabbi explained that his conservative temple in Montreal was a part of the Israeli diaspora information network, and they were linked with many other temples and groups in Canada and the United States. They were tasked with the need to identify Jews who would go to Israel to settle and populate the new nation. He explained how the large population of non-observant Jews in North America, including in Mexico and Central America, were very liberal in their views on abortion. He believed that single Jewish women who became pregnant often turned to abortion. He wanted a program like Remy's to help them during a pregnancy, and he wanted then to place the babies with families in Israel, which he said he could easily make happen. During the entire conversation, Shlomo looked at Remy and confidently nodded in silent agreement with his uncle.

In addition, Rabbi Heitman informed Remy that for any other women who were in the program in Ottawa and did not wish to keep their baby, that he and his staff would rigorously examine the family background of the mother to determine if there was any Jewish blood, and if they could document it through searching records, then those babies could also easily be adopted by families in Israel as per the Israeli law. Remy liked what he heard. He explained to the rabbi that the program was starting as a small program but would expand as needed, and that Remy, JOA, and Chaucer would also expect that the rabbi and his group would then become financial contributors to the program. Rabbi Heitman agreed and said that he would visit Remy in Ottawa in a month, after Remy had returned from his upcoming business trip.

Pastor Leo also faced problems in convincing other clergy to help recruit for the program. The pastor and Remy decided that the two of them, along with JOA and when Chaucer joined them in Ottawa, would begin individual visits to each and every Catholic church in the Ottawa and Montreal area. They also planned to visit the many college towns in Vermont and northern New York state and meet with the clergy there. It was an ambitious plan, but the program had now become the spiritual calling of Remy and JOA as well as Chaucer and Pastor Leo. They would spend all their available time and energy on it.

Within months, the available beds at the program's dormitory in Ottawa were filled. Similar to the success of the program in New

Orleans, the volunteer physician and nurses were meeting with the pregnant young women as were education and vocational counselors. What was disappointing to Remy and the others was the small percentage of women who wanted to keep their babies.

Chapter 56

For Love

FOR THE NEXT TWO YEARS, the two programs in Ottawa and New Orleans filled every client room and bed available. The volunteers kept coming, keeping their word to help. Little by little, each month brought positive upgrades to the program, whether it was building a better library, expanding the outside cultural programs that the clients could participate in, a better choice of daily foods from the kitchen, or more options for education and job training for the clients.

Again, of disappointment to Chaucer and Maggie, JOA, Remy, Jasper, and Margola, was the small number of women who opted to keep their babies. Of the 221 babies born in the two programs in a little over two years, only forty-three babies went home with their mothers. Of the remaining 178 babies, 110 had been placed with selective, adopted parents and the remaining sixty-eight were being cared for in the two orphanages. Yet slowly, the rate of babies staying with their natural mothers was increasing, and the time between child birth and placement with adoptive parents was decreasing.

Much of the this was due to the help of the increasing numbers of churches, temples, and civic organizations that worked in concert with the programs. Because of strict oversight by Chaucer and Maggie and senior staff, not one problem of an ethical or legal nature occurred. Only three total employees were dismissed for non-performance of their duties over the first two years. The two programs were proving to their donors that they could be assured that the babies were well cared for and placed with good adoptive parents.

* * *

About the middle of the second year of operations, after an audit visit by Abraham and his small staff from the Hollywood Studios Charitable Foundation, the HSCF decided that the programs had proven their value and had met the objectives of the HSCF. To the delight of the founders, the HSCF decided to become a permanent funding source for both programs with a ten-year funding contract developed, reviewed, and signed by both parties. Other funding organizations soon matched the HSCF's commitment, thus giving the programs a level of security not seen before.

After Abraham announced the funding decision at a board of directors dinner in Ottawa, he told Remy, Chaucer, Maggie, and JOA that he and Olivia had decided to end their informal personal relationship. Apparently, she had met another man, a wealthy film producer from London, and they had been spending considerable time together in Los Angeles and London. Abraham said that while he did not know the man well, he had heard he was an "OK guy," as Abraham put it.

Abraham told them that he did miss his joyous times with Olivia but her writing schedule and the demands for her screenplays had also sequestered her away in her writing studio at times for many weeks. During those times, she did not want his company, and thus the frequency of those many lonely periods had already convinced him that he could be without her if it ever came to that, and now it had. He said he would miss her but he and Olivia had learned that they were fundamentally different people. Upon hearing this from Abraham, Remy, JOA, and Chaucer just grinned at each other. They too had lived this type of life with Olivia. They knew the experience well.

* * *

About a month after the meeting with Abraham, Remy got an unexpected phone call from Olivia. He was amazed, as he had not spoken to her in at least two months. She called to check in on JOA and Chaucer and the grandchildren, and to hear the latest news on the orphanages in Ottawa and New Orleans.

"Well, hello, stranger," Remy said cordially. "Nice to hear your voice again. How are you?"

"Very busy, so many projects to work on. You know me. How are the children and the little ones?" she asked.

Remy filled her in on everyone, and then they spoke about the orphanages and the idea of perhaps starting a third orphanage in California and perhaps another in Glasgow too.

"Remy, that is a good idea," Olivia said emphatically. "These kids today are just so irresponsible. They just seem to think that abortion is like having a toothache. Pull it out and let me go on with my life," Olivia voiced in a fine state of annoyance.

"Yes. What is western culture coming to if the babies that God creates mean nothing to these young people. Frankly, it is shameful," Remy replied.

"Yes, it is...Thanks for the information on Chaucer and JOA and the grandchildren. I also want to tell you about my new friend, Tobias Wrightman from London." She paused. "Well, he and I have decided to do something that I never thought that I would do, something that had never really interested me before."

"And what is that? Are you going to bike across Canada or France?" Remy asked with a little laugh.

"Nooo...actually we are going to sail his boat from Los Angeles to Hawaii, stay there for a while, then sail back! I've set aside two whole months from my screenwriting projects, something that I have never done before," she said with a small amount of joy in her voice.

"Wonderful, that sounds wonderful, Olivia," Remy said, surprised. "And will you be writing on the boat or not working at all? You have been working so much lately; tell me about the boat you will be sailing to Hawaii."

"Of course, I'll probably be working on some new fiction outline or something. I can't just stop working because we are sailing, now can I?" she said laughing a bit. "His boat is a 45-foot Morgan with all the latest instruments, he tells me; it practically sails itself. He's bringing along a couple of cases of good Bordeaux and champagne so I imagine that we'll relax with that. Depending on my work, we may fly back and then sail the boat back to L.A. a few months later. I'm really looking forward to this trip."

"OK, well, enjoy the trip and please call us from Hawaii. I'm sure that JOA will want to hear about your travels. She is so busy with the work at the orphanage that I may surprise her soon with a trip to Barbados. She has been a real blessing for those little babies and the clients we have."

"Yes, Remy I am very happy that she has found herself in doing all this work with you and Chaucer and the others. And yes, I will phone you from Honolulu when we arrive. We leave in a week and plan to be on the water for about two weeks or so to get there, according to Tobias. Please give Chaucer, Maggie, and JOA my love, and you take care of yourself too. Bye for now," and she ended the call before Remy could reply, as was her style.

Remy, still holding the phone receiver, smiled and thought, "Olivia, Olivia. You'll never change."

* * *

About three weeks later Chaucer called Remy from the company office in Tampa, Florida.

"Dad, all the manifests for the ships at the Panama Canal have been cleared for passage. They have their assigned pilots, and the six of them will be in the Pacific by this time tomorrow."

"Great, thanks for the update, Son. When will you be going home?" Remy asked.

"Looks like I'm driving to Mobile tomorrow to meet Jasper and review the new port assignments for us, then he and I will drive home the following day unless some issues come up there," Chaucer said.

"OK, good to hear. Anything else?"

"Dad, have you heard from Mother yet? She should have gotten to Honolulu by now, don't you think?"

"No, she hasn't called yet. She was hoping to have a two- to three-week passage depending on the winds. I believe they left L.A. about a week after she called me the last time. Why do you ask; is something wrong?"

"Well, not really," Chaucer said slowly, "but today at the port here, during lunch I was talking to a couple of guys who are old mariners who have sailed the L.A. to Hawaii passage, so I told them about Mother sailing to Hawaii the past couple of weeks, and they asked if she was safe, so I asked, 'What do you mean?' and they told me that a typhoon had quickly come up from the Gilbert Islands last week and just missed Hawaii and then stalled out. They just wanted to make sure we knew she was in port now," Chaucer said.

"OK, well, I know that our San Francisco and Honolulu offices filed reports that our ships were kept in port until the storm broke up. Perhaps she is already there or perhaps they didn't leave L.A. as planned. Let me look into this from here and see what I can find out. Call me from Mobile tomorrow when you get there, OK?"

"OK, I will, bye for now."

*   *   *

Remy called his friends at the Canadian National Weather Service and got a hold of an old mate that he knew from World War II. Remy asked him about the typhoon near Hawaii that Chaucer had mentioned. Yes, his friend confirmed, a week ago a Pacific typhoon had missed Hawaii by about 200 kilometers, then veered due north through the shipping lanes and then stalled out and died. Remy thanked him. He felt worried and pondered his next step. He poured himself a glass of port and decided to call Abraham in Hollywood.

"Abraham, Remy Giroux here. Do you have a few minutes?"

"Hi, Remy, sure, how can I help you? Everything all right with the programs?"

"Oh yes, the two programs are just fine. It's actually about Olivia. She and her new friend from London were sailing his boat to Hawaii. They left L.A. about two or three weeks ago, and we have not heard from her. She promised to call me and the children when she arrived, and now I know about the typhoon that almost hit Hawaii last week. Do you know anything that could help me find her?" Remy asked in a calm voice.

"Oh shit. She was sailing to Hawaii last week, are you serious, Remy?" Abraham sounded alarmed, which made Remy feel even more concerned.

"I am," Remy said.

"OK, well, the weather reports here on the West Coast did talk about that storm, and that it did cross into the shipping lanes from

California before it died out."

"Yes, that is the information that I have, too. Olivia told me that her new boyfriend was Tobias Wrightman and he was from London. I know you had said he was an OK guy, but you didn't really know him," Remy said.

"That's right, Remy. I think he has a son at one of our local studios. Let me make some calls, and I'll call you back after I check this out."

Remy thanked Abraham and said goodbye. Remy then stood up from the chair behind his desk and walked over to look at the large, framed map of the Pacific Ocean on the wall. He stared at the wide expanse of water between L.A. and Honolulu for several minutes, sighed, and then went back to work at his desk.

*   *   *

About an hour later the phone rang; it was Abraham.

"Remy, I had my staff find Wrightman's son at MGM, and I spoke to him. He knows his father was sailing to Hawaii a couple of weeks ago, and no, he has not heard from him. He said if his father had been in trouble in that storm, he surely would have radioed him and the Coast Guard. He said the boat was a 45-foot Morgan named Lady Luck. Sorry, I wish I had more information. Let's keep in touch and hopefully Olivia is safe somewhere on Oahu or one of the other islands. She doesn't like to take chances so I would expect we'll have some good news soon."

Remy thanked him and hung up. He then called his friend Carleton at the Canadian Weather Service and asked him if he could use his contacts with the U.S. Coast Guard to see if they had any information.

The next morning, Carleton called him. He said that the U.S. Coast Guard had an SOS from a Lady Luck out of Los Angeles but it was just one SOS May Day signal call and then nothing. "They checked the Honolulu reports and found that a 45-foot boat out of L.A. was overdue. They checked with the harbor master in L.A., and they had a Lady Luck registered in England leave for Hawaii three weeks ago," Carleton paused. "Remy, you're in the shipping business so you know that it does not look good if the U.S. Coast Guard cannot locate that craft in any Hawaiian harbor in the next twenty-four hours. I will check again in the morning or if they call me back today, I'll call you right away, OK?

"Thanks, Carleton. I appreciate what you are doing."

Remy then called his office in Honolulu and asked his manager also to check with the U.S. Coast Guard for any reports of the Lady Luck. Remy poured another glass of port, lit a cigar, and went out on the rear terrace to look at the river.

That night Remy said nothing to JOA about his concerns, and he did not call Chaucer as he did not want to cause any undue alarm. He went to bed but could not sleep. He lay there thinking about Olivia, seeing her in his mind's eye over the years, from the first time he had met her thirty years before and of the last time he saw her in Ottawa two years ago. He remembered the beauty of her smile, her full broad lips, the softness of her warm skin, the smells of her hair…and then the morning sunlight woke him.

*   *   *

Late that morning Remy received a call from Carleton at the CWS. His voice was grim.

"Remy, the U.S. Coast Guard has told us that two vessels have not been reported in any port in Hawaii, one is a Canadian cargo ship out of Vancouver and the other is a London-based boat coming from L.A., and it is the Lady Luck. They said that they have started an air search out of Honolulu, and they will let us know if they have any sightings. Let's not give up hope, Remy. They may have lost their mast and power and are floating and waiting for air rescue."

Remy decided to call JOA and Chaucer and let them know about their mother. The calls were painful for him, and for his children. They agreed to continue praying that Olivia would be found.

The next day Carleton called Remy again. "They have located the Lady Luck about 300 miles east of the big island of Hawaii. She was capsized and rolling, her mast was snapped in half. They sent a chopper out and lowered a man on to the boat. He found no bodies, so they are resuming an air search looking for a life raft or floaters."

Remy asked JOA to come to his house, and the two of them called Chaucer and Maggie in New Orleans with the latest information. They decided to keep hope that Olivia would be found by the air search. Remy did not show his resignation in his voice or words.

They must keep praying, he urged them. He did not want the children to lose their mother.

Two days later the U.S. Coast Guard informed the Canadian government that they had ended the air search efforts. They had found debris from the Canadian freighter near the location of the coordinates of the last radio message from that vessel but that was all. The air rescue search had located no life rafts from either of the two vessels. Carleton called Remy with the information. It was over. She was gone. It was June 1976.

* * *

Three days later Chaucer and Maggie flew to Ottawa. They and JOA spent time with some of the other Ottawa relatives at the house. Kathleen, the twins Ollie and Jean Marc, and their parents came from Geneva, New York, to console Remy, Chaucer, and JOA. Cousins Logan and Clint Giroux were out of the country but called their uncle and cousins in Ottawa. The family remorse was palpable. It was extraordinarily difficult to lose Olivia this way, so very unexpected.

After a few days, Maggie flew back to New Orleans as she was needed at the program and in her job with the diocese. The other family members from out of town also returned home. Remy took his children to the golf club to relax over dinner. He asked Pastor Leo to join them.

During dinner, Remy announced, "I'm going to Victoria in a few days. I want to lock up her house and decide what to do with it. Chaucer and JOA, it would be good if we all went together. Will you come with me?" Chaucer and JOA immediately agreed it would be the best thing to do.

"Olivia would want you to do this, Remy," Pastor Leo said. "It will be good if you all do this together. God will guide you and help you in this. It will help you all heal and find the best memories of her. She will be in that house with you when you are there. Her spirit will bring you joy, not sadness. Perhaps we can plan a memorial service for her when you return." Remy, Chaucer, and JOA agreed, and for the rest of dinner, they told funny and loving stories of Olivia.

Chapter 57

A Secret Hidden in Victoria

A WEEK LATER REMY, CHAUCER, AND JOA landed at Victoria International Airport, rented a car, and drove south down Highway 17 to Olivia's house near the water. Neither Chaucer nor JOA had been there in the past three years, and Remy had not been there in twice that time. The property always had a special serenity about it that they still felt as they drove up the one-lane road to the house. Over the years Olivia had done little to trim back the vegetation or the trees that lined the road, so now the acreage had the feel of a haunted property of sorts.

When they arrived at the house, a Royal Canadian Mounted Police car met them. Remy had called their office before he left Ottawa and explained the situation about Olivia. They agreed to keep a regular watch on the house once Remy and the children were gone.

Both JOA and Chaucer still had keys to the house. Once inside, they found a meager amount of food in the refrigerator and in the cupboard. JOA and Chaucer looked at each other and laughed. "It seems like nothing has changed with Mother over the years, whether we were here or not," JOA said with a smile, recalling all the times when Chaucer and she had to figure out their meals as Olivia stayed sequestered with her writing.

The trio walked to the barn and up the stairs to Olivia's writing room and desk. Just like before, it appeared that she had been sleeping in the writing room, her habit for years. She had added a small refrigerator and a hot plate, probably to allow her to eat and continue working. The room was bright from the windows that Olivia had installed, and it smelled musty after being closed up for over a month. Again, JOA and Chaucer smiled, telling Remy how Olivia would be secluded in the room for days, sometimes working in her bathrobe all day. She was that kind of a driven, compulsive writer, and they all knew it.

On her large desk and the shelves nearby were stacks of papers held together with rubber bands and marked "Draft #1" or "Draft #2" or "Final." In the past fourteen years since Olivia had been working in this room, she had written sixteen novels and six screenplays. All the novels sold well, and three reached the top seller list in Canada, and two did the same in the United States. All six of her screenplays were purchased and made into movies. Her nephew Jean Marc Giroux had helped her on the final drafts of two of her screenplays when she was in Los Angeles gaining the final approvals prior to filming. While doing that work, Jean Marc told her about the time that Chaucer and he had driven across country years before, and how Chaucer had visited him during his college days. Olivia had missed all this because by then Chaucer had left British Columbia for college in Toronto, so she appreciated hearing these stories from Jean Marc.

As Remy, Chaucer, and JOA surveyed the room, they also found piles of bank statements, bills, and investment statements. This was a room where she did everything it seemed, and very little was organized. She had a professionally made sign over her desk that read "Get your ass in that chair," apparently her daily credo. It was signed by one of her writer girlfriends in Victoria.

All this work, all these books and screenplays had made Olivia a very wealthy woman, yet to look at her writing room in this barn you would not discern that. She remained an unencumbered woman, not beholden to money or men or status. She had often told Remy that writing was a passion for her, not making money. Ironically, just two years before Olivia had sent Remy the names of her agent in Hollywood, her investment advisor, and her accountant in Vancouver. She wanted him to know their contact information, for the sake of JOA and Chaucer and Chaucer's children as well. Her investment advisor had advocated her writing a will and keeping it on file with him and her banker in Victoria should anything ever happen to incapacitate her. Equipped with this information, Remy contacted all of them from Olivia's house.

Remy explained that Olivia was missing at sea. Her banker told Remy that British Columbia law required a legal determination of death at sea via a hearing with a judge, with evidence supplied by the Canadian Coast Guard in conjunction with reports from the U.S. Coast Guard and U.S. Navy in a situation such as this. Remy called his attorney in Ottawa and instructed him to commence the necessary work to obtain a valid death certificate in British Columbia and then communicate with the Victoria bank and the Vancouver investment manager. He also asked his attorney to advise Olivia's agent in Hollywood as well. Since Remy and his attorney had negotiated Olivia's first writing deal, she had allowed Remy to participate with his lawyer in her future contracts, so both Remy and his attorney were well informed of the location and terms of her documents and contracts.

While Remy was on the phone with these others, JOA and Chaucer were in her studio in the barn going through Olivia's files and drafts and outlines. They were amazed at the work that she was doing, both the amount and the quality. Their mother had certainly worked her way into being a top-level writer, one of the best in North America, they had been told.

JOA decided to make some English tea that her mother had in the cupboard. She was tired from the long day, and she sat in her mothers' writing chair at her desk. She put her feet up on the desk and sat back sipping the warm, delicious Earl Grey tea. Her eyes wandered over the desk and she smiled. Chaucer also was having tea but he sat on the floor across the room flipping through one of the book drafts.

Suddenly, JOA saw it. On the bottom right drawer of the big desk was a label, written in hand, that said "Diary notes only." She pulled her feet off the desk top and bent down and pulled on the drawer but it did not open; it was locked. "Chaucer, can you come help me with this, please?" she asked.

Chaucer walked over and determined that the lever holding the drawer closed was a small latch, so he found Olivia's letter opener, inserted it slowly and moved it to release the small lock. Seeing that there was just another book in the drawer, he went back to his pile of reading on the floor across the room.

But JOA realized this was no ordinary book. It was an expensive, large, leather-bound journal, a beautiful book seemingly for a special occasion. JOA took it from the drawer, put it on the desk, and opened it to the first page upon which Olivia had written in script, "Summer, 1962." JOA started reading.

After a few minutes, she called to Chaucer again, "Brother, come see this, it's amazing!" Chaucer got up and slowly walked to the desk. "Now what, the Holy Grail?" he said semi- annoyed by the interruption. JOA replied, "Well, almost, look at this!"

The siblings sat and read and turned the pages. This was a draft of Olivia's autobiography. It started with the title "My first year in Vancouver," and Olivia wrote about her leaving Ottawa and her family. Several pages later, the book was loaded with regrets about leaving Remy. She had written: "He was a good a man, the best that I would or could ever find to marry, but as much as I loved him, I loved my writing life more, and I could only live it if I moved away from our home in Ottawa and his business life. I know it hurt him badly, and I hoped that someday the grace of God will forgive me for what I have done to him and to our family."

JOA blurted out: "Oh my God, Chaucer, she did suffer, she did have remorse. I never imagined she felt like this when I was younger." Chaucer, standing behind JOA and reading over her shoulder, put his hands on JOA's shoulders, and kissed the top of her head. "I didn't either, Sis. I was just mad because I had to move here and leave Dad and Ottawa. Go ahead, you read it first, and I'll read it later." Chaucer returned to his spot on the floor and continued perusing a stack of papers.

JOA kept reading. At one point, out of curiosity, she flipped to the last few pages where there a small section entitled "just notes, not to be included." She kept reading and reading and reading until she came to the paragraph that read, "My worst mistake ever. How I ever did this still amazes me, even after two decades. That Englishman that my mother introduced me to at the party celebrating her birthday at her house. His name was Phillip Pennington, I think; I don't even remember for sure if that was his name anymore. Why I went with him to his hotel room, I still don't know, perhaps I had far too many drinks or perhaps I was upset about something. That one night and the next morning with him, what was I thinking? It was so wrong, too sad for me to ever explain to Remy so I just told him the baby was his. He had been in England and France for two weeks. The timing worked out to be our second child, so I never told him, and JOA looks so much like me so that was that, done. But still I was wrong. My weakest and worst moment, the opposite of what Churchill said during the war."

JOA's eyes were as big as saucers, so she read it again, and a third time, and finally she realized that Remy was not her father. She laughed at first then started to weep softly.

Chaucer looked up and saw her crying. "What's wrong, Sis, did you read something sad?"

JOA wiped her nose and eyes, then laughed again. "Nope, just something funny that Mother did. I'll tell you later."

She stood up, put the leather book under her arm and walked down the stairs. Once she was at the bottom of the stairs, she ripped the last pages from the journal and stuffed them into her pocket, then went in the house where Remy was on the phone. She found some of her mother's wine and poured herself a full glass, drank half quickly, and refilled it. Then she went back to the barn, climbed the stairs, and sat at her mother's desk and continued to read the journal.

For the next hour, she read, looking for any other mention of the Englishman and her mother's affair with him. She found none. What she did find were many pages of great thoughts, ideas, and her dreams of being a writer, a poet, some story lines she wanted to work on, interesting reflections on Remy, their life in Ottawa, her interest in her children, and occasionally her "terrible mistake," which was always written as either "terrible mistake" or just "tm," but never more.

JOA finished the entire journal that night, never saying anything about it to her brother or father. Near the end, in the section "not to be used," she again saw one last reference to the "tm." Olivia had written simply, "In the first year after I left Ottawa, Mother received a letter from the tm in England that was marked for me, but I didn't want to see it, so I told her to burn it; hopefully, she never read it and burned it, but I'll never know now." JOA quickly ripped out this page and stuffed it into her pocket with the other pages.

The next morning JOA awoke with a hangover from her wine binge the night before. She had a dream during the night of meeting a strange man who came to the Ottawa orphanage in the middle of winter. He came in asking for help. He said that he was looking for a baby born to a woman named Juliette long ago. She said that the orphanage had a strict policy of not disclosing the names and backgrounds of any of the children unless a formal adoption process was started. But this man, a very handsome man with an upper-class Eton or old Sandhurst accent, pleaded that he had come all the way from England to find this child. JOA insisted he follow the rules, and when he became belligerent in an arrogant English entitlement manner, she called for her co-workers, who came and escorted him out. Then she woke up in a fog of sleep and dreams and with a big hangover thirst. After some breakfast coffee and toast, she took the journal from her bedside and handed it to Chaucer.

"Please take this, I never want to see it again. Give it to Father when you are finished. I think it will be good reading for him. He'll see that all the things that she has said over the years about being in love with writing were true, and that she did love him but that her desire to write and be alone was the most important thing for her, more important than him," she paused, "and us. At least I can respect her honesty even if she screwed us up and didn't show us much affection." JOA seemed on the verge of tears. "Oh Chaucer, so many days and nights I just wanted to have us be back in Ottawa with her and Father together." JOA sighed deeply.

"Me too, Sis. She messed me up. I really didn't understand why I had developed a dislike of women...especially after Tessa and Joanie rejected me, just like I felt Mother had done...so what I was doing to women that liked me, I just wanted to be rude to them, probably taking out my anger with Mother and Tessa on them. I was really stupid to be like that...purposely hurting women...and then I met these two girls from Boston on my trip in Portugal, and they helped me begin to sort out my life, and then I met Maggie. She helped me realize what I was doing was wrong and how I was not listening to God who was there for me all the time."

"Yeah, same for me, I guess. It's just that I didn't hurt others, just myself. Then fortunately, Dad brought me back to Ottawa, and you both trusted me enough to bring me into the orphanage management in Ottawa. That was when I really found myself, Chaucer; seriously, it was the right time and for the right reasons." JOA looked closely at Chaucer and squeezed his hand.

"Sure, JOA," Chaucer said holding the leather-bound diary. "I'll read it and then give it to Dad." The siblings had each other to help deal with the loss of their mother, and in turn, both JOA and Chaucer did all they could to comfort Remy.

* * *

Over the next week, Remy, JOA, and Chaucer continued their work at Olivia's house and writing barn. They separated all her papers and files. They created boxes labeled "archives" and boxes labeled "trash," which they later burned. They made arrangements for a local church's charity arm to collect all the furniture and household goods and give it to needy families or sell it, with the proceeds going to the church's food pantry. Because Olivia was originally from Ottawa and a Carleton College alumna, they developed a plan with the college library to accept all her archives since she had become one of the top Canadian novelists. What clothes and jewelry that JOA did not want were donated to local charities. Chaucer and Remy kept a few personal items as keepsakes for themselves, too.

Remy, JOA, and Chaucer all agreed that none of them felt any attachment to the property, so the family would not keep it. Remy went to the Victoria government center and spoke with the land use director. He explained that his former wife was the writer Olivia Wellesley, that she had gone missing at sea, and the family was going to list the property for sale soon. Remy suggested that the local government and the British Columbia provincial government consider placing an Historic Canada sign at the property so visitors would know that Olivia had lived in the house when she wrote all her novels. The official said that he would put the proposal before the local historic commission.

Neither JOA nor Chaucer had any emotional investment in the property even though they had once lived there with Olivia. They also agreed that neither of them would likely return to Victoria again because it harbored mainly negative memories for them. This was a collective truth for both of them.

A few days later, they finished their work at the house. They then flew back to Ottawa together.

* * *

In the succeeding months, Remy went to England and then Glasgow for business and to spend a few weeks with Teasag and Jockie. He was emotionally drained and needed some time away from Canada and to be with his loved ones in Glasgow. Before he departed, he met with Pastor Leo, JOA, two other local ministers, and a priest to review the continued fund-raising efforts and the operational plan for the orphanage and the program. JOA had loved working with the program and orphanage, so with the blessing of the local clergy, Remy informed them that JOA, even at her young age of 26, would now be the manager of the program and the orphanage. She was elated that Remy was following up on the prior discussions that they had regarding her expanded role. After the announcement at the meeting, she stood and thanked her father, and said she would do her best to keep the trust that he had placed in her, then she kissed Remy in front of the others. Remy looked at them with a big smile and quipped: "Now don't we want motivated young people like this to help us make our program be even more successful?" They all laughed and agreed with him.

Chaucer returned to New Orleans, taking with him McCarthy and Mickey, who were both now 5 years old. Chaucer wanted them to spend time with their cousins in New Orleans. It all went well, and after a month as both boys were about to begin school, Chaucer returned with them to Ottawa as Remy had returned from Glasgow.

When Chaucer and the boys arrived back in Ottawa, they greeted the two new "official" members of their family. Remy and Teasag had gotten married the week before in Glasgow in a very small ceremony. Remy had flown JOA into Glasgow as Teasag wanted her to be the maid of honor, and Remy asked his son Jockie, now 12, to be the best man. After a few days honeymooning at a hide-a-way on the isle of Skye, Remy and Teasag returned to Glasgow, packed their bags, rented Teasag's house to another faculty member, and flew with Jockie and JOA to their new life in Ottawa. Prior to the wedding, Remy called Chaucer to let him know about the plans. "You'll always be my best man, Chaucer, but I know you just got back to New Orleans after being away for so long, and Maggie and your children need you there right now. Plus, I want Jockie to feel good about me marrying his mother, and I want him to be a part of the marriage ceremony." Of course, Chaucer completely understood and told his father that.

*   *   *

In December 1976, Remy's lawyer in Montreal, Quinton Marshmonte, called for a family reading of Olivia's will. Marshmonte had read it and reviewed it with Olivia's long-time financial advisor and accountant in Vancouver. They saw nothing new that they had not known so they declined to travel to Montreal for the reading with the attorney and the family. The provincial court in Vancouver had officially declared Olivia dead and issued a death certificate, which was sent to Marshmonte the week before. Olivia's mother, Photina, had passed away two years prior, so the only heirs to her estate were Chaucer, JOA, Remy, McCarthy, and Mickey. At the reading of the will, Remy, JOA, and Chaucer learned that Olivia's estate, due to her earnings from books, writing screenplays, royalties, and the sale of the Victoria property, etc. now totaled $5.2 million Canadian and that her expected annual royalties for the ongoing sale of her books and movies would continue at approximately $450,000 to $500,000 per year for at least a decade or more. The will indicated that both JOA and Chaucer would receive an initial $1.5 million each, and then $100,000 a year from the royalties. Olivia had set up a $500,000 trust fund for each of Chaucer's children (from Tessa and Stephanie), and Remy was named the executor of that money. The remainder of her funds and the forthcoming royalties would be split in three ways: one-third to support the two orphanages and programs that the Hollywood Studios Charitable Foundation had originally funded; one-third to support a prestigious Writer's Workshop to be set up at Carleton College in Ottawa and named for Olivia; and one-third to support a similar program at the University of British Columbia in Vancouver. The language of the text read "at all times, these writer's workshops/programs shall be held twice a year at each institution, and the maximum number of students shall not exceed forty and at all times females SHALL constitute fully two-thirds of each workshop, and at all times two-thirds of each workshop SHALL be constituted by citizens of Canada. Other than complying with these two restrictions, no other discriminatory criteria may be applied to admission." When Marshmonte read the stipulations, Remy, JOA, and Chaucer smiled broadly, knowing that was their wife and mother Olivia speaking from heaven, from her isolated writing room there.

Chapter 58

Mobile Bay

WHEN CHAUCER RETURNED THIS TIME to New Orleans with the knowledge of the money that his mother had left for him and the two boys, he really needed time alone with Maggie. He asked her to see if her boss in the diocese and her colleagues at the orphanage could manage things without her for a few days. Jasper and Margola agreed to take care of Lyla and Jackson.

So much had happened over the past months that Maggie and Chaucer both agreed that a nice three-day retreat could re-energize them. Chaucer, thinking of Maggie, called the very old and elegant Magnolia Hotel in Mobile where he had had a few business dinners while working on shipping company business. He reserved a second-floor suite overlooking the bay. It was a two-hour drive to Mobile, and the spring weather was perfect for the ride. For the next two days, they hardly left the beautiful grounds of the hotel, choosing to walk hand in hand under the hanging Spanish moss of the large, old oak trees and be charmed by the abundance of azaleas on the property.

On the first night, after a wonderful dinner with fresh seafood and a bottle of a fruity French Sancerre, they walked back to their room and sat on the wicker love seat on the second-floor porch, watching the sun sparkle off the water of the bay. Chaucer put one arm around Maggie and held her hand with his other hand. She looked at him with her most incredibly beautiful smile, and they kissed for a long time. Each was now without words, and each realized that no words were needed. Chaucer rested his head against Maggie's, and for a long time they just let their touch do the talking. Soon the sun was way off to the west, behind the trees, and Chaucer stood, took both of Maggie's hands and led her into the room. They kissed and embraced softly. He unbuttoned her blouse, and she unbuttoned his shirt. The breeze ruffled the sheer curtains from the French doors at the porch opening. They sat on the bed, and Chaucer said, "We are so lucky to have each other." Maggie put her finger to his lips and whispered "shhhh."

When they awoke later it was near midnight, and that was just fine for them both. Chaucer thought about his life before Maggie, and how she had changed so much for him by just asking him to be quiet, be still and listen, and let God talk to him and enter his life.

And I've seen the way
Hearts can go astray
And the damage it can do
And my mind's made up
That no matter what
No one else will do
Sometimes fools will rush right in
And promises are made
But like whispers in the wind
Their words just fade away

And so on and on we go
Till someone comes along
Who can make this half seem whole
And make this heart beat strong

'Cause I've seen the way
Hearts can go astray
And the damage they can do
But my mind's made up
That no matter what
No one else will do
No one else but you

—Written by David Hoffner, Bill Miller

Tom Rush - No One Else But You - YouTube

*   *   *

Over the next two days nothing happened except that Maggie and Chaucer walked, talked softly, ate well, slept late, and made love. It was as it should be for them. They wanted to be nowhere else but where they were. They were without want or troubles or hunger. They were deeply in love, a love that had been earned and cultivated. God's reason for putting them together was so clear to them both during those days together at the Hotel Magnolia.

In their days alone in Mobile, they discussed the idea of expanding their program for expecting women and the orphanages. The two original programs had been successful and had resulted in both having very good fund-raising efforts and outstanding audits from two charitable organizations that review the performance of 501(c)(3) organizations for donors. Many babies had been saved, many women had decided to keep their babies, and many orphaned babies had been successfully placed.

Could they save more babies, help more pregnant women, and find great parents and homes for the orphaned children? Chaucer and Maggie knew that the money that Olivia had left them would help. They agreed to continue discussing the idea with some trusted friends and colleagues, their family and most of all, to have an extended conversation with God in quiet moments together. In the last discussion, Chaucer and Maggie would be mostly listening. They thought of how their listening to God had provided them with answers on their walk on the Camino de Santiago five years ago, and how it had changed their lives. They decided to listen even more intently in the days ahead.

Chapter 59

Life Happens

SUCCESS USUALLY BREEDS FURTHER SUCCESS. That axiom proved true for the work of Chaucer and Maggie. In the next five years they learned and better understood that their calling by St. Joseph had been true to them. Their research and the addition of some very qualified professional staff, along with the positive advice, friendship, and blessings of other clergy, allowed them to open a third program in Toronto, a fourth program in Houston, and a planned fifth program in Tampa. Due to the dedication of Maggie and Chaucer in adhering to high standards of ethical and moral conduct as defined by civil statutes and their Christian values, their programs were without operational or legal issues. They had indeed been able to work true to their original intent and plans. More and more civic and religious groups joined to help them, thus ensuring even greater success in the cities where the programs were located.

Tessa, the mother of McCarthy, continued pursuing her singing career, focusing on live theater and musicals. She was talented enough to make a good living. She had a strong labor union behind her and lots of contacts from years of work. She never married. She did visit Mac regularly and actually created and maintained a good relationship with Chaucer and Maggie, even spending a few Christmas days with them. After her parents passed, she no longer had a home in Buffalo, and her small apartment on the upper West Side in Manhattan was not a good environment for Mac to live permanently, although as he got older, he would occasionally spend more time with his mother when she was not traveling and working. Mac loved Ottawa and his friends and his school there. He was a Canadian citizen, and as he continued to grow, Tessa recognized he was content and well cared for in Ottawa. She loved being in the performing arts, so her heart and her soul had spoken well to her, and her child was happy. She had the life that she had wanted since that first summer in New York City.

Stephanie, the mother of Mickey, was very different from Tessa. After Mickey was born and she reached her agreement with Remy for custody, she and Sissy did follow their plan to go to Australia, where they stayed for over a year, got jobs and saved money for more travel. Eventually they left for India, swayed by the mystique of that country from their teen years of listening to George Harrison and Ravi Shankar's music. They flew to Bombay and walked the city for days, soon becoming disenchanted by the poverty and congestion. While there, Stephanie contracted a bad case of hepatitis, and it was only through the efforts of Remy's company's office in Bombay that she was able to get to a hospital for proper medical care. She eventually recovered, and then she and Sissy met two male travelers from New Zealand. The guys, Gavin and Heath, were headed to an isolated Zoroaster religious retreat center near Diu in the far western Indian state of Gujarat. Stephanie and Sissy decided to join them as Stephanie felt the need to ground herself in a spiritual discipline, so she wanted to explore this religion given the opportunity. The New Zealanders explained to her the tenets of Zoroaster faith, the eternal Adar fire, and the concepts of striving to be like Ahura Mazda.

Soon the four of them were on trains and buses through Ahmedabad, Bhavnagar, and finally to a small Zoroaster/Parsi retreat in the hills overlooking Diu and the ocean. They paid a small fee indicating that they would stay for a week. On the fourth night while sitting near the Adar fire, Stephanie was staring into the flames for a long time, quietly saying a prayer, asking for God to help her with her life, to find more meaning and perhaps a new inspiration. And that was the night she experienced a pareidolia. She saw the Virgin Mary and Jesus in the flames of the fire. She stared and was motionless for a long time. She did not say a word to the others then, but rather she quietly went to her quarters and fell asleep. And she dreamt that night that Mary told her that her happiness would be to serve others, less fortunate people, like the ones on the streets that she had seen in Bombay. After this, Stephanie rarely spoke to the others, rather she was quiet in prayer for much of her time. She spoke only to Sissy about her experience, and Sissy encouraged her to believe it, to work to understand it, and to pray for answers.

When Stephanie and Sissy returned to Connecticut a month later, Stephanie went home for the first time in more than four years. Her father had died in New Bedford, and her mother was living alone in near poverty. Stephanie moved in with her mother, found an office job at a local social service agency, and started meeting with a priest at a Catholic church not far away. Slowly through prayer and meditation, she had found her purpose — to care for her mother and train to care for others. She converted to Catholicism, enrolled in a nursing program in the local community college, and then became an associate of the Monastery of Our Lady of Grace in Guilford, Connecticut. Over the next two years, she began calling Remy and JOA periodically to inquire about Mickey and update them on her life. Eventually, JOA took Mickey to visit his mother in Guilford. It was there that Stephanie saw Mickey for the first time in years, and the first time that JOA had seen Stephanie since she had brought the baby to Ottawa five years before. This started a series of visits by Stephanie to Ottawa to see Mickey, and JOA bringing Mickey to see his mother in Connecticut. On one visit when JOA brought Mickey to Guilford to stay for two weeks, as she was leaving for the drive back to Ottawa, Stephanie hugged her tightly, looked her in the eyes, smiled so softly and said in a quiet voice, "Yes, JOA, God does work in mysterious ways."

As JOA learned more about Stephanie's life and her transformation to Catholicism and nursing, JOA gained a great respect for her over time. Soon JOA asked Stephanie to move to Ottawa to help with the orphanage there. Thus began the building of a new, expanded relationship among Stephanie, her son Mickey, and the Giroux family. Over time, Remy, JOA, and Stephanie began to plan for Mickey to live with his mother full time in Ottawa in a small house just minutes from Remy's house. They all came to believe that was the way God wanted it to be.

Over time, Chaucer accepted that his sister had been the catalyst for this family reconciliation. He and Stephanie started to act as cooperative parents for Mickey. Chaucer understood that Stephanie was not the woman from the days in Mexico or the forlorn daughter from a bad marriage. She had mended herself through her spirituality and her nursing career. When Maggie met Stephanie, the two found respect and friendship for each other, what with their common interests in their Catholic faith and their mutual desire to care for others. Her Catholic faith had helped Stephanie live a better and bolder life. Maggie understood this well, and she and Stephanie became good friends with time. No one was more sincerely at peace with this than Remy, JOA, and Pastor Leo.

Chaucer and Stephanie's forgiveness of each other from the conflict of years ago was settled, and Maggie both approved of it and had encouraged it. On a Sunday morning after Chaucer, Maggie, Stephanie, and Mickey had attended a 10 a.m. mass in Ottawa, Chaucer asked Stephanie if she would go for a walk with him in the gardens behind the church. Maggie took Mickey for an ice cream treat at the local soda fountain a block away.

Chaucer began, "It seems to me that it was a lifetime ago that you and I were in Mexico together. So much has changed for you...and me too. You seem really happy, Stephanie, and I am glad for you. Maggie likes you very much, you know."

Stephanie looked calmly at Chaucer, with a small grin. "It's been a long journey to get here, Chaucer, and once, years ago I never thought I would make it. You know that you hurt me in Mexico, and it took a long time for me to get past that, but your wonderful father did things for me that I never expected any man to do for me, given what I had seen growing up."

Chaucer smiled, knowing that Remy had done all these things to care for Stephanie and Mickey. "Yeah, my father is an amazing man. He's not perfect, but he seems always to see things far ahead of me and others. Maybe it was his time in the war, or maybe it was how he was raised by my grandparents, but something inside of him keeps him centered, calm, hopeful, and looking forward. I am glad you have come to care for him like I do; he will never let you or Mickey down." Chaucer decided it was time. "Stephanie, it was my fault in Mexico, I should have never done what I did, to be with you and let you think that I was going to stay around. I was only thinking of myself, not you, and I hope after all this time now, that you can forgive me. I really want us to be good parents for Mickey. He is a great little kid, and we are lucky to be his parents." Chaucer made the most humble face, a face of complete contrition, and Stephanie saw it in full.

She did not look surprised, just calm and understanding. "I'm not the girl I was then, Chaucer. I have learned to forgive, forget, request, and accept God's grace and it has changed my life in so many ways. I've come to love JOA and Maggie for the wonderful women that they are, and that must mean that you are like them, too, or why would they love you so much. That is what I said to myself. So you see, we can heal the things between us, and we have made a good start, don't you think?" and she smiled at him.

Chaucer took her hands in his, the first time that he had touched her since the day on the beach in Mexico when he told her he was leaving. He hugged her, and she kissed his cheek. The reconciliation had begun in earnest.

Later in the car, after Maggie and Chaucer had taken Stephanie and Mickey home, Maggie smiled and looked at Chaucer who was driving. "So Romeo, I saw her kiss you as Mickey and I were walking back to the church. So are you dating her again?" she said with a cute laugh.

"Yeah, I was going to tell you tonight. Actually, we are leaving for Mexico tomorrow." And with that, Maggie punched him in the right arm and they both laughed, seeing the humor and the reconciliation in his words.

"Mickey saw her kiss you, and I think that was beautiful for him, and for us, too," Maggie said.

It was soon apparent that Chaucer and Stephanie had healed their past. Maggie was happy for them, and it benefited Mickey greatly as he began to see more and more of his father and mother in their new state of forgiveness and friendship.

*　　*　　*

During the five years since Remy had asked JOA to manage the Ottawa orphanage and program, JOA had made a fine life for herself. Remy had been confident that JOA would do the job well, yet her transformation had been nothing short of spectacular. She had found a challenge bigger than herself and had accepted it with unmitigated energy. Was she perfect at it? Certainly not, but she was rigorous and energetic, much like her father had been when he started the shipping company after World War II. Chaucer, Maggie, and of course Remy and Teasag, were her biggest supporters and advocates as her talents emerged. She even earned an award as Executive of the Year from the Ottawa Canadian Federation of Private Service Programs.

Shortly after her five-year anniversary of leading the orphanage and program, JOA took time off for a much-needed vacation. She drove to Geneva, New York, to see her cousins Katherine and Ollie, and her Aunt Elizabeth and her uncle, Remy's brother Le Guerrier. She wanted to share with them all the news about herself, Chaucer, and the family in Ottawa. It was to be a special visit in many ways.

Ollie had started a small winery on the west side of Seneca Lake on land that he had bought with the help of his parents. Ollie had been in the Army, serving in the Vietnam War, and he lived on the family farm. He had survived a helicopter crash in Vietnam but his left leg below the knee was so badly damaged that the Army doctors had amputated it at the base hospital. His recovery had been slow but steady and within a year, being young, he found the use of the prothesis leg to be manageable. His biggest issues had been the mental adjustments needed to carry on as before. But he did work through it all with the help of his family, Pastor Wagner in Geneva, and physical therapy.

During the week that JOA spent at the house in Geneva, Ollie gave her the full tour of the winery operations, including the vineyards, the wine-making process, the marketing, and the distribution. JOA was fascinated because she had not been exposed to such detail in the wine business before. Ollie introduced her to his vineyard manager, Thomas Burton. Thomas had been in the Marines for three years and was now a senior at the Cornell University Agricultural School specializing in developing hybrid grapes at the Experimental Station in Geneva. Ollie had planted half his vineyard land with them. Thomas was from nearby Corning, New York, where his parents worked for the Corning Glass Co. Ollie's oldest brother, Logan, had introduced Ollie to Thomas, as Logan was on the faculty at Cornell and had met Thomas though a colleague at the Cornell Industrial and Labor Relations School.

"So, Logan put you and Ollie together, that was so nice," JOA said with a beautiful smile, noticing how handsome and polite he was with his sandy hair and strong arms. Thomas was shy and grinned saying, "Yes, that was really nice of Logan. He thought that with me being a veteran and having been injured like Ollie, that would be a good bond for us, and it has been." Thomas did not mention his specific injury or other details of his time in the Marines. Thomas was too modest for that, and JOA, although curious, was too polite to ask.

In the next days before JOA returned to Ottawa, she and Thomas spent many hours together. Thomas invited JOA to walk the vineyards with him and examine his new plantings, then he took her for a tour of the Geneva Ag School campus, showing her the labs and experimental hybrid sections. They walked the pathways in the park at the north end of the lake in the late afternoons and twice went with Ollie and his girlfriend, Karen, to dinner in town.

On the morning that JOA was to drive back to Ottawa, Thomas came to the house to say goodbye. JOA's beautiful smile, long brown hair mostly kept in a braided pigtail, and her gentle way of walking and talking had captivated Thomas on the first day that they had met. She was like no other woman that he had met at Cornell. Knowing that she was Ollie's cousin was special to Thomas too because Ollie was the best and most kind friend that he had had since his Marine days. Both men had an essential quietness, and they seemed to understand one another well, which made them a good team to operate a successful vineyard.

"Next time you come back, I'd like to drive you to Ithaca and show you around the Cornell campus," Thomas told JOA. "If Logan is in town, perhaps we can have lunch with him and his wife, Marcy."

"I'd really like that, Thomas. Will you be working here after you graduate?" she asked with a hopeful tone of voice.

"Well, I love the Finger Lakes, and I hope that Ollie can hire me full time, so yes, if he wants me to stay, I will," he said in his modest manner.

"OK, great, then I'll use my family influence to make sure he does," JOA said with a big bold smile and a wink. Then she reached out and gave Thomas a warm hug. She looked Thomas straight in the eyes. "Will you write to me, Thomas?" she asked in her typically direct and confident manner.

Thomas looked in her beautiful eyes, and with a very soft smile and quiet voice, said, "Yes, but only if you promise to write back."

"I will. You take care of yourself, Thomas Burton. I've had a lovely week here, and I want to see you again." Then she released his hand that she had been holding. Thomas smiled and turned and walked to the barn and went back to his work at the vineyard.

JOA watched Thomas walk away and thought that they had made a special connection that week. She grinned and nodded with a self-confident assurance that she would see him again.

From where she was standing at the winery, she could see the overwhelming beauty of Seneca Lake; the houses on the far eastern shore, the small boats sailing and fishing that day, and the sun shining off the calm water. The buzz of bees and the flutter of large butterflies were subtle and kind sounds, the soft chirping of birds in the adjacent trees was God's music. The smells of the farmland and vineyards were new and beautiful to her. She liked it here, and she knew that Thomas and Ollie were happy. She wondered if she could ever be happy living here, among the lakes, farms, and vineyards. But now it was time for her to go back to Ottawa and care for all the babies in the orphanage and the expecting mothers in her program. She missed Remy, McCarthy, Mickey, Jockie, and her work...

The End

Epilogue

Chaucer's Journal Entry 1:
July 14, 1995

OUR WORK TO PRESERVE CHILDREN and their mothers has now been going on for twenty years, and Maggie, JOA, Father and all the others who helped us start these programs have stayed with us in their support. We do miss Abraham Pearlman, whose wisdom and generosity at the start was a blessing. We helped him through his illness. His memory will live in the success of the programs, including the program that we established on Vancouver Island with the Catholic church and the leadership of the First Nation tribes. He is with us in our hearts and minds forever.

Our programs have remained the same as when we began. We continue to provide medical care, spiritual counseling, education classes and vocational training, and internships for the women who want to keep their babies. For the babies that we keep, our adoption services continue to expand, and now we have many babies born in our care who have started college and others who entered the work force and are successful. A small group of our alumni have taken the wrong road in adult life, including a few who are incarcerated. For them we pray, and we visit them in prison when possible. We never give up on them as God created them and gave us the resources to help them in life. We believe that they will one day let God into their hearts to come home to him and accept his true plan for them.

Father is now 73 and finally fully retired from the company, with the exception of maintaining his position on the board of trustees. His health is good, and his life with Teasag remains happy and joyful for them both. This pleases JOA, Maggie, and me very much.

Jockie has taken his Canadian citizenship seriously. He is studying at McGill University Medical College in Montreal. He tells us that he will remain in Montreal or Ottawa when he graduates and completes his internships and fellowship training. We all have come to love Jockie very much over the years. JOA and I smile so big when we see Father with him, for Jockie is our sibling who helped Father so much with his recovery from losing JOA and me after the divorce. I cannot help to smile each and every time I see Jockie. He is a good lad and loves his parents and us without reservation. I believe that God sent Jockie to Father and Teasag for that reason.

Journal Entry 2: Remy's letter to the family on Canadian Thanksgiving Day, Monday, October 9, 2000

AT THE LONG TABLE in the large Ottawa house dining room, the entire family assembled to listen to Remy read his letter. Chaucer, Maggie, Lyla, Jackson, Remy Jr. and Suzette (the son and daughter of Chaucer and Maggie); JOA; Le Guerrier and wife Elizabeth; Ollie and wife Karen; Kathleen and husband Tony and their children; Tessa and McCarthy; Stephanie and Mickey; Teasag and Jockie.

"What a joyful day for us all — our Canadian annual Thanksgiving Day tradition. This is a good time for me say some things about our family, things for which I am thankful. I am also thinking today of Father Etienne DuBois at the Eglise Monolithe in St. Émilion. He is now 87 and remains active in St. Émilion. God sends us angels, and Father DuBois is one of those angels sent to me and the people of France. I think of you today and send my love, as does Chaucer.

"Let me start by offering a prayer; please hold hands and bow your heads:

> Dear God, thank you for the splendid family that you have blessed me with, that you have blessed each of us with. We bow to your wisdom, your mercy, your grace, and we give you thanks. We ask for your continued blessings as we all work to be the best people we can, and to fulfill your plan for each of us. Grant each of us this day and every day the patience we need to be good people, good students, good colleagues, and good stewards of the beautiful earth that you created for us. Grant us wisdom as we continue

Epilogue 391

our programs for the children and their mothers to save the many babies that you send to us, and grant us the wisdom to help their mothers and fathers to love them, to keep them, and to be good parents to them. Lastly, let us remember the faces and names of those who have left us: my parents Gillian and the General here in Ottawa; Suzette and Rufus, the parents of Lyla and Jackson; Olivia, the mother of Chaucer and JOA; and Abraham Pearlman, our original benefactor from the Hollywood Studios Charitable Fund. Let us all keep them in our hearts and minds in the year ahead. Amen.

"And now just a few more words before our meal. I am now 79 years old, and that helps me to focus on the important things for the time I have remaining. As the Roman philosopher Cicero wrote two thousand years ago, 'If you have a garden and a library, you have everything you need.' Well, I have my retirement garden and my library in my office here, but I need more than that. I need my family, all of you. You are the most important matter for me, not the company I helped create years ago, not the money that we made and saved and invested, not this house. The important thing to me now is helping each of you to become the best person that you can, today and every day ahead. We have been granted much and from those granted much, then much is expected, and that is all of you at this table. You all have great lives ahead of you, and I want you to make sure that every day when you wake up, that you say a prayer and give thanks to God for who you are and how you will live in love and kindness each day. If you do this, you will find that the goals that you have — the honorable goals of service, love, kindness, and grace — you will have those with you all day and every day. And sometime in the days ahead, you can stand up in front of your family as I am now and tell them that you love them with all your heart...and I do, all of you, each of you."

With that Remy nodded to them, smiled, and sat down slowly. The room was quiet and then one by one, Chaucer, JOA the other adults and then the children, all said, "Thank you father, we love you" or "Thank you Grandpa, we love you." Lastly, Teasag stood up, looked at Remy from the far end of the long table and said, "Remy my husband, father and grandfather to all of us, thank you for all the love you have given to us over the years and on this special day. We are grateful to have you in our lives." Then everyone stood and clapped.

Journal Entry 3: Chaucer's letter from Christmas 2018 to his children

"To my children McCarthy, Mickey, Lyla, Jackson, Suzette, and Remy, Jr:

"Fifty years have passed in my life, seemingly quickly. I am now 71. Before you were born I was near faithless, confused, angry, lonely, and contemptuous about myself and life. I am glad that you were not born then. I was but a shadow of the man I am today.

"I write to tell you this because my earthly father, your grandfather Remy, and God, my father in heaven, never gave up on me. They nurtured me, loved me, guided me to become the better person I am now; your father, your Abba, guided by the love of St. Joseph.

"You range in age from 30 to 48 years old. You have seen much already. As you live you will see and experience much more. I pray for all good things in your lives, and if you fall, I pray that you will remember the strength of your family, your faith in the love of God, and lessons that I hope that I have taught you about love, kindness, sharing, building, and teaching.

"Fifty years ago some wonderful people filled with faith, love, and friendship helped me turn my life around and guided me to the best person I could be. First was your grandfather Remy, my guiding light. He never let me down, he never let me fall so deep that he could not pull me up. He is the saint of our family, and I always want you to remember that. His physical body has been gone from us for three years now yet his spirit and love will be with us every day of our life, so always think of him the way you think of God. They both are with you every day; they both love you; you are never alone.

"The second person was and is Maggie. She challenged me to change, to open my eyes to the vast love of God and how my life could surely change if I listened for the message. Her wisdom and faith was the daily discipline I needed to begin to change and see my life in a very different way. I was so fortunate to meet her, and I am so fortunate that she has been my partner for all these years.

"You will meet and befriend other angels on this earth and they too will guide you if you listen and discern what they are teaching you. Please learn to distinguish true friends and earthly angels from the pretenders. True friends give to you, so learn to accept them. False friends will take from you, so know the difference and seek the truth always in relationships. Your joy will depend on it.

"Here are two examples of what I mean. When I was young and traveling in Portugal, I met two young women from Boston. Lisa and Teresa are cousins. In the three weeks or so that we traveled together, they listened to me, talked with me, illuminated circumstances of our travel for me. They started me down the road to a great sense of spiritual development and honesty. Over the years we have remained friends through letters and some personal visits. They both have been angels to me.

"The other person is an older German man whom Maggie and I met on our pilgrimage to Santiago, Spain. His name is Rudy, and he introduced himself to us one day in a church along the Camino de Santiago. Rudy was a German Lutheran who was on a 33-day pilgrimage, one day for each year of the life of Christ on earth. He was walking the entire length of the Camino to Santiago, more than 500 miles, to where St. James is buried. One night Rudy awakened me at the hostel where we were staying. It was in the middle of the night, and he insisted that I come outside and speak with him. He held a candle in his hands. He said that God had sent him to shine a light for me. We talked for hours, until the first rays of light, then he stood up and walked west towards Santiago. Maggie and I saw him again four days later sitting near the Cathedral de Santiago, and we prayed together inside at the Porto de Gloria. Everything we prayed for that day has come true. Rudy was my light, our light. He wanted nothing from me, just my attention directed towards God, which I had been neglecting to my own detriment. Rudy redirected me, and for that I have been grateful each day since. Rudy and I still write to each other and remain friends. He has been my most special angel, next to my father and Maggie.

"So these are my words to you children at this time. Learn to see the angels in your life, keep them close. You will be a true and joyful person if you do. God will guide you with his angels and his love. As your father, your Abba, I strongly recommend it to you.

"I love you all. Be kind and loving. Peace be with you in all your days. This is a good earth."

Father

Acknowledgments

FIRST AND FOREMOST, to the saintly woman from Iowa, my editor, moral compass, and my rock, Jane E. Sutter Brandt. Her experience, knowledge, attention to detail, and love of words are a thing of beauty never experienced before by this writer. I always defer to her judgement. Thankfully, I am also married to her.

To Susan Welt of Pittsford, New York, for her creative work in the design of my books; thank you.

To my many Canadian friends, present and past, who have always been a source of special joy, inspiration, and admiration over the years, particularly Pete Tufford; Billy, Peggy, and Andrew Thorne; Sean and Larry Greenhalgh; Pastor Bob Zimmer and his wife, Shirley; Barbara Astman; Patrick Kavanaugh; Susan Coles-Provenzano; the late Marnie Welt; and lastly, the remarkable twins from Winnipeg — our Cornell team captain Shalen Kouk M.D. and our goalie Tristan (Cheese) Kouk MHA. A group of wonderful men and women who enrich all those around them. Thank you all.

In remembrance of Stan Rogers (1949-83). A philosopher, poet, songwriter, performer, and saint of Canada, who captured the essence and spirit of Canada and its people in his short lifetime, to wit: "Northwest Passage," "The Mary Ellen Carter," "Free in the Harbour," "The Field Behind the Plow," etc. You are not forgotten, mate.

And lastly, a fond thank you to the staff of the Toronto Youth Hockey Academy at Tam O'Shanter who molded me into a better hockey player and person. You were the best when I needed you most.